# All The Devils

# All The Devils

## CATELYN WILSON

MICHAEL  JOSEPH

PENGUIN MICHAEL JOSEPH

UK | USA | Canada | Ireland | Australia
India | New Zealand | South Africa

Penguin Michael Joseph is part of the Penguin Random House group of companies
whose addresses can be found at global.penguinrandomhouse.com

First published 2024

001

Set in 13.5/16pt Garamond MT
Typeset by Falcon Oast Graphic Art Ltd
Printed in Great Britain by Clays Ltd, Elcograf S.p.A.

The authorized representative in the EEA is Penguin Random House Ireland,
Morrison Chambers, 32 Nassau Street, Dublin D02 YH68

A CIP catalogue record for this book is available from the British Library

HARDBACK ISBN: 978–0–241–68394–1
TRADE PAPERBACK ISBN: 978–0–241–68395–8

www.greenpenguin.co.uk

MIX
Paper | Supporting
responsible forestry
FSC
www.fsc.org   FSC® C018179

Penguin Random House is committed to a
sustainable future for our business, our readers
and our planet. This book is made from Forest
Stewardship Council® certified paper.

To Courtney and Camille – my sisters, my better thirds, my everything. From the time we were born as three tiny, ugly babies, you've been at my side, guiding me through my own Underworld. I would go to hell and back for you, always.

'Hell is empty
And all the devils are here.'

William Shakespeare,
*The Tempest*, Act 1, Scene ii

# I

*February*

I've never understood the concept of open-casket funerals. Lines of mourners queuing to stare down into a rectangular box where a loved one lies covered in makeup to hide the gray pallor and blue lips. The sickly-sweet smell of funeral homes and the suffocating aroma of an endless sea of flowers.

Funerals are macabre enough. So, as I look down at the oak casket and at my sister, her hands folded unnaturally across her stomach, all I can think is how this is so very wrong.

That isn't Violet. It can't be.

'I am so sorry for your loss. She was such a wonderful girl.' The same damned line delivered over and over again passed from grimaced lips over the body of my sister and to my parents.

I ignore the people filing into the funeral home and crossing over the faded pink carpet to the coffin, their coats dusted with melting snow.

I stare down at Violet, my jaw clenched tight to keep the tears back, and finger the crumpled note she sent me a little over a week ago, deep inside the pocket of my black dress.

*Acta deos numquam mortalia fallunt.*
Watch for Tooth and Talon. Follow the path of Anubis.
  —Violet

The wax seal has crumbled from my constant picking and the edges of the thick paper curl inward. The Latin scrolls across my tongue as I repeat the translation silently.

*Mortal actions never deceive the gods.*

When the line thins out while mourners file into the adjoining chapel to await the service, my mother sags.

'Almost over, Andy,' she says to me, a tiny, weak smile flickering on her thin lips.

Dad doesn't speak, he only looks down at Violet with a vacant expression. He's trying to be strong, to not cry. But he can't mask the sheen in his eyes as he reaches down to squeeze one of Violet's limp hands. As soon as the last attendee enters the chapel, Dad flees to join them.

I know I should go too, but my feet won't cooperate. I can't move, can't breathe, can't think. The mysterious note pricks at my thoughts, at my already tender conscience. I can't shake the feeling that I am missing something.

I look down at Violet. *Wake up*, I plead.

She doesn't.

*Acta deos numquam mortalia fallunt.*

'Come on.' Mom extends her hand, a tremor rippling across her fingers. 'Grandpa Emmerson is giving the eulogy.'

I glance over at the open doors and the waiting crowd. The second I leave this room the funeral director will shut the lid and seal the casket. And I'll never see Violet's face again.

A rushing sound skates over my ears. I shake my head, trying to clear it. My heart races, pushing blood past my ears.

I rub my eyelids, jostling my tear-smudged glasses, spreading even more mascara across the bags under my eyes. 'I need a second. Please.'

Mom's face breaks a little more. She's faded like a painting left in the sun. Losing a child is the worst kind of pain, they say. I've seen it over the past week since we got the call from the headmaster at Violet's school. How Mom screamed and dropped her phone. How Dad's face went white.

Me? I ran to my room and was sick all over the carpet.

2

Dead at eighteen. Violet would grumble about that in her obituary and insist on it reading eighteen and a half. She is particular like that.

Was.

Mom puts a delicate hand on my shoulder, but I hardly feel it. 'Alright, take a moment. But, Andy, I know Violet wouldn't want you to torture yourself.'

It's on the tip of my tongue to say the same thing to her, but Mom looks too delicate. She's probably slept even less than I have. Her hair, as dark brown and curly as mine, hangs limp around her hollowed face. A ghost of a person.

'Don't take too long to say goodbye.' Mom leans over and presses a kiss to Violet's cold forehead. Wiping at her cheeks, she braces herself, pulling her tiny frame taut, and heads for the chapel.

Finally, I'm alone. I know the funeral director is hanging in the wings, his oiled black hair glistening like a grease spill. But I don't care. I study Violet's face. It's her . . . but it's not. The expression is too slack, there's no spark or fire. Her black hair is straight and arranged too neatly. Her eyebrows have a few strays the mortician must not have plucked.

The thought of someone's hands running over my dead sister's body sends a jolt of nausea through me. I curl my fingers around the edge of the casket, my throat tight and stinging.

'I'm so sorry, Vee. I should have talked to you, made you listen.' Reaching out to clutch her leg, a half-sob rattles from my lungs.

It's so cold. There's no comfort here. There's nothing but a raw, gaping hole my sister left behind.

Violet should be preparing to start her final year at that academy, the one so pretentious it had 13 grades instead of the usual 12. Violet was smart, the star of the family. A light that blazed so bright it always burned, but I was happy to bear a few scars if it meant Violet could be happy. Be seen.

She shouldn't be buried by parents who aren't even gray.

'You can't leave me here,' I whisper, the fabric of her skirt scratching my palm. 'What were you trying to tell me? What does it mean?'

Of course, Violet doesn't answer. My thigh burns and I rub at the itchy tights covering my leg and the tattoo my parents don't know about. The one that matches Violet's.

I study her wrist where a bracelet identical to mine rests against her stomach. The charms are all there: the silver antlers, the golden crescent moon and the pewter moth. My fingers graze my own charms, all identical except for the last one. The one Violet sent me with that cryptic note only three days before she died. A curved tooth, like a wolf's incisor.

Mortal actions never deceive the gods.

The funeral director walks deliberately by me. His shadow streaks across the hallway as he paces. I take a ragged breath and straighten, my hand resting on Violet's cold leg. My tattoo burns again, and on impulse, I'm desperate to see Violet's. That was the last time we saw each other, getting those tattoos on her eighteenth birthday.

The rushing sound returns to my ears, louder this time. My fingers shake so badly that I can only bring myself to nudge her favorite skirt a few centimeters. I expect to see the bloom of black ink against her chalky-looking skin. The kiss of a pattern: antlers cradling a moth and a crescent moon.

There is nothing but blank skin.

My tongue lodges to the roof of my mouth. I move the hem again. Nothing.

Ice creeps into my veins, and lodges in my stomach. Makeup. It has to be the makeup. They put that on dead bodies, right? A way to make them look less *wrong*. Clinging with one hand on the lip of the casket, I press my fingers into Violet's stiff, cold skin and rub. The pale canvas of her thigh remains the same. I grit my teeth, lick my thumb and scrub harder.

Gone.

I snatch my hand away from the body, stomach heaving. *No, no, no.*

The room spins, dizziness swirling my thoughts and senses. I stumble back but my shoes stick to the carpet and I collapse to my knees, staring in horror at the body.

The hair, the face, the skin. That sense of wrongness curdles my stomach. I bury my fingers in the carpet and struggle to breathe. Blackness tinges the edge of my vision, vast and endless. I can't feel the scratch of the rug on my fingers and knees.

A heavy thud resounds in my ear. My heart flies into my throat and I jerk aside. The funeral director stares down at me with strained sympathy, his comb-over glinting. He secures the casket's lid, sealing the body from my vision.

Cold sweat slicks my skin. I shiver, hunched like an animal on the faded, musty carpet, still gasping for breath. Beneath my fingers, the fibers are damp.

He extends one hand down to me and nods towards the chapel. 'The service is starting. You should join your parents now.'

I stagger to my feet and follow the director as he wheels the casket towards the chapel. Each step sends something burning through my veins.

*Acta deos numquam mortalia fallunt.*

Mortal actions never deceive the gods.

The strange charm, the cryptic note, the missing tattoo. And something clicks. Something that makes that terrible sick feeling scald the back of my throat. Because it's my fault. I missed the signs. She was trying to warn me.

She *is* trying to warn me.

I sit down next to my mother as the service begins, but I don't cry. Sniffles brush past my ears and my fingers curl into fists because there is only one thing I am sure of: the body in the casket is *not* my sister.

Violet is alive.

# 2

*August*
*Six Months Later*

The cab driver stands at the set of wrought-iron gates illuminated by two weak orange sconces. Rain falls, dripping steadily over the brim of his hat and into his eyes. He pushes the call button again and again.

I press my nose to the half-open window, ignoring the way it smudges my glasses. Although it's only the last week of August, the air is chilly and choked with an oppressive mist. The call box crackles to life amid the sound of gently falling rain.

Jones, the cab driver, replies to the garbled words and tugs his cap lower over his face before he retreats to the taxi. 'Cursed intercom is getting soaked in the rain. They could hardly hear me, miss.'

'It's alright.' I use my sleeve to clean my glasses before perching them back on my nose. 'They're expecting us.'

Jones doesn't reply as the iron gates stretch wide open. A shudder skates along my skin as we drive towards Ravenswood Academy, gravel crunching beneath the tires like dried bone.

Darkness encases the cab as we wind through the narrow road lined with thick pine trees. The air smells both clean and putrid, like fresh rain and decaying leaves. Life and death. I rub absently at the tattoo on my upper thigh.

All at once, the stately outline of the school emerges

from the mist and rain. Lights blaze in almost every window. Ravenswood Academy stands imposing, a sprawling four-story Victorian mansion studded with gothic architecture. The car rolls to a stop under a covered drive leading to a stone staircase and intricately carved front doors.

Gray stone and red brick blur together as Jones opens the door and my glasses fog up. I pull my cramped body from the back seat and twist the silver bracelet around my wrist, charms tinkling. The front doors are flung open and a man in a brown tweed suit stands at the top of the stairs, his graying hair slicked back.

'Miss Emmerson.' He descends the stairs as Jones grabs my two suitcases and hefts them from the trunk. 'I am glad you arrived safely. Follow me, please.' He looks down his hooked nose at me.

My heart beats frantically.

Headmaster Madden is everything that Violet had described. Dark, beady eyes peer out of a face that has wrinkles mixed with subtle nips and tucks that speak of facelifts. It's clear he doesn't approve of my presence here. My fingers tighten on the strap of my backpack.

I remember the dull monotone of his voice speaking on the other end of my father's phone, that cold February morning. How he had so calmly described the very event that tore my life apart – that tore my parents apart.

I hate him already.

'Now, since you are coming in a few weeks after the start of the school year, your teachers are aware and have arranged packets to make up for readings. Our counselor approved your schedule this morning.' Madden opens the door to the administration wing and strides into a large office. 'You'll have a roommate and a hall chaperone.'

I make a non-committal nod. Just enough to acknowledge

that I heard him. He doesn't look at me as he types a password into his computer.

'We are glad your parents insisted we admit you for the fall semester instead of waiting for spring.'

I can taste the sarcasm in his voice.

He tried to keep me from coming to Ravenswood for as long as possible. He'd said he didn't want to 'upset' me or remind me of 'unpleasant' things. But I know he fought my parents so hard for one reason: Violet.

I remain silent, perched lightly on a hard wooden seat across from him. He clicks around on a computer as I stare vacantly out the window, imagining what things may look like in the daylight. How they might have looked to Violet. She'd loved this school. Loved the art and the history and the exclusiveness of it all.

I can't see why.

'You'll be with the rest of the year eleven ladies,' Madden says absently. 'Your room is in the east wing, overlooking the gardens and cove. Lovely, I hear. You've missed dinner, and students are required to go to bed at half past ten, so your tour will have to wait until tomorrow morning, before breakfast. Here is your schedule and some things from your teachers.'

I take the bundle of papers, careful not to touch the headmaster's skin. He continues to prattle on but my focus fades as I study the names of the wings, halls and many rooms on my small map and schedule. They're all so familiar but strangely alien at the same time.

I interrupt his speech about the school mission, without waiting for so much as a pause. 'Can I see Violet's old room?'

Madden's lips purse into a thin line. In the low light of the office, he looks pale and washed out. I can't see the whites of his eyes. I swallow, fighting against the lump in my throat.

9

Could he be covering up the truth of what happened to my sister?

'Andromeda —'

'Andy,' I correct automatically.

'Yes, well, *Andy*,' his nose wrinkles, 'your sister's room has already been searched by the police. It is empty for now, as most students here have a habit of spreading silly ghost stories, but it will need to be occupied soon. And besides, your sister's belongings are all gone, mailed to you shortly after we, ah, contacted you . . . about her situation.'

'I know.' I try to keep the malice from my voice, digging my fingers into my thigh, my tattoo. 'I just want to see it. See where she lived.'

Madden stands slowly and shuts off his computer. Disapproval and haughtiness radiate from him. He motions towards the open door and I follow him out into the foyer.

'I am afraid you will have to wait for a while yet. We are trying to keep all of that under wraps, to comfort the parents, and to avoid scaring some of our younger students who are easily swayed by their elders.'

Violet, my vibrant sister, reduced to a ghost story. I bite down on my tongue to keep from screaming. I bite so hard that my eyes water. Blinking away the tears, I look away from Madden.

My shoes ghost over white marble tiles inlaid in patterns of ivy. Madden stops at the foot of a massive staircase, a grand entryway opening like the throat of a Leviathan, ready to swallow me whole.

Every inch is cavernous and opulent and reminds me of my sister. Of nights bent over books carrying the heady scent of old paper and history. Of tracing pictures of ancient art beneath my fingertips while listening to her tell me the stories and symbols behind them. My chest squeezes the breath in my lungs and I rub at my burning tattoo.

'I will show you to your room. Breakfast is at seven. I will ensure you have someone to give you a tour before then.' Madden turns towards the large staircase and climbs. I follow him, my eyes glued to his ramrod-straight back.

We pass small nooks with plush chairs, and skirt past the darkened classrooms. Rain slithers down tall arched windows lining the walls. Below I see thick mist curling around ornamental trees and statues, obscuring my view of the cove beyond. I imagine I can hear the ocean pushing relentlessly against the rocky shore.

Finally, we reach the end of the long hall. Here the ceilings are lower than normal and covered in white plaster. A door opens into a large square room filled with couches, chairs and small tables. Girls sit and lounge all over, dutifully typing on laptops, scribbling on paper or scouring huge tomes. They look up as Madden guides me to a set of doors that lead into a long hallway.

A cacophony of whispers erupts behind us as we disappear into the dorm rooms.

'Violet . . . sister . . . dead . . .'

*Wrong*, I think.

A woman with long blonde hair – no doubt the hall chaperone – appears from a room at the end.

'Mrs Bianchi, this is Andromeda Emmerson. She will be in room 13A with Miss Al Soori,' Madden says.

The woman smiles brightly and hands me a brass key dangling from a ribbon. The handle is in the shape of antlers. I shudder as my fingers close around the cool metal.

'Welcome, Andromeda.'

I give Madden a pointed look. 'It's just Andy, please.'

Bianchi seems to smother a smile at Madden's huff of breath. 'Well then, Andy, it's lovely to meet you. Your bed is all set up. The laundry is on the floor below and is accessed with your student ID card.'

I nod, acutely aware of Madden's presence beside me, like he's watching. Waiting for something. Suppressing a shiver, I cross my arms.

'And curfew is strictly enforced,' the headmaster says crisply.

'Lights out at ten thirty on weekdays, but the weekends permit a little more leniency,' Bianchi says softly. 'Midnight on Friday and Saturday nights. Next year you'll be allowed into town, with parental permission. The bathroom for this hall is right there,' she points to a richly carved door with two brass handles, 'and right here is your room.'

She opens the door to my room, painted in soft taupe. Inside there are two beds on opposite sides of the room flanked by desks and bedside tables. Two separate closets meet the foot of each bed. It's small. I can't imagine Violet enjoying shoving all her clothes into such a tiny closet.

One side is taken. It's decorated with a flag of the United Arab Emirates, plenty of pictures, and a thick pink velvet cover is draped over the bed. No one else is in the room, and I'm relieved not to have to meet my roommate yet.

Madden sniffs and checks his watch. A Rolex. Figures.

'I will see you in the morning, Miss Emmerson. And do let your grandparents know we at Ravenswood Academy appreciate their continued patronage.'

Right. My father's parents are the only reason they let me into this school with my crappy GPA and low test scores. Both of them are alumni from Yale. Since Violet started attending, they have donated money yearly. They paid her tuition, now mine. I'm sure it's to make up for their absence when my father was a kid. Dad's a professor and is respectably middle class, but it's only because of my grandparents' deep pockets that I'm even here. That Violet could go here too.

The headmaster leaves with a crisp stride to his steps. He can't wait to get away from me.

I clench my teeth and watch him go. I drop my bags, a little wet from the rain, at the foot of my bed.

'I was sorry to hear about your sister. She was an excellent student,' Mrs Bianchi says, crossing her arms.

'Thank you.'

The words are hollow at this point. Meaningless.

'Her death was a true tragedy,' she continues as she sidles to the door. 'I hope you can feel some peace by being in a place she was so fond of.'

She waits, watching me. Her eyes are dark blue, made darker by the low lamplight, but filled with pity.

'Let me know if you need anything at all, Andromeda.' Finally, she slips out, leaving me alone.

I take a few deep breaths, turning her words over in my head. Violet's death was not unfortunate. It never *happened*.

I make quick work of unpacking my clothes. I brought little by way of pictures or personal touches. I don't plan on making a life here. If I do, this place will chew me up and spit me out, just like it did to Violet. Ravenswood won't sink its claws into my flesh.

It's ten by the time I crawl under the covers and shut off the light. My pulse hammers in my throat as I trace the path in my mind, picturing the map of the school I've all but memorized.

A light flickers on as my roommate stumbles in. I don't flinch or turn over as she drops something heavy on a desk. She looks over at me, but I keep my eyes slitted, feigning sleep.

In a matter of minutes she is in her bed and everything is dark once more. Slowly, the chatter in the common room fades until the only sound is the patter of rain on the window and the creaks and groans of the old building.

As I lie staring at the ceiling I know what I need to do.

Once everything is quiet, and the rest of the students are

asleep, I must hunt for the answers to my questions about Violet's life here.

I roll over, staring at the wall.

The school is hiding something dark and wicked, and I will uncover the twisted truth. Even if it kills me.

# 3

I lie in bed until the last sounds of slamming doors and murmuring voices fade away. I leave my room and the hallway without a problem, the corridors entirely abandoned this late at night.

Floorboards creak beneath my bare feet. The long stretch of the year 12 hallway looms ahead, and I search for Violet's old room. I move slowly, measuring my breaths. The storm that followed me here picks up, and rain pelts the roof and windows.

A door catches my eye. The brass number, 14D, shimmers. Violet's room. The air feels thick and heavy. I touch the door. A chill licks across my shoulders.

My pulse quickens. Sweat gathers at the nape of my neck and I creep forward until the tips of my fingers, poking out from my thick sweater, touch the knob. I twist, and the door swings open. Stale air floods my nostrils, and I slip inside and shut the door.

I'm not sure exactly what I expected. Violet's room doesn't look like the pictures she sent. It's cold and dark. The heater in the back of the room doesn't whine and growl like mine. Dust hangs heavy in the air, coating the sterile white sheets that are rumpled on both beds. It's empty. Devoid of life. There isn't anything left of Violet.

I drift around the room, and my heart slows its frantic beating to a disappointed thud. One closet hangs half open, and I run my finger along the door. It should be bursting with Violet's designer clothes, the ones she begged desperately for and couldn't bear to part with during the school year. But we boxed those up and hid them away in the garage of our home after the funeral.

I push my glasses up my nose, squinting. Violet must have hidden something for me in her room. The note she sent made that clear. Why else would she leave it so cryptic, so strange? She knew someone wanted to hurt her, silence her, and that I would come looking. She relied on me. Her room has to hold the answer: a password, a flash drive – *something*.

I make another pass around the room, crouching to look beneath the beds and lifting up the mattresses. I open both closets and bedside tables. But there is nothing – just school-issue oak furniture and dust motes. I press my fingers to my temples and try to keep from crying out in frustration.

The window panes rattle in their thick wooden casings. Tiny cracks in the caulking let in the drafty air and whistle like demonic birds. I jolt away from the window and clutch my arms to my chest.

There's nothing here. Nothing.

Months of planning. Weeks of begging to come to this godforsaken place. A school so exclusive and elitist no kid like me could get inside without my grandparents' money. I've devoted every inch of myself to discovering what Violet had been trying to say. And now all I have to show for it is a looming year stuck at a boarding school I never wanted to go to, and a lonely, dusty room haunted by memories.

There is nowhere else to look.

I slide down the wall until I am sitting with my knees folded against my chest. Grasping my head, I tug at my dark brown ringlets. Violet is alive. *Alive, alive, alive.* I'm sure of it, or she wouldn't have sent that note, that charm. As I slide my hands along the plaster to push myself upright, the pads of my fingers brush a lump on the skirting board.

I suck in a breath and lean close, squinting in the darkness. Rain pelts the small window that overlooks the rocky headland and cove below. Shadows of large pine trees lurch across the wall, their fingers scraping and reaching for me.

'A crawl space,' I whisper aloud. Only the barest hint of a raised outline whispers that there is more here than meets the eye.

I inch forward, tracing my fingers along the skirting board at the base of the wall until I feel it. A notch carved into the section attempting to disguise the small frame of a hidden crawl space.

Wind howls outside. Branches scrape the roof of the old building. But despite the clammy air sticking to my skin, my blood feels like fire. I claw desperately at the skirting board, prying it off with my thumbnail until it lifts. And where the board was, a series of symbols, so painfully familiar, wink at me in the bleak darkness.

A moth. A set of antlers. A crescent moon. And a fresh carving surrounded by curls of wood also glares back. A tooth, sharp and long, like a fang.

I push softly on the carved tooth. The plaster dimples slightly, separating with a groaning sound. Fumbling with my charm bracelet, I hold up the silver tooth. I squeeze the bracelet off my wrist and gently fit the tooth charm into its carved twin. And then I push harder.

The panel bows inward, giving far too easily, as if there is a hollow spot behind it.

Footsteps slither outside the door to the dorm room. The scuff of a shoe and the sound of the knob being hastily tested. Biting back a gasp, I slap the skirting board in place, hiding the carvings, and grab my bracelet before diving into the closet. I shut it just as the door to Violet's room opens.

I stagger in the small space, knocking my chin against one

wall. My glasses tilt across my face but I can't reach up to fix them. The air feels like syrup, so thick I can't move or even blink. Fear sets in.

I hear a voice as the figure enters the room, but the words are difficult to piece together. Another language, ancient and full of sharp vowels. They speak a string of fluent words. But my ears catch on one that I know: *Violet.*

I peer through the tiny crack of the closet. A dark shape, lithe and tall, stands near the window, hands hovering in the air like they're trying to summon something. He speaks again, a chant.

I stagger, chin knocking against the door again.

The chanting man freezes and stares right at the closet. I press my spine against the back wall and my heart hammers against my chest.

A loud sound, like stamping feet, echoes through the hall. The man curses, speaking in English this time, and I glimpse wavy hair and a flash of dark eyes as he whips his head around.

More voices trail through the hallway as cold sweat slips down my back. I'm going to be found.

The man shoves the window open and a blast of cold air rattles the closet door, tugging it open a few inches. I pray my dark sweater will cover my pale skin and the knobs of my bare knees. The voices get louder and the man pulls himself out the window, holding on with far more strength than should be possible. I edge closer to the opening of the closet to see what he's doing, my breath catching in my throat.

And then he lets go of the frame. I fight back the instinct to scream as he plummets from view.

I drop to my knees, gasping a lungful of air. That man, that stranger, just jumped from a third-story window. I stare at the growing puddle of rainwater on the floor below the open window frame. The pounding of feet in the hall grows louder and the door swings open once again. This time, the beam of a flashlight cuts the darkness.

I tuck my knees to my chest and ease the closet door shut until just a narrow crack remains. It seems my sister's room is far more popular than Madden gave it credit for.

A group of young girls, freshmen by the looks of it, huddle in the center of the room, each holding a dripping wax candle. One has a Ouija board tucked under her arm. The girls titter and squeal about the cold.

Bile creeps up my throat as one slides the window shut and the rest gather in a circle on the floor and set their candles down.

'Violet, are you there?' Wind pummels the windows again and a girl shrieks. 'We wish to speak with the spirit of Violet Emmerson.'

I clench my fingers into tight fists and bite down on the inside of my cheek. This is my sister's room, not a haunted mansion.

'Violet, tell us what happened to you on the day you died.'

'No,' another girl hisses. 'Ask her to spy on the boys' locker rooms!'

More snickers erupt.

Wind beats against the window frame like fists. My teeth clench so hard I taste blood, like my gums have split.

'Leave,' I snarl, speaking before I can stop, my voice so ragged and torn I don't recognize it.

The girls scream and the Ouija board goes flying as one of them kicks it. They scatter, clutching their candles to their chests.

'Violet,' a girl with blonde hair, their leader I'd guess, says. 'Is that you?'

I'm too disgusted, too enraged, to be clever. Instead, I grab the inside of the closet doors and slam them back and forth.

The freshmen flee, their screams and yelps causing the rest of the hallway to stir.

My breath comes in shallow gasps. I move numbly, stepping out of the closet.

I need to leave, fast. But I see the slightly cracked window and the Ouija board lying on the dark wood floor. I can't abandon it there, an ugly reminder that everyone believes my sister is dead.

I rush across the room and grab the board like it's a filthy sock and nudge the window open. Cold air slaps my skin, dank and bitter. Holding my breath, I peer into the dark gardens, looking for a broken body. There's nothing but a dent in a shriveled rose bush.

Impossible.

Wind whips through my hair and dances across my scalp. For a moment, I think I see a dark shape, a set of shoulders in the treeline. Lightning flashes, bright and sharp. The trees rustle, their needles quivering. And as thunder rolls through the valley, reverberating against the mountain tops, I see the outline of bodies strung up in the trees by their necks. Shadowy limbs dangle, spines bend at ugly angles, and the groan of the dead fights against the boom of thunder.

A scream catches in my throat as the world plunges into darkness once more. The cold puddle of water stings my bare feet. When another flash of lightning arcs across the clouds, there is nothing but a normal forest outside my sister's window. A trick of the light.

Doors open down the hallway and the rumble of voices picks up. I fling the board as hard as I can and it sails into the maze of waterlogged greenery. I slam the window shut. Before I make my escape, I pause and look over at the wall with the carved symbols. The skirting board is still a little loose and I stoop, moving to push it against the wall.

I push the skirting board firmly in place so no one else can see the carvings. But as I do, a crinkling sound, dry and brittle, whispers to me. Quickly, I pull the skirting back again and see a small gap on the flat side of the board, like a tiny door has slid away. My tongue sticks to the roof of my mouth as I look back at the carvings. The gap matches up perfectly with the carving of the tooth on the wall. Like when I pushed my charm into the socket of the carved incisor, it triggered a mechanism when the board was replaced. I dig my finger into the gap, and paper rubs against the pad of my thumb. I pinch, pulling it free.

Heart hammering, I secure the skirting. Easing the door to Violet's room open, I peer through the gap and spy shoulders clad in bathrobes. For once I'm glad of my stick-like physique because I can slip through into the crowded hall easily. Ducking my head, I push my curls over my face. Everyone is too confused and bedraggled to pay me any mind. To them, I'm just another face.

'What's going on? Cindy, I can't understand you when you're blubbering snot all over my sleeve.' An older girl with dark brown skin and long black hair stands in front of the sobbing ringleader as she wails about ghosts.

A woman with cold cream on her face and her hair in a strange mess of home-made rollers comes barreling out of the room at the end of the hall. 'Enough of this! It's four in the morning. What are all you year nines doing here? Get back to your rooms before I call your dean.'

There's a rush of activity and I leap into the thick of it. Cindy, the blonde girl, is grabbed by the tall one with the smooth dark skin and hauled towards the faculty member. Excited chatter flies through the air and I make my escape while everyone is distracted.

I'm back in my room before anyone can see my door shut. My roommate's bed is empty, the covers pulled back. She'll be back soon, once the adults get the situation under control.

I clutch the paper, wax seal cracking as I unfurl the parchment. All thoughts of Ouija boards and strange men leaping from windows flee my mind.

I know this handwriting as well as my own. My stomach drops to my toes as I squint at the parchment. Another clue from Violet.

The path of Anubis begins in the greenhouse.
*Acta deos numquam mortalia fallunt.*
–Violet

Wax crumbles onto my chest as I dig my fingers into the thick paper. I was right. Violet did want me to come to Ravenswood. She left me those carvings, the note in the skirting board, and whatever sits inside the hollow of her wall. Hands trembling, I unfold the paper the rest of the way, and suck in a breath. Below the note is a hastily drawn map of the school grounds with an X marking a spot just inside the edge of the thick forest.

I hear Mrs Bianchi herding the other girls in our hallway back to bed. My roommate must be out there as well, trying to find the source of the commotion. I move towards my bed, ready to crawl under the covers and reread Violet's note all night. But I hesitate.

My bed is rumpled, like someone sat on it, and my pillow is tossed to the side. As I peel my covers back something litters my mattress, small lumps against the dingy cream sheets. I lean forward, squinting in the dark. Tiny bodies, delicate hairs, and soft green wings curling like dried leaves.

Dead moths. Dozens of them. They're luna moths, identical to the one inked into my thigh. And below the graveyard of insects, right where my pillow is meant to be, is a red X painted in blood.

# 4

The next morning the school buzzes with tales of ghosts. I stand at the top of the staircase, my teeth gritted and my backpack crushed to my side.

The rain continues to drizzle outside and the mist rolling in from the sea is thick and dense. I can hardly see past the border of the gardens and greenhouses lining the back of the school.

Every time I blink I see the dead moths on my bed. The bloody X where my head would have been had I not slipped out of my dorm. Someone sent me a message, one that left little to the imagination. I'm not welcome at Ravenswood Academy.

While I wait, I unroll the note in my fist, the one from Violet's room, and read it again. The map below her short note depicts the outer grounds of Ravenswood with an X marked beyond the base of the grassy hill where the school rests. The border between civilization and the deep forest. I roll the paper back up and run my thumb along the edge.

A group of students, all dressed in the mandatory neutral colors, skirt past me and head downstairs. They let their eyes linger a little longer than necessary. I wonder if it's curiosity guiding their eyes, or something more sinister.

'You could have just waited for me in our room, Andromeda,' a girl grumbles as she comes to my side. I turn from my view of the soaked gardens and fogged windows.

'Andy,' I correct automatically. 'You're my roommate.'

It's not a question, and she doesn't take it as one.

'Well, Andy, my name is Munia Al Soori, thanks for asking.' She gives me a perplexed look as she finishes pinning a silky hijab in place.

'Sorry. I got in late and didn't sleep well.'

I study her face as she adjusts the scarf around her neck and head. She's pretty in a delicate sort of way. Her eyes are a dark amber, and her hijab complements her light brown skin.

'I think everyone could hear the squealing, even in the boys' wing. Usually, I sleep like the dead, but that sure got me out of bed.' She stops fiddling with her clothes and looks me square in the face as if just realizing who I am. Her eyes widen before she looks away, a flush darkening her cheeks. 'I'm sorry. All this talk of ghosts is upsetting, I'm sure.'

Shrugging, I walk down the staircase. I want this over with as quickly as possible so I can run outside and search for the greenhouse.

Munia follows me. Her long trousers swish elegantly as she walks, and I feel a twinge of envy. Violet would have loved Munia's style. Every piece of her clothing is tailored to perfection, she looks more put together than any fashion model.

When we hit the base of the stairs, I feel her staring at the side of my face, studying me. I dart a quick glance at her.

'Right.' She lifts her brow, as if in a question. 'You saw the foyer when you came in, and the admin offices of course. Over there is the cafeteria and dining hall, and through there is one of the libraries . . .'

I shut my mind off and follow dutifully behind Munia. She pauses now and then, waiting for me to reply, but after the third stretch of silence on my end she stops trying. We see the first two floors of the school. She points out the hallways that lead to the English and math classrooms, indicates which rooms are primarily history and fine arts, and so on.

As she leads me through libraries, study rooms, offices and

the gym, my thoughts are far away, nestled in the pine trees where my sister's secret greenhouse waits.

When Munia finally stops by the dining hall doors, and the smell of eggs and burning pancake batter hit my nose, I tuck my backpack closer to my ribs and take a step back.

'Thank you. I'm going to go back to our room for a minute. I forgot my pens.' Giving her a tight nod, I turn to the little alcove. A door leads directly into the back gardens.

'There's an alumni lunch today,' Munia calls as I look back over my shoulder. Her brow is furrowed. 'All the students, from year eleven on, are required to go. An alumni panel speaks and answers questions. If you want to sit with me, I can save you a spot.'

'Okay, thanks.' I nod, eyeing the clock on the wall above her head.

'If you need anything, you can ask me.' Munia frowns a little and watches me go. 'I'm at student council meetings most days and in the library studying, but you know where I live.' She laughs a little.

I give a half-hearted smile and back away again. When she turns towards the dining hall, shaking her head, I bolt for the back door.

I take in a deep breath and fill my nose with the scent of pine and saltwater. The rain has let up a little, but the mist still clings to the ground even as weak sunlight filters through the low cloud cover. My plaid brown trousers, tucked into boots, and my thick navy sweater stick to my skin.

A low brick wall cuts a path through the grass. Greenhouses are lined up against the back of the property and flower beds burst with herbs, shrubs and saplings. But none is the one that Violet indicated. The forest she marked waits beyond the stretch of the grassy hill, past the school grounds.

The property ambles down, tumbling towards the rocky

beach far below. I walk along the edge of the manicured lawn, studying the area. There are crumbling outbuildings in the distance and low stone walls from demolished portions of the old school near the treeline. It would take days to scour the place properly.

My boot catches in the tangled, wet grass. As I crouch to tear the toe of my shoe free, my eyes snag on a crushed bush near a gutter.

I crane my neck up and count the windows. The bush is directly below Violet's room. My jaw clicks as I recall the dark figure leaping from the room above and disappearing into the night. Hiking my bag up on my shoulder, I march towards the flower bed, searching for signs of footprints.

The rose bush is tangled and bruised, lying in a broken heap. Ruby-red petals lie crushed and sodden beneath the outline of a boot. The divots are full of water from the rain and barely visible, but they're there. Besides the footprints, there's nothing to hint of broken bones or blood.

Impossible. But I've encountered the impossible with Violet.

'Looking for this?'

A hand, a soft golden brown, is outstretched, elegant fingers wrapped around a muddy Ouija board. Attached to the hand is a boy in school colors. His angular brows, thick and black, are like slashes across his face, accentuating the alluring dark brown, almost black, eyes.

'No.' I adjust my bag and step out of the bushes, gasping as my lungs slowly fill with the damp air. 'Just looking.'

The boy drops his hand to his side and pushes his damp black hair from his forehead. 'Anything in particular you're after?'

'Nothing you could help me with.' I step around him, ignoring the bitter taste in my mouth and the memories of squealing girls clustered around the very board in his hand.

'You'll find digging around in the rose bushes isn't on the list of extra-curriculars that Ravenswood offers,' he says, one hand tucked into his pocket.

He's handsome, in that annoyingly perfect way that makes you ache to look. His limbs are long and lean, his neck graceful, his lips so perfectly sculpted he looks like marble. The exact preppy trust fund brat I expected to encounter in a place like this. Except mud is caked onto the knees of his immaculately pressed navy trousers. The sleeves of his crisp white button-down are rolled up to his elbows, and those long fingers have dirt beneath the perfect oval nails.

'It looks like you've been doing some digging yourself,' I say, narrowing my eyes to study him more closely. No one else is outside in the gardens, it's too cold and misty.

'Botany class. I was looking for wild mint,' he says absently and shrugs. 'What do you think this is doing out here?' He waves the Ouija board around, and I resist the urge to curl my lip at the sight of it.

'What do I look like, a ghost hunter?'

A short, barking laugh erupts from his lips as a bell rings, high and grating, through the air. He trots along beside me as I duck my head and let my hair tumble around my face, heading across the lawn and back to the door I came through.

'I'm Jae Han.' He offers his free hand, but I ignore it, shoving my own deep into the pockets of my sweater.

I say nothing as he opens the door for me. Our boots squeak, leaving little smudges of mud on the pristine tiles. My skin itches and my throat burns. I rub my eyes. Hard. When was the last time I slept a full night?

'Hello? Did you hear me?' Jae asks, waving his hand in my face.

I squint up at him. 'What?'

'I asked if you knew where you were going.' He produces

27

a shockingly white handkerchief from his pocket and wipes his hands clean. 'I can take you to your class if you like. Don't want you to get lost in the gardens again.'

'I'm fine.'

'Come on.' He gives me a dazzling smile, the kind I'm sure he uses on everything with a pulse to get what he wants. 'I promise I won't bite.'

I ignore him, my fingers trailing the outline of Violet's new note in my pocket.

'Listen,' Jae licks his lips, hesitating before moving an inch closer, 'if you need any help getting settled –'

'I don't want anything from you.' I turn abruptly from the strange boy still holding a dripping Ouija board.

# 5

Voices murmur from within the gym. The doors are flung open wide and posters on easels announce the alumni lunch. With a heavy sigh, I curl one hand around the strap of my bag and duck my head, walking inside.

Circular tables trimmed with crisp white tablecloths dot the polished wooden floor. Expensive silverware and china are artfully placed on each one. A small stage is set up at the front with a long banquet-style table coated with lush floral arrangements. The alumni panel file in and take their seats.

I skirt around the back of the gym, zeroing in on an empty table.

The room fills with year 11, 12 and 13 students. All look eagerly – almost enviously – at the panel of slick, chic adults lined up at the front of the gym. A man with salt-and-pepper hair and a sleek Armani suit lounges gracefully in the center of the head table, his steely-blue eyes hard.

'Everyone, please take a seat.' Headmaster Madden stands at the microphone, off to the side of the stage, as he smooths his hair and smiles graciously at the wealthy patrons on show. 'Food will be served before the question-and-answer session with our esteemed panel.'

The buzz in the room, the noise of frothing animals hungry to make lucrative connections, pushes into my skull. I keep my eyes down as staff flit about, serving soup and seafood dishes with names I can't pronounce.

When a few other people join the table, I don't look up. I don't want anyone to recognize me. Not right now. I study the floral arrangement in the center of the table and twist my napkin in my lap.

The red petals look like roses for a moment. But the stems are all wrong, jet-black streaks peeking through artfully arranged ferns and sprigs of baby's breath. Thorns encrust the stems and creep up towards the jagged petals, like drops of blood on an obsidian blade.

'On behalf of the student council, Ravenswood welcomes you.' A clear feminine voice rings out through the microphone after the food has been served. 'On our panel, we have three alumni from Ravenswood, all of whom have studied at illustrious universities and are pioneers in their fields. We have Dr Neeraj Joshi, one of the premier epidemiologists at the CDC. Senator Catalina Jimenez, who recently led the charge on the bipartisan bill on student debt relief. And finally, Mr Salvatore Russo, CEO of Russo Oil Corporation. Please join me in welcoming our gracious guests!'

My breath catches at the name of the father of Violet's ex-boyfriend. I stare at Mr Russo, at the crisp nod he gives and his cool blue eyes.

Enthusiastic applause rings through the crowd. I will myself to look away from him and instead study the girl at the microphone as she reads questions to the panel. Glossy black hair hangs pin-straight to the small of her back. Her skin is a smooth brown, her brows thick and her eyes dark and sharp. My breath catches in my lungs. I know her. That's Regina Kumar – Violet's best friend.

The grip on my napkin tightens until the cloth cuts off the blood to my fingertips. But I hardly notice. Instead, my eyes are riveted to the tall girl who smiles and laughs at all the right times and knows just when to nod her head or ponder thoughtfully over a panelist's answer.

Regina. She was there the night Violet died. I haven't heard from her since the funeral. She'd sent a bouquet of roses but hadn't come to the service. Something about being in Hyderabad. I thought it was just grief that kept her away. But now, looking at her carefree expression, my stomach twists in time with the napkin in my fists. I have to talk to her.

The panel stretches on endlessly. I spy Munia sitting closer to the front, an empty chair left thoughtfully to her right. She catches my eye a few times, a question on her face. I give her a nod and ignore the guilt in my gut. I didn't come to Ravenswood to make friends. It's better this way.

Finally, after the last question about Ivy League interviews is over, Madden calls the end of the panel. 'But tonight,' he continues as students stand, ready to latch on to the nearest of the alumni and beg a prestigious internship off them, 'a few students will be hand-selected by our alumni for a private dinner. This is an excellent time to make connections for university and beyond.'

Excited chatter ripples through the students. I stand on my toes, scanning over shoulders for a glimpse of long dark hair. Finally, through a gap in the navy and gray cashmere, I spy Regina thumbing through a stack of papers as she speaks to Senator Jimenez. Before I can talk myself out of it, I grit my teeth and weave through the crowd, heading for the buffet tables.

'I attend every Model UN.' Regina leans closer to the senator, handing her a veritable laundry list of academic achievements. 'My father, Varun Kumar, is the Indian ambassador to the US. I'm sure he'd be willing to support your relief efforts in Turkey if you'd be so kind as to write me a letter of rec –'

Regina glances up as my shoes squeak on the polished floor. As I approach, her face pales and her mouth flattens. But I blink and her expression is neutral, and I wonder if I imagined it.

'Regina,' I say, my voice breathless.

Her lips part, but she turns her sharp eyes back to the alumna before her. 'Pardon me, Senator, I'll be right back.'

Regina motions for me to follow her, and we step closer to the empty stage. She crosses her arms, tapping one patent leather loafer against the floor. 'I heard you were here, but I was hoping it wasn't true.'

'I haven't heard from you.' My throat is dry, and I swallow hard. 'You didn't come to her funeral.'

Regina grimaces and looks down at the stack of papers in her hand. 'I couldn't. I hope you understand. Really, I wanted to come. But the last time I saw Violet was when we pulled her body out of the ocean. You don't just get over something like that.'

'You know what I'm going to ask.'

'I don't know what you're hoping to hear that you haven't already.' Regina twists away from me and gathers the vases of flowers from the head table. 'The police, the school board – they've all heard the same story from me.'

I cross my arms over my chest, hugging my soft cable-knit sweater. It was one of Violet's – a cast-off, before she started begging for designer and high-end clothes from our parents and grandparents. She had to be identical to the kids she went to school with. Had to be well-liked and fashionable and everything else the Ravenswood students were. The soft wool is worn in places, but warm, and still smells faintly of Violet's strong vanilla and patchouli perfume. My fingers tingle and my nose itches, but I breathe the smell deeply once more.

'I need to hear what happened that night. Not from Madden. Not from the police. From you.'

Regina watches me for a moment before sighing. She wears a black turtleneck and black leather leggings. She looks chic. Golden hoops brush her shoulders as she adjusts the vases in her grip again, eyes hungrily searching the room for Senator Jimenez.

'She drowned in the cove, Andromeda.' Her voice turns brittle. 'That's all there is to it. You know the police only investigated because she was a student here and they have to avoid any hint of suspicion or blame.'

'But there was more. Why were you at the cove in the first place? How did she just drown, and why was no one else in the water with her?'

I step closer, imagining Regina standing over the water-bloated corpse of my sister. Or did she simply make up that story to hide some darker truth?

Regina straightens, tucking her hair behind her ears. 'Now is hardly the time or place to discuss this. I have to clean up and organize the alumni dinner tonight.'

I reach out, grasping her wrist before I can even think. As I do, my silver bracelet slips free from the sleeve of my sweater. The charms – moth, antlers, moon and tooth – glint in the incandescent light. Regina's eyes snap to the bracelet, narrowing slightly.

'Listen, Andy.' Regina sets down her armful of floral arrangements before carefully plucking one of the strange, jagged-looking roses from a crystal vase. 'Violet had been acting strange since winter break. Our friends were out in town that night, in the middle of the week, without permission. We were drinking – Violet way more than everyone else. We lost sight of her for a moment and,' she snaps her fingers, 'just like that, she was gone.'

I shake my head firmly, the sickly-sweet scent of the flower filling my nostrils. 'She never drank, Regina. Violet said she hated the taste.'

The older girl smirks, quirking a dark eyebrow at me with a wry look. For a moment I think she might even pat my head, mock my naivety. 'Oh Andy, she probably told you that to protect you. Her "little star". Of course she wouldn't want you to know about all that.'

I stiffen at the nickname.

'Violet wouldn't lie to me, something else must have pushed her to act out of character,' I insist. But even as the words slip past my lips, I know they're not true. The note in my pocket crinkles, and I wonder if I really know my sister at all.

'You tell me. Like I said, she wasn't the same after she came back from winter break.' Regina levels me with a look. Accusing.

A queasy feeling takes over my stomach and burns the back of my throat. Winter break. When we got our tattoos. When we saw each other for the last time. When I said those awful words I can't take back. I push the memory firmly to the back of my mind.

'We fought,' my voice squeaks, 'but it doesn't explain what happened to her here.'

'Take some advice, Andy.' Regina twirls the flower in her hand, looking down at it like it's a bouquet of funeral roses. 'Violet is gone. I miss her every minute of every day. But making yourself sick with worry and unanswered questions will only hurt you. Sometimes people die. I've accepted that, and I think it's about time you did as well.'

I want to open my mouth to speak but she lifts her hand and snaps off the long black stem before setting the flower behind my ear. The petals tangle in one humidity-frazzled curl and I reach up, brushing my fingertips over the waxy bloom.

'Violet wouldn't want you to torture yourself. Focus on your schoolwork, on honoring her legacy here. Chasing ghosts will only lead to heartache.' Regina lets her hand fall from the flower, and that slight movement causes one of the long thorns to bite into my thumb and another to scratch behind my ear. I wince. Hot droplets of blood well up and burn my skin.

'But –'

'I have to get back.' Regina turns on her heel, heading for Senator Jimenez, when an alumnus, the CEO with the gray suit and salt-and-pepper hair, moves to her side.

Salvatore Russo, father of Violet's on-again, off-again boyfriend, Luciano. His dark blue eyes are stormy. I tighten my hands into fists, blood smearing from my thumb over my knuckles.

'Mr Russo.' Regina smiles tightly. 'Come with me; our art history teacher and GSE club faculty guide, Mrs Bianchi, will show you to the lounge where you can make some calls.'

'You told Luciano about what I said?' He looks at his watch impatiently, and Regina's smile grows taut. 'He begs me to come to this panel and then runs off to the city for the day to forget his responsibilities?'

She glances at me, lips pressed together. 'He'll be here in a few hours. I'll make sure of it.'

Salvatore Russo looks up at me, taking in my appearance with a flat gaze. He recognizes me. Maybe the tilt of my lips or the shape of my face. The features I share with my sister. Salvatore's face hardens, like he might say something.

'Follow me, sir.' Regina clears her throat, loyal as a dog as they cross the gym and join Mrs Bianchi. I watch as she murmurs something to Mr Russo. They share a terse conversation. Probably about Luciano's absence.

I turn from the head table, stomach in knots and fingers shaking.

'Hey!' Munia's voice rises above the low murmur. 'I saved you a seat but you didn't come. Is everything okay?'

'Fine, thanks. Do you know when we'll find out if we're picked for the alumni dinner?'

I have to see Regina, Luciano and his father.

Munia scrunches her face. 'Only GSE club members will be invited.'

'GSE?' My ears prick up. Regina said something about that to Mr Russo.

'Yeah, the Global Social Enterprise club. You have to be a legacy practically to get in.'

'Legacy?'

'You know, the child of someone else who was in the club. Right now, it only has four members – well, it used to be five with your sister.'

I step closer to my roommate. 'Violet was in this club?'

'Violet, Regina, Luciano, Melinda, Eric – they've been in it since year ten. No one else can join unless they're invited.' She flicks her hijab over her shoulder and rolls her eyes. 'They get all the best internships and field trips. Bianchi is their advisor, and Mr Russo is a donor, so of course Madden won't stir the pot by letting anyone else join –'

'Thanks.' I cut her off, backing away from the gym as my head continues to pound and my thoughts swim with unanswered questions about this exclusive club. 'I'll see you later.'

I turn away from Munia's puzzled expression, clutching my scratched hand to my chest. My heart is beating too fast. I know Regina is involved with whatever happened to Violet.

As I leave the bustle of the gym, I shake out my throbbing hand. I won't stop looking for answers. Because Regina and Luciano know more than they're letting on. And Violet's life depends on me tearing the truth from the grasp of Ravenswood, no matter how badly it hurts.

# 6

The intense headache I've been nursing since the alumni lunch throbs a dull beat at the base of my skull as eighth-period art history class ends. Projected on the board is a grisly painting. Rich oils depict a savage old man using his bared and snarling teeth to rip the limbs off a child. It does nothing to help my head or stomach.

'Francisco Goya used the imagery of Saturn devouring his children deliberately.' Mrs Bianchi speaks at the front of the room, leaning against a podium off to the side. 'Why do you think he would evoke images of the gods from another time?'

Regina, at the front of the class, leans forward, hand shooting into the air. I've been trying to focus; art was Violet's favorite class here and is only offered once a semester for all grade levels. But my head is killing me, and my hand and ear burn from where the thorns punctured my skin.

'Go ahead, Miss Kumar . . . '

'I think Goya was trying to paint an allegory for his own time.' A familiar voice from the back of the room makes my spine snap straight up. 'He was probably trying to show the fear and corruption that happens when someone is afraid of being usurped, just like what was happening in Spain.'

'Excellent, Jae.' Bianchi nods approvingly, even as Regina slumps in her seat, fingers fisting a wad of notebook paper. 'And the constant dichotomy of sons overthrowing fathers – and each trying to thwart those fates – is seen in the painting. Look at the eyes, wild and wide, and the crouching position.

Saturn is desperate to gain control, no matter the consequences or the means. An astute allegory that applies today.'

'Power is something that must be taken, no?' a musical voice asks.

I stiffen, fingers digging into the smooth wood of my desk. Luciano. He leans back in his chair, long legs sprawled lazily. He looks rumpled, somewhat the worse for wear, like he hasn't seen a bed for the past three days. His olive skin is wan and his curly hair disheveled.

'Perhaps, Luciano.' Bianchi shrugs. 'But it is the results that Goya was trying to show. An endless cycle of taking and losing, and the desperate means one employs in order to retain power and control.'

'Power and control are easy things to lose. Maybe the artist was simply trying to say that the rewards justify the means. Saturn may have been defeated, but his sons were no better and did much the same thing. Maybe the only way to keep power is to destroy all your enemies, no matter who they are.'

Regina shifts uncomfortably in her seat next to Luciano. She elbows him and shoots him a glare.

'A very nihilist approach,' Bianchi says drily. 'Perhaps we can have a Socratic seminar on this very subject, if you still feel strongly about it, as we move through Goya and Caravaggio this next week.'

The bell rings and Luciano and Regina stand quickly. They look over their shoulders, whispering together. I stand, following them like a moth to a flame. Before I can race through the doorway after them, an arm shoots out and blocks the way.

'You left this.' Jae holds my backpack out.

I make a grab for it and am about to clutch it in my hands when he takes my wrist. Before I can yelp or smack his arm, I notice what it is he sees.

'What —?' I try to speak but the words are lost.

Jae turns my fingers over to inspect my thumb. A long angry gash appears along the pad. But that isn't what concerns me. Where the thorn punctured my skin, ribbons of black are running through the veins of my hand like ink. I touch the spot behind my ear and wince at the burning, aching flesh.

'I have something that can help,' Jae says, turning my hand over to inspect the cut.

I pull out of his grasp and clutch my hand to my chest. 'No! I have to go to the hospital. This could be blood poisoning.'

'Did you get bitten by a spider? Punctured by a nail?'

'No – it was a flower. The ones with the thorns . . . f-from the lunch,' I stammer a little, feeling foolish at the admission.

Jae sets his mouth in a hard line. 'It's not blood poisoning. I can help. I'm very good with botany.'

'Right,' I snort, my hand aching fiercely. 'That's why you were digging around in those bushes below my –' I catch myself in time. 'Below that room.'

'Andromeda . . .' Jae sighs like I'm an annoying toddler. 'I know who you are.'

'Andy,' I correct, my skin burning, 'and if you'd move, please, I'd like to go see the nurse and then a doctor before I lose my entire hand.'

Jae moves aside but snags my elbow as I try to make a beeline for the nurse. 'Come with me. I know how to help. I swear.'

My hand convulses, fingers curling inward involuntarily. I choke back a gasp. Bright red stains slither down my fingers, and black bruising eats at my nails.

He glances back into the room where Mrs Bianchi is packing up her laptop and books. But he isn't looking at her. By the window, a potted plant with blood-red petals and thorns as black as midnight wilts rapidly. A souvenir from the luncheon?

Jae glances at my hand, then back at the small potted plant, before returning his attention to me. His eyes trace over my face, as if debating something. 'Would you listen to me if I said I have something of Violet's?'

My mouth gapes. 'What? What is it?'

'Not here. Let me fix your hand and I'll show you.' He drops my elbow. Without another word, he turns on his heel, marches out the door and into the grounds, clearly expecting me to follow.

I grind my teeth together, partly to keep from screaming obscenities within Bianchi's earshot, and partly because my hand burns so badly I almost faint.

'Miss Emmerson,' Bianchi calls before I can open the door.

Shoving my arms behind my back, I turn to face her.

She walks past the plant with the thorns, turning it to face the weak sunlight streaming through the cloudy windows. 'How are you doing?'

'Fine.'

'How are you, really?' Her voice is deadpan, but her smooth blue eyes crinkle at the corners in concern.

My stomach tightens and I swallow back the lump in my throat. Bianchi doesn't look away, just waits patiently, a soft expression on her face.

I dig my teeth into my bottom lip. 'It's been hard. But I'm coping.'

She gives a half-hearted smile and nods, smoothing her sleek pencil skirt with one hand before leaning against the lip of one of the long, oiled desks. Her blonde hair is arranged in a neat chignon, stray wisps dangling by her face. She waits for a few beats, never looking away, as if waiting for me to break apart. In that moment, all I can remember is Violet gushing over her. Over the art history teacher who turned down an adjunct position at Oxford to teach at a high school and find students like her and nurture their love of art.

'I can't even imagine how difficult this has been, Andy. If there's anything I can do, truly anything, please let me know.'

Nodding tightly, I move to step away. My body isn't cooperating, and I'm not sure I can speak without my voice breaking.

'You know, the GSE club I advise has an opening,' Bianchi says before I can retreat. 'I spoke with Mr Madden and Mr Salvatore Russo, both donors to the group. I said you may be interested.'

I catch her cool blue eyes. Study them.

I consider her offer. An excuse to be close to the people Violet spent the most time with. They'd know about her final days at the school. How she spent her time. 'Won't other people be upset?'

She shrugs. 'Violet was a member; I don't see why anyone would have an issue. It might do you some good to see what she was doing, how she loved it.'

I remember the way Mr Russo spoke to her at the luncheon. The way he looked at me, like seeing a ghost. I would wager *everyone* connected to the club has an issue with me joining.

'I'll think about it and let you know.' I dig my fingers into my sweater, hoping Jae is still waiting for me.

Bianchi shifts, her elegant heels making a soft clicking sound against the hardwood. 'If you're worried about Regina and Luciano, don't be.'

'That's not –'

'I know they can be . . . obnoxious, for want of a better word.' She laughs lightly, and the tension in my spine slackens. 'But the club is a fantastic resource. It could do so much good for you, just like it did for Violet. She told me so much about you, Andy. If you're anything like she said, you'll excel in the club. It could take you far, if you let it.' She lifts one shoulder. 'Think about it. And don't forget what I said; I'm here for you, whenever you need me.'

Smiling weakly despite the nausea cramping my middle, I stumble out of the classroom and after Jae. He is waiting impatiently in the back foyer, the door to the grounds open behind him.

The air feels too thick as I follow him into the winding gardens, past the greenhouses where students are finishing up their lessons, and over the crumbling stone wall at the far end of the main lawn.

'Where are we going?' I gasp for air, feeling like a wet rag has been slapped across my lips.

Jae looks over his shoulder and slows his long strides. 'A place I found. There's something there that can fix your hand.'

I want to ask more questions, but my eyes feel like they might explode if the pressure in my head doesn't ease. I stumble again and Jae catches me, slinging my arm across his shoulders. Black visions swim in front of my eyes. Antlers. Missing tattoos. My knees give out again. Jae adjusts my weight, but our height difference means he practically drags me through a wide grassy field and towards a thick line of trembling pines.

We lurch into the woods. A thought crosses my racing mind, bursting between flashes of darkness and pain. Maybe he poisoned me. Maybe this is all a ploy to eliminate me and get rid of the last person who cares about Violet's mysterious death. The blood drains from my face and hands at the thought. Cold sweat creeps along my skin and violent shivers convulse my limbs. My eyes close.

# 7

The world spins and suddenly I'm sitting on a rough wooden seat. My head sags against a hard wall. A flashlight burns against my eyelids, and I feel someone's warm hand smoothing my aching one.

'Here,' Jae murmurs, his voice soothing and entrancing all at once, 'this should feel better.'

Something cold and wet is smeared across my hand, stinging the punctures in my thumb.

I yelp, my eyes flying open as the last remnants of delirium vanish almost painfully fast. 'What is that? It smells awful!'

Jae smirks as he spreads a sticky green salve across my hand, his thumbs massaging it into my palm and dragging it down my fingers. The initial sting fades until the pain in my hand is nothing more than a numb suggestion. I expel a shaky breath, which rips through my teeth.

'It's a mixture of different healing plants. You'll get used to the smell in a minute.'

I look around. We're in a dilapidated building, the ceiling half glass and mostly broken. Moss and ivy cling to every surface. A rickety wooden table and shelves full of jars and old books are the only pieces of furniture. Leaves are piled up in the entryway, rotting in a mushy heap. It's an old greenhouse.

'How do you know this is going to fix it? There's something wrong with my hand . . . my head, I –'

'Your head hurts? I imagine so. The plant that cut you can have some very strong hallucinogenic effects if it enters the bloodstream.'

'What plant are you talking about?' I reach back to touch the swollen skin behind my ear. But even as I look at my hand, and see the black ribbons disappearing, I feel a cold tingle.

'The one in Bianchi's room. It was the same one from the lunch.'

'The rose?'

'Not a rose.' Jae lifts my hair from my neck and I breathe in sharply, stiffening. He smooths more of the ointment on the wound behind my ear, warm fingers tracing the contours of my jaw and neck.

'Then what was it?' I try to keep a tremor from my voice, sharpening the edges of my words like a blade. 'How can your disgusting grass paste fix whatever is wrong with me? My skin looked almost dead.'

I shudder as his fingers skate along the sensitive skin behind my ear.

'*Subitae mortem* is extremely rare and only grows – well, nowhere near here. And this salve isn't made of *grass*, it's a bunch of herbs to counteract the poison from the thorns.'

'Poison?' I choke.

Regina couldn't have known that this little flower with its odd, jagged leaves and wicked thorns was poisonous, could she? Why would she decorate an entire gym with them if that was the case? But my pulse pounds at the side of my neck, jumping at the gashes in my skin, and I let myself wonder.

Jae nods and steps back, wiping his hands clean on a handkerchief. He tosses it behind him and crosses his arms, leaning against the lip of the table to study me. 'It's a very dangerous plant. It shouldn't be near the school.'

'They were the centerpieces,' I mumble, my tongue sticking to the roof of my mouth.

'Not the smartest idea. I told Regina so, but the head of the

44

GSE club bows to no one. Besides, it's not exactly a common plant. I doubt anyone else recognized it.'

I shut my eyes, recalling Regina deliberately plucking the reddest, angriest bloom and tucking it behind my ear as I questioned her about my sister –

I stand abruptly, my legs knocking the stool out from underneath me.

I glance around, noting journals, books and jars. Strange items to store in what looks like an abandoned greenhouse. 'What did you mean when you said you had something of my sister's?'

'Violet?'

'Did you know her? Were you here when they say she drowned?'

Jae pushes his inky black hair off his forehead. 'I wasn't at Ravenswood when it happened. This is my first year.'

Hope drops like an anchor, sinking into oblivion. 'Then how do you know about Violet? Why do you care?'

'It felt suspicious to me. The other kids in my year still gossip about it, but I've learned that besides one local article, the school hushed it up. Even Violet's closest friends have refused to speak about it. And then, well, I found this place.'

I sit up straighter, twisting to look out of one grimy window pane. Through decades of sludge, I can just make out the roof of the school, up a steep hill. This isn't just any greenhouse, it's *the* greenhouse. The one Violet had sketched out in her map.

'How did you find this?' I demand.

'I was just wandering one evening and came across it. Most students stay out of the woods, it's expressly forbidden. There are bears, the occasional wolf, and endless acres to get lost in. But I like plants and wanted to look around. I knew it was hers when I looked at the books. She wrote her name inside each cover.'

'What do you know about her death?'

'Nothing more than you.' He holds up his hands. 'But I got interested after I found this greenhouse and all her things inside it. Do you have any idea what your sister was into? What she and her friends were doing?'

'Why get involved in something the police aren't investigating and you don't have any personal connection to?'

He shrugs and traces a line in the wooden tabletop with a long finger. 'Maybe I know a little something about girls dying in schools like this.'

'What does that mean?'

'I want to help you.'

A red-hot anger flashes across my eyes and blisters through my veins.

*Help me?*

Indignant, I clench my fists, ignoring the squelching sound the ointment makes. 'You don't have the right to poke into Violet's life here. Leave it alone. If anyone is going to get answers, it should be *me*.'

'It seems you and I are the only ones who still care that a girl died here.'

Heat blooms in my belly, angry and sharp. 'Stay away from me and from my sister. You're just a bored, rich asshole who wants to play ghost hunter like everyone else here.'

I take a step towards him, my hands trembling with the effort it takes to keep from striking him. How dare he use Violet's memory as some sort of game to entertain himself?

'It's not like that.'

'Then what *is* it like?' I don't move.

He stares, his jaw so tight a muscle jumps. A brief shrug tugs my attention to the broad shoulders I'm so near to. 'I just want to help, Andromeda.'

'I don't need your help. And my name is Andy.'

I wipe the green ointment from my hand across his crisp white shirt. He smiles, his perfectly shaped lips parting over equally perfect white teeth.

'See you in class, *Andy*,' he calls as I storm from the crumbling building.

Even as I plot my return to my sister's strange greenhouse in the woods, I can't help but look down at the cut from the thorns. I barely keep myself from whipping my head around to catch sight of Jae. Because my hand, which only minutes ago burned and looked a sickly shade of red, is perfectly healed.

# 8

It's late afternoon by the time I slip back into the school, wiping the last of the green paste off my hand. I have to find Luciano before the alumni dinner.

It isn't difficult to find him. I follow the sound of obnoxious laughter from a rec room that is centered between the boys' and girls' wings.

A tall boy and Luciano are lounging in the room. He looks up just as I walk in, and for a moment his face flickers with recognition. And something darker.

'Can I speak with you for a moment?' I ask. The other boy gives me a funny look, as if he recognizes a hint of Violet in me. Or is it wonder at the audacity of some new girl speaking to the star student?

The boy, tall and stocky as a lineman, straightens. 'Find another rec room. This one's for club members only.'

I square my chin, matching his glare with one of my own.

Luciano holds up his hand before I can say anything. 'I'll catch up with you, Eric. Tell my father I'll be there in a moment.'

Eric stands obediently, shooting me a look so full of venom a chill slithers down my back. Soon the room is quiet. A grandfather clock ticks in time to my racing heart.

'Must be an exciting club if you get a whole rec room to yourself.'

Luciano waves his hand dismissively. 'Eric is territorial about what's his. Comes from being the son of a very successful soccer player and sharing his life with press since before he could talk.'

I don't reply. I couldn't care less about Eric Lindgren, son of famed Swedish soccer captain Johan Lindgren, and his pissing contest with school property. He's Luciano's oldest friend and most loyal lackey. Violet never liked him – and I share the sentiment.

'You know who I am?' I ask, just because I want to hear him say it.

His sea-blue eyes darken a shade. 'Of course. You look like your sister. I knew you'd want to speak with me at some point.'

'You and Violet dated . . .' I pause, but continue when he flicks his hand as if urging me to get to the point. 'I wanted to hear from you what happened that night.'

'Do you not think it unwise to go digging into something like this? Regina already spoke to me. You know Violet drowned. You know I was there. You and I both know the police cleared me of any wrongdoing.' His accent rolls the words so that, though they sound beautiful, they bite with a vicious warning.

I narrow my eyes but don't back away. Violet and Luciano's relationship was turbulent at best, fraught with tears, fights and cheating. I could never tell who was to blame for their rocky relationship, only that they were both stubborn and their passions burned hot, getting in the way of others' feelings. I don't trust him. Never have.

He can play the pretty, rich Italian playboy all he wants. But he's holding something back.

'I just want to hear it from you. My parents, the school, the police – they've all tried to protect me. The only way I can get any closure is to come here and ask for myself.'

His smile, movie-star white, fades. Crumbles to dust. 'Okay, I'll tell you. I didn't want to admit this but . . . we got into a fight. It was stupid and immature, and I would take it back in a second. Violet was drunk. She walked away. I should have followed her. I didn't. And then she drowned. And I just feel so awful, and that's why I didn't go to the funeral.'

I shake my head once. 'And you called the police yourself?'

'Yes.' He looks up at the ceiling, blinking fast, and rubs his hands under his eyes – his completely *dry* eyes. 'Couldn't stand to see the only girl I've ever loved lying cold in the sand.'

The word 'love' seems to be torn from his mouth like a rotten tooth. Something flashes in his flat blue eyes as we look at one another, and I feel a cold tremor jolt all the way to my toes.

His father and Headmaster Madden are friends, graduated in the same class at Harvard. He's here for the alumni event. Hand-picked. A donor. They could have worked together to protect the golden-boy image of Luciano Russo, heir to a massive oil company.

My eyes turn to slits. 'Your dad flew in the next morning, didn't he?'

'Of course. He knew I was in pain and came to make sure I was alright. Not surprisingly, I was a wreck.'

I flick absently at a thread on the cuff of my sweater. 'Didn't he go to the local paper and have the story axed?'

He stands, all six foot three of him towering over me, as his jaw ticks and he clears his throat, brushing a hand over his mouth. 'Seeing your first love dead and cold breaks something in a person. Father didn't want to see my name dragged through the mud when I'd done nothing wrong. He helped the locals see that.'

'Huh.' I'm making a humming noise. The grief shadowing his face doesn't quite reach his eyes as I lean closer, my jaw aching as I grind my teeth and force out my words. 'Strange that you were there the night she died, and were so overcome with emotion that you couldn't bear to attend her funeral. But you jetted off that same weekend to – where was it, Mallorca?

Just partying it up while the "only girl you've *ever* loved" lay in a casket.'

His Adam's apple bobs, and his brow furrows. Those famous crystal-blue eyes of his are still bone dry. But he doesn't say anything as his lips remain parted. And then he turns on his heel and walks away from me.

Madden, Mr Russo and Luciano are connected to Violet. I feel it in my bones. I glare at the disappearing shadow of Violet's ex-boyfriend, surer than ever that I'm staring at the reason my sister is missing.

Not dead, like Luciano claims, but vanished.

Like smoke.

# 9

Night falls over Ravenswood Academy. Munia sleeps soundly in her bed as I stare out the window and look over the grounds, waiting once more for silence to fall before I return to the greenhouse. I absently trace the tender skin behind my ear. The cut is gone, but all I can think about is Luciano and Regina. Her deft hands tucking the flower – just so – behind my hair. The thorns kissing my skin.

A few more minutes slip by as I listen for signs of movement. When I'm sure all is quiet, I yank on my rainboots and open my backpack to shove in my flashlight. As I do, something wet and sticky touches my fingertips. Grimacing, I withdraw my hand and hold it up to the weak light. My fingers are stained dark, like paint.

The smell of copper invades my nostrils and I freeze, the moaning wind making the hairs on my arms stand on end.

Blood. Blood coats my hand and seeps into the cracks of my nails. I smother a scream, jolting back so hard I collide with my bedframe. Munia doesn't stir as I pry my backpack open and look inside.

Antlers – small, like they belonged to a young buck – poke out between my binder. Everything swims, the world tilting, like I can't get enough oxygen. Maybe I'm imagining this. Maybe it's a nightmare. I hold my breath and pull the antlers out. The smell of blood and rot is sickening, and I gag as a decomposing deer skull glares at me with hollow eye sockets. Insects and maggots crawl between the bared teeth and dangle from strips of flesh.

Blood pounds in my ears and my breath comes in sharp, shallow gasps as I stumble to the door.

Holding my bag and the dripping skull at arm's length, I slip from my room into the empty hallway, ducking inside the bathroom. The light is harsh, accenting the grooves of bone and the prongs of the antlers. The jaw dangles grotesquely, swaying as my hand shakes uncontrollably and tremors convulse my limbs.

I fling the head and backpack onto the floor, feel the shudders crawl across my skin. My knees are weak. My throat burns. I touch the flesh at the base of my neck with an ice-cold hand and imagine someone sawing through it, ripping, tearing. Just like they did to the deer. Blackness creeps into the edges of my sight and I sway.

The skull settles, the jaw sliding to the side. Something stained pink sits on the half-rotten tongue. Nausea swells in my gut and presses on my ribs, but I grit my teeth and reach inside the mangled jaw. I pull out a piece of blood-stained paper and set it on the counter. Holding my breath, I drop the skull into my backpack, zipping it shut, and hurl it into the garbage bin.

The paper flutters to the ground as I lean over the basin and heave, turning on the stream of hot water to scour blood and viscera from my nails. Someone was in my room again. Snuck inside and left a dead animal for me to find. Somewhere between dinner and lights out. It couldn't be Munia; she was studying with her friend all evening long in the common room.

So, who was it?

Who would want to not just frighten me away from Violet, but threaten me too? The moths, the bloody X, the severed deer head – they add up to more than just a warning. Someone wants me dead.

Once I can control my breathing, I stoop down and gingerly unfold the foul-smelling note. I'm not surprised when

I see another blood-red X on the paper with a single word below it, scrawled in angry, harsh capitals.

LEAVE.

I *am* surprised at the symbol blazoned at the base of the note, like a coat of arms. A curved tooth crosses a wickedly sharp eagle's talon, surrounded by a wreath of bones. They look like human femurs.

Tooth and talon. This is who Violet warned me of.

I look over my shoulder, but the bathroom is empty. Swallowing hard, I finish drying my hands and fold the new note into my pocket. I zip my jacket up to my chin and hold my flashlight in my fist. It's heavy enough to bludgeon someone with, if I have to.

Whoever is threatening me knows something about Violet. The tooth and talon symbol proves that whoever – or whatever – that is, they scared her enough to warn me. They want me gone from Ravenswood. Away from Violet's clues.

I stand up straight and meet my eyes in the mirror. I can't let this break me, or frighten me away. No one can stop me from saving Violet. Dead bugs and a rotting skull aren't enough to keep me from her. If someone wants me to leave, they'll have to personally drag my dead body through the gates.

I spin on my heel, leaving my ruined backpack and the skull behind.

I sneak through the halls and down the stairs. The same back door, quiet and nestled in the strange alcove, is deserted. The door shuts noiselessly behind me.

Once I exit the low wall that rims the main gardens, I tug my hood over my hair. For once, there isn't any rain, but the air is damp from the humid wind blowing in from the ocean and the grass is sodden with dew. My sliver of light cuts through the darkness and I cross the wide-open field leading to Violet's greenhouse.

I clench my teeth and touch my ear. Regina and Luciano know I'm asking questions. It can't be a coincidence that I've had a confrontation with each of them and just so happen to be threatened soon after.

That same uneasiness I felt when pricked by the strange flower grows as the shadows thrown by the approaching treeline grow longer. Deeper. I retrace my steps from earlier, when I left the greenhouse and Jae behind, trying to remember which break in the foliage leads to the dilapidated building.

I shut off my flashlight as soon as the listing building comes into sight between thick branches, feeling my way blindly for the next few steps. Pausing, I listen for the rasp of breath or the whisper of voices. For the crunch of footsteps. But it's silent. Eerie.

The smell of mildew and rotting leaves hits my nose as I gingerly pick my way inside the greenhouse, nudging a piece of sodden plywood aside that serves as a makeshift door. It's a little drier inside; half of the gaping hole in the roof is haphazardly covered by a blue plastic tarp.

I set my flashlight on the table, and rummage through discarded candles and matches in a dirty plastic bin. The smell of smoke flits briefly to my nose as I light a few stubs, placing them around the small space. Soon, the warm flickering light is enough to see by.

I rub the spot behind my ear again, stomach churning.

My breath plumes in front of my face. I trace my fingers over the books on the shelf. Some are so old, I wonder how Violet got hold of them.

I drop to my knees and dig through the books on the lower shelves until I see something glimmer – a leather cover with gold embellishments.

*Clavis Inferni*. 'The Key of Hell'.

It feels like someone punched me in the gut. The cold

earth seeps into the knees of my jeans as I reach forward with trembling fingers and flick the cover open. The thick yellowed pages are heavily annotated. Smudged ink bleeds into the margins. I recognize Violet's neat, looping handwriting.

Biting down on my cheek, I scan the book in the low candlelight. Strange spells and incantations litter the pages. Questions and underlinings and ideas.

*Could this work for controlling familiars?*

*Does this spell work during a waxing crescent?*

*Similar to incantations used in the cult of Hecate . . .*

I put the book back on the shelf and stand, kicking aside a pile of sodden and rotting leaves. Bell jars, misted over with condensation and smudged with dirt, line the wall. They're also labeled in Violet's handwriting.

I study the stickers and pinch my lips together. Mugwort. Cardamom. Hemlock. Wolfsbane. Narcissus. Rosehip. Belladonna. And on the shelf below are some I have never heard of. Other labels are scrawled in ancient languages. Bundles of sage and smudge sticks litter the low table in the center. Crystals, stones and bags of salt line another rickety shelf. Tarnished silver bowls, cracked teacups and blades of various metals are scattered about.

I peer at something on the table, half covered in leaves. Flecks of something dark stain the blade of a large knife. I dust away the rotting foliage and look closer. Rust? But then I see the way it sticks to the metal; how dark it is. Blood.

I stagger back until I hit the bookshelf.

A ball of dread lodges beneath my sternum as sweat slicks my brow. I want to run from here, from these strange secrets. But I can almost hear Violet encouraging me to look beyond what is in front of me. To perceive the truth hidden behind the mystery.

But this isn't right. This isn't Violet. A breeze flaps the blue tarp, slapping it against the broken roof. And then a pile of small bones near the silver bowls rolls gently back and forth, back and forth.

Blood and bones. Knives and spells.

'What were you getting into, Violet?' I whisper to the wind.

It seems to answer, a low and mournful groan that rips through the thick branches. The temperature is dropping. I smell rain coming in the distance. All I see are the bones. The blood. And what looks like teeth in a silver bowl.

Blood.

Bones.

Teeth.

Magic.

My hip hits the rickety table, and it shudders, crystals spilling across its grimy surface. I reach out to steady myself and feel the familiar crinkle of paper. One of the boards on the tabletop is loose. I turn, shaking from the cold and something else. Prying the wood up, I reach in and yank hard, freeing a beat-up folio from the hidden compartment. It's hastily bound by silver rings and a cardboard cover. But there's no mistaking the messy, scrawled note on the inside cover.

To my little star. Follow the path of Anubis. I know you can
do it.

I press my fist to my lips, gasp for breath. Fingers shaking, I flip open the first page.

Inside are printed pictures I've seen tacked up on the walls of Violet's room. Paintings by Caravaggio, Da Vinci, Goya. Dark oil paintings with vivid splashes of color and strange images of demons, witches and monsters.

On each page are symbols I recognize well, and some I don't. There's an Egyptian ankh, an eye of Horus, a moth, antlers, and glyphs in many languages. Something dances at the edge of my mind, something I can't quite grasp. Violet was the historian, the artist, and a genius. She knew seven languages, and she read more widely than anyone I have ever met.

That terrible knot in my chest tightens. I realize something that hurts almost as badly as the poisonous plant.

I didn't know Violet at all.

I spin round, hands on my head as I struggle to breathe. The candles flicker, the light dancing across the broken, dirt-choked window panes. A familiar trickle of cold dread slides down my spine. Like I felt in Violet's old room. A sense of . . . something otherworldly. The flames dance wildly, cavorting with the shadows from books and jars and broken teeth.

Reflected in the shattered pieces of the filthy glass, I see Violet's face, cold and bloated with water, staring at me with black eyes. Her hair is a wet, stringy mass plastered across her chalky brow. She opens her mouth to plead with me to keep trying, to keep searching. But no words, only water tinged with blood, dribble out.

I scream. The sound is stolen by the wind as it returns, fierce and violent. The candles are extinguished, smoke swirling in the air as whatever I think I saw in the glass disappears. I stagger outside. I have to leave.

The wind bites. Like that night I saw her for the last time. When I said those awful things and ignored the fear on her face when she told me she needed help. I didn't believe her. Didn't listen.

My hair whips against my cheeks as I clutch the folio to my chest. I left the flashlight somewhere in the crippled greenhouse. There isn't much moonlight; I look up at a faint hazy halo in the thick clouds. I don't care. I run. From the truth. From the memories I try so hard to forget. From myself.

Her little star. The reason she's gone.

But I can't outrun secrets.

## 10

Thunder rolls in the distance. Over the sea, lightning strikes. A ghostly purple and blue light illuminates the bank of rolling black clouds. Without a flashlight, I can hardly see. Branches whip my face and grasp at my hair, tugging me back, pulling me into their embrace.

After a while, I stop running and brace my hands on my knees, gasping until the dizziness fades and my chest rises and falls in a steady rhythm. Tears sting my cheeks and I hardly notice that my hand is still closed around the tattered folio with the grotesque yet fascinating oil paintings.

What do the bones, the blood or the magic have to do with anything?

Another sob is torn from my throat. Replaying the last time I saw my sister. Those words we threw at each other. How she all but told me she was in danger. I thought it was emotional dramatics. Another break-up with Luciano. But now I see she knew what was coming.

*Enough! Violet needs you.* She isn't dead. *Isn't dead.* Alive.

It doesn't matter that I don't understand.

I need to go back to her room before Madden can scrub the place clean or put new students in there. Maybe these paintings contain a pattern. The symbols she's scrawled on each work must mean something. A cipher of some kind, like she tried to teach me to use as a kid.

I take a deep breath and wipe my cheeks.

Distant thunder rolls. I tuck the folio into the deep inner pocket of my rain jacket and zip it back up. The sharp corner digs into my side, reminding me I have so much to do. Turning, I look for the path I charged along in my race from the greenhouse. But the wind shakes the branches, and leaves roll across the ground. I can't find my footprints. I'm totally lost. Have I really come so far?

The smell of impending rain, that rich, earthy scent, is suddenly marred by something else. Bitter and choking. Smoke. I straighten, eyes straining in the dark. Flashes of distant lightning momentarily illuminate the tall trees, the rocky boulders and the soft, spongy ground.

There in the distance, a speck of orange light. Smoke swirls through the trees, growing thicker by the moment. The smell isn't like any campfire. It's rich and multilayered, like incense mixed with something else. Something acrid.

I only ran for a few minutes, but the trees all look the same to me, the mossy rock and leaf-littered ground underfoot. I try to locate the sea or the lights from the school through gaps in the treeline, but it's impossible with the clouds rolling in and mist rising amongst the branches. I must be further away from Ravenswood than even the greenhouse is.

I drift towards the mysterious firelight, drawing closer to the smoke that is so strong my eyes burn. My lungs tighten and I choke between rasping coughs. Despite the thunder and the distance, I think I hear voices. A melodic, chanting sound. It pulls me forward. A call in the darkness just for me.

The flames grow brighter, and I skirt around trees, stumbling over roots and stones.

The fire can't be more than a hundred feet away when the chanting stops. So does my heart. I listen, straining, feeling foolish for wandering in the deep woods where there is so much mystery and potential danger. Where Violet could have been hurt and taken captive.

The flames grow brighter, reach higher, licking the air

and casting immense shadows. Four people stand in a circle around the fire. Something is thrown onto the pyre, and sparks and embers erupt and scatter in the air. Through the swirling flames I see four hooves lashed together, the fur on the animal turning black before it burns too.

The chanting resumes. When the group members move, their shadows look deformed. No, they're wearing hoods. Hoods with antlers attached. Like the rotten deer skull in my room.

The words wash over my skin and pull me forward again. Just as I take another step closer, the fire disappears, extinguished, and the voices stop.

The air tastes wrong – almost sick, and poisonous. The chorus resumes, but it's different from before. Voices, furtive whispers in tense strains, far too many for the few figures I saw clustered around the dead fire. Then rain, sheets of it pouring down, sizzle over the hot embers. Mist and smoke and rain collide, and I'm momentarily blinded.

Bleached white bone stares up from the ashes. Smoke curls through ribs, dances over the knobs of a spine. Dark blood, black and congealed, trickles through the fire pit in roiling bubbles. Like a river. I stare in horror as the bones settle, clacking together. It's a deer without a head.

An animalistic sound, deep and reverberating, echoes around the forest. Birds scatter, their wings beating out a rhythm that echoes my pulse. The bones shift again, disappearing into the pit. It's as if the carcass of the deer is being consumed. Something darker than the deepest shadows emerges from the bonfire. Hunched. Broken.

The harsh, bitter smell is so strong, it catches in my throat. I cough, the sound echoing in the sudden silence, and the figures turn towards me. One taller than the rest, misshapen and hulking, steps forward out of the bonfire.

Everything inside of me screams to run. So, I do. Fleeing in the opposite direction, as fast and as far as I can go. I think I hear footsteps following me, shouts. My boots slip as I stumble over the slick ground, and water runs into my eyes. The rain hammers down with even more fury and I collide with a tree, the rough bark tearing at the skin of my palms. I cough again, my lungs still full of that awful smell.

Lightning flashes, and for a moment I can see the unmistakable thinning of trees, the promise of the clearing near the greenhouse.

Darkness again. I pick my way forward, soles slipping, soft ground sucking at my heels. I reach out blindly, using my hands to save myself from the worst of the whipping branches and the sideways rain pelting my eyes and cheeks. My hood blows back and my hair whips around my face in wet clumps like a blindfold.

Peeling the hair off my eyes, I surge forward. Lightning flashes once more, and I dart a glance over my shoulder. There is an outline of something behind me. Something tall and moving. As the darkness returns, the deafening clap of thunder overhead makes my skin tingle.

The blackness of the night swims before my eyes and I push forward, hands outstretched. The toe of my boot catches on something – a root, a rock – and I fall forward, landing on my elbows. Sharp pain radiates down to my fingers, but I crawl forward. Slow, measured steps make the ground beneath my hands vibrate. Leaves and undergrowth shudder from the force of heavy feet. A steady rhythm that draws closer.

I suck in a breath and scuttle on my hands and knees, rocks tearing at flesh and cutting through my jeans. The *thump, thump, thump* gets closer. I claw wildly, struggling to my feet. The rain lessens but the mist doesn't, and I heave my body forward, clutching at a tree.

Another flash. A clearing bathed in brilliant white light tinged with blue. The soft orange lights of the school in the distance.

I twist my head and a scream sticks in my throat. The roof of my mouth is dry with fear. Mist swirls around a set of antlers rising from the head of an impossibly tall figure. Darkness obscures the clearing for a moment before a web of bright purple scatters overhead.

Empty eye sockets. Elongated skull. Twisting horns rising high and piercing the heavy lid of mist. Black robes open at the waist. A sound, low and throaty, erupts from the creature's mouth, coated half in flesh while the rest is bone. Its hand reaches towards me. Blood drips from the huge fingers big enough to grab and crush my entire head. The skin is wrong – thick and textured. Black lines form a heavy tattoo, crawling up the hand and over the wrist, undulating like liquid ink.

Everything shifts. The world tilts sideways.

The breath is knocked from my lungs as someone decidedly human-sized flattens me to the ground. Golden skin and slick, wet black hair.

*Jae.*

He rolls off of me in a flash before colliding with the monster, keeping it from ripping into me, saving me from certain death. An animalistic grunt is ripped from the beast's throat, the antlers sway as it crashes to the earth, blood dripping from its mangled jaw. All I can see is the skull in my backpack.

Blood and death.

'Come on!' Jae shouts, crouching down to grab my shoulders.

'What is that thing?'

Jae's face is ashen white as he grabs me underneath the arms and hauls me to my feet.

'Run, Andy. We have to get back to the school!' Jae jerks

my arm hard, and I stumble after him. His legs are long, and he practically drags me through the rest of the trees and into the clearing below the school.

Jae's fingers wrap around my waist, half holding me as we stagger through the clearing and up the hill. He whips his head round to look behind us and curses, his teeth gritted as rain drips down his sculpted cheekbones. I make the mistake of looking as well.

Every flash of lightning acts like a strobe light. With each blink, each step, the antlered monster gets closer. The black ink moving across its arm shudders and rolls like the waves of the boiling sea. So close. So far from safety.

'Come on! He can't enter the grounds of a building unless he's summoned there. Hurry!' Jae shouts over the thunder.

The hair on my arms stands on end, even under the fabric of my jacket. I blink at Jae, uncomprehending, as he hauls me over a large rock.

Another curse rips from his lips and he runs faster. The wall of the garden is only a few steps away. Jae looks over his shoulder once more before he reaches out and pushes me to the side, knocking me onto the soft grass. That's when I see it.

The monster with the half-fleshed face and the twisting antlers. He's so close the smell is suffocating, like burnt skin and boiled blood mixing with the salty air. And then the scent of ozone, distinct and crisp. A flash so bright all I see is white.

A split-second later, thunder shatters the world. The monster staggers, his antlers singed, as ribbons of electricity from the lightning rip across his skin. Jae crawls to his knees and hoists me up, throwing my limp body over the stone wall. I can't hear anything as he shouts at me. His face is a huge white blur. He turns back to the monster.

For a moment, I can't tell if it's a trick of the endless flashes of lightning overhead or the unrelenting rain, but Jae's profile seems to change as he stalks towards the smoking beast. It's as if his face has changed with the flashes of light – elongated, or shifted somehow. But when I blink hard, his face looks normal.

The beast lowers its antlers towards Jae's chest. I see Jae's lips move around alien words, and the beast replies.

Jae shakes his head, and his face looks strange once more. Inhuman. Almost like an animal's. But then it flickers back to normal with the next flash of lightning overhead. My ears pop, and for a moment I think I can hear something intelligible.

'. . . go from this place before your time on Earth runs out,' Jae snarls.

The monster responds with a flurry of words I can't decipher, before it turns, still smoking from its brush with the storm, and is enveloped in the swirling mist.

# 11

I don't remember how we got inside. Jae carries me like I weigh nothing and drops me onto a musty couch in a room I don't know. We're somewhere deep inside the school – a forgotten storage room, if the stacked desks indicate anything. A radiator hums in the background, vibrating angrily.

Jae strolls around the room, peeling off his jacket and tossing it in the corner. I look around while my ears ache and my eyes slowly adjust to the low light.

Jae shucks his soaked sweater over his head, leaving him in black jeans and a dark blue T-shirt. Our eyes meet.

'Andy, can you hear me?' He squats in front of me, but I can't focus on his face. All I see are the antlers and the textured skin of that monster and the way Jae's profile shifted with the light.

I lick my cracked lips and clutch my fingers in my lap so hard my nails pierce my palms. 'What was that thing? Th-the monster. The thing with the antlers. You talked to it!'

Jae's face darkens and he holds a finger to his lips. 'We're not meant to be down here.'

I shake my head fiercely, hoping I'll wake up in my bed and that everything was just a strange dream. But I'm not that lucky.

'Tell me what it was. You talked to it.' My breath sticks in my chest as I recall the mottled skin and the rotten smell of decay.

Jae swallows hard. His eyes are narrow and wary as he crosses his arms and stands up straight. 'I don't know.'

'That's a lie. I heard you speaking to it. You told it to leave.'

'Something bad. Something that shouldn't be here.'

'Tell me,' I demand, forcing myself to stand, even though my legs shake and my wet clothes make my skin so cold I can't feel my fingers.

'Not until I can trust you.'

I choke on a bitter laugh. 'Are you kidding me? You followed me into the woods. You're the one digging into my sister's actions for no reason, and you wonder if *you* can trust *me*?'

He stares at me, jaw clenched. I ball my fists and try to push past him roughly, but it's more like a wobble on my weak legs. A set of white-painted steel stairs lead up to a narrow door, like an old servants' wing.

'Wait, Andy.' Jae catches my elbow. 'I needed to keep an eye on you. And I was right. I saw you leave from the window in my room. In the middle of the night, in a rainstorm. You have no idea what you stumbled into.'

'Then explain what the hell is going on!' I shout.

He sighs, struggling for words, and rakes his fingers through his wet hair, combing it out of his eyes. It's glossy black and for a moment I'm reminded of the way he looked beneath the stormy sky. Almost . . . inhuman.

The radiator rattles and we both jump.

'Tell me why you're looking into Violet,' I demand. 'I can't trust you, can't believe anything you claim, until we start there.'

Finally, he turns aside, crossing the room to a pile of dusty boxes and wooden crates stacked in the corner. Jae opens a chest next to a rolled-up Turkish rug. He digs inside and the scent of mothballs wafts towards me. He holds out a dry sweater. I don't know who it belongs to, but I take it and unzip my jacket.

He turns his back to me and faces the cracked plaster wall. 'I never really considered going to Ravenswood,' he begins.

'But my parents decided that the school I was at held too many bad memories. I lost someone important to me there, and nearly went mad with the grief. My mom heard about the academy from friends and decided I should come here,' he continues, his voice stilted. 'So, I started researching the place I was going to live at for the next two years, and came across a news article about your sister. My parents sent me here early, before the end of the summer. I asked about her, and it seemed odd that no one was talking about a girl who drowned in a cove at an elite private school. I dug into the school's history, and I found something.'

His voice drops, low and accusing. 'Your sister isn't the first mysterious death at this place. I've found a pattern going back to the first cohort of Ravenswood. At least *sixty* similar deaths have happened over the years. All young girls. All drowned. Though some bodies were never located.'

My stomach hollows out. A history of girls drowning in the cove. I grip the hem of my drenched sweater and tug it over my head, putting the folio on the ground by my boot. I want to retch, to vomit. But what Jae says is eerie. Is this what Violet wanted me to know when she disappeared in the cove? Maybe these other girls point the way to the path she mentioned, littering it with their bodies.

I think of the moths in my bed. The deer head.

'And you think Violet is another one of these girls, that she's part of the pattern?' I fling my wet clothes aside, memories tangling so badly I don't know how to unwind them.

'I know she is.' He turns around and his face is grim. 'It can't be a coincidence. Each one is hushed up. It took a lot of time and digging through town and church archives for death records, and reading reports from newspapers that haven't been in print for five decades.'

'So, you think the school is covering something up?' I

shiver, imagining dozens of girls, all like Violet, floating in the cove. Forgotten. Abandoned.

'They have to be involved somehow. I know that much. But your sister isn't the first, and I'm afraid she won't be the last. Each time a girl goes missing or turns up dead, it's never a one-time thing. Two more always follow soon after.'

I press my hand to my forehead. Drops of water drip from my hair and stain the shoulders of the borrowed sweater. 'How have the police or the FBI not gotten involved? Or at least the girls' parents? The victims are not nameless wanderers. They're from elite families – socialites and diplomats.'

'That's what I want to find out. There has to be something murky going on for so little to have been done. So little notice taken. Sometimes it's local girls who disappear, other times it's students. But the deaths have occurred at intervals since the 1890s.' Jae rubs his jaw and I notice his knuckles are bruised. 'That's why I'm interested in your sister.'

'That thing in the woods – the monster. Is that what's killing the girls?'

'I don't think so. Why would something so big drown them and not devour them?'

I press my lips together, sinking my teeth into the flesh to keep them from trembling. 'What is it, then? Tell me.'

'I really don't know what it is. A monster, yes. Or maybe someone dressed as one to scare the hell out of you and push you away from the truth.'

I think back to the bizarre ritual I witnessed in the woods. Those people in the robes, they weren't just having a meeting. They were . . . feeding that thing. The body of the deer was consumed faster than time or fire would ever allow. And the way it emerged from the ashes . . .

My jaw clicks as I grind my teeth. 'Well, it worked!'

But the idea of a murderer dressed up as a massive monster

made of rotten flesh and exposed bone doesn't sit right. Not after that smell. Not after the way it chased me. Like it wanted *me* specifically. To savor the taste of my blood spilling over its tongue as it tore me apart.

'You followed me into the woods, saved me from a monster or a deranged serial killer, because you're interested in true crime?' I straighten and force air into my lungs. Being alone with him in a forgotten part of the school feels like a bad idea. I feel caged. Trapped.

His eyes turn almost black in the low light. 'No. I have my own reasons to stop these deaths.'

'Another vague answer.' I bend down and grab the folio, ready to launch myself up the stairs. 'If you want to help me find my sister, then tell me the truth.'

'Your sister is dead, Andy,' he says, his brow furrowed.

I bite the inside of my cheek to keep from correcting him.

'Fine.' My cheeks flush and I face the stairs again. 'You think someone killed her, and got away with it. You say you're doing this to help others – I don't need to understand your savior complex. I just need you to either help me or stay out of my way.'

'You know nothing about this place,' Jae counters. 'You don't have to believe me, but I know this world. I know the people Violet was friends with. You don't. If you want justice for your sister, you'll need me.'

'Then maybe start by telling me the whole truth,' I snap.

I turn to run up the steps. His hand reaches out and snakes around my wrist, keeping me in place.

'Listen. I don't think you're safe here. Whether the school is involved – or the town, or the students – someone knows you're here and that you have suspicions.'

I suck in a breath. Does he know about the note, the dead animals in my room? I yank my wrist out of his grip, the heat of his skin too much for me to bear.

'We can help each other, Andy. I know you don't trust me, and you don't have to. But we both want the same thing. We are the only two people who want to stop more deaths.'

*You're wrong.* I want to find my sister. She's alive somewhere, scared and waiting for me.

'I'm fine on my own.'

'What plan do you have, besides rifling through her greenhouse and confronting her ex-boyfriend?'

I'm about to retreat up the steps when I hesitate. I don't have a plan anymore. I found the folio in the greenhouse, but there's no map this time. No clear direction. My shoulders stiffen as I force myself to turn back.

Jae continues, 'Do you know anything about schools like this? About languages and history, and everything else in your sister's greenhouse?'

The moths in my bed. The threatening note. And then that monster chasing me through the woods. Someone knows I'm following Violet's path, and they want me gone. I press my lips together, shivering from the cold and something more.

Jae could be useful, and if I'm going to survive Ravenswood, I have to be cunning, like my sister.

'What did you have in mind?'

He doesn't need to know my secrets. He'll simply be another tool for me to use. Violet would want me to do this, to use him to get what I need. It's what she would do.

Jae lets out a slow breath, the tension easing from his shoulders. 'We work together; share resources. Violet was your sister, so you know her better than anyone else. I can read and understand what's in those books and notes. We figure out who is responsible and then stop them before they can kill anyone else.'

'You make it sound easy.' I hate that I'm almost useless. I can't read Hebrew or solve ciphers. I have a rudimentary knowledge of Latin at best. I'm not Violet. I never will be.

'It won't be.' He shakes his head soberly. 'But it has to be done. Who knows what will happen if we don't?'

*I* know. I'll probably be killed for sticking my nose where it doesn't belong. And then Violet really will die, and I won't be here to save her.

'Fine,' I say again. I thrust out my hand and he shakes it once. 'But know that if you cross me, I'll have no problem taking you down. This is my sister we're talking about.'

His eyes glitter like black jewels.

'Where do we start?' he asks.

'I'll meet you here tomorrow after lights out. Then you can help me break into Violet's old room.'

# 12

Jae meets me in the hidden storage room the next night.

'What do you hope to find in her room?' he asks as we creep slowly up a back staircase that leads to the third floor, each holding a dull flashlight.

The school creaks and moans; another storm, fiercer than any other, beats the roof and walls with fists of wind and rain. It helps to cover our footsteps, the ragged sound of our breathing.

'She hid something in there. She wanted me to find it.'

'How do you know?' Jae pauses at the top of the stairs, peering out and looking both ways before he waves me forward.

We pad silently into the common room of the girls' wing.

I consider what to tell him before deciding on the truth. 'I found it my first night – before those freshmen broke in for their seance. I haven't been able to sneak out again since then.'

It's the only place I can think to look for another clue.

'So, she knew something was going to happen to her?' Jae says.

I nod, and for the first time in six months, I feel that someone believes me. Like someone else hasn't given up or forgotten. I blink rapidly, ignoring the tears misting my eyes, and focus.

We get to the door of Violet's room. There's a padlock hastily clamped in place.

'You don't happen to know where the key is, do you?' I sigh.

Jae grins, and a small dimple creases his left cheek. Cute. Not that I'm taking notice.

'How do you think I got into that storage wing?' He drops to his knees and pulls out a set of tweezer-like tools.

I hold his flashlight steady for him as rain beats down on the roof. It's quiet, no roaming students looking for ghosts.

A gentle *click*. Jae unhooks the padlock and pushes the door open with a soft creak. He stands, puffing out his breath so that his hair flies out of his eyes.

'Don't get too big of a head,' I say and slip past him, our shoulders brushing. 'It's one little lock.'

But he only smirks, making me want to roll my eyes and flush at the same time.

The flashlight beams cut through the dark. The window is tightly shut, the radiator silent. The room is cold.

'Where's the secret compartment you mentioned?'

'Here.' I crouch and adjust the flashlight in my free hand. The curls of newly carved wood look back at me from the cleverly fabricated skirting board. Warmth radiates from my side. Jae crouches beside me, his head tilted.

I take a deep breath and peel the board back so I can access the wall panel. I hand my flashlight to Jae and he juggles his and mine for a moment. I feel the uneven texture of the wall beneath my fingertips, and I dig in my nails, prying the panel away. Dust from old plaster sprinkles on my clothes.

'I can't believe it,' Jae says, his mouth open. 'This must have been here for years. I wonder how Violet found it.'

A piece of sanded and painted plywood has been wedged in place, covering a small hollow in the wall. A crawl space. I set it down and dust motes swirl in the air. Inside is a four-foot-deep nook, kind of like the ones you see under stairs in older houses and apartments. The air inside is musty and stale. I crawl forward, the ceiling too low to allow me to stand.

Inside are boxes of notebooks and leather-bound books.

A stack of scanned images rests on top of a dented box. I pull a few off and fan them out on the floor. I recognize the repeated image immediately.

'"Saturn Devouring His Son",' Jae says softly at my side, stooping so he doesn't hit his head. 'Goya. Why would Violet have this hidden away?'

My mouth feels dry as I shuffle through the stack. More paintings, the dark oil ones that Violet loved so much. They're almost all identical. The same image from art history class glares back at me. The wide black eyes, the teeth tearing a small limb from a small body. The grotesque features. What had Luciano been arguing? It's all about power. The image depicts the tenuous balance of power, the things man does to attain it. I shudder.

'There's more over here,' Jae says as he crawls to the other side of the narrow alcove. 'Why does she have so many?'

I shake my head and reach the end of the stack. There are multiple copies of each painting. Some are crumpled, others have rambling notes on the back.

'There are some books back here. Do you want me to take a few and translate them? It looks like she annotated them pretty heavily.' Jae blows dust off the cover of a black leather-bound book. 'Another copy of the *Clavis Inferni*? Your sister sure had interesting tastes.'

I hardly listen. There's something that pricks at the back of my mind. I stare at the copies in my hand, the same images we study in art history. The class Violet was taking last year when she disappeared. The same ones she hid in the greenhouse.

I feel the stirring of cold excitement in my bones. Now I remember something else, something I didn't catch last night during the fevered chase and lightning storm. The images in the folio are *wrong*.

I tear through the pictures until I find a pattern. There

are three images copied, again and again. 'Narcissus' by Caravaggio. 'The Nightmare' by Fuseli. And then there's the hideous image of Saturn tearing apart one of his sons with his bare teeth. I take the folio out of my jacket. I couldn't bear to leave it in my dorm, not after the note that Violet had left in it.

I compare the image tucked into the battered folder. Saturn's eyes are wrong. In the original painting they stare off to the viewer's left and the brow is furrowed with fear. But in the image in Violet's folder, he is looking up towards the sky, and in what should be a blank foreground there is the hint, the suggestion of water – like a river.

'What are you looking at?' Jae scoots closer to me and I spread the images in front of him: the three copies of the original paintings from the cupboard, and the three weather-worn ones from the greenhouse.

'Narcissus' by Caravaggio. One of Violet's favorites. The rich, dark colors swallow a young man as he peers longingly over the still surface of the water, gazing at a shattered reflection of himself.

'That's weird.' Jae leans forward and squints. 'This one is wrong. The reflection doesn't match, it looks more like . . .'

'A jackal,' I finish.

*Follow the path of Anubis.*

We're both quiet for a moment. Jae swallows hard, his face pale and drawn in the low light and odd angles. He looks away from the painting, a grimace marring his smooth jaw, and moves to dig through another box.

I run my fingertips across 'The Nightmare'. The horse in the corner, the nightmare, looks wrong. Like Narcissus, its shadow on the red drapery doesn't match. Antlers instead of the triangular ears of a horse.

My heart speeds up and I flip the images from the stack over. There is a hasty scrawl in pen, smeared by a hand. But the shape is clear. An ankh, the cross with a loop at the top. And something else, one I have to stare at for a moment before I can recall what it is. A djed, another ancient Egyptian symbol.

'What does this mean?' I point at it. It looks like a column with multiple steps at the top. I know Violet was obsessed with art of all cultures and periods. Her fixation apparently ran deeper than a dash of Renaissance art or postmodernism. This feels . . . ancient. Powerful. Almost sacred.

Jae squints at it. 'It typically means resurrection or rebirth. Like the myth of Osiris that it's linked to. He was killed by Seth, his brother, after he conceived Anubis with Nephthys, Seth's wife. But Osiris returned, in a way, as Lord of the Underworld.'

'I remember,' I say softly. The symbols litter the backs of the copied paintings. They're in Violet's familiar hand-writing but much harsher, like she gouged them desperately in with a pen.

*Follow the path of Anubis.*

Follow the path of Anubis. It's here.

Cold sweat breaks out across my neck, and my stomach twists into a painful knot. What are the symbols of eternal life and of rebirth doing written on the backs of old paintings? What is Violet trying to say?

Life and death. Cycles.

I grab three of the images, one of each painting, and tuck them into the folio. I need to research the symbols and the myths associated with them. Violet's clues feel more tangible than ever, and anxiety beats at my skull like a fist. I must be on the path.

But the rush of victory is short-lived.

'Andy.' Jae's hand grabs mine and his fingers are cold. 'Do you see that?'

'What?' I tear my eyes from the folio.

'There in the corner. The black blanket.'

I follow his pointing finger and my heart stutters. Wadded up and tucked near the foot of a tattered box is an inky black robe, the hood gaping like a black maw. And there, resting in the center of the pile, is something white. A mask. Antlers attached to the top.

'What is that?' I recoil from the empty sockets staring back at me.

'It looks like . . .' Jae pauses, his Adam's apple bobbing. 'It looks like the ones that group wore from the woods last night.'

'Why does my sister have that?' I reach out, fingers closing around the cold antlers. The mask is heavier than I thought, more like plaster than flimsy plastic. I shudder to think what the original cast was made of, all too familiar with dead deer for my liking.

The mask is small, and so is the robe. My sister's size. Nausea inserts its fingers into my stomach and twists, *hard*. Violet couldn't have gotten mixed up with that *thing* from last night. It wasn't human. It looked like those strangers in masks and robes had tried to help it. Summon it somehow. There is no way Violet would be involved. No way.

Jae ghosts his fingers over the antlers. 'Maybe she got mixed up with that group from last night. Made them angry.'

A sound echoes down the hallway, soft at first. I stiffen, and our eyes meet. Jae scoots back and exits the alcove. It feels stifling inside the small space and I crawl out after him, my sweater sticking to my skin. I clutch the folio with one fist and my flashlight with the other.

Whispers float through the air and slip under the door. Footsteps, careful and measured. They're almost impossible to hear over the sound of thunder and rain. Jae throws me a look.

'This isn't the first time someone's been lurking around my sister's room,' I whisper and slide next to him against the farthest wall. 'A person, a man, was in here my first night, looking for something.'

'Maybe he's back.' Jae holds a finger to his lips, and I nod.

The voices grow loud enough to discern.

'She's looking into it, Lu.' Regina's strained voice is muffled by the door. 'You're not concerned at all?'

A masculine scoff, sarcastic and pretentious all at once. Definitely Luciano.

'Of course not. We did nothing wrong, why should we be nervous?'

'Because he was there in the woods last night! She saw!' Regina whispers harshly. Her voice sounds like she's directly on the other side of the door.

'She won't know who he is. Relax,' Luciano says.

'Are they talking about the thing that chased me?' I grab Jae's arm, digging my fingers in.

He shakes his head and presses two fingers to my lips, his eyes wide.

'That was a mistake,' Regina almost whimpers. 'We shouldn't have done that. I knew she was nosing around.'

'We'll take care of it,' Luciano sighs.

'Your father seems to think you can't handle this. Can't take over from Violet. Maybe –'

There is a heavy thud. A footstep. Regina breathes in sharply, and her shadow falls under the crack of Violet's door.

'My father has doubted me for long enough,' Luciano hisses. 'Violet may have found the path, but I'm finishing it.'

Regina huffs. 'He and the other alumni of the society won't be happy with you if we mess up. It doesn't help that you showed up late and drunk to the meeting. What were you thinking?'

'Thinking?' Luciano huffs. 'I was thinking that my father could only dream of the power we'll have, when he was at Ravenswood. He might bluster and rave at me for being an irresponsible screw-up for an heir, but we both know he needs us – needs *me*. I'm the only one who can do this. We'll show him. And Andy won't be a problem for long. We'll make sure of that.'

'Tonight?' Regina's voice wavers. 'We don't know how to do this without Violet.'

'You think she was the only one who knew how to call in favors?' Luciano whispers, the sound silky and cold. 'There's a lot Violet never knew about me. Come on, we'll start the process tonight.'

Their feet retreat down the hall. Jae and I stay still. A few beats of silence.

I step back, my heart thundering in my chest. 'Is it safe to go out?'

'I think so.'

'We should follow them, see what they're up to.'

A crease appears between his brows. 'No, they're clearly trying to stop you.'

'All the more reason to follow,' I say and yank the door open. The warmer air from the hall spills into the space and rustles the papers in my hand. I tuck the folio tighter to my chest, the symbols racing through my mind.

'We don't know where they went,' he protests.

'I'll go by myself. I don't need you.' I race down the hall.

Jae curses behind me and fumbles with the door, clamping the padlock in place.

The hallways at the back of the building are narrow, criss-crossing between the two wings and many floors of the old building. Faint voices trail ahead. I follow.

A door, thickly painted with peeling white paint blocks our

way, but it's slightly ajar, as if someone just went through. A brass plaque on the front says: *No Admittance*.

'Andy, wait!' Jae whispers harshly. He comes to a stop behind me just as I push open the door.

Steel stairs, also painted opaque white, lead down in a spiral. It looks like a service entrance from when this place was a mansion. The air is heavy with dust.

'I think they went in here.' I point down the stairs and gesture at the half-open door. It's dark and too risky to use my flashlight. The cold metal is tucked in my pocket, next to the folio. I'm so close, I can feel it – taste it in the air. Answers are here, I just have to follow.

'Slow down!' He grabs my arm but I yank it out of his grasp and grab the railing.

I descend, moving faster and faster into the depths of the school. The air grows thick with humidity. The staircase ends in a narrow hallway that turns sharply to the right. There aren't any windows. It must be another basement or some sort of storage area.

I creep around the corner, pressing my back to the wall, ignoring the dust it stirs up. Another door blocks the way. A faint orange glow flickers through the cracks. Like lighted candles. Jae appears, his face strained and coated with sweat.

'Can you pick this lock?' I wiggle the handle.

The door is shut tight.

'This isn't a good idea,' he murmurs, but drops to his knees anyway, as if the frantic energy crackling in my veins scares him.

A few moments later, a *click* sounds and the door wheezes open. Voices speak in low, rhythmic tones. I follow them. Pressing my shoulders to the wall, I peer around the corner as the corridor comes to an end. I try to place where we are in the bowels of the school. Somewhere near one of the libraries – below it, maybe.

The hall opens into a chamber with a tall ceiling. Heavy tapestries and painted symbols in a riot of colors line the walls. The scenes are a mixture of grisly and angelic. Images of demons consuming children, human sacrifices, and angels staring into heaven war with one another for dominance.

Furniture from a bygone era is pushed to the sides. A narrow bed. An antique armoire. Suits and jackets and smoking pipes are laid out on a low table. It's as if someone – a man from the last century – lives in this basement. A rickety narrow staircase lines the back wall, leading up to the first floor of the school.

Candles with thick, dripping wax are lined in a circle, smoke wafting from their wicks as if someone barely blew them out. A bowl, polished silver, sits in the center of the circle and I see something inside – not liquid, at least, not quite. It's thicker, darker. Almost like blood.

'Andy, we have to leave.' Jae grabs my arm, more forcefully this time, and yanks me back.

It's on the tip of my tongue to yell at him, to demand he leave me alone, but I never get the chance. Another door slams, one that connects the staircase to the chamber. Feet shuffle, as a group of four descends the stairs. I drop to a crouch and press back into the shadows of the corridor.

They kneel together near the bowl, heads bowed. I stagger, the strength sapped from my muscles. A breeze slithers in, hot and humid. I taste smoke in the air. And something metallic.

A knife is held aloft before slashing across someone's palm. They extend their hand, squeezing their blood into the vessel. An offering. A feeding. Each member repeats the process until the bowl is brimming with blood. And then they speak again, together, and somehow, I know what they're asking.

82

They want a favor from the monster in the woods. But for what?

I strain to see in the dark. Jae curses again and grabs my arm as if to make his way back towards the spiral staircase, away from this place. His face is coated in sweat. But he doesn't pull me aside. Instead, he freezes. The weight on my chest intensifies as one member of the group stands and lifts his hands. The air in front of him seems to ripple.

'Is our offering accepted?' the standing man asks.

His voice sounds warped, too deep and slow. My ears feel like they're full of water. A rumble replies. Inhuman.

In the middle of the room, the scene is changed. The four figures stand before the strange patch of air that looks too thick. It's almost like a two-way mirror. I peer inside, trying to figure out what it is. A flash of antlers. A face only half covered in flesh. I jerk back, bumping into Jae.

'Quiet,' he mouths.

I look harder, my eyes warring with my brain. The leader, the one who spoke, converses with the antlered beast, but I can't hear what they're saying. A booming rush, like the sound of a torrential river, echoes in the chamber.

The warped image of the monster disappears. Instead, through the slash in the air, a river, black and oily, cuts through like a ghostly hologram. The banks are lined with thick mud and tall grasses, grayish in color. Flowers dot the scene, bone white with sickly purple centers. And on one side is an army of pale creatures with gaping black eyes, their vaporous bodies pressing desperately forward, hands reaching frantically across the shore.

'Do you see that?' I whisper to Jae.

He lets out a pained breath. 'It's the thing we saw in the woods last night.'

'No, there's a river.' I shake my head in confusion, trying

to focus. Jae gives me a strange look, as if he can't see what I can. But everything feels slow and fuzzy, like looking through water. My tattoo burns and I clutch my thigh.

I turn back to the strange vision. I can see the fear in the gray beings' eyes. They want to cross – *have to* cross. Life and death exist on these banks, cut in half and separated by this river.

And then on the other bank, I see something.

Someone.

Violet.

# 13

Daylight streams through my bedroom window. It feels wrong, warm rays kissing my cheek. I sit up with a strangled gasp. The storm from last night is gone and the sky is a mixed tapestry of blue and white. Munia's bed is empty, her covers neatly tucked against the mattress.

How did I get here?

I swing my legs out of bed and move to the window. It's early, the sun still too watery to light up the forest that presses around the school. And then it hits me. *Violet. I saw Violet.*

A river. The basement. The hooded figures.

I drop to my knees as my head pounds. That strange room and the chanting group. They were feeding the monster with their blood, asking for a favor. A sick feeling creeps into my stomach, freezing like ice. Are they trying to find Violet too? Did she show herself to me as a warning, pleading for me to hurry?

Sweat sticks to my brow. I don't have the answers. My world feels off kilter, spinning on an axis that doesn't quite align. Jae. I have to find Jae and see what happened. What he remembers.

I rush to get dressed, my thoughts swimming.

There are a few students milling around as I make a beeline for the dining hall. The smells of breakfast wafting through the air turn my stomach as I enter the room. The walls are streaked with early morning light.

Jae sits at a far table, a pensive look on his face as a plate of eggs sits untouched in front of him.

Combing my wild curls with my fingers, I rush to his side and sit down.

'What happened last night?' I ask him urgently.

'Andy,' Jae breathes out, 'maybe you should stop looking into Violet's death. It isn't safe.'

I sit back, my stomach hollow. 'Jae, we saw Violet –'

He leans forward, cutting me off, eyes darting around the quiet room. 'I think it's better if you aren't involved. Clearly, that group Violet was involved with is still in the school. They know about you, and sooner or later you'll get hurt.'

'But the paintings, the symbols . . . you said you'd help me!'

'I will help you.' He darts his gaze around the room, as if afraid we're being watched. 'But you need to make sure they don't know what you're doing. They could do to you what they did to Violet.'

I scoff. 'So, just wait around for them to make a move? I knew this was dangerous. You don't need to protect me.'

He pushes his hair back from his face roughly. 'They're experimenting with magic, Andy, if the abandoned green-house and Violet's notes are any indication. What we saw last night – what they did – they could be planning on killing you next.'

*Magic.* The word feels strange spoken out loud. Laid bare like that.

'Even if they did perform some magical ceremony against me,' I swallow hard, my throat bone dry at the thought, 'I can't just stop. Violet needs me. I saw her, Jae.'

My sister. Alive. Waiting for me to save her.

My words must spark something in him because his face hardens.

He looks over his shoulder again, twitching with anxiety. 'I need to go. I have homework.' He stands up, his breakfast forgotten. 'Just . . . just lie low for a while, okay?'

86

I watch him retreat; no doubt headed for one of the school-sanctioned greenhouses to dig in the dirt while my sister's ex-boyfriend plots something sinister.

'Andy,' Mrs Bianchi says with a smile, appearing at the end of my table. 'I wanted to see how your schedule works for a GSE meeting later today.'

I shake my head, tearing my gaze away from the door through which Jae disappeared. 'What?'

She lifts a brow. 'The GSE club. The one I'm a faculty advisor for. You said you'd think about coming – and the others want to close the trial period soon.'

Regina, Luciano and Violet's other friends trapped in a room together where they can't escape my questions?

Ignoring Jae's warning, I set my jaw. 'Yes. I'll be there.'

'I can't believe you've just been invited to the club like it's no big deal!' Munia throws up her hands as she leads me to the second-floor library and the private study room where the GSE club will meet later tonight. The club meets late, when most other students are required to be in their common rooms. Another perk of exclusivity, I suppose.

The floor is checkered black-and-white marble, with long cherrywood tables in the center of the room and matching bookcases on either side. Marble busts and what look like original oil paintings dot the walls. I can't focus on Munia, though. My thoughts are consumed with Violet. My sister standing on the riverbank, where those ghostly figures cried out in pain and hunger. It can't be a coincidence that she appeared while her friends were summoning that monster. Slicing their palms.

'You said it yourself, that legacies get in,' I say absently, but my eyes are focused on the half-open door where the club meets.

'Still,' she huffs, flicking her hijab back over her shoulder, 'I've been on the student council for three years now and I've never even been invited to a trial meeting. And you know they kept Melinda Delgado despite her dad being thrown in jail.'

'What does that have to do with the club?'

Munia sighs enviously again. 'Because her dad funneled money from his brother's drug ring into the school and the club. It's dirty money, traceable by the FBI. But instead of trying to keep the club's reputation impeccable, they kept her in . . .'

I shrug one shoulder, only half listening as she goes on about nepotism and its inherent follies. My eyes are trained on the open door, on Bianchi's furrowed brow as she stands in front of the seated Luciano. He's spitting words so fast I can't hope to read his lips.

Munia's voice trails off as we stop outside the study room.

'Why does he send you to scold me?' Luciano's accented voice clips the words. He's angry, furious even. I can see the emotion ripple below the calm mask he wears, marring his features. Bianchi crosses her arms, an exasperated look on her face.

'Your father won't stand for it. Your rogue behavior can't continue –'

He leans forward in his chair, blue eyes cold and dead – masking his fear, perhaps?

'My father doesn't like to know my failures. So, why share them if it makes both our lives more difficult?'

Bianchi lowers her voice. 'He asked me a question. I simply answered it.'

'He thinks he controls me. Don't let him control *you*.' Luciano sits back, clenching his jaw as if he is biting back what he truly wishes to say.

'And has Salvatore sent a message for the club?' Bianchi

doesn't seem fazed by Luciano's sulky behavior. Her eyes are sharp, but her mouth is set in a hard line. It could be an argument over his absence at the alumni lunch.

'Remember who pays for this club, this school, for *everything* you need in order to continue.' Luciano sighs, as though the words are too familiar to mean anything anymore.

But Bianchi's forehead creases with worry lines. What role does Salvatore Russo play in this club? I wonder.

Luciano straightens, catching my eye. His lip curls as he smooths down his buttoned shirt. 'I think this meeting is over, don't you?'

Bianchi turns, her lips parted, as Luciano walks out of the room and into the main library. Munia and I stand still as statues.

'What's going on, Luc?' Regina's voice floats through the room, sounding brittle as it bounces off marble and wood.

I whip around, heat expanding in my chest. She stands with Eric and Melinda, the other club members. Four of them in total. Four members of the GSE club. Four people in robes in the woods. And four figures in the darkened basement last night.

I step forward, fingers curling into a fist. They did something to my sister, their friend. And I saw her last night. It has to be connected.

'The meeting is canceled,' Luciano says stiffly, breezing past me. 'Sorry, Andy, the club is closed to new members.'

'Now, that's not up to you.' Bianchi stands, her blonde hair making her complexion appear even more ashen. 'Mr Madden and your father agreed she should be interviewed –'

'That was a mistake.' He shoves his hands into his pockets, looking down his nose at me. 'She has too much of Violet in her to be of any use to the club.'

He strides away. Regina, Melinda and Eric follow dutifully

after. The library is as quiet as a cemetery. Bianchi expels a breath sharply through her nose and tucks a strand of hair behind her ear.

Munia looks between us, nervously toying with the cuff of her jacket. 'I . . . maybe I should go.'

Bianchi nods. 'That would be best, Miss Al Soori.'

'I'll see you later, Andy.' She takes off in the direction of the common room.

Awkward silence stretches between me and my art teacher. Part of me longs to search for the basement from last night. Maybe Violet is still there, shimmering in that strange veil. But the air in the study room hangs heavy after the altercation, as if there was more behind Luciano's anger than I know. After a few heartbeats, Bianchi smooths her skirt and gives me a tiny smile.

'Sorry about that. Arguments about funding can always get a little dicey.'

'He said his father pays for the club. What kind of funding problem could there be?'

She rolls her eyes. 'Luciano does not like to obey his father. Sometimes it feels as if this club is merely a way for me to babysit Salvatore's delinquent child. It's nothing.'

My heart beats against my ribs. 'Did Mr Russo tell Luciano to keep me from joining?'

Was that what they were doing last night? Making good on their threats with the moths and the deer?

'I rather think it was the other way around. Don't worry, Andy. I'll talk to the donors and see what I can do.' She purses her lips into a tired smile. 'You have a little under an hour before lights out.'

I glance at the darkened corners of the library, my mind mapping out where I was last night. There could be a staircase leading down to the basement.

Last night, the folio, the candles, the robes. Four people. They were trying to enact something last night. Maybe against me. My tattoo feels hot, like it did last night. The vision of Violet on the riverbank, in that strange portal they conjured, must mean something. I saw her, even if Jae didn't. She needs me. She's warning me. The burning sensation in my tattoo spreads to my fingers and toes. I'm close to getting answers. Tonight. They can't run from me any longer.

I leave the library and Mrs Bianchi without another word.

It's Thursday night, so the upperclassmen can't leave campus until tomorrow. Regina will be in her dorm. I stomp up the stairs. Throwing open the door to the common room, I stride into the year 13 corridor. A few of the older girls give me strange looks as I march past them, but I don't care.

'Regina!' I pound my fist on her door so hard the number rattles. 'Regina! Open the door.'

A shuffling on the other side. It creaks open and Regina looks down at me. Her hair is glossy and immaculate, but there are circles under her eyes. Like she was up late last night.

'What are you doing?' She tugs her sweater close and shivers. 'The meeting is canceled. You're not going to get into the club, I'm sorry.'

I jab a finger at her and she takes a step back. 'I know what you did.'

'Andy. Are you alright? You don't look so good.'

'Last night. You were talking about me in the hallway outside Violet's room. Then you vanished into the basement!'

'Andy,' Regina sets a gentle hand on my shoulder, 'you need to calm down. You're white as a sheet.'

I shake her hand off. 'You and Luciano are hiding the truth. You did something to Violet! I saw her last night . . . by the river.'

91

'You're not making any sense.'

I laugh derisively, the kind that erupts from your throat and shakes your shoulders. 'And you're hiding something!'

'Reg?' A girl calls from inside the room. Melinda Delgado appears, her stick-straight brown hair braided tightly. 'What's going on out here?'

'You were there last night too,' I hiss at her, cold sweat slicking down my spine. 'You're working with Regina!'

'This is Violet's sister, huh?' Melinda sneers as she peruses me with an unimpressed flicker of her eyes. 'I expected more than this.'

I grit my teeth and shove Regina, my fingers tingling. 'Where is Violet? What did you do to her?'

Melinda's face turns red and she takes a step forward. Regina raises her arm and stops her, the picture of calm.

More people are gathering in the hallway, heads craning to see the commotion. Regina breathes out slowly. 'Your sister is dead, Andy. She died last year – drowned.'

'She *isn't* dead!'

Arguing draws more girls like moths to a flame. I see taller figures pressing in from the common room. Teachers. A flash of white-blonde hair is visible above the other heads crowding around me. Mrs Bianchi. Her slate-blue eyes wrinkle at the corners with concern. I look away, turning my attention back to the liar standing in front of me.

'You're not well, Andy.' Regina draws her eyebrows together. 'But Violet's gone, you have to accept that. Stop imagining someone is out to get you.'

I lower my voice. 'Violet isn't dead. I saw her body. She didn't have a tattoo on her leg – the one we got together. It *wasn't* her.'

I lean back, scowling. There. The proof I've hidden from everyone, laid bare for my sister's former best friend. Our eyes meet. She has to realize I know Violet is alive. That my sister sent me to find her.

Regina's eyes darken. She shakes her head and raises her fingers to her mouth. They're trembling.

'To think of what you've been putting yourself through for the past six months . . . I can't imagine it.' A tear slips down her cheek and she places her hands tenderly on my shoulders. 'But Andy, you have to know Violet always covered that tattoo on her thigh with makeup, like you use for stage productions at school. She didn't want anyone to take pictures, or for your parents to find out.'

It feels like a punch to my stomach. I stare at her, hard. But her face doesn't change. She just keeps looking at me, her expression heartbroken, like I'm a lost puppy.

I step back, the blood draining from my face. My hands and feet are cold. 'But if she went swimming in the cove, the makeup would have washed off.'

Melinda scoffs, crossing her arms. 'It was waterproof, you idiot. What else would she wear when she went swimming?'

'Melinda, please,' Regina sighs.

'What?' Melinda rolls her eyes. 'This twig comes to our room, screaming about her dead sister? I never liked Violet to begin with, but now we have her little sister calling us killers?'

'You're lying.' My knees almost buckle. 'The mortician wouldn't have bothered to hide the tattoo when cleaning her up.'

Regina tightens her grip on my shoulders and shifts us away from Melinda, speaking softly. 'They could have, if they saw she'd used makeup to cover it before. I saw Violet's body when they dragged her out of the water. She's dead.'

'What about the moths? The deer? You're trying to force me out of the school before I find out what you and your club are really doing – what you did to my sister!'

'Deer? I don't know what you're talking about.' Regina blinks her large brown eyes at me, even mustering a misty sheen that promises tears. Like I'm the one scaring *her*.

I lean forward, my jaw tight from the effort of keeping my voice down. 'I saw you in the basement last night . . . and earlier, in the woods.'

Melinda scowls as Regina removes a hand from my shoulder. Is that a flicker of fear in her eyes?

'You don't know anything.' Regina touches my arm and I feel a pinch, a sting. For a moment her mouth moves but I can't understand the words. I look down, but my vision blurs. My tongue feels heavy. My arm throbs. When I blink, it looks like moths are dancing around her head.

I reach out for Regina's arm, yanking her hand into the light. There's a Band-Aid on her palm. She closes her fist and the Band-Aid disappears. I could have sworn it was covering a cut inflicted by a knife.

'What's going on here, Miss Kumar?' Bianchi shoulders her way through the crowd behind me.

My teeth clench. The world tilts, and I stagger. My head is fuzzy and pounds with a throbbing headache. Last night I could have sworn I saw Violet stranded on the bank of that river. But the tattoo. The makeup. The missing cut. Maybe Regina is telling the truth . . .

I feel dizzy. Detached.

'She hasn't been sleeping or eating. I've been keeping track,' Munia says, though I have no idea when she appeared.

Everything sounds like my head is underwater, or my ears are blocked.

'Let's take her to the nurse, Munia.' Bianchi lowers her voice and hooks one of my arms around her shoulders. 'Quietly and quickly now, we don't need to make a bigger scene. She looks like she's going to be sick.'

Another set of hands steers me by my shoulders. I try to resist. But the only thing I can do is think of the absent tattoo. It can't be as simple as makeup, can it?

Suddenly, we're in the nurse's office. A light shines in my eyes. Words like *dehydrated, malnourished* and *sleep deprived* float around my head in vague snatches of thought. But I can't listen. All I can do is close my eyes and see Violet.

My sister. Standing on the other side of the black river, pleading with me to save her.

# 14

My mouth is dry and my throat stings. I shift, dragged down by the tangled threads of a strange and unnaturally heavy sleep. I open my eyes and clutch my neck. My throat doesn't just hurt, it *burns*. My tongue feels fuzzy, thick and bloated. Something tickles the roof of my mouth. I want to gasp, but my airways feel blocked. I can't breathe.

Shooting upright, I claw at my lips. I feel the brush of tiny feet. The flutter of wings against my teeth. The taste of dust. A scream catches as moths crawl from my throat, over my tongue. I retch their little bodies onto the sheets. Their damp wings unfurling, their eyes staring up at me. I feel them in my ribs. In my lungs. Choking, climbing . . .

I sit up with a gasp. It's dark outside and the air smells like pine and damp undergrowth. It's cold. Turning my head, I peer around the darkened room. It's the sickbay. A row of empty beds takes up one wall, the clean white sheets pulled tight across narrow mattresses. A lamp shines at the desk in the corner. There aren't any moths at all.

'You've been asleep for a while.' A magazine thumps down on the foot of my bed.

I turn my head. Munia sits in a wooden-framed chair with sage-green upholstery. A silky blue hijab is pinned expertly around her face and neck, and she's wearing gray trousers. Her mouth turns down at the corners as she scrutinizes me.

'What happened?' I croak and wince, brushing my fingers over my throat. It felt so real, those moths in my mouth. Crawling. Searching for something.

Munia leans over to a small table and hands me a glass of tepid water. 'You were screaming at Regina and her room-mate in the year thirteen hallway. You kept saying someone was lying and that your sister was alive. Bianchi had to drag you to the sickbay. You must have been exhausted, you fell asleep and have been out since last night.'

I look ahead as I sip the water. My fingers are cold and my limbs heavy. Everything hurts like I've been bruised all over. I hardly have the energy to hold the glass. Munia watches me, her fingers gently tapping one knee.

'You didn't have to stay with me.'

'You haven't been eating or sleeping. You're gone at all hours of the night, and your teachers say you haven't been doing any of your work. That you're distracted in class.'

I shrug, still fighting the repulsion making my skin crawl.

'Andy,' Munia leans forward, her thick eyebrows furrowed over her long lashes, 'you can't just fall off the face of the earth. You're not taking care of yourself. You're depressed and anxious, and you're making yourself paranoid by encouraging your own delusions.'

'What should I do instead?' My voice catches. 'Act like Violet was never here?' I face the wall. I take another sip of water and wish I was anywhere else.

She sighs and uncrosses her legs. 'Madden wanted to call your parents. He wants to pull you out of the school. Regina said you were talking about rivers and ghosts and your sister walking in the basement. Melinda said you tried to attack her.'

I almost gasp in outrage at the accusation. They're trying to hurt *me*. Regina did something last night. That pinch on my arm, the way the world went black. I rub my biceps, and feel a strange lump there, like a bug bite. I push the thin cotton sleeve of my shirt aside. There's an angry red and black lump. Like before, with the flower, only this time it seems to be healing itself. I sit rigidly, remembering the way I passed out. The familiar confusion and headache.

I am *not* crazy.

'When are my parents coming?' My heart pounds.

'They aren't.' Munia stands and plants her hands on her hips. 'I talked Madden out of it. The nurse said you're probably experiencing post-traumatic stress and we need to address it.'

'Why would he listen to you?'

'Because my parents are donors to the school. They paid to refurbish the gym and acquired fifty volumes of rare manuscripts. And I'm very convincing – kind of a necessity as student body president.' She flicks the corner of her hijab over her shoulder before giving me a challenging look.

I scoff. 'Of course. The only thing Madden or anyone in this school cares about is money.'

'I didn't do it because I have a superiority complex, Andy.' Munia purses her lips. 'I did it because I can see you're lost and hurting and you feel alone. You don't have to be, you know. Don't let a tragedy like this derail your entire life. It isn't worth it.'

My stomach plummets. Every nerve ending tingles like I've been burned. I sit up straighter in the bed, trying to look indignant even wrapped up in the tangled white sheets.

'Listen, I appreciate you calling Madden off. But you don't know the first thing about what this is like – or what *anything* in the real world is like.' Tears sting my eyes and envy gnaws at my stomach. Her perfect life and perfect parents. Endless amounts of money to throw at every problem.

Munia's back straightens. 'Just because my family has money doesn't mean I don't know what it's like to lose someone.'

I turn my head and stare out the window. 'I'm doing just fine, Munia.'

She crosses to the door and for a moment I think she's going to walk out. But then she stops, one hand grabbing the carved wood of the door frame. 'Andy, you don't know me. You don't know the people here. I just want to help you; you don't have to accept it. But running around the school, screaming at prefects, and letting your health deteriorate – you're not just hurting yourself. You'll hurt your family too. Believe me.'

And then she's gone.

## 15

I stare down at the soup in my bowl. The eyes of the head counselor are glued to me from across the dining hall. Mrs Bryce has been watching me like a hawk for the past two weeks. Between her and Bianchi I feel like I'm always being monitored for my next meltdown. Every five seconds I turn around and one of them is there, watching me with pity-filled eyes.

The hall is full of students, clustered around the long, dark stained wood tables, chattering about the homecoming dance at the end of September. It's on Saturday, just three days away, which explains the frantic mood from the staff and student council.

With her gray hair pulled into a tight bun at the nape of her neck, and wearing an elegant pant suit, Mrs Bryce is the picture of professional decorum. She sits with the other staff members and teachers at the head of the dining hall, with Bianchi to her right. But her eyes never stray far from me, and she never fails to count the spoonfuls of soup I bring to my lips.

Besides the counselor and Bianchi, no one sits near me. An invisible wall separates me from my peers. Regina and the other year thirteens give me a wide berth. I see them in shared classes and in the common room, but it's always brief glances. My outburst is old news and, for the most part, the gossip has faded. But one thing hasn't.

And the only person I can talk to about this, Jae, is nowhere to be found. Not in class, not in the common room, and not in the greenhouse. When asked, his roommate said he was sick. I don't buy it for a moment.

I *saw* Violet. I dream about her every night. Her terrified expression, trapped on the bank of the river as her old friends cut their hands and bled into a bowl. I know they tried to hurt her, but I'm no closer to figuring out Violet's riddles.

'Is this seat taken?'

I look up from the swirling eddies I've been idly creating in the surface of my soup. 'What do you want?'

Jae sits across from me at my empty table and neatly plucks a napkin from his tray. 'I wanted to check on you.'

I snort harshly and scoot away so his knees won't knock against mine. 'You've finally decided to make an appearance, I see.'

'I've been researching.'

'Is that so?' I bite back my sneer. 'Well, after you made that fuss about helping more girls like Violet and then abandoned me for two whole weeks, it turns out that I don't trust a word that comes out of your mouth.'

'Why's that?' He leans his elbows on the table and looks right at me.

'A thousand reasons.'

'Tell me one, then,' Jae challenges.

'You've got to be kidding me.' I dig my fingers into the over-sized cuffs of my sweater. He lifts his eyebrows and tears apart his roll. I lean across the table, my voice low and tight. 'After the basement, you disappear for weeks on end without a trace, while I'm accused of being crazy. No word, no explanation.'

'And you were drawing everyone's attention. I needed to let things die down –'

'What is wrong with you?' My fingers grip the lip of the table. 'You begged me to let you help, and then you just run off by yourself?'

'We are partners. That hasn't changed. Regina and her club have been watching you.'

'We followed them into the basement! They were there and they did something to my sister.'

'I . . . Look, I went to Hemlock Cove and did some research without anyone being the wiser. But now we need to go into town, Andy. There are archives, and people who know the stories – or at least have suspicions, like we do.'

'Why do you need my help, Jae? You threw me under the bus. I don't know if I can trust you ever again.'

'Because . . .' he hesitates, 'I lost someone the same way you lost Violet.'

He picks at his roll again, long fingers tearing at the bread and spreading crumbs across his plate. His sleeves are rolled up to his elbows, exposing golden skin that's so smooth it almost seems fake. His hair is a little curly and longer on the top and disheveled in a stylish way that boys like Luciano always try to copy but can never quite pull off. Is his clean-cut, caring facade a front? A disguise?

Finally, he takes a short breath. 'My aunt was close to my age; she was almost seventeen years younger than my mother. We grew up more like cousins than anything else. She and I were both at a boarding school in Edinburgh two years ago, in a place a lot like Ravenswood – exclusive and hidden. She was in year thirteen and I was in year ten. One day she was out with friends in the town center and she never came back. They found her body floating in the river a few days later. Nobody did anything. Nobody seemed to care that some Korean girl living in Scotland was alive one day and then suddenly wasn't. Even my parents and grandparents accepted it as a drunken accident. But I knew Min-Jun better than anyone, and she wouldn't do something like that. I was the only one who seemed to think so.'

Chills crawl along my skin. His face is ashen, his eyes shining with an emotion I can't quite name.

I swallow hard and hug my sweater closer to my skin. 'Were you able to figure out what happened to her?'

Jae's face darkens and his knuckles turn white as he twists the last of the roll to shreds. 'Nothing came of it, no one believed me, some fifteen-year-old kid versus a well-respected, prestigious school.'

'Is that why your parents decided to send you here?'

He nods stiffly. 'They wanted me as far away from my old school and memories of Min-Jun as possible. But it's why I want to help you. I don't want what happened to Min-Jun to happen again. I don't want something like this to keep going on in places like Ravenswood, to young and vulnerable girls. I wanted your help because I know you're like me, you care like me – you're probably the *only* one who cares. No one else is going to figure this out, or stop it from happening. Only us.'

Jae's jaw sets in a firm line, contrasting sharply with the smooth contours of his lips and the gentle sweep of his hair. I rub my forehead and take a slow, measured breath, ignoring the way the soup curdles in my stomach at the thought of another Violet. Another girl dead.

'Why didn't you tell me sooner that you knew exactly what I was going through?' My voice shakes at the end.

'It's difficult to talk about Min-Jun.' Jae clears his throat and looks away, his eyes red-rimmed. 'So what do you say, partner? Will you come with me?'

I swallow back my emotions. Pity. Regret. Anger. Betrayal. It all swirls in a sour stew of confusion in my stomach.

Jae forces the traces of grief from his face and looks at me head-on. His aunt died too. Girls are dying at these places. Falling like flies. Why? And why does nobody else care?

'I'll come. Just don't hide things from me anymore.'

'Thank you.' Jae exhales and the tension leaves his body. 'And for what it's worth, I'm sorry. I should have talked to you, tried to help. If anyone can understand remotely how you're feeling, it should be me.'

I blink at him, my lips frozen around a reply. We hold each other's gaze for a few breaths. My skin heats up as my fingers go cold. Someone at the head table moves, snapping us out of the strange spell. Mrs Bryce stands aside so Bianchi can leave the dining hall. She passes by our table, shooting me a thin-lipped smile before disappearing into the heart of Ravenswood.

'We'll have to wait until the homecoming dance this weekend. It's the only time all the staff are busy and won't be able to catch us slipping out.' Jae goes back to picking at his food, like the ripple of emotion we just shared didn't happen.

'Can't you go to town on the weekend? You're in year twelve.' I fold my arms and study the half-eaten food in front of me.

I don't want to look at Jae's face, at his eyes that suddenly seem too piercing – too full of understanding. I want to pull my grief back around me like a cloak.

'There's no way we'll make it back before curfew. We'll need to take a bus or taxi into town and visit someone who's been helping me gather information. If I take my car, the teachers will know I'm gone.'

'So, what do we do?' I rub my lower lip. I want to trust Jae, to have someone on my side who hates this place, these people, as much as I do.

'I can get my roommate to cover for me. Can you get yours to do the same?'

I grimace at the thought of Munia. The more I ignore her, the more I feel the stab of guilt twisting in my ribs. She was right, I run the risk of hurting myself and my family, but I can't leave this alone. It feels like a betrayal of Violet.

Even though my sister isn't dead, the grief of losing her has been tearing me apart just the same. And I've let it make me reckless and callous.

I force myself to meet Jae's eyes. 'I can convince her.'

# 16

The last day of September arrives with another storm. The past two weeks have been almost warm, with the sun slipping between the patchwork of clouds. But now the gray lid has slid back over the sky, sealing us into the mountains and cliffs of Hemlock Cove.

I have yet to work up the courage to speak to Munia and ask her to cover for me.

I wait until Munia is getting ready for the dance. She's finishing pinning a soft blue hijab in place and wears an elegant gray and blue dress that looks both effortless and stylish. Her eyes are lined with kohl in a way that emphasizes her long lashes.

'Are you going to say something or keep staring at me?' she asks my reflection in her mirror.

My pale cheeks, still hollow from months of struggling to eat, flush pink. 'I just wanted to apologize.'

'For what?' She stands and slips on her shoes.

I feel frumpy, drowning in another one of my endless sweaters, with my curly hair a little frazzled from the humidity. I push my glasses up the bridge of my nose and look away from the mirror. 'For that night. What I said to you, it wasn't fair.'

Munia pins an earring in place and leans against her dresser. 'It's fine. I just don't want to see you fade away. There is more to life than beating ourselves up over the past.'

I nod, fingers picking at the hem of my sweater. 'I think I'm starting to understand that.'

'My sister died too, you know.' Her face doesn't change. 'She was younger than me. We were in a car with our driver in Manhattan, on our way to elementary school. We were involved in a crash. I made it but she didn't.'

'I'm sorry.' I swallow thickly.

'It was a long time ago. I stopped blaming myself and started living life without guilt. It's hard, but worth it.'

'I'm not sure I can live my life without guilt,' I whisper, not sure I even say the words aloud. The last night I saw Violet is still burned into my mind, crushing me every time I remember it.

'I want to be your friend, Andy. If you'll let me.' She looks right at me as she says it. I'm a little taken aback. She's direct, and so pulled together. It's as if she's so comfortable in her own skin, and with her own desires, that nothing can scare her.

'I think that might be nice,' I admit, unfolding my legs so they dangle off the edge of the narrow bed frame. 'I actually wanted to ask a favor.'

One of Munia's sleek eyebrows raises. 'A favor?'

'Yeah.' I adjust my position again, my palms sliding against the fabric of my duvet. 'I need to go into town today. If anyone notices I'm not at the dance or in the common rooms, I just wondered if you'd be able to cover for me. Say I'm sick or asleep upstairs or something.'

'Why do you need to go to town?'

For some reason I don't feel comfortable lying to her. Maybe it's because she's one of the only genuine people I've met at Ravenswood. She doesn't fit into the mold I've made for the students Violet went to school with. They're meant to be like Luciano and Regina, even like Madden: cold, calculating, and richer than sin. The kind of people who would stab you in the back and then use your body as a stepping stone to climb higher and higher.

But Munia is only concerned with her schoolwork, with being the best version of herself. The lack of worry for how others see her is foreign within the walls of schools like Ravenswood, where name and reputation are worth their weight in gold.

'I'm going there with Jae. Jae Han. He's in year twelve. He wanted to show me something in town and figured tonight would be a good time to go without anyone else from school crawling around.' I'm babbling, but I can't seem to stop. Besides my arguments with Jae, this is the most I've ever spoken while at Ravenswood. My vocal cords feel rusty from disuse.

'If he wanted to take you out, why didn't he just bring you to the homecoming dance?'

I shrug and look at my lap, studying the lint covering my jeans. They desperately need to be washed. 'I don't think it's a date so much as sharing a common interest.'

Munia makes a thoughtful sound. 'Well, I'm glad you've found someone you can be friends with. I don't know Jae very well, he's new this year too. But he seems nice enough – a little single-track-minded, maybe, but nice.'

'So, you'll do it?'

Munia nods, a warm smile lighting up her face. 'Sure. As long as you promise to be careful.'

'Okay.' I blink at her, surprised she agreed so easily.

'I'll see you tonight. If you aren't back before breakfast, just know I'll probably call the police,' she says and opens the door.

'Fair enough.' I can't help but laugh.

'If anyone asks me, you're upstairs with a migraine. Lock the door behind you, will you?'

'Thank you.'

As soon as she shuts the door, I pull out my phone and text Jae.

*Ready to go. Where should I meet you?*

He responds only a moment later.

*At the front gates. See you there in fifteen.*

A rush of students, dressed to the nines, swirls around the staircase and main foyer. Couples posing for pictures, teachers ushering the groups towards the main gym where music spills out and lights flash. It's an elaborate dance for a high school, but no one seems shocked by the crystal glasses and serving dishes, or the extremely expensive DJ testing his sound equipment.

My black jeans, boots flecked with mud, and dark gray coat are like a disguise. I walk out into the gardens and round the side of the school. The light is fading fast as the sun sets slowly behind the clouds that have temporarily stopped spitting rain.

I jog from the gardens and the school grounds and walk down the long gravel drive to the main gates. The air is crisp and nips at my bare cheeks and nose. The pines are tall and covered with the most recent rainfall, the drops rolling down their needles to beat gently against my shoulders.

A breeze pushes through the branches with a groan and I walk faster, keeping my eyes straight ahead, avoiding the deepest shadows of the forest.

Finally, the tall gates topped with scrolled iron come into view. The haloes of orange light burning from elaborate sconces illuminate Jae's profile. He's looking effortlessly sophisticated again, wearing a dark blue button-up covered with a tan coat that reaches his mid thighs. He wears tan boots, and his hair is slightly damp.

'All set?' he asks.

I tuck my fingers deeper into my pockets. 'My roommate has it taken care of. How long do you think we'll be gone?'

Jae opens the pedestrian gate framed with dark gray brick

and ushers me to go first. He shuts the gate with a clang and then pulls my elbow to guide me down the hill. 'We should be back with the last bus of the night. Probably three in the morning or so. There's a bus stop about half a mile down the road.' He releases my elbow, lingering slightly.

We walk in silence for a moment, occasionally brushing shoulders as we breathe. Nothing but the sound of the creaking pines and the crunch of leaves beneath our feet disturbs the eerie silence.

'Will you tell me where we're going now?' I turn my head to look at him, wiping my glasses clean with my sleeve.

'There's an old church that houses the archives in its basement. I've been in contact with the minister and his wife; she runs the library in town. They have everything I've asked for in boxes and ready to go.'

'And what did you ask for?' I wipe my glasses again as water drops from the tall pines.

Jae had refused to reveal too much about where and who he got his information from. Said he didn't trust us not to be overheard in the school.

Jae keeps his eyes focused straight ahead. 'Death certificates and cemetery records. Police reports and newspapers stretching back since the school was founded. A few things about the man who built Ravenswood. I've been piecing together a timeline with what I could access in online archives.'

'You're looking for a pattern? A hint for who started this and who's continuing it?'

He bobs his head in agreement.

'But why would someone keep this pattern going? If it's been happening since the school first opened, that's well over a hundred and twenty years. It can't be the same person murdering all those girls.'

Jae pushes his curling damp hair back from his eyes. 'It feels similar to what happened to Min-Jun – mysterious deaths covered up and quickly forgotten. The work of a group that passes down their knowledge and secrets.'

I wince at the reminder that Jae isn't merely sating a morbid curiosity. He's got skin in the game too. 'You think a secret society is doing this?'

'Something like that.'

We're quiet for a moment before I work up the courage to ask what I've been wondering since he told me about Min-Jun. 'What . . . what happened to your aunt, exactly?'

Jae makes a sound in the back of his throat but looks sideways at me with his piercing dark eyes. 'Drowned in the Water of Leith after a night out at a pub with friends. When they found her in the morning she looked . . . awful. They ruled it an accident, like your sister. Except no one knew how she'd gotten into the river, or when she'd disappeared.'

The road is dimly lit by a few street lights spaced far apart. We walk between the patches of light, our boots skating along pebbles and flicking water from the damp asphalt. A lonely bus stop with a single bench and a rickety roof painted bright green sits below one of these circles of light.

'You said nothing came of your investigation.' I twist my fingers inside my sleeves. 'Did you find out anything else?'

Jae and I sit beneath the dingy plastic covering of the bus stop.

He shrugs. 'Just that more girls died at that school. That someone was responsible. My parents sent me to a few different schools before I could discover more, hoping I'd work through my grief. I never saw who killed Min-Jun with my own eyes.'

We sit in silence after that, until a bus rumbles up the steep hill and screeches to a stop. We board and sit near the back.

111

The bus is largely empty, just a man in a windbreaker asleep against a window.

Hemlock Cove is a tiny fishing town nestled deep in the rocky coast. The seas are rough but full of all kinds of fish and shellfish, rich pickings for the most intrepid of sailors. I haven't had the chance to see much of it, and the drive in the dark leaves the place shrouded in mystery.

We pass the sign for the high school that serves this section of coastline. The bus rumbles past the post office, which is situated in an old mercantile painted in flaking white paint. I can barely make out the profiles of a few businesses lining Main Street and the signs indicating where the docks are. The bus turns onto a narrow road and stops, brakes hissing and air condensing from the exhaust, next to a lonely park with a sorry-looking playground.

Jae stands and I follow him. We step down onto the sidewalk. The bus lumbers away, steel body reflecting the warped images of darkened storefronts. There is hardly anyone out on the sidewalks, just a stray fisherman or two working their way home after logging and selling their catches.

'The church is a few blocks this way.' Jae takes my elbow again and keeps his hand there as he sets a bruising pace down the long, dark road that runs past the park and its clinking chain-link fence. Soon, we're walking so fast we may as well be running.

'What's the matter?' I hiss as he pushes me ahead of him. We stumble out onto another road, this one lined on both sides with low brick walls.

'I think I see one of the other students' cars,' he says as he guides me across the road and towards a low iron gate cleaving the brick wall in two.

'So? Ease up, you're half a foot taller than me!'

Jae opens the gate and purses his lips like he's biting back a snide remark. 'We can't be seen by anyone at the school. If they know we're meeting the minister, that we're here, it could get to the wrong ears.'

I let him guide me down a gravel path, even though I'm starting to develop a blister on my heel from my wet socks rubbing in my boot. His eyes are frantic, his face pale instead of its usual smooth golden color.

'Fine . . .' I relent and shake his hand off after he tugs my hood over my hair. 'I can walk by myself.'

Headlights sweep across our faces and shine harshly on rows of stones in all shapes and sizes that surround our little path. I stumble, momentarily blinded. A cemetery. Monoliths of marble and granite are mottled with moss and grime, the etched names obscured by decades of neglect. I don't know how many acres of moldering bones lie beneath our feet, but the chill in the air seems sharper than it did a second earlier.

Jae grabs my hand again and squeezes it hard, his long fingers suffocating mine in a stranglehold. 'Relax, Andy. We need to blend in and not look like Ravenswood students.'

'Is this really necessary?' I tug feebly at Jae's grip as the headlights search again, the car turning sharply to make another pass along the outskirts of the cemetery. Despite my complaints, my heart rate kicks up a notch. The headlights turn again, bright halogens seeking our figures for a third time.

'Come here.' Jae tugs me under his arm and adjusts my hood. 'Look like a bereaved couple for a minute, alright? It will look suspicious if we break out into a run.'

I follow his eyes, catching a glimpse of the passenger window as the car does a U-turn in the street. Bright blond hair. A hard frown. Eric, Luciano's friend and a member of the GSE club. My heart beats a little faster, my pulse a little more frantic. What is Eric doing circling a cemetery, and who is driving the car?

'Careful!' I gripe as Jae pulls me so fast my feet almost fly out from underneath me on the wet gravel.

He selects a grave at random and we step onto the spongy grass. Jae bends his head and looks down at the headstone. I copy him. His scent wraps around me, swirling like incense. He smells like spices and rich wood, far more appealing than the pungent, cloying cologne the other boys at school wear. Not that his scent *appeals* to me.

A few seconds pass like this, the headlights shining and our heads bowed in pretend grief.

'Should I pull out a handkerchief and blow my nose?' I whisper.

'Very funny.' Jae digs his elbow into my side and I feel the urge to smile. Almost.

The car turns, tires kicking up water on the road as they screech against the wet concrete. Bathed in darkness, we seize the opportunity to hide. Jae pulls me to crouch behind a marble angel, cold wet moss pressing against my knees. My breath fogs, lifting past the tips of the angel's wings like a soul ascending to heaven.

Headlights. A fourth time. Columns of brightness that slap against our legs. I half expect them to burn my skin. Jae's arm tightens around me, his warmth almost a balm as it seeps into my bones. We squeeze further behind the weeping angel. A car door opens and I peek through my dripping curls and over Jae's shoulder.

I'm not quite sure in the dark, but I can just make out the body of an old, sleek sports car, painted a shiny metallic color. The engine roars as it idles. No one in a fishing town would have the money for something like that. Another door opens and two darkened figures stand in front of the car, their bodies dark spots against the bright headlamps. One of them is definitely Eric Lindgren.

'Stay still,' Jae whispers into my hair.

My throat tightens. Even I have to admit that this seems suspicious. Jae's fingers are tight as they dig into my side, anchoring me to him. The voices, male, discuss something urgently in low tones that drift in our direction, muffled by the engine as it purrs and growls.

My vision swims as I experience a jolt of inexplicable fear. I lay my cheek against Jae's arm, hoping that, if they do spot us, it sells the image of two people mourning the loss of a loved one. He stiffens for a moment before he seems to hold me closer. To keep me from running, I'm sure.

The car doors slam again and tires screech as the vehicle roars down the road at blinding speed. We're submerged in darkness and silence again. I blink a few times to clear the spots from my eyes and try to suck in a deep, calming breath.

Jae's thumb runs up and down my side, smoothing the notches of my ribs under my open coat. His lips are still pressed to my head, like we're lovers caught in a moment. My skin tingles and, almost regretfully, I pull myself away from the tangle of his long limbs. Part of me immediately misses his warmth and scent, the unanticipated shiver that wants to race down my spine at his touch.

'Do you think they were looking for us?' I clear my throat and wrap my arms around my middle. The damp air is even colder without Jae's form blocking the worst of the misting rain and ocean breeze.

Jae looks fixedly away. 'I'm not sure. We haven't been away that long. Let's go. The church is just up the path.'

We walk quickly, but this time he keeps his distance and doesn't reach for me. I try to ignore the imprint of his fingers on my side. The ghost of his thumb caressing me is harder to dismiss than I expected.

A gray stone church, surprisingly large, emerges around the

bend and towers above the sea of headstones. The windows are arched and inlaid with swirling metalwork in the gothic fashion. Jae leads me to the minister's house at the rear. Lights glimmer in the windows and a cheery-looking fire blazes in the front room.

Jae knocks on the door, and I push my hood back. An old man dressed head to toe in black opens it. His hair is shockingly white and thinning on the top, and his dark blue eyes study us from a face lined with wrinkles carved by weather and time.

'Mr Han,' he says, voice gravelly but not unkind.

'Pastor Carmichael, this is my friend, Andy Emmerson.'

The minister stares down his hooked nose at us. His eyes flick between the two of us before resting on Jae. He grunts, hardly a reply, and steps back. Jae motions for me to go first and I do, the warmth of the church a welcome reprieve from the damp night.

As I cross the threshold, I feel a strange sort of shock run down my spine. I roll my shoulders and neck and urge the sensation away.

Beneath my boots is a worn red carpet covering equally worn wood-planked floors, narrow, like they're original. I peer through the crack of an open door and spy a study filled with leather furniture and bookshelves. Straight ahead, the chapel yawns, only a few candles near the front providing any light.

'Well, come in from the cold, my boy,' Pastor Carmichael says in that gruff voice of his.

Jae stands, his hands in his coat pockets, and his face strained. He doesn't meet my eyes but I can tell he's troubled. He forces one foot across the threshold from the porch and into the church. The other follows slowly, like it's being dragged against his will.

I turn around and slip my coat from my shoulders, letting

the minister take it and hang it to dry on a small rack by the door.

'Sorry, I just got dizzy for a moment,' Jae says, and shakes his head. His fingers brush deliberately against the door frame and a tiny brass symbol I didn't notice before.

I squint, trying to figure out why the symbol looks familiar. It almost looks like a djed, the Egyptian symbol for rebirth. But that doesn't fit with a protestant church in a small town.

'Come into the study,' Pastor Carmichael says in a measured voice, looking sympathetically at Jae. 'I have everything we discussed there.'

Jae nods tightly, his jaw clenched. His fingers drop from the symbol, but before I can bend my head to study it myself, the pastor closes the door. Pastor Carmichael waves his hand and leads the way into the study.

I move to follow but take a quick glance at Jae. His face is pale and coated in a thin layer of sweat. His skin almost seems to ripple, to shudder. He closes his eyes and takes a deep breath.

His eyes, blacker than ever, snap open. 'Go ahead, Andy. I'm right behind you.'

A blast of cold air dissipates the warmth from the burning fire, and I turn to follow the pastor without a peep of protest. The heat from Jae's body presses at my back as he follows me.

'This is all I have on the disappearances. We pulled them from town archives and our own records.' Pastor Carmichael spreads his hands and gestures towards the boxes strewn about. 'There's a section over here on Richard Greene, the man who built the house and sold it to be turned into a school.'

'Thank you. And be sure to thank your wife as well.' Jae extends his hand and the pastor shakes it with a firm grip.

'Of course. If I could do more, go to that academy and tear

117

it apart brick by brick, I would,' the old man says, his fathomless blue eyes pinning me in place.

I look at him in surprise, my mouth hanging open.

Jae nods. 'You've helped me more than you know.'

'It's about time someone looked into that godforsaken school. I hope you find the answers we've all been looking for. I'll be upstairs in my apartment. If you need anything, let me know.'

Jae nods coolly and the pastor steps out into the hall, wrinkled hands shutting the door behind him. I hear the heavy footsteps of Pastor Carmichael retreat across the church. I wait until they fade and the rafters have swallowed the sound.

'What was that about?' I cross my arms and pretend to study a few yellowed newspapers at my hip.

'The pastor? He's harmless, but rather spirited about his hatred for the school.' Jae shrugs his coat off and tosses it onto the back of a leather chair. He lifts a box from the floor, sets it on a long table and rifles through the contents before he pulls out a few promising-looking headlines.

'I mean, he seems to know more than I expected.'

'Oh, he does. He was alive when the last killings rocked the town. He thinks it was a secret society too.'

I make a thoughtful sound. 'And what about just now at the door?'

'What do you mean?' Instead of looking at me, Jae hands over a bundle of newspapers dated from the mid-1920s. The pages smell like mildew but I undo the twine and tap my fingertips against the dry and curling paper.

'You acted strange, like you were in pain or something.'

Jae shrugs, his shoulders moving with far more grace than they should. 'I'm fine. Like I said, I just felt dizzy for a moment.'

Pursing my lips, I decide not to push further – for now.

Instead, I focus on the papers and shuffle through them. Some articles are circled in faded red and black. I bend my head to study them closer. 'What am I looking for exactly?'

'Dates of disappearances and deaths of girls in town and at the school. As far back as 1896, and as recent as last year.'

'And you couldn't find this stuff online?'

Jae shakes his head and picks up another set of boxes. These hold certificates, neatly bound and sorted. Death certificates, by the looks of it, issued by the church and courthouse. Most are in faded ink. Some look much newer, bearing the neat imprint of typewriters, or printed on embossed paper.

'No. This town is too small and doesn't have much of a police presence. Most of the girls' deaths have been covered up anyway. I had to earn Jonas' trust for him to even admit he had these documents. If Ravenswood knew about them, they would have destroyed them. I convinced him, eventually, that I wasn't just another Ravenswood student throwing my weight around, so he would let me take a look.'

'So he knows the school is covering up the deaths, right? Or he wouldn't have hidden these away.' I sit on the floor and lay out my stack of newspapers. I sort them by date, hunting for articles about girls that fit the age range, and then begin to read.

Jae is quiet for so long I almost forget he's there until he speaks, his voice a little raspy. 'The townsfolk don't like Ravenswood students. They think we're rude and entitled and ruin their peace.'

I murmur in agreement, pull a pad of paper into my lap and begin to jot down notes. 'I can't really blame them. I don't think I'm a fan of the students at the school either.'

Jae joins me on the floor, so close his knee almost brushes mine. 'Not all are bad.'

'No, I suppose not. But you seem to agree that places like

Ravenswood – the kind that cater to privilege, that groom kids to become ego- and money-obsessed adults who feed back into the school – have their own agendas. Their own secrets.'

I mark another date on my legal pad. Another name.

'I do,' he says. 'But your sister went here. My aunt went to a place like Ravenswood too. You and I are both here.'

'That's different. I'm not here to go to an Ivy League. I'm here to get justice for Violet. No one else cares. No one in that school cares. Besides you.'

'Besides me,' he agrees, his voice soft.

# 17

'Andy. Andy, wake up.' A warm hand nudges my shoulder. I groan and rub my eyes before I blink up at the face peering over me. For a moment I forget where I am.

'What's going on?' I sit up as Jae scrambles around the room and plucks my notepad from the floor at my side.

'We need to go.' He tears out a few sheets of paper and folds them, tucking them into the breast pocket of his coat. He throws my coat at me and it slithers into my lap. I pull myself to my feet and look out the windows. The sky is that blue-black of pre-dawn.

'What time is it? Munia is going to call the police if I'm not back by breakfast!'

'It's four in the morning,' he says, his hands tearing pages from notebooks and shoving them into his pockets. 'We need to get back.'

I throw my coat over my shoulders and shove my arms into the sleeves. 'Why didn't you wake me?'

'I fell asleep too!' Jae opens the door to the study. The church is dark and quiet, and the candles in the chapel have gone out.

'Where is Pastor Carmichael?' I ask

As if summoned, the old man comes down the steps, still dressed head to toe in black, but this time it's topped off with a thick wool cardigan. 'You should get back, Mr Han. The last thing I need is that blasted school breathing down my neck.'

'Thank you for your help.' Jae nods and extends his hand. 'We might need to come back.'

The pastor clasps Jae's hand gingerly, like it might burn him, but shakes it just the same. 'Martha would like to see you again. To thank you in person.'

Jae's cheeks turn a little pink. 'It's not necessary. Your kindness is enough.'

Jae opens the door. The cold wind whips at my cheeks, a shock after the toasty warmth of the fire. I rub my eyes, trying to remember what happened before I fell asleep. Before we can step out into the chilly morning, the pastor speaks, his voice so grave it sends a chill straight to my toes.

'You know what day it is, Mr Han.' Jonas looks at me uneasily before he leans in. 'The closer it gets, the more reckless they'll become. And the more you visit *that place*, the more attention you'll draw.'

Jae's mouth flattens into a thin line. 'I understand. We'll stop them before time runs out. You can be assured of that.'

Pastor Carmichael nods, his startling blue eyes shining even in the dimness. 'Be careful wandering these mountains and forests just before dawn. You might not know you've been dead for hours.'

And with that the pastor retreats back up the narrow steps leading to his apartment above the chapel. I stare at his back, at the dark gray pattern of the wool cardigan. Jae steps out into the cold air of the porch and stands aside, waiting for me.

'What was that?' I join him, my fingers drumming against one leg.

Jae checks his phone and I do the same. There are no texts from Munia or anyone else. That must mean she's still asleep, that we still have time to get back to our dorms before anyone grows suspicious.

'Nothing really. The pastor and I have been talking for weeks now.' He descends the steps, his long legs eating up the distance between the church and the gates of the cemetery.

I hurry after him. 'What was he talking about? He said something about the date, and you visiting somewhere. And what was the thing about dying in the woods?'

Jae doesn't look directly at me but I can still sense his eyes, studying me with his peripheral vision. 'Just that he suspects the same thing we do, and that we need to hurry before the next girl is killed. It's been months since Violet. Too long a gap.'

'The pattern,' I recall. 'There's going to be another death soon.'

He nods, eyes troubled. 'I wondered if it could be related to the tides. The girls almost always die at night, drowned in the cove.'

'No. Not the tides.' I stop walking, my head pounding. I pull my cellphone from my pocket and pull up a chart. And I remember what I was looking at before sleep pulled me down. 'Look. The murders in the fifties all took place on full moons. And look, the three in the twenties. These happened on equinoxes – summer, winter.'

Jae takes my crumpled wad of paper and unfolds it, scanning the dates. I look up at the darkened sky, the hazy whisper of the stars through the clouds menacing somehow. Jae jams the paper into his pocket and starts walking again.

He moves fast, and if it weren't for the sleep still making my eyes feel gritty and bleary, I could swear smoke or fog clings to Jae as he moves. His outline flickers for a moment. Changing shape. But then we reach the outskirts of the graveyard. Jae opens the gate and I'm glad to be free of the cemetery. The sky is dark blue-black, not morning but not night either. It makes it hard to see the road, to make out the shapes of buildings as we walk back the way we came.

He stops, catching my gaze. 'We can only talk about this when we're alone and away from school grounds, do you understand?'

'Of c-course,' I stammer, surprised at the fire crackling in

123

his dark eyes. 'These deaths. All of them happened during celestial or astronomical events. Why?'

Jae sighs and rakes a hand down his face, his thumb skating along the short stubble beginning to cling to his sharp jaw. 'I don't know. But whoever is doing this, whoever is keeping these deaths going, picks these events for a reason. I should have seen it earlier.'

'Those things can be predicted and tracked years in advance. That means we can guess if, or when, another girl is due to be killed. We can be a step ahead of them,' I say slowly even as he begins to walk again, moving with purpose.

Rain mists steadily down on our shoulders, and I hunch against the cold and the wet.

'The last death was your sister,' Jae says as we come to a halt at the bus stop. 'There hasn't been anyone from the school or town who has gone missing since then.'

'That's a good thing, isn't it? When Violet died, that night was a partial eclipse.' I point at my phone. 'If all three deaths need to be around the same kind of event, we should be safe. Another partial eclipse won't happen anytime soon.'

'Unless they don't need an eclipse,' he murmurs. 'Something else could have happened that night. A moon phase, a comet, something like that.'

I rub my brow again and bend forward to study the beat-up schedule taped to the side of the plastic cover. The next bus isn't due to return to Ravenswood for two hours. I text Munia, and hope it helps her hold off a little longer.

'There are multiple events coming up this month. A new moon, a full moon,' Jae muses. 'We have no way of knowing which one they'll pick. But this is the longest stretch of time I've seen between a grouping of murders. Remember they always happen in threes and are usually a few months apart, staged to seem like accidents.'

'Why do they need to pick a time related to the sun and moon anyway?' I'm starting to feel irritable, sleep deprivation making my head ache.

'Celestial and lunar events charge magic. They're powerful, if you know how to use them. The problem is there's a new moon tonight and tomorrow. And tonight, it will be exactly seven months since Violet.'

I press my lips together. 'There hasn't been a gap that long between any of the deaths I found.'

'Exactly. They might be getting desperate. Something could be wrong. Or they could be waiting for something.'

'So, they could be drowning another girl right now? We should go to the cove to check.' I stand up straight, my eyes burning a hole on the horizon.

'No, there isn't enough time for them to kill someone and leave before the fishermen are out on the water. Someone would see from the docks. If they are going to kill again, it will be at night. Let's go back to the school and watch Luciano and the others. We'll follow them if they leave the school.'

I knead my forehead with my knuckles, thoughts spinning.

'We have to get moving. The bus will take too damned long.' Jae grabs my arm and hauls me towards the trees. My heart flies into my throat and I dig my heels in, but my boots slip and slide over the wet grass.

'Where are we going?' I screech. He can't take me there.

Jae stops for a moment, studies me. A line creases the space between his black brows. 'Our best chance of getting to the school before they notice we're gone is through this hiking trail. It goes up the mountain towards the school and loops back around by the river. It used to be part of the town when it was first settled to pan for gold.'

I dig the heels of my hands into my eyes and breathe slowly. The air feels strange here at the mouth of the forest, and I can't help but remember what Jae said about it. That it's off limits for students. Dangerous. A warning sensation pricks at the back of my neck, and I try to push it away.

'Are you okay?'

I shake myself out of his grip. 'Fine. Come on, let's go before my roommate decides you killed me.'

'If we hurry, we can be back in an hour.' He cocks his head to the side, clearly concerned.

*That makes two of us.*

# 18

My foot sinks in the muddy riverside up to my ankle and I pull it back with a disgusting squelch. Jae plods along easily as dawn begins to approach, barely illuminating our little path through the forest with gray light.

'Careful, there are some stones and bricks that are covered by grass over here,' Jae calls from a few yards ahead.

I grumble under my breath but push forward, my boots slipping back each time I try to move faster. The river churns past us, tumbling over rocks and kicking up spray into the morning air.

I reach the section he mentioned. It's a mess of half-destroyed foundations and the crumbled walls of a settlement long since abandoned to the earth. There are a few imprints of small houses left that I can barely make out over the tumbling grass and low brush. But here and there the riverside is dotted by partly intact chimneys, a few feet of old mortared wall, or an empty arch.

Pausing to catch my breath, I lean against one of the few archways and tip my head towards the sky. The base of the hill where Ravenswood sits is directly above us. We should be back soon if we climb hard. But that same warning chill is tightening around my chest and it's sapping any strength from my limbs.

Jae doubles back and stands beside me, his hands on his hips. 'Everything alright?'

'Peachy.' I give him a half-smile, half-snarl. 'I love being dragged around in the rain for twelve hours by a guy who keeps more secrets than a Freemason.'

His mouth quirks up a little at the jab, which kind of takes the fun out of it. 'Are you hurt? Do you need me to carry you?'

'No. I'm just tired. We had a long night.' I ignore his outstretched hand and straighten up, keeping one palm on the decaying arch.

'We're almost back,' he says encouragingly. 'Once we are, we'll need to make a plan for tonight.'

I nod, my vision swimming. I keep my hands on the arch as I steady myself and then step through it, wondering for a moment if the people who lived here, worked and dreamed in this little village, are sleeping beneath the grass at my feet. Maybe they're watching me right now.

Jae follows behind, his hands hovering at my back as if he expects me to fall over. We walk together in silence for what feels like an eternity. Soon, I begin to notice black streaks in the sky. Odd.

I turn to look behind me. Jae is a few steps back, his eyes on the ground and sweat beading his forehead. His face is twisted again, contorted with pain like when he entered the church last night. Fog billows behind him. What once was a forest is endless gray nothingness.

Gasping, my fingers digging into my chest, I whirl around again. The sky is now dark and clear. Starless. Vast. The forest looms around us, cradling the river. The water churns so black it looks like an oil spill. My voice is lost somewhere in my throat.

'Andy?' Jae's ragged breath brushes the back of my neck. 'Why have you stopped?' He runs into me and curses under his breath.

I stagger forward, my lungs hardly able to function. It's like I'm stuck underwater. Drowning in the air. I've felt this before . . . in the basement when I saw Violet.

'Where are we?'

The only sound is the river surging beside us. The banks are pockmarked with a mixture of dark mud and rocks and peppered with odd plants I don't recognize. The grass beneath my feet is gray and crumbles to ash wherever I step.

Mist, curling and icy, wraps around our legs and obscures the path we've trodden. A wall of opaque vapor, so thick and tremulous it feels alive. A heart beating in the ether. The trees loom like sentinels above and around us, closing in like a fist.

'Are you seeing this too?' I whisper, my voice rough.

'Yes. Now stay still,' Jae whispers in my ear and takes my hand, anchoring me to him. 'We have to be careful. Don't disturb anything or anyone you see, do you understand?'

*No!* I want to scream it at him. But I can't do even that. So, I nod dumbly and hold tight to his long fingers. They're cold, when they're usually so warm. It feels like an omen. He leads me forward a step, and more grass crumbles beneath our shoes. Everything is eerily silent. I'm not even sure I can hear our footsteps anymore. Or our breath.

We walk carefully, slowly. I feel like the strength is being sapped from my muscles. The black sky, so silky and endless, feels like a great stone grinding me into dust. I stagger, tripping over something, and crash into the ashy earth. I cough and sputter, crawling on my hands and knees. But I don't get far.

Bones, an endless sea of them, scatter at my feet. They move, quivering. And then they begin to assemble themselves, the bones clacking as they join together. Sinew materializes out of nothing, and then slabs of muscle, soon covered by skin as dark as ebony. I can't open my mouth to scream. I can't do anything.

In front of me is a monster, a creature with the head of a . . . dog?

'Andy,' Jae speaks calmly, his hands held out, one towards

me and one towards the monster glaring at me with eyes of ruby. 'Don't move, whatever you do. Don't do a thing.'

He steps forward, almost as tall as the thing made of shadows and power. A headdress covers the top of its skull, the pointed ears sticking in front of the golden band. A wickedly sharp spear, tall and with a flat blade, is gripped in its fist. Its face is elongated. Not a dog exactly. I know this. What is it?

Jae takes something from his pocket. A coin? It shifts between black and gold and back again, like a kaleidoscope. He extends his hand, palm up, the coin resting there.

The monster considers it with a tilt of the head. 'You return. Have you yet finished what you intended?'

I'm frozen on the ground, my knees tucked to my chest. The dog – no – the jackal-headed man has a voice deeper and more melodic than anything I've ever heard . . . until it snaps in place, the realization. I *have* heard a voice like this before. Hiding in Violet's room, the first night I came to Ravenswood.

'We do not return for long. Let us pass unharmed.' Jae holds the coin out again. It's long, its shape oval and uneven rather than circular, as if it were hammered by hand.

'You have only one. The girl wishes to save someone from the bank. You will need two.' The monster with the ruby eyes looks down, meaty fingers curling around a golden spear.

Jae's shoulders tighten. He curses again – at least, I think it's a curse. I don't recognize it. Maybe another language. 'She's here? Alive or dead?'

'Alive.'

Jae stiffens and his free hand fists at his side. His skin ripples, breaking out in sweat as if he's in severe pain. Just like at the church. I can't blink, even though the ash at my fingers is forming clouds around me and getting into my eyes. I know the jackal-headed beast is going to snap Jae in half.

Jae looks over his shoulder at me, a glance. A warning. 'We are unable to reach her anyway. We can find another way.'

'Very well.' The jackal inclines his head. 'I accept your offering and will not stop you. But your window is closing. It is not often mortals such as this girl find their way to the banks of the river and remain intact.'

'You have our thanks.' Jae bows formally and the creature returns the gesture. It accepts the strange coin from Jae and melts into darkness.

Suddenly I can breathe. I cough and sputter and spit ash from my mouth.

'What was that?' I gasp between coughs. My lungs burn like I've inhaled a cloud of bleach.

'I promise I'll explain later but we have to hurry. Do not touch or say anything else until we're out, do you understand?' Jae crouches in front of me and grips my chin, forcing me to look at him. His face is wild, manic almost.

I nod and he releases my chin, helping me to my feet. He takes my hand again and leads me along the bank of the oily river. I try to keep my eyes trained at our feet, at the dust licking our boots and churning around our legs. But I catch glimpses of things. Inexplicable and terrifying.

In the trees, I see figures moving among the dead branches. Heads adorned with wreaths of bones. They dance to an inaudible beat I feel in my teeth. They whisper and point as we pass. At our feet, the ground slithers like snakes are trapped beneath it. Strange birds with sleek golden bodies and the heads of people stare at us with wide eyes, their necks twisting all the way around to watch our progress.

I see bodies hanging from ghostly gallows. They turn their heads to smile at us and ask if we have any water. Their skin is gray and colorless. Drained of life. I lurch, tempted to cup my hands in the midnight river and let them drink from my fingers.

'Hello, little star,' they croon, clacking hungrily. *'We knew you'd come for her. We are so ravenous. Feed us and we will lead you to her.'*

I stare at them, my tongue stuck to the roof of my mouth.

*'Just a drop of blood,'* one corpse begs, the rope around his neck creaking. *'Feed us and we will grant you anything you wish.'*

My head aches worse than anything I've ever felt. I smell the stench of corrosion. A hand cups my cheek, forces me to look away from the swinging corpses that beg and spit at me and cry for mercy.

'Andromeda,' Jae says, his voice so strong and commanding it stabs straight to my heart. 'Look at me. Do not listen to what they say. Do not look at them, only me.'

I nod, licking my cracked lips. 'Only you.'

He breathes out slowly and pulls me close to his side, his arm snaking around my shoulders like a cloak. I shiver against him, my skin crusting over with ice. We walk for what feels like an eternity, until my boots fill with blood and my toenails blacken. I can feel life slipping from my bones.

Jae hauls me up a hill. At the top is a tree, its bark bleached white like dead coral. The limbs twist towards the sky and are adorned with red petals so dark they look like drops of blood. Heavy thorns, long and black, jut outward. It looks familiar. Like the poisoned flower Regina tucked behind my ear.

'We need to go up there,' Jae points, 'and prick ourselves with the thorns.'

I shake my head and clutch at his coat. 'We can't. Last time, the rot almost destroyed my hand!'

'It won't happen a second time. The cure I made ensures you're immune to the poison. It's the quickest way back before we become trapped,' he says calmly. I recall the pinch on my arm, the red and black lump. Regina tried to poison me again after the club meeting. But it didn't kill me. Still, the thought of another wave of the pain makes my palms sweat.

'Trapped?' My chest squeezes.

He nods solemnly, face grim.

We rush up the hill. When we reach the top I pause, the giant tree fading from thought. Below us is spread a fantastical, terrible scene. The river coils through an endless valley of gray. On the other side life springs forth in colors so rich and deep they can't be real.

Giant palaces of marble and obsidian dot the mountains across from us. Boats, long and wide, glide along the winding river. Firelight dances on the decks and happy voices spill over and mix with the water. Gardens gleam in invisible sunlight. Luminescent plants dot the opposite bank.

But on this side, the one where Jae and I have wandered, there are hordes of people cramming the muddy bank. They're gray and almost shapeless. But I can feel what they want. What they need. Life. To cross the river. To make it to the other side. They need payment. They crave blood.

Jae blocks my view, his face somber. His skin is rippling again, his face shifting. One moment it's him, and then he seems alien and unfamiliar. I can't reconcile the images. I don't know what they are.

'Here.' He grabs my hand and yanks a small branch free. 'This will hurt, but it's what we need to get back.'

'Get back?' I ask, uncomprehending, my tongue tripping over the words.

He positions a wickedly long, needlelike thorn at my forearm and slices the skin. It isn't a deep cut but it burns like he's hit bone. I try to pull back but he shakes his head and squeezes so that blood flows over the sides of the wound and drips onto the ground.

'What are you doing?' I gasp and wince as the wound glares at me, angry and red. Jae's fingers are sticky with my blood. He takes a petal, already curling in on itself, and holds it out to my lips.

'You need to eat the petal or you'll die here.'

'Die?' I wheeze. 'You said it wouldn't hurt me this time!'

He steps closer and I notice again how tall he is, how broad his shoulders are. Did he always look like this? His other hand cups my jaw and sends a tickle of surprise skittering across my skin.

'Eat the petal and you'll be fine. It's *Subitae mortem*, a food of the gods here. It's useful to humans on occasion – it has the power to free you from the realm between the rivers.'

'I don't understand anything you're saying.'

Maybe I don't need to leave. A whisper runs along my skin, encouraging the thought. Like the call of a bird, I hear it again. *Stay.* I sway on my feet, listening to the voices of the ghostly creatures spreading through the valley.

Jae's expression is sympathetic, his straight brows furrowed over his beautiful angular eyes. Strangely, I want to trace the contours of his high cheekbones, his proud face. But then he thrusts the petal at my lips and I bite his finger instead.

'Andy!' He barks and shakes out his hand. 'You have to do this! Dawn will be here soon. If we let it pass, we could be stuck here for years.'

I turn my head away but he holds my chin in a firm grip, forcing my jaw to open. I beat my fists against his chest but it's like hitting a statue. I need to stay here in this gray land. No, I *have* to. Those creatures demand it. They'll help me if I feed them my blood. They whisper it through the thick air, over and over again.

Jae doesn't even flinch as he places the petal behind my teeth and then snaps my mouth shut. I taste his skin on my tongue, like amber and incense and ancient things.

Jae's voice shifts into a deeper tone and he speaks. The words are nonsense to me, but beautiful just the same. His eyes shut and he places a petal on his own tongue but doesn't cut his flesh, just swipes my blood in a pattern on his forearm.

The world swirls into nothingness. Colors drain and mix and burst across my eyelids. The petal in my mouth disintegrates, oddly sweet – almost like turned meat. I gag and sputter and fall forward, expecting to hit the ashy earth and choke on clouds of dust. But instead, my cheek hits rough fabric.

My eyes flutter open. I'm in the secret storage room Jae took me to, where the radiator rattles and screeches at us like an angry cat. I sit up, pushing away from the musty couch. Jae leans against the wall in front of me, arms crossed, his eyes wary.

I look down at my arm, ready to see a huge gash coated in dried blood. But the skin is smooth and unblemished. There isn't even any dust on my boots.

My gaze flies to Jae's face and I stand, ignoring the persistent headache.

'What happened?' I step forward and jab my finger into his chest, tilting my head up to meet his gaze. 'And don't even consider lying to me.'

## 19

A clock chimes slowly above us, somewhere on the main floor. I count the echoes. Five. Five in the morning.

I press my fingers to my temples, struggling to balance logic with the truth. 'How did we get back so fast? We wandered that riverbank for hours. Days even.'

'The Underworld,' Jae corrects me again, even though I want to slap him for it. 'Or at least the place between Earth and the Underworld, on the banks.'

Between the living and the dead.

'Is it still the same day? Are they looking for us?' I take off my glasses and rub at my nose.

He's been trying to explain what happened and where we were for the past fifteen minutes. The Underworld and ghosts and jackal-headed sentries. It's not that I don't believe him, I saw it for myself. What crawls beneath my skin is the dawning realization that he already *knew* it was real before tonight.

He shakes his head and sits on the couch, long legs sprawled in front of him. 'Time is different there, fluid. What feels like only a second to us here could be thousands of years there.'

'How did we get there? What was that strange-headed beast that stopped us?' I have so many questions rolling through my mind I can't keep them straight. It feels like a dream. A nightmare. And yet I still have the cloying taste of the petal heavy on my tongue. I hear the awful shouts from the apparitions in the ghostly forest.

'The archway, I should have been more careful. In certain places the veil between worlds is thin. At times of change, liminal places and liminal times, that veil can be pierced.' Jae's hands move as he speaks. He's trying to draw a picture for me, something to grasp. But it slips through my fingers.

I sit next to him and measure my breath. 'You're saying you know about the Underworld, that you've been there before, and didn't think to tell me?'

Jae pushes his hair back. It's tousled and disheveled, but he still looks composed and unruffled, whereas I'm certain I look like I just crawled through a swamp and then through hell.

'I'm sorry, Andromeda.' His jaw tightens, and he looks away. 'I didn't know for sure yet. I didn't want to scare you! And I won't hide these things anymore, because we are stronger together.'

'Together?' I stand, every instinct urging me to run from this room and leave him here, locked inside forever. '*Together* implies we are actually partners. That one of us shares his secrets and explains what is going on before the other person wanders into the Underworld, Jae. We aren't anything. Allies, friends. Nothing.'

'I didn't mean for us to end up there, I would never want you to experience that.'

A sound of outrage slips through my clenched teeth. 'But you knew what to do. You've been there before. How did you access the Underworld? Explain that.'

He stands and paces in front of the door, blocking my exit, his hands constantly raking through his hair. 'Ever since Min-Jun died, I've been trying to speak to her. To know what happened, so I found ways to slip between life and death. It started with archways at strange times and days, and then moved on to using plants and ancient concoctions to transport myself. I've been to the Underworld countless times, searching for clues. I wanted to know, needed to know who killed her and why.'

'You said you didn't know who killed her.'

'I did find out,' he says darkly. 'But I paid a high price to get that knowledge. Higher than you can imagine. And I learned more than I should have. I've changed in my time there, that's why I walk through the Underworld like I belong there. I don't recognize myself anymore.'

Jae stops in the center of the room. His eyes are far away, fixed on a point I can't see. Lost. I hate the twinge of sympathy twisting in my heart. Hate it for making me understand why he's so intent, so focused. Am I not the same when it comes to Violet? Wild and desperate, thirsting for justice, for knowledge – consequences be damned?

'Why didn't you tell me about the Underworld before? There's so much more going on with Violet than I could have imagined, and you kept it hidden.'

He swallows hard, like the words hurt. 'You saw it yourself. It's an awful place, Andy. A terrible place to get lost. And I didn't know if you would believe me.'

'I've never believed for a moment that my sister is dead,' I say sharply, remembering the jackal-headed man Jae paid for safe passage. 'And you suspected too.'

What had the monster said? *The girl wishes to save someone from the bank.* He said she was alive.

'You knew Violet was alive. And all this time you've been able to go to the Underworld. You could have spoken to her!' My voice is shrill, cracking at the seams. My sister is trapped in that awful place that reeks of death. An image of the oily river that keeps her bound flashes behind my eyelids as I squeeze them shut, willing a wave of nausea to recede.

Jae could have saved her.

'I didn't know,' he insists, reaching out to touch my knee. He flinches when I jerk away. 'I swear that I had no clue Violet was alive in the Underworld. And I didn't tell you that

I can access it, because who would believe me? I'm sorry, Andromeda. I really am.'

I get a strange sensation when he says my name like that, like he's caressing each syllable.

'But I didn't think you'd understand or believe me,' he insists. 'Who would?'

'Where is she? How do I get her out?' I press my fingers to my forehead, remembering how I saw Violet on the bank of the river, weeks ago. How scared she looked.

Jae shakes his head. 'If that guardian knew she was there, she's out of our reach. There are places in the Underworld guarded by beings far worse than him where only the dead can go.' His brow furrows as he considers something. 'Or if you know magic.'

Violet's writings and books already told me she was dabbling in the occult, but still, I shiver to hear it said. 'What kind of magic gets you to the Underworld?'

'The dark kind,' he laughs ruefully. 'I think that when the secret society tried to kill her she must have slipped into the Underworld to hide. But the problem is, it takes years of practice to know how to enter and leave the land of the dead. Violet must be stuck, if she's been there for so long.'

'She knew she might be stuck – that's why she left me all these notes and hints. But if a coin can buy a way out, why can't we do it again?'

'I only had that one coin, a sort of bartering chip favored by many ancient cultures, for use in the Underworld. They're incredibly rare. Each coin is a mixture of iron and gold, both dangerous and intoxicating to spirits. It acts as payment to keep mortals safe from unearthly beings interested in collecting damned souls, the living included.'

I glare at him, a memory clicking into place. 'You were the man in my sister's room the first night I was at Ravenswood, weren't you? I recognized your voice when you spoke in that language.'

His jaw clenches. 'Yes. I was searching for answers, looking for clues about what happened. That's when I guessed Violet might not be dead – I could sense the coin hidden in her room. She knew about the Underworld somehow, and I wanted to find out more. But those freshmen came in before I could figure anything out.'

I press my lips together at the revelation. 'Why didn't you use the coin to go save her, if you can travel to the Underworld at will?'

'It doesn't work like that. I grabbed the coin when we went to her dorm that night, and it's a good thing I did. A coin like that only works for one person, and only if you bring it with you. It's why cultures put them under the tongues of dead loved ones.'

'It got you out just fine.'

'The coin was for you. I have other ways of leaving the Underworld. Ways you don't want to experience yourself.' His face is dark, eyes stormy. Regretful.

'Violet is there, still alive. We have to find another way to get her out.'

'We will, I promise. But first things first, we have to stop the next girl's death – or Violet's plan will be for nothing.'

I don't look at him but I can still sense his eyes on me.

'Why do you really need my help?' I ask. 'Tell me the truth. Please.'

His gaze is a heavy thing. Palpable. Like he sees beneath my skin to the secrets buried there. 'Violet left clues; I realized it when I was in her room, that first night you came to Ravenswood. I think she knew she was going to be targeted next and tried to leave a warning. She left things for you to find, things only you would understand.'

'So, I'm the secret key?' I huff, half joking.

'Yes.'

I jerk my head up and stare at him. His face is close and his scent permeates the air. Incense again. What a strange smell for a teenage boy to wear.

'What could I possibly do?' I snap, tearing my gaze away and rooting it firmly in my lap.

Jae's hands tighten around each other. 'You're the only one who understands your sister. She left you everything that's needed to figure out who is responsible. Maybe it's time I realized that too. Stopped my one-man crusade of revenge.' His smile is rueful and sad.

'You said you can travel to the Underworld whenever you want. You saw that there was a pattern before I even got here. All she gave me was a letter and a charm before she died, and our matching tattoos.'

'What charm? What tattoo?' He straightens at my side.

'We both have these bracelets,' I take mine from where I stashed it in my pocket, 'with these charms. And I have a tattoo with all of them as well. Violet insisted, on her eighteenth birthday. I don't know what it means.'

I lay the bracelet in Jae's palm. He brings it close to his face and studies the charms. The moth, the antlers and the moon. The curved tooth. He looks at me, eyes wide.

'Can I see the tattoo?'

'Now?' I splutter.

'Yes, now. I need to see it. To be sure.'

Heat creeps up my neck and licks at my cheeks. My skin feels so hot I wonder how my glasses haven't fogged up yet. 'It's on my thigh,' I hiss, running my fingers over the tattoo beneath the fabric of my jeans.

Jae jumps to his feet, his eyes wide. But I notice the hint of a blush staining his chiseled cheekbones. 'I'll turn around.'

Dutifully, he turns to face the radiator. It's strange. We've come full circle in this room. Just a few weeks ago we were in this same position but we were both hiding secrets so deep we were drowning in them. Now, I don't know if I trust him, but I do understand him.

I hold my breath and peel my jeans off my legs and kick my boots to the side. Goosebumps prickle my skin and I shiver. Sitting back on the couch, I pull my coat across my lap to retain some semblance of modesty.

'Okay. I'm ready.' I clear my throat, hating that my skin is both hot and clammy.

Jae turns and strides to me before dropping to one knee. 'This leg?'

I nod and move my coat just high enough so he can see the ink that wraps around my leg, standing out harshly against the sickly pallor of my skin.

His fingers trace the pattern, sending skitters of electricity up my spine. A crescent moon lying sideways, the tips kissing the points of a moth's wings. Below, a wreath of antlers cradles it like a cupping palm. The details are exquisite, precise. I used to think it was beautiful. But since everything happened, I shudder when I see it.

'I've seen this exact pattern before.' The pad of his thumb outlines the curve of the moon, and my skin tingles in response. I wish his fingers were cold again, not warm and soothing.

'Me too. It's all over the internet. Common Wicca or pagan symbols.'

'No.' He leans so close his breath fans against my skin. 'This pattern, this order exactly. I thought I recognized it when I saw the bracelet. But this is more precise. This is something else entirely, I know I've seen it before.'

'Where?' I ask, fidgeting on the scratchy couch.

'A book in the library, and in some old archived bits and pieces about Richard Greene.'

'The original owner of Ravenswood?' I cock my head. 'What does he have to do with my tattoo?'

'This is what I've been missing. This is everything, Andy.' His fingers brush my thigh and shivers crawl across the tattoo like aftershocks.

Our eyes meet and I wish he'd use my full name. For some reason, I like the way it sounds when it falls from his lips. It sounds . . . beautiful. I always thought it pretentious. My grandfather insisted on it when I was born. It was meant to honor his own great-grandmother, a rich woman from the East who established an empire in steel or manufacturing. To everyone, even Violet, and most importantly myself, I've just been Andy.

But to Jae I feel like Andromeda. Hidden among the stars. Something you can only see if you look just right.

As if realizing how he's holding me, how close he is to brushing his lips against my skin, he jerks back. My face burns even hotter. Is it shame I feel, or something else entirely? Something I didn't know I could feel.

'Sorry, I'll let you get dressed.'

I'm facing his broad back again. I take a shuddering breath, pull my jeans back on and shove my aching feet into my boots.

'What does it mean?' I ask.

Jae turns cautiously. 'What?'

'My tattoo. The charms.' I cross my arms over my chest and hug my sides tight.

His cheeks are still a bit pink and his gaze bounces around the room, avoiding mine. 'I need to go to the library. I need to be sure before I assume anything.'

'Remember when you said five minutes ago that we would be partners?' I gripe. 'You being vague is what puts me in danger.'

It feels safer to bite at him, to snap like a dog chained to a pole. Easier. But Jae doesn't flinch. His shoulders drop and he nods, his jaw tight. Like he's giving up a fight, surrendering a piece of himself he keeps hidden away.

'You're right. Come with me. I think there's something you should see. Something Violet discovered too.'

## 20

After I stop off at my dorm to make sure Munia doesn't wake in a panic and call the police, Jae takes me to the fourth floor. The numerous antique clocks in the school chime softly. It's eight in the morning, and quiet. Most students are getting breakfast and teachers are preparing for their lectures. We have the place to ourselves.

Half of the floor is an attic, the other half is an old library full of dusty tomes with thick, curling yellow paper. Special collections, they call it. Everything in this library is focused on the history of the area: the old boom towns and original settlers. Hardly anyone comes up here. It's more like a museum these days. A mausoleum.

We sit at a long mahogany desk, polished to a mirror-like finish. A green lamp with a pull cord sits between us, illuminating a stack of books Jae plucks off the shelves. Narrow windows feed in a little gray light, but for the most part we sit huddled together in the drafty space with only a few lamps to fight back the shadows.

'Here,' he taps an index finger against a grainy black and white photo, 'this is Richard Greene with the first class at Ravenswood Academy, in 1896.'

I lean forward and squint. Richard Greene looks like anyone I'd picture from the era. He has longish hair and a thick beard. He squints at the camera and stands next to a group of about twenty young men dressed in suits, each with a hand tucked into a vest. A pocket watch dangles from Greene's waistcoat and his eyes, even without color, look glassy and cold.

I scan the rest of the page. It's a yearbook from the first class, or at least a predecessor of what I would consider a yearbook. It's so old the spine is cracking and the glue in the binding is crumbling. The pages smell musty and are a little water damaged.

Jae turns the pages of the thin book and stops. I study the leaf for a moment, trying to make sense of the warped paper and the grainy image. My head snaps up and I gape at him.

'Is that —?' I swallow hard. 'Are they dressed in those robes we saw in the forest?'

Six boys stand in the foreground of another black and white photo. Behind them is a background of thick trees. Richard Greene stands in the middle, his hands holding a small deer skull aloft like it's a trophy. All are dressed in black robes that could be mistaken for graduation gowns if I didn't know better. Some of the boys, turned to the side, reveal grotesque hoods. The antlers. The skull.

'Even though Greene lost this house after he spent all his money, he was still respected in town. Even feared.' Jae points to the caption.

*Tooth and Talon Society, October 1896, with sponsor Richard Greene.*

Tooth and Talon. A secret society dating back to the beginnings of the school. Violet's warning rings in my ears.

*Watch for Tooth and Talon.*

'Violet warned me about Tooth and Talon,' I say thickly.

'The group has probably been around since this picture was taken.'

I take the book and pull it closer. 'Violet must have been a part of it. That's who tried to kill her.'

'Do you know how Greene lost all of his money?' Jae asks, a crease between his brows. 'He spent it all on his research and fascination with the occult. Spirits, ghosts, ceremonies. These kinds of things were fairly popular in the Victorian era, when

146

there was a certain fascination with the spiritual. Societies like this cropped up all over the country in places of higher education – all over Britain too.'

I sit back, feeling numb. 'I've heard of them, like the ones in Yale. I thought they were just fraternities who messed around with ghosts.'

'Maybe some. But Richard Greene is different. He was infamous in the area for his work with the occult. He was convinced he could commune with the dead, that they told him secrets. He lost his fortune paying for expensive relics, often hoodwinked by fraudsters selling fakes. But the fascination spread across the town, rooted in the school. Greene mysteriously made his fortune back after he lost the mansion. He became an important donor and lived in the area until he died. He was always searching for something.'

'What?'

'A way to the Underworld,' Jae says. He hands me a newspaper article that's so old and faded I have to squint hard to make out the words. The title reads: *Greene Returns from Europe, Vast Fortune in Tow.* Another winks at me from the stack: *Greene Establishes Mercantile for the Occult.*

'Why would he want to go there?' The place where the dead either languish in torment or are released into paradise. I shudder at the reminder of the ashy land stretched between two planes.

'The Underworld holds the key to immortality; a way to reach ancient gods. Unlimited power is available if you know who to ask and what to look for.'

'You go to the Underworld.' I clutch my hands in my lap, my fingertips icy cold. 'Is that what you're looking for too?'

Jae drags another book closer to us. 'No. And I'm not immortal either, in case you're wondering.'

I make a face at him.

He continues, 'But I'm less concerned with what Greene wanted than how he was going about finding it. The society is featured in photographs of the school until about 1908. Then it's absent from the yearbooks, from any mention of the academy. I thought it was gone, disbanded maybe.'

'The missing girls . . .' I start, licking my dry lips. 'The first three were in 1896. The next occurred about three years later, right? Then the next group was in 1908, the same year Tooth and Talon disappears from the records, like you said. Isn't that the first year that girls were admitted to Ravenswood? I read articles about two girls from the academy who drowned that spring.'

'You think the society disappeared to cover their involvement in the murders?' he asks.

He hands me another scanned article. A picture of the cove with two bodies on the pebbly shore covered in white sheets. Policemen and onlookers stand around, their faces obscured. The title sends a fresh bolt of nausea through me.

*Girls, 14 and 17, Drowned in Cove Near Horus Mansion.*

'It has to be why Tooth and Talon disappeared. They wouldn't want anyone to suspect them – or to have any proof. It would be easier to just disappear. And we know they're still around, because of Violet's warning.' I shut my eyes, imagining those boys in robes, so young, led by a man who had thirsted after the occult his entire life.

Power. The occult. A quest for immortality.

Jae taps his fingers on the table anxiously. 'Tooth and Talon has to be behind every death and disappearance at Ravenswood. All of them. *Dozens* of girls.'

'Why? Why would some secret society drown girls?' I push my fist against my stomach, trying desperately to beat back the sickness that spreads across my skin. A society, with a secret ideology passed down since the late 1800s, makes more sense than a single killer targeting girls in Hemlock Cove for the past century. But it's also more sinister somehow. More wicked and cruel.

'Here,' he opens the pages of a new book, even older than the rest, 'I don't think they are simply drowning them. The moon is associated with women, and always has been. It's a symbol of divinity, femininity and power. Young women have been sacrificed for thousands of years, across many cultures, in the belief that they can complete complex magical rituals. Their blood and innocence are offerings.'

I flinch, studying the pages as he flips them over. 'Offerings for what?'

The book is a volume on symbols of the occult, from the library of Richard Greene. Flashes of symbols race across the pages. Diagrams. Pentagrams. The Seal of Solomon. Sigils. Moths, moons, antlers. Violet must have studied this book – all of Greene's books. There are notes in the margins in her handwriting. The words cluster around images of moths and antlers, dotted between phases of the moon.

This book is the inspiration for our tattoo.

'I think, based on the ritual sacrifices of young women, that the members of the society were trying to summon beings from the Underworld with the power to grant favors. To give themselves magic powers.'

I recall the animal bones in the greenhouse. Tiny skulls. Violet's wild notes and annotations mentioned sacrificing animals, like pagans used to do, in order to channel power.

'Summon things like demons?'

He winces at the word and shakes his head. 'That may be what Christianity would call them, but they can be anything. They come from the Underworld, from the place between life and death. They feed on fear, blood and sacrifice. They long for carnal pleasures, things they can't experience because they aren't mortal. They're desperate for a taste of life. They'll grant favors, use magic to help those who summon and feed them.'

My skin breaks out in a clammy sweat. Violet. My sister, summoning demons and monsters with blood and death. It's wrong. Sickening. How could she?

'Tooth and Talon is still here and Violet was a part of it. But she became a sacrifice. Maybe she knew something she wasn't supposed to.' The words sound hollow coming from my lips.

I realize I don't know my sister at all. I never did.

'There has been a long gap between the last deaths. Greene died in the late forties, when he was over ninety. The last time a trio of young women died was in the mid-sixties. It's been over forty years since a group of girls was killed. Just scattered deaths, like they couldn't get their timing right. That can't be a coincidence. I think this new society has been resurrecting the old practices, bringing Tooth and Talon back to its former glory, like it was under Greene. But I'm not sure.'

I shut my eyes.

Jae turns to me, his face a little pale and washed out by the lamps. 'The moth and the antlers, your tattoo. They're a sigil, a symbol of power people use to charge spells. The moth symbolizes control over others, like guiding a moth to a flame. The antlers are complex. Typically, stags are harbingers of destiny. Tying that in with a moth and a crescent moon is significant. Each piece together would be used for spells: to bind things together, to tie destinies to a path the creator intends. It seals their fate.'

Binds. Seals. Was Violet trying to control her fate?

I shut my eyes against the memory pounding against my skull. Almost a year ago, during Violet's last winter break. Her birthday. She drove us to a tattoo parlor in the city, far enough away that our parents wouldn't accidentally stumble across us as they shopped for Christmas gifts. The way her eyes glittered as she showed the artist her hand-drawn design. I thought it was just excitement, the thrill of a little bit of rebellion against our parents. They'd been fighting for the past few months. Violet was angry, blaming them for something. She wouldn't tell me what, just said she had to get out of the house and away from them for a while.

We sat together on the leather chairs, our pants rolled high and our thighs bare. She held my hand as the artists got to work. We laughed after the first sting of the needle. Talked of her time at school, and how excited she was to graduate and study at Cambridge or St Andrews or some other far-off and prestigious university. I'd been so happy. So star-struck by my glamorous sister. The genius. The only one who really saw me.

Violet cared about me when no one else in our little town seemed to. To them I was just Andy, Violet's sister. She was the one people always seemed to remember and adore. I didn't have any special talents. My grades were average. I enjoyed reading, but what was that compared to Violet's brilliant mind? The effortless way she carried herself. Each new language she learned, like it was as simple as breathing. The connections she made to brilliant people.

I was nothing.

But to my sister, I was the world. I was enough.

'Come on, little star,' she laughed as the artist swiped the last of the stray ink away, 'you have to admit this was fun.'

'How are we going to make sure Mom and Dad don't see?' I asked as I twisted my leg from side to side, to see every angle in the mirror.

'It doesn't matter if they do or not.' Violet sat across from me, her fingers tracing the pattern lightly over her tender skin. 'This is my choice. Our choice. We can do anything now.'

I met her eyes in the mirror. I remember being struck by her expression. It was so fierce, so haggard. It didn't fit the soft lines of the expression she usually wore. She stared down at her leg, her mouth pulled taut. It was a strange thing to say.

'What do you mean?'

Violet didn't look up. She kept staring at the tattoo, her fingers dancing over her bracelet. The charms she'd given me over the past three years. 'We don't have to do what Mom or Dad want anymore. I can go to university in Scotland and be whatever I want. I could marry Luciano. He's mentioned it before, you know.'

'Violet.' The smile melted from my face. 'You can't marry him. You're barely eighteen. You're being silly.'

Her eyes flared. 'Maybe I am. But I'm sick of people telling me what to do. Who to be. Mom and Dad, Grandma and Grandpa, they think they can control me. They want me to be something else. A doctor. A scientist. They think art history is a waste of time.'

I joined her on the sticky leather chair. 'Vee, they're just worried about you.'

'I don't care what they say! I beat leukemia once, didn't I? I can do it again. You'll see. I don't have to be babied or coddled.'

I remember the feeling I got in my stomach. The cold chill that seeped through each organ. Our parents' worried looks and furtive conversations. Violet's anger at them the past few weeks. There was something they had all been keeping from me.

'You're sick again, aren't you?'

Violet rolled her pants down, hiding the tattoo. 'It doesn't matter. I'm fixing it.'

'What?' The room spun round and round. 'You visited the doctor last month. Is that what you've been fighting with Mom and Dad about? You won't go to the hospital. You won't get chemo?'

She stood and shrugged her coat on, her shoulders tense and hunched. I saw it then. Her face was a little drawn, a little too tired. Her hair was a bit dull, her skin sallow.

Not again, oh God, please not again.

'I'm not poisoning myself again. I won't lose my last year at Ravenswood to vomit and my hair falling out. I told you I have a plan. Doctors can't fix what's wrong with me, not this time.'

She stormed out into the frigid winter air. The clouds had been low that day, the street lights bouncing off the mist and creating a hazy light. Snow crunched beneath our boots as I followed her to the car.

'Violet, what are you saying? You're going to just let yourself die?' I grabbed her arm, yanked her to a stop. My boots slid on the ice.

'I'm in control for once, Andy.' Her eyes burned bright and wild. 'No one can control me anymore. Manipulate me. Everything I do is for myself now, not for Mom or Dad. Not to make up for all the money Grandma and Grandpa have thrown into my education.'

It felt like she had punched me in the stomach. 'You're not making any sense. Please, Violet. Please, you have to get treated.'

Violet yanked the car door open, the dome light illuminating half her face. 'No one can tell me what to do anymore. I'm eighteen, it's my choice. I thought you, of all people, would understand. I'm going to graduate. I'm going to university, and I'm never coming back.'

'What?' Those words hurt worse than the slap of the cold air rolling in from the lake hemming in the city. 'You're just going to leave me?'

'You can't keep relying on me for everything, Andy. It's time you grew up and thought for yourself.'

'Because you're pissed that you're sick again and that Mom

and Dad want to help you, you're just going to run away to Europe to die?' I slammed my hand against the car. Frost cracked across the window like a spider web. 'That's stupid, and you know it.'

Violet glared at me, her eyes burning. I knew what was coming next. My sister could be kind, I knew that. But she was also haughty and controlling. Everything had to go her way, and everyone had to comply. I usually sided with her. I loved her too much to lose her. But this was foolish. Desperate.

'Maybe I am stupid, but at least I have my own life. I can be anything I want; go anywhere I want. What are you going to do with your public high school diploma and crappy grades, Andy? Go to the community college, live with Mom and Dad forever, keep them company into old age? Don't you want anything else out of life?'

'It won't matter if you die, Violet! You're giving up. You're being selfish, and for what?' My face burned, alternating between cold and hot. The way my sister looked at me, like I was ripping her heart out and stomping on it. Like I was a monster for not agreeing with her plan.

'I'm not going to die. I told you, I have a way to fix everything.'

'Luciano? Your stellar cheating boyfriend with a trust fund, is that it?'

Her jaw tightened. 'He believes in me. That's more than I can say for you.'

'I don't even know who you are sometimes. Ever since you went to Ravenswood –' I cut myself off, anger making my head feel light. I bit my tongue, willing the words back.

Violet slammed the car door shut, frost and icicles raining from the bottom of the door. 'What? Finish what you were going to say, Andy. Go on!' She crossed her arms, looked down her nose at me.

I wanted to push her, to slap her, to make her see sense. That look she gave me, that was the one she gave people she knew from middle school. The one she reserved for people she thought were below her. Who wouldn't amount to anything. My fists balled; heat bloomed in my belly. How dare she look at me like that?

'Ever since you went to that school you think you're better than everyone else. You flash your famous friends, the money you make Grandma and Grandpa give you, and you throw it around. You're just pretending to be something you're not. You're egotistical, and that school has turned you into a pretentious, conceited snob who only cares about herself. You'd rather have money than your own family, your own life.'

Violet's fingers closed into fists. She glared at me, a look that could cut through diamonds. She shoved my shoulder and wrestled the door open, pushing me out of the way. My boots slid on the icy pavement and I stumbled, falling into a packed snowbank a plow had left. I gasped at the cold seeping through my coat.

'I hate you,' she spat, and then shoved her keys into the ignition. 'Good luck finding your own ride home.'

That was the last time we had spoken. She'd never responded to any of my texts, calls, or even to the emails I'd sent. She blocked me on everything and left that next morning without a word. Mom and Dad said she'd gone to a ski lodge in Aspen with a friend from school.

Two months after that, she'd been reported dead.

I should have seen then that she was desperate. That she was willing to try anything. She got mixed up with Tooth and Talon because she was sick again. I never should have said those words to her. She was scared, alone. And she couldn't even talk to me. And now she's stuck in the Underworld.

'Andy?' Jae's voice rings in my ears, pulling me back from that night.

'What?' I jerk my eyes up, my heart racing.

'What's wrong? You don't look so good.'

'Nothing. I – I just remembered something. When we got the tattoos. I think I know why she had us get them, why she came up with that design.'

Jae waits, his handsome face sympathetic. It hurts to look at him, so I study the table again.

'My sister was sick. She'd had leukemia as a kid but it came back. I think she got involved in the society to try and fix it, to save her life.'

'She tried to make a sigil to bind her fate, to manifest her health.' Jae nods thoughtfully. 'It's a powerful symbol. She got that tattoo with you for a reason. Maybe to use you to strengthen the spell, your blood and hers mixed in a way.'

I rub my eyes hard. 'Would it have worked?'

'Probably not with the tattoo alone. But your sister is smart. With that tattoo on her skin every spell she makes is charged with power and intent. This society has the means to use real magic. Whatever Richard Greene did, he made that possible. And since Violet can wield magic, that sigil makes it stronger. She was preparing for something big. To summon a familiar that could cure her sickness.'

And I let her go.

I called her names, awful names. She hated me. Hates me.

'Andromeda,' Jae says in his silky voice and reaches out to hold my hand. 'I'm sorry about your sister. About everything. This can't be easy to learn, especially now that we know she's in the Underworld. Trapped in a liminal space between life and death.'

Trapped. Waiting for me to save her.

'We need to find out who's involved in Tooth and Talon,' he

says. 'If we know who they are, we can stop them from killing any other girls and maybe we can learn how to save Violet.'

I'm quiet for a moment, leaving his hand flat and abandoned on the desk. 'The new moon is tonight. They could strike again. Didn't you say the sacrifices need to be close enough together to work?'

Jae nods. 'Whoever or whatever they're trying to summon must be strong, powerful enough to need a sacrifice like your sister to awaken it.'

'What do you mean?' I rub my eyes again.

'It's one thing to sacrifice a random girl. But the society turned on Violet. She had to have been powerful, the brains behind the operation. There's no way she just stumbled into the Underworld, or uncovered the coin, by chance. She's been there before, and that isn't an easy thing to do. Your sister's magic must have been the strongest of everyone in the society. Her energy would have been enough to summon something with the power to destroy almost anything.'

I dig my nails into my palms, blocking the images of Violet murdered and then thrown into the cove by people she trusted. How did she slip into the Underworld? Where is she now? And why can't she get out, if she is so powerful?

'Luciano is part of the society. He has to be,' I say, easing myself from the cramped desk to stand.

'Her boyfriend?'

'Regina is too. And we saw four of them in the forest and the basement. Their friends in that club, Eric and Melinda, they must be the other two. Let's find them and drag them to the police station before they kill someone else!'

Jae scrambles to his feet. 'We can't go in guns blazing. There's no way the police would believe us anyway. We don't have any proof. We have to have solid evidence, or we risk the society finding out about us and disappearing.'

I cross my arms and stare at the spines of books stacked against the wall. 'So, what do we do?'

'Follow them.' He pushes his inky hair off his forehead, and my eyes track the motion. 'Never let them out of our sight. If it is them, then they will have to act soon. Maybe even tonight.'

I clench my jaw and remember the way Violet looked at me the last time I saw her. The hurt, the betrayal. Her illness pushed her into exploring magic and demons and the Underworld. I could have stopped it all, if only I'd listened to what she really wanted to tell me that night. But now I have to save her.

'If they're going to the cove, we'll need to take a car. The bus won't catch them.'

Jae smiles devilishly at me. 'I'll drive.'

## 21

Night falls quickly over the mountains. The stars are bright, shining dutifully between gaps of wispy clouds riding high in the air. The sky is a patchwork of diamonds and cotton.

Jae and I wait in the darkness of his car. We followed Regina, Luciano, Eric and Melinda as they gathered to head into town. A few others join them now, smiling and laughing and pushing each other around in the student parking lot. They wear light jackets and hold cigarettes in their fingers, not bold enough to light them yet.

I grit my teeth as Luciano throws his arm around a girl and plants a sloppy kiss on her cheek. The girl is shorter than him and willowy, dressed in a long dark coat. I can't see her face but I can tell she's looking up at Luciano in adoration. His latest conquest.

'They're about to leave.' Jae's fingers tighten on the wheel of his '69 Chevelle. The engine is quiet. No one can know we're watching.

The fleet of expensive cars roars to life, the headlamps illuminating the fine mist that always clings to the air. Luciano murmurs something into his date's ear before he hands her what looks to be a bottle of liquor. She nervously takes a swig, coughing loudly. He looks pleased as she forces down another gulp. With a few whoops and hollers and friendly shoving, the group piles into the vehicles and screeches down the long drive and into the night.

'I always hated that guy.' Jae puts the Chevelle into gear.

He keeps the headlights off as we follow the convoy of cars

into the dreary town. The shops on Main Street are closing, leaving only a few diners and bars open. The harbor is eerily quiet and still as the group park their cars haphazardly in the lot and pile into a rundown bar.

'Don't the owners know they aren't twenty-one?' I slide down a little into my seat.

Jae keeps one hand on the wheel as the other taps a rhythm on his thigh. 'I doubt they care. Those kids probably throw enough money around in one weekend to pay the bills for a month.'

Neon signs flicker. Bursts of red and blue bathe the pavement in fluorescent light.

Red. Blue. Red. Blue.

Time stretches on.

Sweat slithers between my shoulder blades even as our breath fogs the windows of the cold car. 'Are we sure the new moon is tonight?' I shift in the seat and wipe my glasses on my hoodie.

'For the hundredth time, yes. I can check the internet with the best of them, Andromeda.'

'Andy,' I snap, and he grins. 'They've been in there for over an hour. Won't they need to hurry?'

Jae rubs his jaw where a five o' clock shadow dusts his fine bone structure. 'Relax. We just have to –'

'They're coming out!' I hiss, and slide even further down in my seat.

Jae ducks, half his face bathed in red and the other in blue.

Footsteps crunch on gravel. Doors slam. Laughter erupts out of the bar. Headlights wash away the flickering neon.

'They're heading towards the cove.' Jae sucks in a breath and his fingers latch onto the gearshift. 'Do you have your phone?'

My fingers are clumsy and I fumble in my pocket for my

cell. Finally, I show it to him, the screen flashing in the dark cab for a moment. 'You want me to call the police?'

The engine groans as Jae turns the key and slams on the gas. My shoulder hits the passenger door as he peels out of the parking lot, following a set of lone tail lights as a single car disappears down the winding road lining the ocean. We speed past stumbling groups of a few remaining drunken students. But no one else follows us.

'Ow, Jae!' I smack his arm as he twists the wheel hard. I grasp wildly for my seat belt and click it in place, giving him a venomous glare. 'I said do you want me to call the police? Careful!' I yelp as he rounds a corner so fast, I swear two of the wheels lift off the pavement.

'No.' He twists the wheel again and the belt pulls taut across my chest. 'Once we get to the cove, stay put. If anything goes wrong, call this number. It's Pastor Carmichael's.' He takes my phone and adds a new contact, his eyes barely on the road. 'I'll stop them.'

'What?' I gasp.

Jae's knuckles tighten on the wheel and his eyes flash with rage. He speeds up, cutting through a red light to stay up with the car ahead of us. Soon the tail lights of the car in front turn onto a narrow dirt trail and we bounce after it.

'I'm not letting you go alone!' I grip the door handle and brace my other hand against the roof for dear life. The headlights of the other car bob ahead of us. We're bathed in darkness as soon as it disappears around the last bend. Even over the crunch of the tires and through the closed windows, I can hear the roaring waves. Black cliffs tower high around us, jamming us into a one-way canyon.

The other car rattles away, driving directly onto the beach. Jae turns off the engine, parking next to a group of trees in the mouth of the canyon where pebbles and sand mix in the grass. The smell of the sea is strong: fresh and salty and pungent all at once.

'Stay in the car, Andromeda!'

'No, wait –' I grasp at his arm but he opens the door.

'Stay here,' he commands again, his eyes frantic and wild.

Jae slams the door and darts down the path so fast I lose sight of him in an instant.

I struggle with my belt for a few moments before I finally manage to disentangle my battered limbs. My door jams against the rock wall and with a groan of frustration I crawl out through the driver's side.

It's impossibly dark without street lights or the moon. I can't hear or see the other car, just the vague outline of rocks in the water through the opening in the gorge. The stars shine weakly down as I stumble over stones and shuffle over the pebbly shore. I feel my way along the rock wall, too afraid to turn on my flashlight.

Finally, the ocean opens up, faint starlight shining off the foam cresting the roaring waves. The cove is big, much wider than I imagined. On the far side the lights of the harbor glitter, casting long lines of gold and orange across the black rippling water. I make out the distant, hunched form of an island.

Forming a long crescent, the cove stretches away into the distance. All around, dotting the water, are rocky headlands. Pine trees cling desperately to the boulders and the tiny islands studding the cove. I squint, searching the wet rocks for Jae, and wipe my glasses as the wind blows mist into my eyes.

The air turns bitterly cold. Frost coats my fingers and steals the breath from my lungs. I freeze, tempted to call out to Jae where he slinks along a rocky outcrop near a tiny jetty. I open my mouth to cry out when something moves in the darkness on the other side of the jetty. My lips seal shut.

A group. Off in the shadows. And then a flash of light. A streak of white, as glaring as bone, glints in the water. Darkness moves, pools of ink against the rolling tide. I crouch down, my back sliding against the wall of stone. The society stands in the ocean, maybe a hundred feet from where I'm crouched at the mouth of the cove.

Four figures stand together, calf-deep in the rolling tide. Antlers pierce the sky, attached to masks on their heads. They hold onto a small motorboat, heaving something into the bottom. I whip my head around, searching for Jae, but I've lost him among the rabble of boulders littering the pebbly shore.

I creep forward, straining to hear. It's impossible to make out their words, but a sensation – now so familiar it curdles my stomach – washes in with the next wave. An impression of wrongness, of cold and evil, that sinks into my skin and seeps into my bones. The stench of death – rot and loam and blood – fills my nostrils. I gag as the group start to climb into the small boat.

White skin flashes in the starlight. A girl, her hair falling over her face, is draped over the side of the boat, her hand hanging limply above the water. One of the shrouded figures pulls the cord and the engine roars to life.

They've already killed her.

I crawl forward, another terrible feeling that someone – something – is watching me. Something inhuman and dark.

One of the society members adjusts the girl's body, to keep it from falling. I catch a glimpse of her ashen face. A freshman, one of the girls who had broken into Violet's room. Cindy, I think. She was Luciano's date.

Where is Jae?

I crawl forward on my belly, the sense of heaviness and evil nearly flattening me. My toes slide in the pebbly shore, my freezing fingers dig into the smooth stones. I have to stop them.

A female voice rings out as the wind changes, carrying the words to my ears. 'We offer a sacrifice in exchange for a favor. Grant us your power for a time, my lord, that we may accomplish our goals.'

A wave breaks across the surface of the sea, like the ripple left behind as a jet breaks the sound barrier. Something is listening.

The boat starts to pull away, and I push up to my feet. My fingers close around a stone the size of my palm. I use a bleached white tree stump to pull myself upright. One foot in front of the other.

Another ripple, stronger this time.

I heft the stone in my hand and stagger forward as a flurry of excited, hungry voices, like the ones belonging to the gray and wretched ghosts, echo in the cove.

It's now or never.

The rock sails out of my hand, arcing towards them. It falls short, sinking into the tide with a shallow splash. Before the group can even look up, a body streaks across my vision and collides with the boat, capsizing it as easily as if it were a toy.

Jae.

I lurch forward, my limbs freed from the impossible weight of darkness. The sounds of splashing and struggling fill my ears as someone screams. Jae's head emerges from the water and he grabs the hood of the tallest figure. They go down, wrestling and gasping for air. A burly figure with blond hair grasps the side of the boat, yanking his robe free. Eric. He kicks against the tide, reaching for Jae. Fists collide and the water boils as the boys try to pry themselves from the fray.

'Grab the girl!' Melinda's voice is shrill as she screams and splashes in the water. 'We can't stop the ritual now!'

Antlered masks fall into the grasping fingers of the waves. They've given up the ruse of their disguise. Dark hair tumbles free and tangles in the wind. Regina.

Without thinking, I plunge into the sea. My breath freezes somewhere in my chest as the icy water sinks its teeth into my skin. Salty water grasps me, rising up to my thighs, and then covers my shoulders as I chase the two people dragging Cindy further into the ocean towards the upside-down boat. I kick hard, reaching for the edge of the overturned skiff.

'Regina!' I scream, my throat tearing. 'Let her go!'

She looks wildly over her shoulder and swims to the other side. Melinda's brown hair is plastered to her skull as she moves faster, dragging Cindy behind her.

The water closes over my head, spinning me in the surf. I thrash, my glasses useless as fat, briny droplets obscure everything. Desperation feeds the anger growing in my gut and I fight the water hard, my head breaking free.

'Quickly!' Regina's shrill scream breaks through the air, augmenting the grunts and cries from closer to the shore. 'We have to get to the convergence!'

Regina and Melinda grasp the edge of the boat, dropping Cindy as they heave together to turn it upright.

'No!' I dive forward before a wave crashes against me, knocking me back. I tumble through darkness, overhead and below. I roll, my skin scraping against the rusted bottom of the boat. For a moment my head breaks the surface and I gasp, sucking in water and air.

Regina's hair swirls around her head as she casts a desperate look in my direction. Cindy's limbs flail sluggishly through the water, splashing Regina as she sits in the boat, pulling the younger girl up while Melinda pushes from below, treading water.

Cindy's still alive.

The smell of decay and death fills the air. A crackle of lightning overhead, though the clouds are still high and dispersed. Impossible. Something is coming. Another flash of lightning illuminates a wave as it rises and crashes back down. The outline of an antlered monster, its face half covered in flesh, grins at me from the depths.

I fight wildly through the sucking tide. Regina screams in frustration as I reach for Cindy's ankle and yank. Hard. The girl's body jerks free from Regina's grip and flops back into the water before she begins to roll towards the shore. I don't have time to check if she's okay before Regina lunges at me over the edge of the boat, her hands closing around my throat.

Water rushes into my mouth as I cry out. I beat ferociously at her arms but Melinda grips my shoulders and pushes me down. Water covers my lips and burns as it forces its way up my nose. I twist and thrash and buck against their hands.

I kick frantically and connect with someone's stomach. Melinda grunts and lets me go as she hunches over, air bubbling from her lips as she groans. I take a gasp of air, salt water coating my tongue.

'Do you know what you've done?' Regina wails, her fists beating at my wave-tossed body from where she kneels inside the boat. 'Do you know what he'll do to us?'

'Jae!' My scream turns into a gargle as Regina shoves my head below the water again. The tide is coming in and the sea swells around me, dragging me into its embrace. My skin is so cold, it hurts. I feel like I'll shatter into a thousand shards of ice.

Though I jerk and roll and fight, my head doesn't rise again. Air bubbles rush from my mouth. I scream silently. Regina's hands, Melinda's, they're too strong, aided by the pulsing power of the ocean. Jae isn't coming for me. I'm going to die here.

Water burns my throat and seals my lungs as I take a breath despite the warning bells ringing in my head. It hurts. I try to cough. No more air bubbles slip past my lips or nose. My limbs go slack and the pressure holding me down disappears.

My vision fades. Black spots and flashes of brilliant blue. I don't rise above the surface. My body tumbles with the demands of the ocean. Push and pull. I must be dead. My eyes close and I feel the darkness reaching for me.

*Give in*, it says. *Let go.*

I will.

And then, silence. It's peaceful.

But it doesn't last.

Abruptly, the cold returns and my eyes snap open. But I don't understand what I'm seeing. I still float below the surface of the angry sea, but I'm not inside my body. I'm outside, looking at myself.

'*Hello, little star.*' A voice reaches my ears, spoken, but not.

'*Violet,*' I gasp, though I don't speak the words either. '*Are you really here? Am I dead?*'

A strange laugh, my sister's but wrong. '*I'm not here, not with you. I can't hold this spell for long, so listen carefully.*'

'*Violet,*' I sob. '*Please tell me where you are. How can I find you?*'

'*There isn't time. Listen, Andy. You have to go back. The tattoo will save you, but it will hurt. Once you're at the surface you have to find Cindy, make sure she doesn't die or they'll almost be ready to summon him. You can't let that happen, I'm not ready yet. I need more time.*'

'*Summon who?*'

I can almost hear Violet's voice, as if she's right next to me. But there is nothing besides the rolling sea and my lifeless body.

'*A creature powerful enough for what Tooth and Talon needs to complete their plan.*'

'*What plan? Tell me.*'

'*Andy, I can't answer all your questions,*' Violet scolds. '*The tattoo is imbued with magic I designed. It will protect you during liminal times, like tonight. You have to save Cindy.*'

'*Wait!*' I cry as her voice begins to fade. '*You aren't dead! Please, tell me how to bring you back from the Underworld.*'

'*My little star.*' Her voice cracks with affection and my heart breaks along with it. '*There's so much I can't say – where I am, the things I've done and promised.*'

'*Violet, just tell me how to reach you. I can't do this without you; they'll try to kill me now!*'

'*You have to go back. Save Cindy, stop Tooth and Talon.*'

'*How?*' I plead.

'*The path of Anubis, the path I took, it has the answers –*'

A scream rips from my throat and I feel my windpipe tear. I claw for the surface. Violet's voice fades from my mind as I throw my head back and gasp for air. I cough and hack, the waves pushing me forward, blinded by the stinging salt. My glasses are long gone.

Water spills from my lips. My lungs seize and I kick weakly towards the shore. My shoulder scrapes the pebbles and rock. I flop onto my back, shivering violently. My ears ring. My chest cramps and I curl on my side and hack up more sea water. I don't know how far down the shore I've been pushed. It's quiet.

Violet's warning rings in my ears. I don't know if I imagined it or not, but I don't care. I lift my head and push my tangled, wet hair from my eyes. Squinting, I can make out the shape of a body half in the water, each wave pushing their legs sideways. A white dress.

It's Cindy.

Panic forces my limbs to move and I lurch to my feet, half crawling towards the shipwrecked girl.

She's too still.

I drop back to my knees, still coughing, and place my shaking hand over her nose and mouth. I wait for a few heartbeats. A hint of warm breath stings my palm. A half-sob rips from my throat and I roll her onto her side, hitting her back firmly between the shoulder blades. Water trickles from her mouth and she coughs weakly. Her eyes don't open and her lips are blue.

I lift my head, shivering hard. Where is Jae? Where are Regina and the others? I don't see any robes or antlered masks.

Something strange prickles at my skin and raises the hairs on my arms. There's something buzzing around my ears. Power. Magic.

A gasp slips from my lips. Even through my sodden jeans, a strange, silvery light shines from my tattoo. It burns and aches, but then the light becomes a halo, encircling us. The air grows warm. Cindy breathes slightly easier.

*Violet.* It has to be. She's saving us.

Jae said our tattoos bind us together. That the shared symbol is powerful, that she can use it to cast spells. Maybe that's why Violet had it tattooed on me, for a moment like this.

I gaze wildly around the beach. Maybe a few hundred feet away, near a rocky outcrop on a battered headland, I see the four soaked figures of Tooth and Talon. But not Jae.

The group watches, cringing away from the light bleeding from my tattoo, like it burns them. Behind them stands a flickering being, made of smoke and ash. A scream lodges in my throat. It's the antlered monster from the forest. The one that tried to kill me. But it doesn't move. It appears vaporous, like it's half-formed. It grins with its half-fleshed mouth and stares at me hungrily.

I gape, trapped by its gaze. Images of death, flashes of smoke and burning and suffering, flit before my eyes. My tattoo burns so hot that I cry out, breaking free of the grisly spell. Forcing myself to my feet, I hook my arms under Cindy's and pull. Her legs drag through the pebbles, leaving two long divots. The group don't come after me. Neither does the monster. Violet's spell, the magic imbued in my tattoo, seems to be keeping them away.

It takes a long time, or it feels that way, to drag Cindy's limp form across the beach and towards Jae's car. The ocean tossed us up far enough away that my legs burn as I go. The driver's side door is still open and it takes a few minutes of maneuvering to get Cindy safely inside and slumped onto the bench seat.

Cold sweat slips down my back. My hair is plastered to my forehead and I scrape it away. Salt itches my skin and makes my clothes stiff and heavy. I shiver uncontrollably. The warmth from the protection of my tattoo disappears. Jae! Where is he? I turn in a circle, searching the cliffs. A cold weight lodges in my stomach as I remember the last time I saw him. The fierce expression on his face as he fought Luciano and Eric in the waves. Was he drowned too?

Shouts echo from down the shore. I curse and stumble against the cold frame of the car. The keys, where are the keys? I open the door and fumble around and under the seat, my numb fingers ungainly as they dig around the footwell and steering wheel. Nothing.

I force the lock cylinders in each door down with my fingers. The clicks do nothing to slow the frantic beating of my heart.

*Thud!*

Something heavy hits the hood of the car and I scream. I can't see anything beyond the shape of a dark figure limping around to the driver's side. The door handle is yanked so hard the metal groans. The locks pop and I lunge forward and brace my feet against the side of the car, fighting to hold it closed. My muscles scream in protest.

'Andromeda!' A muffled voice beats against the car in time to a fist. 'Let me in before they stab me already!'

My arms go slack and I stutter, 'Jae?'

'Move over!' He pushes his way onto the bench seat and I slide across, my wet clothes sticking to the leather, and press myself against Cindy's limp body.

'What happened to you?'

'They're coming. That spell from Violet's sigil kept them at bay, but its power has gone now.'

The car roars to life and he jerks the wheel hard. Tires screech and a mixture of dirt and pebbled sand kicks up and pings against the car before it gains traction and we jolt out of the canyon.

'You're alive. I thought you'd d-died,' I stammer, unable to tear my eyes from his face as he turns to look at me in the darkened car.

His hair is wet, his lips are almost blue, and he's shivering as violently as I am. A cut crosses from his left eyebrow and runs down his cheekbone. His lip is swelling, and I have the ridiculous urge to touch him to make sure he's real, that those are his only injuries. I've never been so glad to see someone in my life.

'I'd never leave you.' The words are so fierce, I feel a thrill down to my numb toes. He looks away and continues, 'Luciano and his friend tried to drown me, but I fought them off.'

Luciano, Melinda, Eric, Regina. They're all members of the GSE club. A sickening feeling crowds my chest. Violet was a part of the club, the one they used as a cover. So exclusive no one else can join. And Mrs Bianchi is their advisor. We have to warn her what's going on. Maybe she already knows.

'Where did you go?' I shake my head, trying to get a grip on my thoughts.

'I slipped into the Underworld before I could swallow more

water. I tried to find you, but the waves had pulled you so far I couldn't pinpoint where you went.' The haunted look returns to his eyes and he glances over at Cindy. 'Is she alive?'

The car thunders onto the highway. He hits the gas and we sail through the night and follow the twisting road around the rocky headlands back towards town.

'She's alive,' I say. I look away from the intensity in his eyes. 'We need to get her warm. Take her to a hospital.'

'We'll take her to Pastor Carmichael. He knows what to do.'

'She needs a doctor!' I protest. 'We need to go to the cops.'

He shakes his head and we turn past the harbor, headed down the lonely road that leads to the cemetery and the church. It feels like an ill omen, the moment the iron gates of the graveyard are illuminated by the headlights.

'The police can't help us now. Carmichael knows a hell of a lot more than the cops do. He is our best bet.'

Jae pulls around the cemetery and enters through a narrow parking lot at the back of the church. I don't know what time it is. My eyes are swimming with a mixture of burning tears and saltwater, plus the strain of not having my glasses.

He cuts the engine and comes around to the passenger side, hoisting Cindy's limp form into his arms with a grimace. I barely manage to stagger after him as he jogs up the steps and kicks at the door. It opens easily, the hinges bending in like butter. The air inside is so warm it hurts.

Jae stumbles the moment we cross the threshold, groaning with the effort. I try to reach out, to soften Cindy's fall as he tumbles to his knees, but someone is there first. A shock of white hair. Brilliant blue eyes.

'Jae!' I grab at his shoulder and he grimaces again. His face drains of color.

'What's happened?' Pastor Carmichael asks, his gruff voice steady.

'They tried to drown her. We stopped them but he was there, almost half formed. I felt him with us in the water. He's become more fully manifested since the last time we saw him,' Jae gasps.

The minister swallows a sharp breath. 'You're certain?'

'Wait.' I hold my hand up, and notice my fingers are shaking. 'You know about that . . . that thing with the antlers?'

The pastor looks at me, eyes wide, as he cradles Cindy's limp body to his chest. 'I'm well acquainted with demons, Miss Emmerson. They've been haunting my town for decades. Mr Han and I suspected it must be one of those monsters requiring all those deaths.'

'You didn't say anything.' I shoot a look at Jae, but he's leaning heavily against the wall, eyes pinched shut.

'Martha!' The pastor's booming voice echoes in the empty church. 'Fetch towels and blankets, quickly!'

Jae falls forward onto the carpeted hallway, completely unconscious. I drop to my knees at his side. I shake his shoulder and he rolls over stiffly, groaning in pain.

'What's wrong?' I gasp, my fingers resting on his stomach where his shirt sticks unnaturally to his skin.

He doesn't say anything. His eyes roll back in his head and his skull hits the carpet. Around my fingers blood blooms, seeping into the cracks of my skin and creeping under my nails.

He's been stabbed.

## 22

The rest of the night is a blur. Pastor Carmichael and his wife work with grim determination on Cindy and Jae. I sit uselessly, wrapped in a blanket by the fire with a mug of peppermint tea.

'Is he supposed to be bleeding so much?' I curl my fingers tightly around the burning-hot ceramic. I hardly feel it. Hardly care.

'He'll be sore for a while but should be okay. I've cleaned him up and I'll stitch the wound. I'm a nurse – or was one, at any rate,' Martha Carmichael says.

She bends over Jae, who lies on a stiff-backed couch. His face is drawn and tight but he doesn't make a sound. Doesn't move. She cuts his shirt away. At the sight of the wound slicing across his ribs, white bone showing between red and pink flesh, my stomach protests.

Jae makes a pained groan as she pinches his skin together, blood welling over her gloved fingers.

'Maybe we should call an ambulance. The police.' White spots dance across my eyes and I have to look away.

Martha glances at me as she ties off a stitch. 'They can't help us, I'm sorry to say. The school would simply throw their weight around, sweep it under the rug.'

I pick at the threads of the blanket, hardly blinking, as she methodically stitches the gaping skin back together. 'How can we protect Cindy from them? From the society?'

'She can't stay at the school. If she remembers anything from tonight she could be killed.' Martha snips at her thread with a pair of scissors. 'We'll think of something to convince her parents this school isn't a good environment for their daughter.'

I clutch my mug so hard my knuckles are bleached white. 'Cindy could call the cops just as easily.'

'If that society hasn't tampered with her memory already,' Martha says. 'They manipulate people's perceptions of them all the time. I wouldn't be surprised if her version of tonight is totally different to yours.'

Cindy is somewhere upstairs, wrapped up in blankets, safe and dry. The pastor checks on her periodically, trying to get her to drink water and swallow warm broth. Meanwhile, my thoughts are clouded with monsters and the voice of my sister from the Underworld.

Sometime around three in the morning, the pair stop working. Jae is as patched up as he can get, and Cindy seems to be doing better. Though my eyes are scratchy and the lack of sleep from the past few nights is making my limbs heavy, I keep a vigil by the fire.

'Are they going to be alright?' I ask.

Martha hands me another warm cup of tea. The smell of peppermint and licorice rises from the steaming mug.

The pastor sits heavily in an armchair, wiping a hand down his face. 'They're both half frozen and exhausted. But they'll be okay. Don't worry about Mr Han, my girl,' he says drily. 'That boy could survive far worse than a little knife.'

'Why are you helping him? Helping us?' I study Jae's sleeping face for a moment. His hair flops onto his forehead and his expression is smooth in sleep. He looks peaceful. Young and innocent.

'We've known our whole lives that evil stalks that school. That it's been covered up and hidden. Deaths, endless deaths, for decades. My father was a young man when Richard Greene died. His sister disappeared in the mid-sixties before the killings stopped. No one said anything, did anything for a poor, unimportant local girl.'

'They serve the devil in that school, make no mistake,' Martha says harshly, spitting out the words through clenched teeth.

I wince at the accusation. At the prickles of fear it sends down my spine. In a way it's true, isn't it? Tooth and Talon and the history of the school are so intertwined, it's like the roots of a tree. Impossible to separate.

'My family has been trying to find a way to end the cycle since then. My father never forgave and never forgot what happened to his sister. And neither did I. The deaths have paused for the past few decades, but we knew they'd resume. The darkness that lives in that school was waiting to claim new victims.'

'And Jae contacted you this past summer, is that right? He wanted to find out what was happening and stop it himself.' I rub the skin of my arms, fighting to dispel the chill caused by his words. 'And you all thought it was the work of a demon.'

The pastor nods. 'Your friend is clever. And persuasive. I'd never have let someone whose soul is so corrupted set foot in the grounds of this church unless I knew his intentions were to rid the valley of the curse of that school.'

I stare blankly at him, my eyebrows pinched together. 'Corrupted soul?'

'His time in the Underworld has done damage.'

'Jonas, she shouldn't have to hear –' Martha begins, her voice full of warning, but he shakes his head and holds up a firm hand.

'Look at her, Martha. She knows about the society, the truth behind the murders. And now she has the right to know what she's getting into. What she's working with.' He sighs heavily, eyeing Jae to ensure he's asleep. 'We can't do anything to control that school. No one in town is able to stand up to them, to get answers. Who'd listen to some old townie bleating about girls that died last century? Someone like Jae – a person touched by the Underworld – was our only hope for peace. We had to let him help us, and aid him in return. We owe him, after all.'

'What do you mean?' A cold feeling spreads through my gut.

Martha Carmichael purses her lips and exchanges a look with her husband. 'We can't say much, my girl, but we can say this. If what he says about you and your sister is true, you can put an end to all this. Stop the deaths.'

'My sister?' I feel like I'm dreaming.

'You can destroy the thing that connects the school to the world beyond ours.' Jonas leans forward. 'Demolish what Richard Greene did to pervert and pollute the ground Ravenswood sits on. That's the only way those monsters can tap into the power required for their rituals. Close the connection, the gate, and you can cut off the power source. You have your sister on the other side. You can work together.'

'I don't understand.' I shrink back into the seat, alarmed at the gleam in the pastor's wide eyes. He looks half mad, his sleeves rolled up to his elbows, his white hair wild and in disarray. The firelight dances off the wrinkles of his haggard face.

'That's enough, Jonas,' his wife says, attempting to lighten the atmosphere. 'We will get Cindy back to the school. Call her parents. We have a few connections with other academies; we'll make sure she's taken far, far away from this place.'

The pastor stands, nodding to his wife. 'I'll take her right away, call Brigham on the way there. He's the headmaster of an exclusive school in upstate New York. I studied theology with him in my university days. He can contact her parents, convince them to ship her away somewhere more prestigious than here. I doubt Ravenswood will put up a fight once the parents learn they allowed a young girl to slip into town and get drunk with irresponsible upperclassmen.'

The fire crackles and pops. Jonas disappears upstairs. His wife stands and peels back the blanket over Jae's body, inspecting the wound. She covers her expert stitching with a wad of gauze and bandages.

My eyes trace the gauze covering his ribs and stretched across his abdomen, noting the lean muscles tensed beneath his skin. Strangely, I want to reach out and touch him. Run my hands across his chest.

'Don't worry too much about Mr Han. He heals quickly,' she says, her dark green eyes catching mine.

'How do you know so much about him? He's only been here since late summer.' My cheeks are hot; I blame the fire, tearing my gaze away from the contours of Jae's torso and looking up at the woman leaning against the mantel.

'I learned about him and his kind through a friend in Edinburgh who is the chaplain at a school there. He told us about Mr Han's abilities.' Her fingers tighten on a silver tray she's holding. 'Jonas and I knew it was only a matter of time before more of those foolish children got themselves caught up in that world once more, seduced by the promises the beasts on the other side make.'

I shake my head, ignoring the way the firelight casts shadows on Jae's face. Familiar shadows, like the ones I've seen play across his skin before. Changing it into something else.

'But what do you mean by "his kind"?' I lean forward, desperate to know, to understand why they look at him with a mix of reproach and admiration.

'Mr Han has surrendered himself, in a sense, to something

bigger. He's not what he used to be, and he never will be again. Tampering with things not of this world will affect a person's soul irrevocably. He's tainted, in a way. But we owe much to him for his help keeping our daughter safe in the Underworld.'

I choke on my sip of tea. 'Your daughter is stuck there?'

Martha looks into the fire, her eyes far away. 'No. She died.'

The peppermint and licorice turn bitter on my tongue and I set the mug down on the coffee table.

'My husband – he dabbled in things he shouldn't have. He learned about the Underworld, about the demons and gods that call it home. He's always been protective of this town and thought he could find a way to keep Hemlock Cove safe from that school forever. Instead, he drew attention from demons on the other side who were eager to use another man of the cloth for their games.' Her jaw tightens and she looks out the window. 'Eventually, they got our dear Lucille. Jae here, with his connection to the Underworld, is able to travel its planes freely. He has suffered for that gift. He'd met Lucille on one of his many trips to the Underworld and helped her cross the river. That's the first time he heard about our town and its problems, from our little girl.'

I look over at Jae, his smooth face, his hair flopped over his forehead.

'So, you see,' Martha wipes under her eyes with her free hand, 'we owe the boy quite a lot.'

'He wants to help people,' I say softly.

The shadows swim across his bare skin. His face seems to change again, imperceptibly. I can't tell what it is.

'He does. He guides lost souls. Part of me thinks it's because he can't guide his own. Together – you and your sister and Mr Han – you could break this endless curse. Save other girls. Keep those monsters where they belong.'

'How?' My voice catches. I study Jae again.

'He told us about your sister's connection to the Underworld a few weeks ago. I just know something about you two feels different. It's curious.'

'Martha.' Jonas trundles into the room, a heavy coat on his back. 'Cindy is awake, but can't remember anything beyond driving to town. We should go now. Brigham has everything lined up. We can say we found her passed out at that infernal bar that serves those kids. No one will question it.'

'Let me take this to the kitchen,' Martha says and turns to me. 'Once Mr Han wakes up, give this to him.' She passes me an envelope with something hard and small inside. 'You can head back to the school. Keep an eye on the kids who did this. You're running out of time to stop them before it's too late.'

Before I can ask her what she means – if feels like for the thousandth time that night – she and her husband slip into the hallway. A moment later, the front door shuts loudly and then I'm left alone with nothing but the crackling fire and endless questions for company.

# 23

'Andromeda?' A raspy voice wakes me from dozing. I sit up on the uncomfortable couch and look into the dim light of the small study. The fire has gone out, leaving nothing but softly glowing coals.

'Jae, you're awake. How are you feeling?' I stagger off the couch, shaking the tangled blanket from around my arms and legs.

He sits up, the bleak gray morning light making the hollows beneath his eyes look like bruises. I try to ignore the way the blanket slides off his shoulders and down to his waist.

'I'm fine. Is Cindy okay?' He swings his legs over the side of the couch, his bare feet flexing against the cold wooden floor.

'The Carmichaels are taking care of everything. They said she'll be gone by this morning.'

Jae rubs at his jaw. 'Good.'

I reach into my jacket and thrust out the envelope. 'Martha wanted you to have this.'

He takes the envelope with his long fingers and unfolds it. I expect a letter, but instead the only thing inside is a coin. Jae tips it into his palm and I squint at it.

'Another coin from the Underworld? How did they get that?'

Jae shifts on the couch, wincing as his stitches pull. 'I gave it to them, after I . . . well, after I did something for them. A token to prove who I was.'

I stand in front of him awkwardly, keeping my eyes on his face. 'They told me what you've done for them.'

He freezes. So still, I can't even tell if he's breathing. Slowly, he stretches out his injured side, gathering himself to his full height. I'm painfully aware that my skin is crusted with salt and my hair is a wild, tangled mess.

'They told you?' His voice is breathy, quiet.

'You saved their daughter in the Underworld.'

His eyes soften a little and I see his chest rise to take in a full breath. 'Oh, that. I met her on the banks a few months before I came to Ravenswood. I don't usually talk to the families of those I help to cross – it can be painful to hear about. But I wanted them to know their daughter was safe, and that I wasn't . . . evil. It helped convince them to let me look at the records and enter their church.'

'And you gave them a coin to prove it?'

He rubs his chin absently. 'I wanted Jonas and his wife to be safe, in case any demons came after them again.'

'Why is he giving it to you now?'

'I think it's for you. We both know I don't need it.' He reaches out and turns over my hand, pressing the coin into my palm. 'Tooth and Talon will come after you. Keep this. I know the Carmichaels want you to have it. *I* want you to have it.'

We stand there, close enough that I can feel the heat of his skin. He looks down at me, his face so perfect even after what happened last night. I'm tempted to touch it, to see if he dissolves into smoke beneath my fingers.

'Why didn't you tell me about Lucille?' I ask, pocketing the coin.

'Guiding lost souls – talking to the dead – it isn't something I can bring up in normal conversation.' He smiles ruefully. 'And I didn't know if the Carmichaels would want you to know about her. I suppose I didn't want you to know how inhuman I've become. I don't want you to be afraid of me.' Slowly, his hand comes up to brush my hair from my face.

I shake my head. 'I'm not afraid of you.'

He swallows once, his expression shuttering. 'I remembered something last night, at the beach, when I felt Violet's spell protecting you. I know I've felt that before – her energy. Her power.'

'How?' I curl my fingers into hard fists, needing to ground myself.

'Months ago, I met her soul while she was wandering the banks. I thought she was just another lost mortal, mourning her life. But she turned down my offer of helping her cross to the west side of the river. I thought nothing of it. It's not uncommon – lots of spirits hang on to the life they had before, refuse to move on. If I had known she was alive, I would have helped her, you have to know that.'

My knees feel weak, my breath short. Violet is alive in the Underworld, and Jae saw her. My heart aches. He saw her. Tried to save her. But she needed *me*.

'Was she alright?' I croak.

His eyes soften, his gaze reassuring. 'She appeared calm. And if the Cynomorpha knew of her presence, she must still be alive and safe. When I slipped into the Underworld last night, I tried to find her energy. It's like she's hidden. I couldn't sense her. She's somewhere I can't go, maybe where no one can go. To be somewhere between life and death for so long – she's tapped into magic so dark, I can't save her. The only person who can is you.'

I pull back from him. 'Why didn't you tell me?'

'I only remembered when I felt her energy tonight – when she cast the protection spell. I'm sorry, Andy.'

'Why me? What can I do to help her?' I relax my fists and rub a hand down my face, trying to think.

'You're connected by something stronger than any magic I've ever heard of. Your tattoos, your charm bracelet – it's just the surface. She's been calling to you since she disappeared. I think you're the only one who would be able to find her, wherever she is.'

'Do I need to become like you, go to the Underworld whenever I want, wander wherever I want? Is that what I need to do to save my sister?'

'No,' Jae barks, and I flinch. His hand moves to cup my chin, to force me to look at him. 'I don't want you to end up like me. I told you before, after Min-Jun I went down a dark path. I don't know who I am anymore. You can't become what I am.'

I don't try to pull my face away. Everywhere his skin touches mine I feel strange jolts of electricity. It feels . . . good. His eyes burn, that unique shade of dark brown that is almost black.

'What are you, then?' I whisper.

He opens his mouth to speak, but nothing comes out. He shakes his head and shuts his eyes before leaning his forehead against mine. For a moment we stand like that, his hands rooting me against him. His breath is warm and smells of all the things I associate with him: wood and incense and spices.

I want to close the space between us for a brief moment of insanity. With his warm hands, his scent – everything about him calls to me. I wonder what it might feel like to kiss him. To tip my chin up and feel his lips against mine. Would it fix this aching I always feel? The hollowness in my chest since Violet left?

My fingers itch to touch him. Slowly, I lift one hand to cup his face, to feel the sharp planes of his cheekbones against my fingertips. He leans into my hand, his breath hitching. Even though the fire is out, heat licks up my spine as his arm wraps around me, pulling me against him. I feel his stubble scrape against my neck as he presses his face to the hollow of my shoulder and pulls my hair to the side.

'Andromeda,' he whispers against my neck, his lips brushing my skin in a way that makes my muscles tighten.

I can't answer. All I can do is stand there as his lips trail across my collarbone and skim the curve of my jaw, featherlight. His fingers brush the base of my skull, and for a moment I think he's going to tip my chin up, kiss me like I want him to.

But instead, he stiffens and pulls away. I open my eyes to the dim morning light, and his eyes are guarded. Instinctively, I step back and pull my hands from his bare skin, flinching from the burning sensation in my palms and the way it makes my heart twist in a strange new way.

What the hell was that?

'We need to go,' he says, his voice rough as he lifts one of his hands to his bandage and peels it back. It takes me a moment to see that his skin isn't raised in an angry red scar or dotted with any blood. The stitches are dark against his ribs, but the cut inflicted by the knife is pink. Come to think of it, his swollen lip and cut face are perfect. Healed.

'Okay,' I answer, so softly I'm not sure I've spoken.

'Andromeda,' Jae says, his voice rich and smooth and almost hypnotic.

'Andy,' I snap, forcing myself to turn and face him. 'For the millionth time, it's Andy!'

His face is impassive. His shirt is back on and I feel I can at least look at him dead on without my face turning as red as a tomato.

'Sorry. Sorry for – I didn't mean to . . .' He clears his throat and looks away. 'We need to get back. Regina and Luciano and the others will be there. They'll be furious we stopped their ritual. We ruined their ceremony, so they'll have to start all over again. They'll need to kill two more girls but won't have the chance until later this month.'

'Why?' I snap.

'They've missed their window with the new moon last night. We aren't safe yet though, Halloween is just around the corner.'

'The phases of the moon aren't enough anymore; they need a specific holiday?' I ask.

His full lips tug up at the corners as he shoves his feet into his boots. I hate that smile. I want to wipe it off his face.

'There aren't any strong enough lunar or celestial events until next month. Their only chance to harness enough power to finish their ritual will be on Halloween. They're getting nervous, Andy. They know we're going to try and stop them. If they use a night like that, so full of energy and connected to magic for centuries, it will be more than enough to finish what they've started. As long as they kill two more girls that night, they'll raise that monster from the Underworld for however long they can hold him. He'll grant them whatever they want.'

'That thing from the forest? The one with half a face?' I wrap my arms around myself as Jae tugs his coat on and limps towards the door.

'He's a powerful demon with enough magic to grant them anything. Eternal life, endless power, all the riches in the world. The moment he's fully revealed on Earth, a hell you can't even imagine will spread. Every time he's been raised in the past, there has been destruction and death wherever he goes.'

My skin turns cold at the thought. 'But he was here that night I went to the greenhouse, and at the beach. Why isn't he causing all this destruction now?'

'He wasn't really here, just a shade, an echo of his true self. He won't be manifested on Earth in all his power until the ritual is complete.'

'Why would they want him to cause mayhem and kill like

that?' I clench my fists as Jae opens the door for me. The air is chilly and damp on my skin.

'Demons give favors to those who sacrifice to them. To those who raise them from the Underworld, like Tooth and Talon. A demon can cause a plague somewhere that benefits a family member who works for a pharmaceutical company. Or he can wipe out a crime syndicate that is threatening the vested interests of the group. Demons don't care who they hurt, just as long as they feed and are free.'

An uneasy thought pricks at my skin as he shuts the door. 'You said once that killing Violet would give the society untold power. That she was different. What could a demon do with someone like her as a sacrifice?'

'Anything he wants.' He swallows hard and walks down the porch steps. 'The demon wouldn't be forced back into the Underworld once the magic from the sacrifices wears off. He would stay on Earth.'

I follow him into the gray morning. His car is parked haphazardly across a few lines. There is no sign of the Carmichaels' vehicle. I half hope we don't see them again.

Jae sighs and carefully eases himself into the driver's seat. I wish he wasn't so close to me, that he didn't look so good, even after almost drowning in the ocean and getting stabbed. I shut my door, keep my eyes fixed firmly ahead and my hands folded neatly in my lap.

'Tooth and Talon knows about us, Jae.' I rub my temples and try to take a full, calming breath. 'They could kill us. There's nothing stopping them.'

'We have to protect ourselves. They won't outright try and murder us in school, in history class,' he says, a determined look stealing over his features. 'But they'll try other methods. Poison, hexes – you name it.'

'We can't protect ourselves. We're around them every day.' I

187

bite the inside of my cheek as I think. It's an impossible task; just the two of us trying to bring down an ancient society. 'Maybe we should just leave Ravenswood.'

He shakes his head. 'And leave every girl there defenseless? Without anyone to protect them, they're at the society's mercy. I'll cast protection charms in the girls' wings, put antidotes in the food, or alter memories. Whatever it takes.'

'There's only two of us, Jae. How can we do all that *and* watch our own backs?'

I look at him for the first time since the moment when I thought we would kiss. He appears preoccupied. Determined.

The car climbs steadily up the switchbacks and through the tunnel of tall pine trees that leads to the school.

'You're not going to like my idea,' he says, his lips pressed together. 'We should spend our nights in the Underworld.'

'What?' He winces at the decibel level I manage to reach, but I don't care. 'I'm not spending another minute in that place!'

'We're too vulnerable, asleep in our dorms, where anyone could get to us.'

'That's the best plan we have?' I ask, forcing my lips shut.

'I said you wouldn't like it.'

Silence passes between us, the atmosphere fraught with tension and unspoken words.

'It's not what I want either. But we'll be careful, stay in the safest parts. I promise I wouldn't do this unless I thought it was our only choice.'

We pull up at the gates of the school. My stomach twists at the sight of the iron railings. I'm going to die here. Regina and Luciano will slit my throat and use my blood to raise a demon who will terrorize the world.

'Andromeda – Andy.' Jae turns to look at me as the gates slowly swing open. 'We will survive this. You just have to trust me for a little longer. Once Halloween arrives, we'll either have stopped them from raising that demon or –'

'Be dead? We're sitting ducks for a month while we hope we can convince Luciano and Regina and the others not to raise a demon?'

Jae's jaw tightens. The car crawls towards the school, and a feeling of dread pools in my stomach. I lean my head against the back of the seat as the dark roofline, jutting terraces and conical turrets come into view. The windows are dark. It's Monday morning. I can't comprehend sitting in algebra class while I watch over my shoulder for Regina to curse me or turn me into a toad.

'I won't let them hurt you, Andy,' Jae says.

We pull into the student parking lot. Luciano's car is there, a sleek silver Porsche. They're back. They're waiting for us.

'How can you promise that?'

He's quiet, his shoulders tight. He twists the key and the engine shuts off, but he doesn't answer.

My throat burns and I squeeze my eyes shut. I have to enter the land of the dead, the place of nightmares and evil. As I stare up at Ravenswood, I fear that the moment the Underworld has hold of me, I'll lose my sister forever.

# 24

I scrub my limbs in the shower for so long my skin turns pink and raw. The smell of the sea takes a bottle of shampoo to get out of my hair. Once the reek of the demon is completely gone, I shut off the steaming water.

It's still early, around five in the morning. No one else is in the common bathroom yet.

I lean against one of the basins in the long row of sinks, a towel wrapped around my middle. My skin breaks out in goosebumps as the steam slowly leaves the room and the mirrors along the wall clear. Brass hardware gleams at me and I rub my eyes before putting on my spare glasses. The frames are round and thin, fashioned in rose gold, but a little crooked from the time I accidentally clipped them ducking my head into the car.

The ink of my tattoo spills out from beneath the hem of the crisp white towel. I brace my hand against the sink and trace my fingers over the pattern. Antlers, a moon, a moth. They meant nothing to me only a few weeks ago. Now they connect me to my sister, to something she had planned for me before she slipped into the Underworld.

The memory of Jae's fingers following the same pattern as mine – warm and smooth, and good – flashes through my mind. I pull my fingers back immediately and look at myself in the mirror.

I hardly recognize the reflection. Wild hair, limp curls falling over my knobby shoulders. Collarbones too sharp, cheeks sunken. My blue eyes look flat and dull, with dark circles making the dusting of my freckles stand out too harshly against my skin. Does it matter what I look like when I'll be dead soon? No matter what Jae says, there's no way he can protect us. We live in the same building as these people, have many of the same classes, and they know how to use magic so dark it twists my stomach.

I clutch the edge of the sink and shut my eyes. My chest feels too tight. I struggle to gulp down a breath and force the air into my lungs.

Jae is wrong. I don't think we'll survive until Halloween.

The door creaks open and I hear someone shuffle in. I look away from the reflection in the mirror and yank a comb through my hair, trying to look casual – not like I spent the night nearly drowning, and communing with my undead sister.

My glasses fog as one of the showers is turned on. I take them off, wiping them with the edge of my towel. My head yanks back suddenly as a hand grabs the back of my hair. I yelp, my feet slipping on the cold, wet tiles. My temple slams against the edge of the sink and stars burst behind my eyelids. I slump to the cold floor as something sticky and warm slips down my cheek and drips onto my shoulder.

A girl leans down, her face blurry. I see braided brown hair and narrowed, hateful eyes. Melinda. I scrabble across the tiles on my hands and knees, blood dripping from my split scalp and down my shoulder. Red dots mar the white towel wrapped around me. I have to get to the hallway. Jae is waiting for me in the common room. If I can just call out for him . . .

'Do you have any idea what you've done?' The girl stalks towards me.

I scoot back until I'm trapped against one wall. My head aches. I can't see straight.

I throw my hands up to protect my face as she reaches for

me again. But she doesn't slam my head against the sinks. Doesn't try to bash my brains out. Instead, she grabs my face and forces me to look at her.

'You should have stayed out of our way. Now you're going to end up just like your sister,' she says, a scornful smile spreading across her face.

Melinda reaches into the pocket of the jacket she's wearing. I flinch automatically, expecting a knife or a gun. But she holds a strange-looking flower. It has pale white petals and a sickly purple center, like a bruise. Where have I seen it before? Gray grass. Ash in the air. The Underworld.

She pinches my cheeks so hard they graze against my teeth. The flower comes towards my lips and I know I can't let it touch my tongue. I bash my fists against her arms and twist my face to the side. She curses and grabs my hair again. I yelp as she tugs at the fresh cut on my scalp.

'Melinda!' Regina's voice calls harshly from the entrance to the bathroom. 'You can't kill her yet. He wants her.'

'She stopped our ritual, and let the girl go! How will we ever get Ossivorus to –'

Regina stalks over. My distorted vision blurs her long legs and fluttering dark hair. She grabs the other girl's hands and yanks them away. 'Don't be stupid, Melinda. Asphodel flower wouldn't kill her, Violet made sure of that. And we agreed we'd just have a little chat with our friend Andy here.'

She crumples the white and purple flower in her hand before throwing the petals into a nearby trash can. I wipe blood from the corner of my eye, hating the sticky, warm feeling on my fingers.

'Go on then,' I snarl at Regina, 'Kill me. Drown me, stab me – whatever you did to Violet. She trusted you. She loved you! How could you betray her like that?'

Melinda moves like she's going to snap my neck or dash

my head against the wall, but Regina holds up a hand. She crouches in front of me, her elegant features twisted in an expression so full of hatred I wonder how I ever missed it before.

'Your sister is the reason we're doing this. *She* reformed Tooth and Talon, *she* wanted power and magic. But one night, out of nowhere, she wanted it all for herself. You talk about betrayal, but she was the one who turned on her friends. She got what she deserved,' Regina spits.

'Some friends,' I retort. 'She's been there for you through everything, Regina.' I lift my chin towards Melinda. 'And Violet never cut you out when your father went to jail, like everyone else did. And this is how you pay her back?'

Melinda hunches her shoulders and throws a murderous glare at the crumpled asphodel flower in the trash. 'You think she didn't rub my family's dirty laundry in my face? You think she didn't whisper about me and how pathetic the Delgados are, whenever my back was turned? Regina's right – your sister got what she deserved.'

I press my back against the wall as heat and anger crawl across my skin. 'You're murderers. And for what? So you can become even richer?'

Melinda scoffs and Regina's cool facade slips for a fraction of a second. She reaches out, long fingers tipping my chin up. I try to slap her hand out of the way but she holds tight, nails digging into my flesh.

'You have no idea what your sister had planned, do you? You and Jae run around playing vigilante without knowing what is truly going on. We're saving the world, saving ourselves. Casualties will happen in any righteous war.'

'You're insane.' I manage to push her hand away.

She smirks before standing up slowly. 'Violet always thought she was better than everyone. But look at us now.'

'You've always been jealous of Violet,' I snap. 'You always wanted to be like her. Better than her. It's why you fling yourself at every internship, every teacher. You want so badly to be as good as she is, but you know you never can be.'

The faucets drip. Regina stares at me, her nostrils flaring. She considers her reflection in the mirror for a moment before she flings a towel from the shelves at me.

'Clean yourself up. And if you breathe a word of this to anyone, just know they'll never believe you. You're no one, Andy. The little sister of a dead girl whose grandparents had to bribe her way into the school.'

'I don't need anyone to believe me,' I say through gritted teeth, ignoring the way my vision swims. 'I'm going to stop you. And you're going to lose everything.'

Melinda's full lips tug into a sarcastic, cloying smile. 'Our master has given us more power than you, or your sister, could ever dream of.'

'Then why was it so easy to stop you last night?' I spit, my head pounding.

'Maybe we should just kill her now.' Melinda balls her hands into tight fists and stalks forward, her eyes cruel and cold.

Regina sighs, like this is a frequent argument with the other girl. 'Not yet. You know he wants her alive, just in case. Take our advice, Andy, and stop meddling in things you don't understand.'

The doors creak open. Reflected in the misty mirrors I spy a silky hijab and Munia's wide eyes. Regina and Melinda stiffen as my roommate hurries over the slick tiles and kneels beside me, her gaze riveted to the blood on my face.

'What are you doing?' she demands, whirling to face the older girls.

Melinda sneers, crossing her arms. 'It doesn't concern you. Go back to running your little student council.'

194

Munia freezes, holding the towel to my cheek. I glance between her and the two girls. They'll hurt her. Kill her even. My stomach twists at the thought.

'You really want me to get Madden involved? Neither of you will ever get into a university now that you attacked another student!'

Regina's face pales just as Melinda's warps into a furious scowl. Without thinking, I stagger to my feet and move between them, my heart beating in my throat.

'It's nothing. Just a misunderstanding.'

'A misunderstanding?' Munia gapes, my bloodied towel in her fist. 'They hurt you!'

Melinda moves forward but Regina places a warning hand on her arm. 'Just a little initiation. Violet was a part of our club – I'm sure you get it.'

At the sweetness in Regina's tone, Munia falters. She looks at me, gaze wide and unsure. I meet Melinda's cruel smile over Munia's shoulder. She mimes slicing her throat. But it isn't a threat against me.

My teeth grind together but I manage a curt nod. 'It's true. Nothing to worry about.'

'At least let me take you to the nurse –'

'I'm fine. Just slipped when they scared me.'

Melinda crosses her arms. 'Why don't you get a Band-Aid or something, Al Soori?'

Even though I want to punch Melinda across her haughty face, I force a smile to my lips. 'Would you? I'd really appreciate it.'

Munia drops her shoulders, handing me the bloodied towel. She looks between us, at the blood on the wet tiles, at the bruise already marking my pale cheekbone. She chews her bottom lip uncertainly, but then nods, backing out of the bathroom.

'I'll be waiting in the dorm, Andy. If you're not back in two minutes, I'm going to Madden.'

Relief slams into my chest as soon as Munia disappears. At least for now, she's safe.

A few seconds pass as we three stare at one another. Waiting for a sign of weakness. A twitch. Something that will give away the next move. My head starts to pound and I grip the towel tighter around me, wrenching open the door. The hallway is quiet, like I expected.

Except when I step outside, setting one foot gingerly in front of the other, I see a head of white-blonde hair scraped back in a tight bun. Mrs Bianchi. She looks over her shoulder, eyes catching mine. In her hands is a flowerpot brimming with asphodel flowers.

Bianchi looks quickly away before she scurries out of sight into the teachers' dormitory.

'Watch your back, little star,' Regina says behind me. 'Now that you know who we are, your life is ours. Enjoy what little of it you have left.'

By the end of the day, in art history class, I'm so on edge I feel like my teeth are being ground into dust. I replay Melinda's attack in the bathroom. The coldness and determination in Regina's face. Tooth and Talon are monsters. Murderers. I peer at Bianchi as she shuffles her notes. A sense of distrust winds through my gut as I stare, unblinking, as if I'll perceive the truth if only I look harder.

Jae and I sit at our usual desks on the far side of the classroom nearest the windows. The rain has stopped but the air is cold enough that frost nips at the edges of the window panes. Jae sits at the aisle, presumably shielding me from anyone who might want to shiv me on their way to sharpen their pencil.

'Is your head okay?' he asks as Bianchi dims the lights and projects an image onto the screen.

I rub absently at the scab on my hairline. The cut isn't deep, and once I got the blood cleaned away it wasn't too bad. A bruise the size of my palm extends from my temple back into my hairline, but makeup has done a suitable job covering the worst of it.

'It's fine.'

'I should have been there. I didn't even see them from the common room. Didn't hear a thing. You're lucky Violet marked you with that tattoo or the asphodel flower would have killed you, desiccated you like a mummy.'

I laugh under my breath. 'If you had been there, you would have been in the girls' bathroom. I don't think that would have gone over very well.'

His cheeks turn ruddy and he kicks me under the table. 'I'm serious, Andy. They could have killed you.'

'I know. But they weren't trying to kill me, just scare me. They said something about the demon wanting me alive.'

I still can't quite meet his eyes. After last night, I'm too confused to get lost in his gaze. I should be worrying over Regina and her cronies plotting to kill us. I shouldn't let myself wonder if the bruise on my temple makes me look even paler and more sickly to him.

The door swings open and Regina and Luciano stride into the classroom. They walk slowly past us, eyes glittering and knowing. They take their seats, close enough that we can see each other's expressions, even in the darkened room. Luciano twirls a pen between his fingers and crosses one leg over his knee. His cold eyes glint and he winks at me.

'We have to go to the Underworld as soon as curfew hits tonight,' Jae says softly as Bianchi begins her lecture.

My palms go clammy at the thought of spending my nights in the land of the dead. 'And you sure it's our safest bet?'

He nods. 'There's someone I know in the Underworld. If I can convince them to help us, maybe we can learn exactly what Richard Greene did that connected the Underworld, and that demon, to Ravenswood. That is our only hope of stopping them, unless you're eager to kill Luciano and Regina and get thrown in jail before you can save Violet.'

I slump lower in my seat. Jae is right. Tooth and Talon has its claws sunk deep into the school. There are parents and alumni that have been in the club. Madden has to know about what they do. Bianchi is involved somehow. And I have no doubt if we tried to kill Luciano, or any other member, someone hiding in the shadows would make it so we never existed.

'I know I haven't done the best job of it, but I'll keep you safe, Andromeda. I promise,' he says, his breath tickling the hair by my ear.

I feel hollow at those words. Jae can claim he wants to help me all he likes, but there's no way he can keep that promise. Even if the words send a thrill of longing down my spine.

'Fine.' I cross my arms and look out the window. 'But whoever we talk to better not be as freaky as that jackal guy from last time.'

He laughs softly; it almost elicits an answering smile from my lips.

Later, when the bell rings, Jae jumps to his feet instantly. The class files out quickly, eager to get away from studies for the rest of the afternoon. Before we can follow, a familiar tall figure blocks our row.

'It seems you've discovered our little secret,' Luciano drawls, his arms crossed as he leans against one of the long tables that serves as a desk. 'You interrupted something very important last night.'

I glance at Bianchi, who is talking to another teacher in the doorway. I can't let her get away before I have a chance to talk to her. Demand to know what she's doing for this group. Why she would betray Violet.

'Consider my deepest apologies for stopping you from killing a fourteen-year-old girl,' I snap through my gritted teeth.

Regina scowls but Luciano puts a hand on her shoulder. 'I didn't come here to fight with you, Andy. I have a proposition, one that could benefit both of us.'

'We don't want to hear a thing you have to say,' Jae declares.

Luciano smiles thinly at him before turning his penetrating gaze back to me. 'What you saw last night is an unfortunate downside of what we must do to achieve a better world.'

'Please,' I scoff. 'You're sick, and I'm going to make sure you pay for what you've done.'

'I am proposing we avoid all the bloodshed and retaliation that will no doubt happen if either of us attempts to hurt the other.' Luciano inspects the cuffs of his argyle sweater. 'I propose a truce.'

Jae jerks his chin back. '*No!*'

'You'll want to hear what I suggest.'

Jae's fingers curl into fists at his side. I put my hand on his arm, pulling him back a step so he's no longer nose to nose with the other boy.

'Why should we trust you? Just this morning your friends slammed my head into a sink.' I cross my arms to control the urge to lash out at Luciano. 'A truce sounds as far-fetched as anything to me right now.'

Luciano flashes his too-white teeth. 'They acted without my permission. As head of Tooth and Talon, it's my job to ensure that anyone who comes into contact with our society is treated well.'

'Unless they get in your way, or are marked out for death, is that right?' I scowl back at the playboy smile permanently pasted on his face.

'We underestimated you, that's clear to me now. But I have no desire for senseless killing. Stay out of our way and we can make a deal with the one we serve. He will be generous. He may even be able to save your sister.'

The floor seems to drop out from beneath my feet. My fingers tighten painfully on my forearms, pressing so hard I wonder briefly if my fingernails have punctured the skin.

'You wouldn't know how to save her,' Jae says.

'True.' Luciano cocks his head, a triumphant look in his eyes. 'But Ossivorus would.'

Jae pushes the other boy back, opening a path into the aisle. 'You're messing with things you can't begin to understand. You'll doom thousands by summoning Ossivorus.'

It's strange to think of that monster with half a face having a name. And one that sends such a chill through my bones.

'He can offer us anything we want,' Regina says, her eyes wide. 'We can control him while he's on the Earth. We're more powerful than any other society before us.'

'I wouldn't trust you with my homework, much less my life,' I snap at her. 'You tried to kill your best friend! You can't control this demon like you say. I think he controls you.'

Regina laughs darkly. 'You're wrong. The other societies before us couldn't summon a lost key, much less a demon. We're strong. We have what he wants, and he'll give us anything in return.'

Luciano's mouth contorts and he reaches out, grabbing my wrist. 'It doesn't matter if we want you dead. He is interested in you, in your sister, in the power you could give him. Think about my offer. If you turn us down you will die, one way or another.'

My muscles twitch at his touch, my skin heating like an inferno. I want to do something crazy: smash his forehead on the table and see how he likes it. But we're in a classroom. Students are milling around.

Before I can throw his hand aside, Luciano curses, smoke curling from his fingers. He draws his hand back. 'What did –?'

'Ready for the club meeting?' Bianchi's heels click as she juggles her books and laptop and stops at our group.

My spine goes rigid as Luciano glares at me, holding his hand to his chest.

Regina smooths her expression. 'The others are already in the library.'

Our art history teacher gives me a curious look. But my mouth has gone bone dry as Luciano studies me with a piercing expression, eyes narrowed to slits. When he turns, barking at Regina to follow him, I catch a glimpse of his hand.

It's red and blistered.

'Will you excuse us for a moment, Mr Han?' Bianchi asks, her eyes still glued to me.

Jae stiffens, clearly weighing up the need to drag me to the relative safety of the Underworld against the need to be inconspicuous.

'I'll meet you outside, Andy.'

The door clicks softly shut. Bianchi flips a stray lock of pale blonde hair behind her ear and sets her stack of books against one hip. My heart is somewhere in my throat. My hands still feel too warm – like I stuck them in a furnace.

I glance down. On the worn denim of my pant leg is a black mark. Charred. Burnt. A brand. The crescent moon, moth and antlers. My tattoo.

'I've been meaning to check in on you, Andy.' Bianchi furrows her brow, following my gaze.

I quickly push my coat over my legs, trying to keep my breath normal.

'You know.' I confront her.

Her brows lift as she jerks her head back. 'What?'

I step forward, grabbing her wrist, panic whipping my

pulse into a feverish tempo. 'You know what they are, what they've done.'

Bianchi laughs lightly, even as her face drains of color and her fingers slip on the bundle of books in her arms. 'Don't be silly. I know what you saw at the last meeting was concerning. But believe me, I've spoken with Mr Russo and Headmaster Madden. Luciano gets a bit hot-headed, that's all.'

She's lying, badly.

'You helped Regina and Melinda corner me this morning,' I say accusingly, my pulse pounding in my bruised temple. 'You gave them the asphodel flower. You had one of the *Subitae mortem* plants as well. Is that what you do? Get them what they need for their spells? Why are you helping them?'

Bianchi steps back. 'I don't know what you mean, Andy.'

'You know about Tooth and Talon. You know they're trying to raise Ossivorus, and you know what they did to Violet.' I clench my fists. 'Is that why you tried to pull me into the club? So they could use me like they used my sister? Trick me like you tricked her?'

The trees groan outside. Voices from the hallway slip under the door like ghosts. Bianchi breathes hard, her face flushed, her eyes darting around. I brace myself, ready for her to try and attack me, to silence me. But it never comes.

'Andy, you don't understand.' Her voice shakes, and the shadows on her face make her look wild. Untethered. 'Those plants – I wanted to destroy them when I overheard Melinda and Regina arguing in their corridor early this morning. I was taking the pots away to burn them when you came out of the bathroom. And I swear I didn't know Melinda had taken one! I wanted to warn you. Violet . . . you . . . I never wanted either of you to get hurt.'

I glare at her as she steps closer, her mouth trembling. Tooth and Talon is everywhere. It has eyes among the staff.

The members of the society have alumni as parents. Madden is in their pocket somehow. And Bianchi is getting something from them, I'm sure of it

'I don't believe you.'

She makes a strangled sound in her throat and I watch as she reaches into her bag. She pulls out a crumbled wad of half-charred leaves and petals. I recognize them immediately. The telltale purple tinge. My gaze snaps up to meet hers. I see the fear in her eyes.

'You don't know what they have over me,' she whispers.

I chew on my lip, considering my words. 'It's a matter of time before they discard you when they no longer need you as a cover.'

The room is deadly quiet. Even the wind outside, the constant rustle of pine needles and heavy oak branches, seems to hush. To listen. A muscle twitches by Bianchi's eye and she darts a quick glance out the window.

'Madden knows where every member of my family lives. Where my friends work. My cousins. Everyone. I didn't take this job because I wanted it. I took it because I owe Tooth and Talon a favor.' Her breath catches and she drops the books on a nearby table. 'When I was in university, years ago, Salvatore brought me to a club meeting they held with other alumni of Ravenswood at Harvard. I thought it was a joke, the magic they talked about. But they killed a bird and did some sort of ritual. Suddenly the program I was waiting to get into opened up.'

A coldness seeps into my blood. Her eyes stay wide, unblinking. I can see the rigidity of each muscle, of each expression that flits across her carefully arranged features. And I know she's afraid, just like when Luciano threatened her in the library.

She continues in a light, sing-song voice, like the birds

outside. 'It felt like a dream, gaining such a prestigious fellowship so young. I was afraid to question it. To even acknowledge their part in it. They didn't talk about it again. Not for years. Not until they needed a convenient pair of eyes in this school. And by then it was too late to back out. I'd accepted their help, kept my mouth shut.' Bianchi laughs bitterly, wiping her eyes. 'And now, my career is in their hands, and my only purpose is to cover up their children's crimes. Provide alibis.'

'Turn them in,' I whisper. 'Before they hurt someone else. You knew Violet . . . don't let it happen again.'

Her jaw clenches, her chest shuddering as she tries to control her emotions. 'It isn't that simple. What they can do is unlike anything I've ever witnessed.'

'Believe me, I know. But I can stop them. If you help me –'

Bianchi shakes her head once, a strangled sound coming from her throat. 'Each one of them has something on me, Andy. If I even breathe a word of this to someone outside of their circle, I'm as good as dead. My PhD is not the only thing hanging in the balance. Their parents, their relatives, they're all connected. If I don't help them, cover for them, everything is over.'

My heart sinks as she raises one hand and deftly wipes at her cheek. In a split moment, the flash of terror disappears from her face. She looks prim and proper and scholarly once more.

'Maybe I can help. We can go to the police; you could give a statement as evidence.'

'My career will end, my family will get hurt, Andy, and nothing will come of it. Please, it's in your best interests if you pretend we never spoke about this. I really need to go before they notice I'm late.'

Bianchi arranges her features into a controlled, blank mask.

She opens the door and pauses, looking over her shoulder at me.

'Be careful. And I hope you find what you're looking for, for both our sakes.'

I meet Jae in the back courtyard near the greenhouses.

'Everything okay?'

I shake off the memory of Mrs Bianchi's terrified expression, and look away. The black scorch marks on my jeans stand out harshly in the daylight.

'I'm fine. What do we need to do?'

Jae's brow puckers but he doesn't press me further. 'Do you remember the flower, the one Regina pricked you with?'

'You mean when my hand almost fell off? Yeah, I won't be forgetting that anytime soon.'

'We need to harvest the petals. There should still be some left over from the pot I swiped after the lunch. I'll need to make a tincture that you can take before the moon rises every day. It's the only way we can get you safely into and out of the Underworld without waiting for a liminal time or place.'

My lip curls as I recall the taste of the petal Jae gave me in the Underworld. 'Then let's go. We don't have long before it's dark.'

# 25

Jae and I huddle together in the cold greenhouse. The sky is streaked with gray and orange as the sun is about to set completely. Moss and ivy block what little light remains, so our surroundings are illuminated by the glow of a Bunsen burner powered by a small propane tank.

'It's almost done.' Jae twists a knob, cutting off the flow of liquid through spiraling narrow tubes. 'Hand me the tongs, will you?'

My hands scrabble over the rough wooden table until they close over freezing metal. Jae takes the tongs and carefully lifts a vial, the bottom a little charred from the heat of the flame.

The remains of the plant with the wickedly sharp thorns lie in ruins on the table before the mess of tubes, vials and beakers. We harvested ten petals in all from the plant in Mrs Bianchi's classroom, grinding them into powder. Jae added ingredients I didn't recognize, mixing the powder with something called Abramelin oil.

He lets the mixture cool, the chill in the air quickly stealing the steam from the mouth of the vial. I hand him a rubber bung and he stoppers the bottle, gently swirling it.

'And that's it? That's all we need for me to travel through the Underworld at any time?' I squint at the vial. Silvery liquid forms webs around the dark red tincture, like mercury and blood refusing to mix.

'It will let you pass through the veil easily, without assistance from magic or celestial timing. You will be harder to detect, but you're still mortal – you can still be hurt there, Andromeda.'

I swallow hard, studying the hypnotic pattern of silver and crimson liquids dancing, fighting against one another. Jae hands the vial to me, placing the slightly warm glass in my palm. His fingers linger, his hand cupping the back of my own.

'Place three drops under your tongue, quickly. The sun will set in twelve minutes.' He checks his watch.

I grimace and twist the bottle open, pulling out the glass pipette connected to the stopper. The smell is odd. Both floral and fetid. Holding my nose, I close my eyes, open my mouth, and squeeze. One. Two. Three.

The taste is metallic and pungent and vaguely like charred rose petals. It explodes under my tongue before curling to coat the rest of my mouth. Gagging, I twist the cap back on and cough, wishing I had water to wash the taste away.

Something warm tugs at my stomach before turning ice cold. I feel the drops move down my throat, spread through my gut, and branch out through each vein and capillary of my body. Cold and dark. A change. In me – in the way my body reacts to things not of this world. The feeling recedes slowly, but a tingle lingers in my fingers and at the base of my skull.

Jae looks grave. Our eyes meet in the dim greenhouse.

He licks his lips, face a little pale. 'As long as you stay with me,' he says softly, 'you'll be safe. I know the Underworld well. No one will harm you if they see us together.'

My heart twists and the same rush of cold and heat returns, making my skin both clammy and feverish. Like last night, when he looked at me and spoke soft words. When his lips whispered over my skin.

I avert my eyes, my pulse pounding in my neck. 'What makes you so untouchable in the Underworld? Why do demons and jackal-headed guys listen to you?'

Jae takes the vial back, his long fingers brushing mine. 'They aren't *jackal-headed guys*. They're called Cynomorpha.'

Jae scowls at the vial before securing it in a leather bag. He tucks it into the inner pocket of his own coat and then heads out of Violet's greenhouse. I trail after him, shoving the rickety plywood door back over the opening.

'When Min-Jun died, I learned how real magic is. The Underworld too. I wanted, needed, to see her, to speak to her and prove I wasn't crazy. To prove she was murdered. I had to change myself, Andy, in painful ways and by means of dark spells,' Jae says, leading us away from the glowing lights of the school and deeper into the forest. 'But now I can travel to the Underworld, talk to spirits and gods and other beings. They listen to me because I can offer them deals, trades in return for their help, because I'm not just another spirit. I can walk both sides of the veil.'

I chew on my lip as we walk for a few moments, heading far enough into the treeline that no one from the school, or Tooth and Talon, can see us. 'What happens if you die in the Underworld? Do you just waltz your way into your afterlife or are you stuck like those gray ghosts on the banks of the river?'

'You would probably be able to pass through the river and onto the next life.'

'I asked about you.' I step over a large rock, nearly slipping on a bed of wet pine needles.

Jae is quiet for a few moments. 'If I die, I wouldn't move on. I'd keep doing what I do now.'

'What do you mean?'

'Travel the Underworld. Guide souls across the river. Look for answers like I always do – since Min-Jun.'

I squint in the fading light. Jae helped the Carmichaels' daughter cross the river. I'm no expert on the Underworld and afterlife, but even I've deduced that eternal rest lies on the west bank of that oily black river. Is Jae cursed? Doomed to wander the Underworld forever?

I wet my lips, the ashy air thick and oppressive. 'Do you think Violet is like you? Is she going to be stuck there forever?'

'I wish I knew what your sister did to herself.' He shakes his head, dark eyes glittering. 'We won't know until we find her. She knows more about magic than me, and has far more skill. Maybe she's just trapped, and nothing more.'

I try to nod, to convince myself not to assume the worst. But how can I not?

Jae's shoulders are tight, but he looks down at his watch. 'The moon is rising soon; we have to go. Take my hand.'

The taste of the tincture in my mouth grows stronger as the last rays of light slip behind the forest and encase us in a tomb of pine trees. I tentatively reach out and place my palm in his.

'This won't be pleasant. It isn't as easy to force travel to the Underworld as it is to accidentally wander into it.'

I grip his hand tighter as he begins to mutter words in a deep, flowing language. The words wash over us and even though I don't understand them, they feel familiar. His voice is hypnotic, deep and sonorous. My eyes shut of their own accord and I forget about the slap of the cold wind on my cheeks, the taste of copper and rotten rose petals on my tongue.

Those words, they're ancient but they don't feel evil or wrong. Instead, they're warm, wrapping their syllables around my arms and legs, sinking into my bones.

And then the warmth turns to scorching heat. Liquid metal flows under my skin, replacing the marrow of my bones. I gasp and try to cry out, but my lungs are encased in ropes of fire. I hardly feel Jae's hand holding mine. I can't smell the salt of the sea in the air or the musty smell of decaying foliage. Instead, all that remains is heat and ash.

Moments pass. A silence so heavy I'm crushed by it.

I open my eyes. A field of gray grass waves in a stale warm wind. Two glittering black rivers cut through the valley, separating the opposing banks. The beautiful, glimmering city with mansions of obsidian and gold sits on one side, and the endless press of moaning ghosts and scenes of stagnant decay take up the other.

'Are you all right?' Jae's voice echoes, the last notes of his chant still ringing faintly in the air.

I gasp and press my hand to my chest, wincing. 'That hurt. Is that what it's like for you every time?'

'More or less. Now come on, time moves differently here.' Before I can even try to ask for clarification, he continues, 'If we time it right, we'll be back an hour before breakfast. You won't need to sleep, and the hex I cast will make it look like you're peacefully in your bed, so your roommate won't suspect a thing. But if we take too long – an hour here, a minute there – it could be weeks from when we entered, and Tooth and Talon will run rampant while we're gone.'

'How long is too long?'

'Hard to say, there isn't exactly a conversion chart. But what is roughly an hour to us here is more than four back home. Though the longer you stay, the more time shifts and changes.' Jae studies our surroundings.

We're on a hill at the edges of the valley between the rivers. White and purple asphodel flowers sway on the breeze, and dark poplar trees creak and groan overhead. It's like a reverse image of the forest we came from. Only this one is stuck between life and death.

I blanch at the thought. I wonder how long Violet thinks she's been in the Underworld. I reach into my sleeve and grip my charm bracelet tightly. The cold metal reminds me of her. Reminds me I have to find a way to reach her.

'Come on, the goddess we need to meet lives near the east bank of the River Acheron.'

Jae begins to tromp down the hill. Gray soil and dark soot plume around his boots.

'Goddess? What do you mean, goddess?' I call.

He shoots a sly smile over his shoulder. I trot down the hill, sticking as close to him as possible.

My second time in the Underworld isn't exactly pleasant, but I'm not paralyzed with fear so strong I feel like I'm going to keel over at any moment. Not like before. For the most part, the gray, mourning ghosts keep their distance. Strange beings and blood-chilling figures still lurk and whoop behind trees and rocks, but nothing stops us or reaches for the thrill of living flesh.

The landscape undulates around us. Hills climb and fall. Mountains of black granite rise in the distance only to disappear the next moment. The rivers twist like living snakes, wrapping around each other and branching off to create deltas and marshlands. The walk doesn't take long, but once we finally stop next to a crumbling wall of black stone, my feet ache like I've run a marathon.

'You have the coin?' Jae asks.

I hold it up to the light, studying the strange markings. It's rough and hammered, made of brass. The outline of an ancient symbol is visible on one side – a feather with a stylized shape is stamped in the center – and a set of ancient scales on the other.

'Keep it with you at all times. As long as you have it, you possess a way out. If the worst comes to the worst, use it to pay a fee for help across the Underworld.'

I tuck the coin into the inside pocket of my jacket and zip it shut. 'You gave this coin to the jackal guy last time,' I say.

'The Cynomorpha,' he corrects. 'Yes, I did. They're

guardians of tombs and crossroads that lead to the west side of the riverbank. Those coins are to them what favors are to demons. In return for helping you cross the Underworld safely, the coin grants them a moment of mortal pleasure. Payment to them is one way to keep your head on your shoulders, if you're someone who is not yet ready to cross fully into the afterlife.'

'Who else would I pay?' I scrunch my nose up at the thought of a brass coin saving my life. How can a few dollars' worth of dingy metal grant a guardian of the afterlife a moment of mortality?

'Give the coin to any other tomb guardian that would harm a living mortal,' Jae says simply. 'Now, come on. We need to hurry if we're going to speak with Egeria before we go back to Ravenswood.'

The ruins of a grand acropolis rise from the brittle gray grass. Chiseled stones of pure white and stark black are strewn around as if a giant scattered them with his fist. Columns of white marble support the ghost of a roof. The grassy ground turns into a rough cobbled road as we walk. The columns are packed tighter together and the air shimmers.

Slowly, the ruins become less and less decrepit until the path we wander is lined with brilliant rows of polished columns. There's a roof that's painted to look like a starry night sky. Gold leaf adorns every surface. The sound of flowing water greets my ears just as the gray grass and sad, wilting poplars turn into large, sturdy olive trees sprouting brilliant green leaves.

A spring bubbles happily in the center of a grand circular courtyard. The olive trees sway gently, lining the courtyard and penning in a garden of exotic plants of vibrant hues. The air smells sweet, of flowers and warm earth. It looks as if someone plucked the scene from Ancient Greece and deposited it here.

'What are we doing here?' I whisper.

We're alone in the temple. The only sound besides our breathing is the steady churning of the spring. It spits out fresh, clear water that spills over the stone lip of a small pool. In an alcove carved from marble, a statue of a woman in an Ancient Greek chiton bends forward with a pitcher balanced against her hip.

'Egeria,' Jae calls, his voice ringing in the near silence. 'I've come to offer libation.'

I snap my head towards him. Libation? An offering?

The spring's merry bubbling turns into a roaring gurgle, splashing the stones of the courtyard, staining the earthen slabs a darker color. The water grows tall, taking the shape of a column as high as a person. Water sluices through the cracks of the stones as the column marches forward before turning fully into flesh.

'My, my,' says a melodic, feminine voice, 'what do we have here? My dear friend returned to me after such a long absence?'

'Hello, Egeria,' Jae says, dipping his chin in a short, respectful nod.

The woman who steps from the fountain is tall and lithe, with long black hair swept into an intricate series of braids that gather at her crown before tumbling down her back. Her olive skin gleams in the light from the starry ceiling. A powerful jolt lurches through me. My eyes are riveted to the woman – the goddess. She's so beautiful it's almost painful to look at her. She moves with fluid grace; each step forward is like the magnetic pull a sun exerts on the insignificant little moons in her orbit.

Egeria moves closer, the folds of her light blue chiton fluttering in the breeze. 'Why do you come to my spring after so many years of spurning my offer, my dear *dux mortis*?'

My ears prick up at the Latin. *Dux mortis*. I can't quite

recall an exact translation, but I know it has to do with death. Egeria's aura is so potent I can't force myself to focus on anything but her perfect face, so smooth and fair it could be carved of marble.

'I need your wisdom,' Jae says, his face impassive. 'Will you help us in return for an offering?'

Egeria circles Jae like a shark. Her dark brown eyes glitter in the soft light. As she moves around him, studying his face as if looking for faults, I notice that the temple we're standing in isn't as pristine and perfect as I thought. The fountain is deceptively deep, yawning like a gaping blue hole. Ivy clings to the marble columns, choking them in a stiff embrace. And then I see the spatters of dried blood on the stones, so dark they're almost brown.

Nausea churns in my gut and I nod towards the blood. 'Jae . . .'

The goddess's spell weaves tightly around us. The smell of the air, of sweet water, is tainted at once by the scent of spilt blood, coppery and fetid.

Egeria cocks her head at me, lips curling into a predatory smile. 'And who is this little pet you have with you? She looks so very fragile, poor thing. What are you doing with a mortal, old friend?'

'Will you give me the information I need?' Jae ignores her question.

'Of course. As long as you are willing to offer payment. This little human shell of yours is weaker than your true form. You must tell me someday why you've yoked yourself like this.'

Jae's lips press into a thin, hard line. 'How much do you require?'

'Oh, nothing much,' Egeria purrs into his ear, her fingers trailing down his shirtsleeve. 'Just a bit of blood, a drop of your essence, and of course a portion of your soul.'

His shoulders stiffen in response. A few moments pass as Egeria continues to peruse him like a hungry lioness, almost as if she wants him to bolt so she can chase him down and feast on her prey.

'That's the only way to pay?' he asks slowly.

My fingers dig into the muscle of Jae's forearm. 'You can't seriously be considering this.'

The goddess glares at me and waves her hand. At first I think it is only a dismissive gesture, but as I try to speak my lips won't move. My tongue is frozen to the roof of my mouth.

I choke, the sound unable to slip past my sealed lips. It's hard to breathe, the air sticking in my throat. The goddess before me shifts. No longer is she a beautiful woman. Her face is elongated, her skin ashen. Her teeth are sharp and coated in blood. And her eyes are pure white, milky and webbed. A monster.

'Don't play with her,' Jae warns, his voice low.

Her face changes again and Egeria pouts, her full lower lip sticking out like a child's. She waves her hand and the vice on my tongue loosens. I rub at my mouth, my cheeks tingling and numb, and take a gasp of warm air.

'I'll be fine, Andromeda. I know Egeria and her games.' Jae hardly spares me a glance, but his arm moves protectively behind me.

'I don't trust this *goddess*,' I whisper harshly, the words clumsy on my tongue. 'There has to be another way to get information. We need to go.'

'Don't be dramatic, dear,' Egeria sighs. 'I am the safest and most reliable source of information in this entire realm. I helped found the original laws and rituals of Rome, you know. I am gifted with prophecy and knowledge, sought after by kings and emperors. All I ask in return are a few libations in gratitude for my work and efforts.'

'Your price has gone up,' Jae says through gritted teeth.

Egeria waves her hand and dances towards her spring. 'The Underworld and all of its lands and kingdoms have changed with the mortal world. No one seeks my council in the world of the living any longer. So I must make do with what sustenance I can acquire from the occasional lost human or desperate soul.'

'I'll do it.' Jae nods, and I smack his shoulder with my fist. 'A portion of blood, essence and soul in exchange for all of the information I seek.'

'You have a deal, *dux mortis*.' Egeria extends her hand.

They close their fingers in a handshake and as they do, a web of black lines, like the silken threads of a spider web, wrap around their hands and trail up their wrists, binding them together for a moment. Then the web disappears and Jae drops her hand.

'Offer your libations to my spring. Then you will have your answers.' Egeria grins, the sharp points of her canines pressing against her ruby-red lips.

I catch Jae's hand as he steps forward. 'You can't seriously be considering giving up part of your soul for some answers. Haven't you ever read *Dorian Gray*?'

'I'll be fine, Andromeda.'

'Stop it! You don't need to play the stoic martyr. We can figure something else out.' Every nerve ending screams at me to get away from the goddess who is watching us like she's sizing up her next meal. Jae can't be this stupid.

He squeezes my hand before carefully peeling my fingers from his skin. 'We need to know how to break the connection Richard Greene made to the Underworld. Egeria is the quickest way to do that.'

'But losing a part of your soul – what will that do to you?'

Jae's lips curl into a small, sarcastic smile. 'Nothing that hasn't already happened.'

'Here.' Egeria leans gracefully against the marble alcove above her spring. 'This knife is blessed by the first Oracle of Delphi. I will be able to see the web of the future more clearly than even the Fates.'

My eyes widen at the flippant mention of the most famous oracle of all time – supposedly blessed by the god Apollo himself. But Jae doesn't react.

A knife, made of bronze so polished it reflects like a mirror, appears in the goddess's palm. It looks more ceremonial than functional, the hilt too ornate and heavy to allow a balanced strike. Jae takes it in his hand and the air grows colder.

He gives me an encouraging nod over his shoulder before he steps up to the edge of the spring and kneels down. Egeria perches in her alcove, chiton billowing in the soft breeze that drags its fingers down my spine.

'I need to know how to break the connection Richard Greene formed between the Underworld and Ravenswood Academy. Tell me everything.'

I want to cry out, to tell him to stop, that giving up more of himself to the Underworld is the last thing he should do – but I can't speak. I'm riveted as Jae lifts the blade and begins to murmur in that melodic language in a deep, resounding voice that doesn't seem to be his. Deep red emerges from his forearm as he makes a neat cut – not too deep, not too shallow – across the skin. The cut is at least four inches long and blood runs down the sides and drips into the pool below, some splattering on the lip of the fountain.

The drops explode the moment they hit the surface, diffusing like smoke in the air. Egeria's eyes grow bright as she watches. Soon, silver mixes with the red in the water, a tiny wisp of shimmering perfection that slips out from beneath Jae's skin at a command he utters in that ancient language.

He grimaces as the last few drops of blood roll down his

arm. Egeria's eyes, brighter than before, peer fiercely into the spring. No, they aren't just bright – they're completely *white*. Jae pushes to his feet as Egeria remains utterly still, her completely blank eyes searching the surface of the water as if she is reading from a book.

I dart forward, unable to shake the feeling that something terrible will rise from the water and pull us into the depths. Jae lets me reach for his hand and pull him back, and I feel his skin – feverish and sweaty – stick to mine.

'What is she doing?' I whisper, pulling his arm up so I can inspect the wound.

'She's scrying now – using my offerings to fuel her powers. We should have an answer soon.'

I don't have anything to clean his arm with, so I use the edge of my shirt to wipe away the blood on his forearm. The cut isn't too deep and won't need stitches, but it looks odd. The edges look a little silvery. That wisp of his soul was torn from the rest of him, leaving jagged scraps behind.

'You didn't have to do this, Jae.' I swallow and wipe again, dabbing at the edges of the cut. 'If you lose a piece of your soul, if you can't cross over when you die, like you said – what will happen to you?'

'It doesn't matter what happens to me. We need answers; now we'll have them.'

The goddess sits over her pool, white eyes unblinking as they stare into the depths. Her mouth is slack and images flash across her blank vision. I shudder and turn away, preferring to focus on what I can understand – blood and pain – as opposed to oracles and magic.

I sigh and drop Jae's arm, ignoring the blood on the hem of my shirt. 'How do you know her?'

He casts a worried look over to Egeria, but she remains completely still, bent over the spring and its mirrored surface.

Finally, he sighs and motions for me to sit, before he eases himself down on the soft grass growing against the trunk of an olive tree.

'Remember that time moves differently here? Well, when I came looking for my aunt's spirit, I would be gone for long stretches of time. Days to weeks. But it was longer sometimes, almost impossible to track. It felt like years when I was searching. I learned a lot about how the Underworld works. I met some friends, but more often than not, I ran into trouble. Egeria helped me in one of my first long journeys, offering a trade of sorts.'

'Different than offering part of your soul?' I raise an eyebrow.

'I told you once that the beings that live here, demons and gods and spirits, all crave what they can't have – life and everything that comes with it. Pain, pleasure, emotion, power – anything that drives humanity.'

I nod. 'Which is why Tooth and Talon can coerce help from demons, by offering them a taste of mortality.'

'Exactly.' Jae glances once at me and shifts against the trunk. 'Egeria and other gods and goddesses – or rather, aspects of them – find their way to the Underworld once they're no longer worshiped or venerated in the mortal world. They lose their power, the offerings of their followers, and become shades of their former selves. It's why you see bits and pieces of mythology and religion from all time periods and cultures here. This place is a melting pot of what mortality believes in, or stops believing in. On the west bank, where people live out their afterlives, humans see what they believe in. Be it Heaven or Nirvana or an endless cycle of reincarnation. But, if you knew the truth, you would see the Underworld for what it is and be able to travel it freely. Awareness is key here. It leads to knowledge.'

'What does this have to do with you?' I shake my head, eying the ancient temple with new eyes. Egeria helped build Rome, communed with Emperors. Is this existence a shadow of the life she once experienced? Does she crave that influence and power still?

'On one of my trips to the Underworld she offered me knowledge, anything I needed to know to navigate the rivers and banks and abodes of gods and demons. For a price, of course.'

'And it was worse than a piece of your soul?' I feel the blood drain from my face. Is that why Jae was so calm about the offering she requested?

He shakes his head. 'Nothing to do with my soul. Not that. I . . . I had to offer myself to the Underworld – like a servant, in a sense. Completing a spell like that would give her decades of power. She might even be able to wander the mortal plane she once walked, if she tried.'

'What do you mean you offered yourself to the Underworld?' My voice is calm but my stomach twists hard.

Jae shifts again, his eyes darting away from me. 'Exactly that. In order to get the knowledge I have now – which paths to take, which beings to contact and to avoid, how to manipulate things and make them bend to my will – I had to give myself up. When my body dies, I won't cross to the west bank. I'll be stuck here, like those who have been forgotten, some sort of shade of what I once was. I got what I wanted, but Egeria used my mortality to feed herself.'

Ice lodges under each of my ribs. I ponder the thought of being lost and forgotten, and being totally aware of your desolation the entire time. An eternity of being trapped in an ashy wasteland where monsters wander. It's unthinkable.

I swallow, my throat as dry as the grass beyond the acropolis. 'Is that why you can heal so fast?' I nod towards his abdomen, where the knife wound from the night we saved Cindy doesn't seem to bother him at all.

'Yes.' His eyes darken and his jaw flexes. 'That's why I don't care about losing a bit of my soul. I don't need it, and I have so little of it left anyway. I know where I'll be once I die. If I can even properly die.'

I study his profile for a moment – the strong cheekbones and sharp jaw, the full lips, the dark brown eyes. I run my gaze over the clothing that speaks of casual wealth. And I pity him, this beautiful boy with everything at his fingertips.

He's damned, forced to spend eternity in a sort of purgatory while knowing every secret about it. Is that why he is so intent on saving other people? Preventing other girls from being used by selfish, privileged teenagers meddling with things they can't understand? It's both noble and heartbreaking.

And for the first time since that moment in Pastor Carmichael's study, I feel the strangest urge to pull him to me. To kiss him.

A strangled gasp echoes off the pillars. The leaves on the olive trees tremble, shaking and rattling as Egeria staggers to her feet, eyes still milky white. Jae and I lurch to our feet as the starry ceiling shakes and glows brightly.

Egeria stumbles forward, her eyes clearing at the same moment she smiles, her skin glowing like she's been rejuvenated – made whole again. 'Oh, you are in for quite the shock. This may be an even greater vision than the one I received on the Sibylline books!'

'Get on with it,' Jae snaps, his face guarded once more. 'We're short on time.'

'Richard Greene, that man who perverted the ground from which Tooth and Talon draws its power, was involved in some nasty magic so old even I had forgotten the ways to accomplish it.' The goddess looks gleeful.

'What are you talking about?' I ask, my skin prickling.

'Rest assured, *dux mortis*,' Egeria purrs, resting her hand on Jae's cut arm, 'your gift was not offered in vain. I know how you can cull the dark magic that resides in the ground of that mortal school you are so bent on saving. But you are not going to like it.'

'Enough games, Egeria,' Jae says, eyes blazing. 'Tell us what you saw.'

The goddess turns to me, her tall and graceful frame humming with ancient power. 'It would be far easier if I showed your little mortal pet. She is far more interesting than I first realized.'

And as she reaches her hand towards me, I don't have time to cry out before her fingers grasp the sides of my head and my vision fades to black.

# 26

When I open my eyes, everything is blurry. I blink rapidly, my head spinning like I've held my breath too long. A shadowy forest surrounds me – thick pines that smell sweet and are so tall they block out most of the watery evening light. A man kneels at a riverbank strewn with smooth stones. Water spills across the shallow bed, gurgling and lapping over rocks at the shore.

Five black candles surround him in a half-circle. A brazier sits on a bed of hot coals and he murmurs words in Latin, fervently, pleadingly, while slowly dripping something from a bronze bowl. My nose wrinkles when the liquid sizzles against metal. The smell is familiar. Blood.

I try to move, to cry out for the man to stop, but I am rooted in place. My limbs are bound to my sides in an invisible spider web. He speaks again in Latin, the words coming to his tongue easily, like he knows the language intimately. As he speaks, I find myself able to understand each word as easily as if I were Violet.

'Ossivorus,' the man says as the candles grow brighter, 'I call on you to forge an alliance, an offering of blood, to aid me in a great task.'

The river seems to stop its flow. The man lets more drops of blood fall from the lip of the bowl. They hiss as they hit the hot brazier. The flames dancing on the wicks of the black candles freeze. Even the air is still.

The man straightens, lowering the bowl of blood. And I see his face. Richard Greene. He is younger than in any of the photos I've seen. His forehead is smooth and his chin is covered by a thick beard. He's dressed in a fine suit, but it's tattered and old.

'I call on you to make a deal, to bind our fates together.' His eyes are wild and bright with excitement as he stands and looks across the bank of the river into the inky trees beyond.

Something moves. A flash of pale white bone and black horns.

I try again to run, but I'm pinned in place. Every cell in my body wants to flee. I scream but not a single sound comes out.

'*Little mortal.*' A deep, growling voice emerges from the other side of the river. It's so powerful, so low it vibrates in my chest, my bones. '*Drops of blood, as delicious as the offering of human essence is, are nothing to me. Why should I help you, boy?*'

Greene smiles sardonically, eyes narrowed. But he looks into the forest as if he can see exactly where the demon stands in the darkness. 'These drops of blood are nothing but a taste, a promise of what I will give you if you bind yourself to me.'

Silence.

My heart thunders in my chest and my throat constricts. Slowly, a hulking form emerges into the dusk. The huge rack of black antlers, the face – neither human nor animal – only half covering a massive skull. I glimpse broad shoulders, skin mottled purplish and pale, and ragged black robes. The half-formed face of the demon.

'*I will entertain your proposal for a time. The blood you have offered is pure and sweet. But if you call me here to waste my time, I will make you suffer.*'

Greene wipes his brow with his sleeve and wades into the river. He stands up to his ankles in the slow current, moving closer to the monster. 'I have a way that we can both get what we want. You wish for more time on the mortal plane, feasting and tasting of every pleasure the mortal world has to offer. I wish for an unstoppable power whose surface humans have barely even scratched. If you help me get the knowledge that I seek, I will feed you souls for decades to come. Centuries.'

'*Intriguing.*' Ossivorus cocks his head, the ragged flesh dangling from one side of his head. '*But I do not see how that is possible. Human lives are short, pitiful things.*'

There is a warning in the demon's voice. One that even Greene can't ignore. He tugs at his collar and loosens the cravat holding it tight against his throat.

'I have a plan, an ancient spell I found in my time studying abroad, searching the oldest libraries of Europe. A spell that you could complete for me. If we can bind a portion of the River Acheron and root it permanently here, it will provide endless sustenance for spells so powerful they could shake human kingdoms. Magic already flows naturally at this convergence, but with you to bind our world and the realm beyond together, it would grow in power. Grow *my* power.' Greene's eyes are wide and manic as he speaks, his voice trembling.

The demon's black gaze bores into the man's eyes. Neither moves for a time. Not a falling leaf or pine needle or drop of water dares to disturb the silence.

'*And in payment for this grand task, you will somehow feed me the souls of humans long past the time when your little mortal cage will crumble and wither?*' Ossivorus' voice is dangerous, rumbling so deep it shakes the water swirling around Greene's feet.

He swallows hard, mopping at his sweaty forehead once more. 'I have been reading texts from the sorcerers of Egypt, the Assyrians, and the oldest cultures of humankind. If you are able to bind the river conduit to me, my mortal life would be extended. The power I draw from the river would keep me alive far longer than any normal human lifespan. And I would pay you in blood cyclically, at times of celestial liminality – times of greatest power for your kind.'

Ossivorus remains silent, his black eyes unblinking. His antlers, his skin, his skull, all speak of danger. He could snap Greene like a twig, rip his throat out with his teeth and drink his blood. But he doesn't move.

'Can you do it?' Greene asks, licking his lips.

The demon laughs. Rocks clatter together on the riverbank. *'Your ingenuity is surprising, little mortal. I will do this for you. My power will help you tie the convergence to your mortal plane. Your life will stretch on, but your body will wither. I can keep your soul on Earth, but you will need to find a new body at regular intervals. I am a demon of blood and carnage – not of life. Remember that.'*

Greene grimaces, his face turning pale, but he nods. 'Of course. That is why I picked you, Lord Ossivorus. You are the most powerful demon of them all.'

*'And the most vengeful. Each time you sacrifice you will need to awaken me from my prison in the Underworld – a task that will require many rituals. I am feared here, kept in the darkest recesses of the land of the dead. It will take time to raise me, and in that time my hunger will grow insatiable.'*

'I have accounted for that, Lord Ossivorus. I will have help during each sacrifice to guarantee you are awakened. And with this help I will ensure you experience the mortal plane for longer than a few moments. We may even extend it to days. Weeks.'

Ossivorus steps further into the waning light, a hungry glint in his eyes. *'You will keep your word, feed me the mortals I need, and you can have whatever magic and frivolous things you desire from the power of the river. But do not fail in your payment, or I will grind your bones to dust for eternity.'*

Richard Greene swallows hard and stammers, 'I w-will need followers, others who can join my s-sect to help feed you for years to come. A society like those of old.'

Ossivorus waves a huge hand. *'I do not care about the logistics.*

*Your followers will feed me, awaken me fully from this painful slumber. I will continue to siphon power from the Acheron to your site of convergence. You will be the most powerful human in this world and you can have the adoration, riches and control you seek. As long as I get what is mine.'*

'Thank you.' Greene dips his head formally, groveling. 'As a sign of good faith, I will offer your first sacrifice now, to fuel you as you create the connection.'

A young woman comes into view, her hair pulled up in an intricate hairstyle. She wears a heavy-looking velvet gown, a corset clearly cinching her waist. Her eyes are wide. She checks a pocket watch dangling from her waistband.

'Richard!' she calls, her voice breaking the spell of utter stillness. 'This is an odd time for a picnic, you know. If your housekeeper did not tell me to meet you by the riverbank, I would think you were being untoward.'

*Stop!* I scream, though the words can't slip past my lips. *Get away from here; run!*

The girl is blind to me, to my harsh breathing and internal agony. All I can do is watch as she unwittingly moves closer and closer to a hungry demon. The girl steps right through me, like I'm a ghost, and approaches the river shallows where Greene stands. The demon stays in the shadows on the other bank, his eyes glinting fiercely. Cruelly.

'There you are, Amelia.' Richard extends a hand to her and she slowly, trustingly, puts her palm in his. 'I am glad Mrs Hester steered you correctly. I wanted to surprise you, and have a special night together before your family heads to Italy for the autumn and winter.'

'My mother is waiting in your garden. She will miss us if we are gone too long,' Amelia says shyly, dropping her eyes.

Doesn't she see the black candles? The burning brazier? Can't she smell the scent of death and blood and decay that

Ossivorus carries with him? I thrash again, but am rooted to the spot, just as when I first opened my eyes to this terrible vision.

Greene pulls her close and reaches into his pocket. 'We will not be long.'

'If you wish to pretend you did not already ask my father for permission to marry me, I can act surprised when you pull a ring from your waistcoat.'

Greene smiles, but it doesn't reach his eyes. Sickness curdles in my gut and I wish I could close my eyes. But I'm forced to watch as he pulls something much larger from his coat than a ring. It's a knife, made of iron and etched with symbols and markings I don't understand.

Amelia never even gets the chance to scream.

Greene pulls her limp body into the river. She's still alive, her eyes wild as she chokes and tries to breathe through her slashed and mutilated throat. And then there's nothing but a cloud of blood as he pushes her below the surface and finishes an incantation.

'*An excellent offering,*' the voice of Ossivorus calls from the shadows, half crazed. '*You have a deal, Richard Octavius Greene. I will forge the connection now, at the height of dusk during your summer solstice.*'

The last thing I see is Greene smiling, his hands and sleeves covered in blood. And the limp body of Amelia as it floats slowly down the river.

# 27

'What did you do to her?'

Voices echo around me, reverberating against my skull. Arguing. Laughter. Blood. I press a hand to my forehead and crack open my eyes. A starry ceiling and white columns glare back at me, and I sit up.

'Relax, psychopomp.' Egeria's lilting voice echoes above my head. 'She is fine. I simply showed her what I saw in the waters.'

'Jae?' I croak.

'Andy!' He turns from the goddess where she sits at the edge of her fountain. 'Are you alright?'

'I'm fine, I think,' I mumble. 'Just a headache.'

'You've been unconscious for over twenty minutes. Are you sure you're okay?' Jae inspects me, as if I somehow fell into a pit of razor blades while lying on the hard flagstones.

I bat his hand away and glare at the goddess instead. 'Why did you show me that? You could have just explained everything.'

'You intrigue me,' Egeria muses, her eyes back to normal. 'I know of your sister, of her connection to magic here. But I did not expect to see such a gift in you as well.'

'What are you talking about?'

'Do not play with her,' Jae warns, moving to stand between me and Egeria. 'Or you will regret it.'

'There is the fiery spirit I remember, old friend. And your little human pet is fine. I was merely scratching an itch. Testing a theory.'

'Don't test your theories on her. Do not touch her ever again.'

Egeria rolls her eyes. 'You have your answers now, psychopomp. And I have mine.'

'Don't call me that,' Jae snaps, the tendons on his neck taut beneath his skin.

'I cannot call you *dux mortis*, nor psychopomp. What title shall I use for one such as you, then?' Egeria narrows her eyes. She still looks as if she is glowing. Powerful. A veritable goddess, not a shadow of one.

I grab his hand and tug. 'We need to go back. We're cutting it close.' I dig my fingers into his arm when he doesn't move. 'Please, Jae.'

Slowly, the tension leaks out of his muscles and he turns to face the goddess, his lips pulled into a vicious snarl. 'Enjoy what little time you have with your powers, Egeria. I don't plan on seeing you ever again.'

Jae leads me from the crumbling acropolis and back into the dreary land between the rivers of the Underworld. He moves fast, his shoulders tight. I jog to keep up with his long strides, trying my best not to imagine the blood of the girl Greene killed or her wild, frantic eyes.

'I don't like having to go to her.' He shakes his head, fists balled. 'I *knew* she might take an interest in you if you were anything like Violet.'

'Violet?' I stop walking, my heart thundering again.

'Egeria, like the demons and other beings here, craves power. Power that only mortality and human souls can provide. When someone like your sister – touched by magic, connected by something bigger than spells and scrolls – enters the Underworld, demons and gods take note.' Jae scrubs a hand down his face and squints up at the bleak sky. 'When someone like *you* enters, they take note.'

'Take note? Why would that interest them, if they can use magic whenever they want?' I tug at a ringlet falling across my face. I've never done a magical thing in my life. It's Violet the goddess should be interested in. Not me.

Jae pulls the tincture from his pocket and twists the bottle open. The floral smell mixes with the stench of decay and tickles my nostrils.

'They can use magic whenever they want – yes. But a human *born* with magic is special. Different. They can grant gods and demons greater favors, test the boundaries of life and death. Why else would a demon like Ossivorus help a rat like Richard Greene? That coward was touched by magic. He could hold up his end of the bargain when so many mortals who dabble in the occult fail miserably.'

I blanch at the memory. Of Greene and the demon with the vile half-face, striking a bargain so evil it cursed a valley for well over a century. And those girls. So many lives lost to a hungry monster and the greed of one man.

'She told you? Then why did she have to show me in a vision?' I rub at my aching temple. Amelia's choked and dying breaths will haunt me forever. So will Egeria's hungry white eyes. I shudder and try to take the vial from Jae's hand without shaking.

His jaw tightens. 'To see if she could. To test your limits. You have magic in you, Andromeda. And she knows it now. Others will too, and they'll seek you out for favors.'

I stare at him, mouth agape. It isn't possible – I don't have a drop of magic in my blood. How can I be connected to something like that and never know it? It has to be Violet. Her tattoo and charms. It's not me; it can't be.

Jae gestures to the vial and I tip my head back and squeeze three drops onto my tongue, gagging and trying not to cough the liquid back out. He chants the same lyrical words

231

as before, and heat spreads through my limbs, painful and scorching.

The world spins when I open my eyes and find us in the storage room. I stagger and brace one hand against the cold cement wall.

'The vision Egeria showed me,' I close my eyes to keep from falling over, 'I think I know how to break the connection between the Underworld and Ravenswood.'

'What is it?'

His eyes brighten with something like hope, and I can only pray I'm right.

'We need to find Richard Greene.' I swallow hard, ignoring the taste lingering on my tongue.

Jae checks his watch, and I glance at it too. It's early. Five thirty in the morning. We've been gone the entire night and yet it feels like only one or two hours. I shake my head, fighting off a strange sense of vertigo. I'm not tired. I don't feel like I've been awake for twenty-four hours. But there is a bone-deep ache curling in my stomach. Settling in my ribs. A sense of dread.

'The only way to break the connection to the rivers of the Underworld that Richard Greene made is to kill him,' I whisper. 'He's still alive somewhere, inhabiting a new body.'

'He could be anyone, Andy.'

I press the heels of my hands to my temples, fending off the ache in my skull. 'He's here. He's in the society. He made a deal, and he won't risk a demon's wrath if he fails.'

I think of the callous way he killed Amelia. Like she was nothing. The hungry glint in his eyes as Ossivorus agreed to his plan.

Jae looks sick as he presses his fingers to his chest. 'I can call in more favors in the Underworld, see if anyone knows –'

'No.' I hold my hand up to silence him. 'No more favors

232

from gods or demons. We're figuring this out on our own. I can't let you keep risking your life – or your soul – to get quick answers.'

'Andromeda, it could be the only way.'

'Stop! You can't throw your life away just because you made raw deals and hasty choices after your aunt died. I can't do this by myself, Jae. I – I need you.' I turn away, wiping angrily at my damp lashes with the heel of my hand.

I can feel his eyes on me. His gaze is heavy and the tension between us permeates the air. My skin tingles and heat sears my back as he steps closer. Before I can push him away, try to snap and bite like I always do, his arms wrap around me, turning me towards him. He tugs me to his chest. I stiffen for a moment, but then I melt and choke back more tears. My chest tightens again, but in a different way. I can't let myself think about what this means. I bury my face into the cradle of his arms and breathe in his scent, my fingers curling in the musky fabric of his shirt.

'Okay,' he whispers into my hair. 'No more favors.'

'Good.' I sniff. 'Because you're an idiot for selling your soul and playing hero. It's really annoying.'

He laughs softly and the sound vibrates through my cheek where it rests against his chest. We stand there for what feels like forever. I take deep breaths, giving myself this little moment of peace. I can worry about saving the world in a minute. But right now – right now, it feels good to be held and have someone to share this burden with. To trust.

'There are four members of Tooth and Talon. Four possible candidates for Richard Greene's host. We'll need to narrow them down, see which one's motivations are different from the others,' he murmurs, his breath rustling a curl and tickling my cheek.

My spine tingles and I stand up straight, pushing away from

Jae. Four members of the society. Four people with a vested interest in killing innocent girls. But there are more than four people tangled up in the society. There are the alumni. Donors. Salvatore Russo and Headmaster Madden. And then I think of my sister in the same circumstances. Something clicks.

'Violet. She knew about Greene and his identity – she had to.'

'What makes you think so?' Jae shakes his head.

'Why else would Tooth and Talon try to sacrifice one of its own? Violet, if what you've said is true, is the most powerful member of their society. Her magic is more potent. Whoever Greene is must be the one who convinced the society to restart the killings. I know my sister, and she would never murder someone in cold blood. And since she's the strongest, she might have fought back, figured out his secret. Whoever told the other members to kill Violet has to be Richard Greene.'

My mind races with the possibility: Violet is smart enough to have figured out Greene's secret. She would have done anything to stop him. And Richard Greene tried to kill her for it.

But Violet would never go down without a fight. She made sure I would find her, figure out what was going on. And she made sure Jae found me too. An idea, a spark of hope, forms.

'We have to find my sister.' I look up at Jae. 'She's somewhere in the Underworld. She knows who Richard Greene is. If we find her, we can end this.'

His beautiful face lights up with determination. 'We'll find her, Andy. I promise. Every night, from now until Halloween, we'll search for her.'

As we look at each other in the darkened basement, the scent of the Underworld clinging to our clothes, I can't help but feel that spark of hope turn into a flame.

With Jae at my side, maybe we can actually do this.

I'm finally going to find Violet.

# 28

The next three days are the same. I go to class, I watch the members of Tooth and Talon's every move, I eat, and then I enter the Underworld. And each night we search for Violet.

We ask some of Jae's contacts. Ancient spirits, druids and holy men who saw more than normal mortals in their lifetimes. But each answer is the same. Violet can't be found. Her spirit is untraceable – locked in a purgatory to keep herself alive. No god or monster can find her, and she wants it that way.

But it doesn't matter. I trust Jae and my sister. We will find Violet. We're going to set her free.

And every moment of every day I try to figure out who Richard Greene is pretending to be. Which four members of the group have the most to lose. The most to gain. Whose eyes have that same dead, cold hunger that I saw in Egeria's vision.

I sit in the dining hall, four days after we spoke with Egeria. Dinner is being served and we usually eat quickly to make it to the greenhouse before the sun sets completely. It gives Jae just enough time to make sure his enchantments are secure and no one will find our beds empty during the night.

Voices and dishes clatter around me. I sit with Munia at the far end of one of the tables and watch the doors for any sign of Jae's dark hair and tall frame.

'You okay?' Munia asks, poking at her dinner.

'Just waiting for Jae.'

Seconds turn into minutes. I tap my foot, bouncing my

knee under the table as I try to choke down the dinner of green beans and pot roast.

'I know you guys are both being picked on by Luciano's pack of jerks.'

My stomach lurches. 'What?'

'Andy,' she sighs, 'Regina, Melinda, Eric – they're all the same. They want to be the best, the brightest. I've seen how they single you and Jae out. They don't like you.'

I breathe out and glance at the doors again. 'They're just bullies, that whole club.'

'I could report them to Madden. To the board, even.' Munia leans forward, catching my eye. 'They can't just waltz around treating you this way.'

I'm tempted to laugh. If only she knew what they were capable of. But Munia is too good to be dragged into this mess. This darkness. She lost her sister. More death, more of this evil, it won't do her any good.

'There's no point in reporting it. They're richer than anyone else in this school – even wealthier than your parents. Their families are more important, more influential. It wouldn't help, and it would only make life more difficult for you.'

Munia huffs and throws her napkin onto her plate. 'It doesn't make it okay. I don't even understand why they're targeting you. Violet was their friend!'

I smile thinly. 'I don't think any of them are truly friends. And I'm fine, Munia. Really. Jae and I are just lying low until they forget about us and move on to the next person who looks at them wrong.'

'I'll try,' she grumbles. 'Where is Jae, anyway? He's usually here by now.'

I swallow hard, to keep myself from saying anything else, and shrug. The clock ticks on as dinner service crawls forward.

Fifteen minutes.

Twenty.

Thirty.

Still no Jae.

The food settles heavily in my stomach like a rock. Through the windows the rays of the sun dip dangerously close to the sea.

'I'm going to look for Jae. Make sure he didn't run into Luciano or Eric in their common room.' I jump to my feet, leaving Munia behind.

He hasn't answered any of my texts or calls. Anxiety turns into full-blown fear as I shoulder my way out of the dining room and turn in a slow circle, my fingers digging into my sweater and tugging at every loose thread.

'Come on,' I mumble under my breath. 'Pick up, pick up.'

But he doesn't answer my twelfth call. Or my thirteenth. Dread blankets my skin like a coat as the sun slips further and further below the horizon and the light begins to wane. I scour the boys' wing, looking in every common room and study area. I search the storage room. No sign of Jae anywhere.

I pull a coat over my shoulders, ready to walk outside and search the gardens. Dinner is still keeping most of the school busy, so when I skirt around a pillar and make for the door near Mrs Bianchi's room, I'm surprised to see two figures standing in the classroom doorway. Measuring my breath, I duck behind a marble statue.

Salvatore Russo, Luciano's father, leans close to Bianchi. It almost looks like they might kiss, but then I see her cringe back from the force of his cool blue eyes and his towering frame. His graying hair is slicked back. His Armani suit is a stormy gray, and impeccably tailored. But he looks dangerous right now, looming over her like a sentinel.

'You were meant to report his location to Luciano,' Salvatore purrs menacingly. 'And yet you failed to contact any member of the group. It is by sheer luck they intercepted him in the field this morning.'

Bianchi swallows hard, her body rigid. 'I have work to do –'

'I have sunk hundreds of thousands of dollars into this club. Into this plan. All for my son to succeed. For Ossivorus to rise. For our society to grow to what it once was. Your *work*,' he spits, looking at the classroom full of art prints, 'is nothing compared to that.'

'I understand.' Bianchi tries to lift her chin, but I see a wobble in her lower lip. 'If you'll just let me –'

Her voice breaks and she clears her throat to cover it. I press closer to the cold marble, the edges of the plinth biting into my ribs as I strain to hear. Salvatore checks his expensive watch with a casual flick of the wrist, but the movement brings his hand right next to Bianchi's face. A threat.

'My son will hear about this. As will Madden. Remember who you truly work for. The good of the society comes above anything else.'

Without waiting for a response, he pivots on his shiny loafers and heads towards the administration offices. Bianchi stares blankly at the wall in front of her; a tendon twitches in her neck. But then she twists around and heads into her classroom, slamming the door.

Slowly, I creep out from behind the statue, my pulse jumping, thrilling along my fingertips. I know they were talking about Jae. I have to find him before Tooth and Talon can do something truly terrible.

Zipping up my coat, I walk into the gardens. Jae isn't there either. The last place I could hope for is the greenhouse. Tears threaten to spill down my cheeks, and I bite my lip hard to keep them from falling. Everything's fine. It has to be. *He* has to be.

I run to the greenhouse as soon as I'm out of sight of the

school. The air is bitterly cold but no rain falls. The sea is angry in the distance. I breathe hard and run faster, slipping over stones and drifts of dead leaves as I enter the forest.

'Jae!' I cry, as soon as I see the dilapidated glass building. 'Are you in there?' The plywood door is shoved to the side and a candle flickers weakly on the table. I see the blurry out-line of shoulders through a grimy window pane. Relief slams into me and I sag, leaning my arm against the doorway as I catch my breath.

'Where have you been? I tried to call you but you didn't an—' The words stick in my throat.

A long body, lithe and casual, lounges against the table. Luciano strokes his thumb along the side of a lighter, and a flame jumps to life, bathing the planes of his face in shadow and light.

'I'm afraid Jae isn't here,' he says, snapping the lighter shut. He pushes up off the table and nonchalantly brushes at the lapels of his coat. 'He won't be coming to hide you in the Underworld tonight, or ever again.'

My throat is so dry I choke. I take a single, shaking step backwards, but bump into someone tall. Eric. He clamps a hand on the back of my neck. I shut my eyes as his other hand grips my shoulder, holding me in place.

'What did you do to him?' The words are a whisper, a shak-ing sob on my tongue.

Luciano gestures to Eric. He pushes me into the green-house and I'm right in front of Luciano. I keep my eyes on his chin, refusing to look higher. Tears burn the back of my throat, but I can't fall apart. I have to think. To focus. To escape.

Luciano grins. 'Nothing he wouldn't have done to me.'

'What is that supposed to mean?' I flick my eyes up to meet his cold gaze.

'Tooth and Talon isn't foolish. His little enchantments are clever, but no match for what we've been given, what we've learned from Lord Ossivorus.'

He leans in close and I lash out, wanting to bite him, but his hand darts out to grip my face. His fingers pinch my cheeks, pressing painfully against my teeth. Blood pools on my tongue, but I don't wince or cry out.

'You're all insane,' I spit out the words, garbled by his grip. 'You have no idea what you're messing with, what you're risking. And for what? More money that you don't need?'

Luciano's eyes darken and he leans in close. His fingers are so tight on my cheeks, I know I'll bruise. 'You and Jae and your little crusade are pointless. We're using magic so old and ancient we could be more powerful than any society before us. It isn't just money, Andromeda. It's everything. What are a few pitiful lives compared to changing the course of the world? Discovering something that will change humanity as much as the gift of fire did. We'll be gods. You could join us. Thrive where Violet failed.'

'Why would I ever want that?'

Luciano's jaw tightens. 'Lord Ossivorus and Violet have told us about you. You know you're nothing special. An average student and an average girl. The kid sister of a girl so gifted she made everyone around her envious. You're nothing, isn't that right? It was *always* Violet.'

'That's not true.'

'Please.' He scoffs, before his eyes turn to darkened slits. 'Wouldn't you love to make your parents proud, make everyone who ever looked at you like you were an afterthought realize that you were so much more?'

*No,* I want to scream. But a small, wicked part of me wonders. All those years in my sister's shadow. I convinced myself I was content, happy even, to be second best. I didn't even try after a while. What was the point? Anything I took an interest in, Violet could always do it ten times better.

'Then you understand what Ossivorus offers each of us.' Luciano nods, as if he can see the thoughts warring in my mind. Read them in the tears welling up in my eyes.

A memory of Amelia's body floating down the river seems to flash in his eyes. This boy, cruel and callous. The way he spoke to Bianchi. The way he controls Regina and Eric. His father's constant interventions in the school. I look at his face and I swear that there is someone else lingering beneath his facade.

Anger flashes through my body. I lift my fist and swing as hard as I can, connecting with his cheekbone. Eric curses and grips both of my arms, yanking them behind my back. I thrash and kick at his legs, at Luciano's hunched form.

Luciano spits and wipes at the blood spilling down his cheek. I split the skin on his cheekbone. He'll have a nasty black eye by morning. I can't help but smile, even though my hand aches and burns.

Eric jerks on my arms, wrenching them painfully in their sockets. 'Don't you dare touch him again,' he hisses.

'You think this demon you're so bent on summoning will actually help you? He's using you! Once he has what he wants, you'll be as dead as those girls you've murdered. Violet was right to try and stop you. You're monsters, worse than the demon you're serving!'

'Enough,' Luciano growls. 'You know nothing about my mission or Ossivorus.' He stalks forward and draws a knife just like the one I saw Richard Greene use almost two hundred years ago.

My blood chills.

He sets the blade against my throat, his other hand fisting my hair and yanking my head back. 'You, Violet, Jae – you don't understand. They'll all die one day. At least this way their deaths will mean something! Lord Ossivorus will bring in a new age for humanity, grant us more power than we can imagine. You can't stop us.'

I gasp and flail, the angle of my neck threatening to cut off the blood flow to my head. 'Everyone will die but you, isn't that right, Greene?'

Eric's face – upside down, with my head yanked back – pinches in confusion.

'What, didn't he tell you?' I sneer at Eric. 'Your alpha, the person you depend on for every thought in your empty head is hiding a secret from you.'

'What is she talking about?' he barks at Luciano.

Luciano presses the blade against my neck. 'Nothing. She doesn't know a thing.'

Panic slithers down my spine and I have to know. Have to confront this vast ache in my chest. 'Did you kill Jae?'

'I did what had to be done to someone like him. What he is – I should have seen it sooner.' Luciano wipes at the blood on his face again and digs in the knife.

My eyes burn from the pressure on my neck and his fist in my hair but I snarl at his bleeding face. 'You'll never get what you want. You're just a stupid, scared little rich boy whose daddy never loved him enough.'

Luciano's fingers dig into my scalp. 'You made your choice. They all did. And as soon as Halloween is over, everyone who stands in our way will be dead.'

The knife slashes across my throat. I cry out, but no sound leaves my severed vocal cords. Hot blood spills down my chest. Eric lets me go, and I slump to the ground, writhing, slapping my palms to my ruined throat.

'Ossivorus wanted you and your sister alive.' Luciano squats down and pushes a curl from my face with the tip of the bloodied knife. 'He said the power you two hold is immeasurable. If only we could have convinced you to help us. But it's easier this way, he'll see.'

He watches me struggle and gasp and bleed, as if lamenting the loss of a solid work horse. I can imagine him in that black and white photo so clearly. A man leading generations into hell. Through flashes of blackness, my vision fades slowly, leeching out of my body along with my blood. At last, his beautiful, terrible face fades away and I'm left alone to die.

I choke again, the air refusing to enter my lungs. I fumble in my pocket, fingers clumsy and unresponsive, reaching for the vial Jae made for me. I set the dropper against my tongue and mouth the words I can't speak, a spell to take me to the land of the dead. But I can't taste the bitter floral notes or feel the bone-cracking pain of travelling to the Underworld. My fingers are numb. Did I even move my hands? I can't feel anything.

I shut my eyes and picture Jae waiting for me in the Underworld, ready to guide me somewhere where there isn't any more pain.

# 29

The first thing I taste is ash and blood. I open my eyes and see the strange eternal dusk of the Underworld. I test my limbs, moving slowly. My stomach hurts like I got sucker punched, and I sit up, gingerly touching my throat. The skin is smooth, no evidence of the knife wound.

I must be dead.

The endless deltas of the twin rivers of the Underworld spider-web around me. The oily black water separates this gray valley from the land of mansions and gardens and lilies. I'm stranded between the rivers, between the banks. Between life and death.

I shoot to my feet. The taste of flower and oil under my tongue is fading.

The blood on my clothes and skin is gone. I reach into my pocket, feeling for the cold metal coin, and wrap my fingers around it. Jae said I should save it for an emergency. If this isn't the time, I don't know what is.

Twisting the coin in my fingers, I scan the valley for signs that Jae taught me to look for. Burial mounds litter the place between the land of the living and the realm of the dead. Those who were never buried properly, who didn't have the means to pay their way across the rivers, or thought death was an endless void. People from all centuries and millennia and religions.

A platform covered in wilting grass, with a poplar tree leaning near it, catches my eye. There, near the base, is a stone marker with hieroglyphs. It's an old Egyptian tomb for one who wasn't wealthy. I sag with relief and head towards it. If it were a Celtic or Roman tomb, I wouldn't have known what to do. But Jae prepared me for this, and even though my stomach twists and I wonder if my heart is beating at all, I walk purposefully towards the burial mound.

The hieroglyphs on the stone marker mean nothing to me, but I study the woven reed covering that serves as a door. The coin burns a hole in my palm as I push the door aside. Musty air swirls around me and fills my nostrils. It's dark and silent. A single, lonely wooden sarcophagus rests in the center. A few shoddy ceramic jars line one side. There isn't a single shabti or item here to help the dead in their afterlife. It looks like a rushed job. A forgotten soul with no way to find rest.

But I'm not a dead Egyptian from three thousand years ago. And I know the truth of the Underworld and can see what the lost soul can't. In the far corner is an opening, a tunnel leading directly to the river where the dead can cross if they know how to pay. I grit my teeth, ignoring the fear coiling in my belly, and step forward.

'Stop,' a heavy, deep voice calls from within the tomb. 'This is not your path.'

Ice lodges in my skin, cracks deep into my bones. A figure, tall and broad, waits for me in the darkness. A guardian, just like Jae said there would be, to stop wandering souls and intrepid mortals from walking a path not designed for them.

'I am not trying to cross,' I say slowly, testing my vocal cords. I want to drop to my knees with relief. I'm not dead, not yet anyway, or the tomb guardian would have let me through.

'Then turn back,' the figure says before stepping fully into the dim light of the near-empty chamber. One of the jackal-headed men – a Cynomorpha – emerges. He looks just like the depictions on tomb walls, a dark-skinned man with the head of a jackal. But his eyes aren't canine or empty; they're intelligent and they glint in the darkness. He holds a wicked-looking sword at his side, hanging near his delicately embroidered tunic.

'I need help finding someone, and a guide to take me to them and bring us both back to this spot safely.'

The Cynomorpha cocks his head to the side and I glimpse sharp teeth. 'And why would you think to ask me, little human?'

Maybe I should have listened to Jae better. Coming to this dusty tomb was a mistake, but I'm in too deep to back out now.

I square my shoulders. 'I'm able to pay handsomely. All I request is that you guide me. You know the valleys and tombs and tunnels of this world.'

'Payment?' He laughs, the huffing sound bizarre coming from his snout. 'I have been rewarded for valor by gods of my world and others. I have lived a human life and died a human death and have been crowned with endless glory. What could you pay me?' He leans in close and bares his teeth in a warning.

I open my hand. The brass coin glimmers. The Cynomorpha looks down at it and the coin seems to burn like gold for a moment.

Please work.

His human hand reaches out slowly, reverently. 'In exchange you ask that I take you to a soul and then bring you back?'

'Yes, but we both must be kept safe until we leave the Underworld.'

'Whom do you seek?' His deep voice crackles with excitement.

'Violet Emmerson.'

He reaches out, fingers seeking the coin. I snatch it back, holding my hand above my head in warning. His black eyes glint and he snarls, his hand on the hilt of his sword.

'Can you find her?' I demand, making my voice steady and authoritative.

He slowly drops his hand from the hilt of the weapon and rubs his chin. I shudder at the human gesture on such an inhuman face.

'I know her,' he growls, eyes trained on my closed fist. 'All guardians do at this point. She has angered gods from many lands for her actions on both sides of the river.'

'Can you take me to her?'

His canine eyes meet mine in a battle of wills. But then he nods. 'I can. It won't be easy, but I will take you to her and return you to this valley. What happens after is none of my concern.'

'Deal.' I hold out the coin. He snatches it up greedily, slipping it under his tongue. I blanch and try to avoid staring as he shuts his eyes, as if savoring a fine wine.

He shudders and his snout morphs. It takes me a long moment to realize he's smiling.

'Follow me, little human. I hope you are not afraid of hungry gods.'

# 30

The limestone walls of a tomb press down. We are in a low, narrow tunnel. The Cynomorpha walks ahead, his broad shoulders nearly brushing the encroaching walls. After he ate the coin, he waved his hand and summoned a strange passage lined with paintings and mosaics. Egyptian paintings, Babylonian carvings and Hellenistic murals decorate the sides, an eclectic mix of art, undulating and shifting. A peculiar mix of religions and mythologies and beliefs in a constant state of flux.

Amenemopet – apparently, that was his name when he was mortal – walks steadily on, hardly bothering to speak to me. I dragged his name out of him after what felt like hours of hiking through a labyrinth of tombs and tunnels. He acted as if names didn't matter. He hadn't had one since he died.

'Where are we?' I ask, after enduring his otherworldly silence for another few hours. I hug myself to keep from shivering in the dank underground caverns.

'The rivers flow above us,' Amenemopet says gruffly. 'Every time and age in human history runs in that water. We shift and change here, as often as the winds, and let the branches of the great rivers guide us where we wish to go.'

I'm not brave enough to ask anything else. I need to bring Violet home. To get answers. We can find Jae together, wherever he is.

I'm so full of nervous energy that I don't notice when my Cynomorpha guide stops. I slam into his back and bounce off, arms pinwheeling to keep myself from toppling onto the hard ground.

'What –?' I don't get the chance to finish the question.

Amenemopet's arm snaps out, hitting me in the stomach so hard I grunt and fall on my backside. I glare at him before I see what he just saved me from. A yawning pit of darkness, vast and deep, stretches ahead in a long, snakelike canyon. The ceiling above us is high and littered with pinpricks of light. Stars.

'A trial for the dead,' Amenemopet explains, not offering to help me stand. 'You must cross the bridge. The Fates will decide if you are worthy.'

I dust off my pants and rub my bruised ribs. 'What bridge?'

He points. A reed bridge emerges from the darkness, stretching across the expanse of the chasm, flimsy and swaying.

My stomach roils, and I jerk back from the edge. 'I can't cross that, I'm not dead.'

As soon as the words slip past my lips, I pause. I know that I'm alive, the tomb guardian stopping me proved it. But that knife . . . I shake the memory away. Maybe this is how my sister got to the Underworld while she was still alive.

Amenemopet shakes his head and points to the bridge. 'Most who make it this far are dead, little human. Though you live, you must cross that bridge. You cannot expect to travel with a guide, slipping through the Underworld and all its challenges, unscathed. The Fates will determine your outcome.'

I blink, and my guide is gone. Across the chasm I see him, eyes glinting in the low starlight. A neat trick. One I'm positive isn't transferable to me.

I move to the lip of the chasm and test the trembling bridge with the toe of my boot. It groans and gives, and I stumble back, yelping. Amenemopet stands immobile in front of the opening to the next tunnel, arms crossed.

Sweat slicks down my back. I shut my eyes and picture

Violet waiting for me. Jae marooned somewhere, bleeding and cold. The rules of normal life don't apply in the Underworld. I can do this. I *have to* do this.

I step into the darkness.

Below, the trench seems to breathe. Warm, humid air rustles my curls and fogs my glasses. I hold my arms to my sides and shuffle forward. I hear the snap of fibers giving way. I freeze, eyes trained on the endless fall below. Why couldn't I just walk through the land of the dead and not look back – like Orpheus?

'Hurry,' Amenemopet calls. 'You tempt the gods by lingering.'

More sweat trickles between my shoulder blades and I shuffle forward again, knees shaking. The bridge groans and my stomach does a somersault.

Moving slowly isn't working, it's only making it harder to force my frozen limbs to cooperate. Instead, I grit my teeth and run. The world tumbles and the bridge shudders. I leap for the lip of the canyon just as the thick ropes snap. I scream, digging my fingers into the red rock.

Arms shaking, I yank myself over the side and flop onto my back, gasping for air. My arms burn and I'm pretty sure I just ripped all of my fingernails. A shadow looms over me and I squint up at Amenemopet.

'You did not fall.'

I get to my knees, shaking like a leaf. 'You promised to keep me safe!'

The jackal-headed man turns away and makes for the tunnel. 'I cannot interfere with trials. I can only guide you through them.'

Scrambling to my feet, I chase after him. 'Are we close?'

'I believe so. Time to me is fluid and without consequence.'

I scowl and ignore the pain in my feet, in my throat, and –

the worst one – the ache in my chest whenever I wonder about Jae.

Amenemopet and I walk once more through the endless spiraling tunnels of the Underworld.

'Human.' Amenemopet nudges me with a sandaled foot.

I slap his dusty leg away and rub at my eyes under my glasses. 'What?'

'Get up. The time for resting is over.'

My back hurts from leaning against the tunnel wall and I feel like I can't catch my breath. But then I notice the soft filtered light spreading through the tunnel. An opening is near.

'We're here?' I scramble to my feet and strain to see what lies beyond. Where my sister has been hiding for so many months.

He sets his hand on his sword, and immediately my stomach tightens with nerves.

'She is there. I cannot fetch her, that you must do yourself.'

I hardly look at Amenemopet. 'What do I do?'

He narrows his eyes, but begins striding forward. 'She is beyond, hidden away in the depths of the marsh, at the place where all branches of the rivers of the Underworld converge.' The tunnel shifts and moves around him, parting like water before the prow of a ship.

'And I just have to find her?' I confirm, hurrying to keep up, squinting as we break free from the tunnel.

Endless deltas glitter before us, branching off in a thousand directions. A waterfall, bigger than any I've ever seen or heard of, pours from the lip of black granite mountains. The sound of roaring water echoes like a drum. My heart sinks as I take in the marsh. It's vast, full of tall grasses and reeds and low-lying trees. A mix of the Nile, the Tiber and the Tigris. Ghostly imprints of the world above.

Amenemopet grips his sword tighter. 'You must hurry. There are many gods that wander this place, forgotten and starving for the power a mortal can grant. You and your sister are not safe here. It is a miracle she has remained concealed this long.'

I chew my lip, scanning our surroundings. Where do I go? Where do I look? Violet has barely been able to make contact with me, and she never got around to actually telling me how to find her. The boundless glittering water stretches into the distance like a funeral procession.

'Go,' he urges again, pushing my shoulder. 'I will wait here and try to lure away the most dangerous of beings.'

Bile creeps up the back of my throat, but I take a step forward into the soft marshland anyway. The earth grips my boots, damp and smelling strongly of rich soil and near-stagnant water. My guide disappears and I'm alone.

I walk aimlessly, trying to feel a connection to my sister. My muscles burn, my legs working twice as hard to push through the thick, muddy terrain. I slosh across rivulets, soaking my pants to the thigh.

I'm painfully aware of time ticking by. It feels as if I've been in the Underworld for at least a day. How much time has passed back home? What if I'm too late?

A light appears ahead, blue and gentle. I freeze, scanning the low trees and hanging vines. The weak light gleams against the surface of the trickling river I'm tramping along. It winks out for a moment. Then it blinks to life, a few feet farther in the distance, before repeating the process.

Water slaps against my legs as I run. It has to be a sign from Violet. I must be close. My lungs nearly burst from the ragged breaths I'm taking, but I don't care. Finally, finally I'm going to make things right.

The light carries on into the distance, guiding me deeper

into the twisting tunnels of reeds and ancient flora. After a few minutes of trudging through the swamp, I emerge into a small clearing. Fog rolls across the surface of a pool fed by tiny tributaries of the twin rivers. Dark rocks tumble from a cliff face ahead, forming small caves and pockets filled with the strange greenery of the Underworld.

'Violet?' My voice echoes off the rocks and is answered only by the gentle trickling of water. I turn in a slow circle and cup my hands around my lips. 'Violet! Where are you?'

No answer. The little blue light is gone.

'How interesting you are,' a velvety voice calls from within the darkness of a cave. 'And I thought your sister was a delightful curiosity.'

I snap my head up and scuttle backwards through the water until my back hits the trunk of a wilting olive tree. 'Who's there?'

A dark figure emerges from the depths of the rocks. He's tall, with flawless dark skin and deep brown eyes. Long gray robes flow around him like shadows. Behind his back rise two enormous, oily black wings.

'You need not fear me, Andromeda. I am a friend to all,' he croons, stepping closer. But his feet don't touch the water. Instead, he glides across the surface, moving like a dancer until he hovers right before me, wings stretching the length of his arms.

An angel? A demon?

'Get back!' I hold out my hands, wildly looking around me for something to throw.

He smiles, teeth white and sharp. 'Do you know what you are, little one?'

I turn my face as he kneels before me, one large hand moving to caress my cheek. I flinch, my breath coming in ragged bursts as I scoot away. But I don't get far before one of his impossibly strong hands pushes me back against the trunk. I'm rooted to the spot, ice in my stomach.

'You and your sister,' he murmurs, his fingers moving to my thigh where my tattoo burns and throbs like a brand. 'So unique. I have not seen your kind in thousands of years. Yet here you are, so unaware of all you could accomplish.'

'Get away from me,' I demand, tugging my leg out of his grasp.

He grins devilishly before unfurling his wings completely. 'Do you know who I am? What I could do for you?'

I try to speak, but the words stick to my tongue. His eyes flash with images, thousands at once. Babies crying, old men grown frail, and every stage in between. He stands in the shadows, unnoticed, unseen. But when a soul falls, withering to dust, he scoops it up with loving hands and brings it to the gates of death.

'Thanatos,' I gasp, the name coming to my lips without my consent.

He grins. 'Reaper, Thanatos, Xtabay – I am Death. But you may call me what you like.'

'What have you done with Violet? Where is she?' My fingers are cold. I can't move. Death itself kneels in front of me, petting my skin like I'm a lost lamb. Sickness curdles my stomach and I want to heave into the water.

'I have done nothing to her,' he muses. 'She would not accept my offer. Of all people she understands what it means to bind yourself to an immortal. Your sister could be a goddess in her own right. But alas,' Thanatos pouts, his full lower lip jutting out. 'She turned me down and has been hiding in this infernal swamp since she came to the Underworld.'

I crane my neck away as he tries to touch my hair. 'What are you talking about?'

Death takes his hand away and studies my face like a fine oil painting. 'When humans are born with magic, the very essence of power, they draw the attention of powerful beings. Gods cannot exist without man, nor can the monsters that haunt your realm. Power is in short supply these days, magic and belief are entwined like the threads of the Fates.' Thanatos touches my tattoo again and it hurts as fiercely as when I first got it. 'When we work together, share our gifts, we can affect the world of man. Experience what it means to be mortal for a time. It is something we gods and monsters like Ossivorus hunger after. So many years of pleasure, of control and desire. Forgotten to us, mere memories in the world above.'

Thanatos' voice drops an octave and he doesn't seem so pretty and vapid anymore. His teeth are the jaws of a predator. His eyes are filled with a ravenous light and his wings are like jagged knives. Death wants me, hungers after whatever is flowing in my veins.

My tongue is glued to the roof of my mouth. My skin hurts, as if Death's icy hand is spreading disease under my skin.

'Accept my offer, Andromeda. I will spare you and your friends from my embrace. I will help you win your little war against that brute, Ossivorus.' He leans closer, full lips so close to my ear they graze my skin as he speaks. 'All you must do is bind yourself to me. Give me your magic and I will give you mine.'

Something flashes across my peripheral vision and collides with Thanatos' head. He gives a startled cry and touches his temple. Dark golden blood stains his fingers, and he blinks in complete shock.

'Get away from her!' A voice, familiar and foreign all at once, screams from above.

Jerking myself out of whatever trance Death put me under, I roll away as he curses in Ancient Greek and tries to fly. But his wings are wet, and blood streams into his eyes. Clawing at the soft creek bed, I pull myself to my feet and run for the cliff.

I don't stop to think, I frantically dig my broken nails into the jagged rock and climb. I slip over the wet stone, my boots sliding, but when a warm hand clamps its fingers around my wrist I look up, blinking through the droplets on my glasses.

Violet smiles grimly and hoists me to my feet. 'We need to get out of here. Death just doesn't know how to take no for an answer.'

## 31

I've been imagining my reunion with Violet for almost eight months. While I didn't have one specific idea of how it would look, I did imagine tears and apologies and relief. But running through a mythical swamp in the depths of the Underworld from Death himself was definitely *not* on the list.

'Quick, Andy,' Violet pants. 'Through here!'

We dive into a thick line of trees. Palm fronds and the winding branches of olive trees grasp our hair and bite at our skin. Mud clings to our legs and sucks at our feet. Violet looks over her shoulder and grimaces.

'Where are we going?' I shout, the roar of the waterfall so close I can feel the vibrations of millions of gallons of water colliding with the earth.

She pushes me ahead of her through thick brush and tangled grass. 'Behind the waterfall. It's the one place they can't reach us.'

She shoves me so violently it feels like I just got hit by a train. My ears ring and I gasp for air, sucking in a mixture of cold water and dank air. My clothes are soaked and I fall to the ground and roll to my side, coughing up water from my lungs. I reach for my glasses, now with a completely bent bridge, and wipe the lenses.

Violet tumbles through the waterfall, barely staggering as the curtain of water beats against her head and shoulders. We look at each other in tense silence as Thanatos shouts our names from beyond the hidden cave. The thumping of massive wings mixes with the pounding water. A shadow flickers beyond the sheet of the falls. And then it disappears.

Violet slumps against the wall, breathing hard. I lurch to my feet and throw my arms around her neck. Her skin feels warm, and she still smells faintly like designer perfume and expensive hair products. She's real.

'I knew you weren't dead,' I sob into her neck.

Violet wraps her arms around me, squeezing hard. I don't even care that it hurts the ribs I probably bruised jumping from that bridge. I don't care that I smell and look like death warmed over. My sister is alive and I *found* her.

'It's okay, little star,' Violet says, her voice catching as she smooths down my wild hair. 'I'm here. I knew you would figure it out somehow.'

We stand there in the darkness, water spraying our clothes and misting our faces. And we hold each other.

After a long time, I pull away, keeping my hands in hers. 'I saw your body in a casket. Mom and Dad buried you. For months, I was the only one in the world who believed you weren't dead. What happened?'

Violet blanches, her tan skin turning as pale as mine. 'We should get further away. I don't want to risk anyone hearing us.'

A million questions burn on my tongue but I let her lead me down yet another winding tunnel. This one is inky black, and no colorful art adorns the sides. Slowly, the humidity in the air leaks away until we enter a dimly lit cavern. The ceiling is high, stretching above us like a cathedral. Soft light gleams in small nooks and crannies, phosphorescent crystals winking like stars. A bed roll lies rumpled in the center of the floor near a low-burning fire.

I swivel to face Violet, my mouth open. 'You've been camping in the Underworld for eight months?'

'That's how long I've been gone? It feels like only a few weeks.'

I cross my arms and move closer to the fire. But she doesn't say more, only tucks an errant strand of her long black hair behind her ear.

'What happened, Violet? Why did you leave like that? You could have come home, told me what was going on with Tooth and Talon – what they were planning. I would have helped you.'

'I couldn't go back home, they would have killed me.' Violet scowls at the flames and wipes her palms on her jeans. 'It's safer for me here. You should know that, since you've figured out everything Tooth and Talon has done. What I helped start.'

I sit next to her, pulling my legs to my chest. 'It isn't your fault. Richard Greene has been doing this for generations – pulling strings and convincing children that magic will solve all their problems.' I shake my head. 'He would have found someone else to revive the society.'

'Maybe,' she muses, still not looking at me. 'But I let it get out of control. Luciano, Regina, the others, they all wanted more. I did too.'

'Why?' I lean closer, reaching for her hand. 'Your friends, even you, had everything on a silver platter. College, scholar-ships, jobs. Isn't that enough?'

Violet smiles, a ghost of an expression I once knew well. 'We could make people tell us the truth, alter their memories, get their money. Luciano's bastard of a father finally saw that his son was capable. You know he wanted to give his shares of the company to Lu's uncle, right? But when Mr Russo saw what we had done, things that other societies since Greene's death only dreamed of, it all changed. We could do anything we wanted, Andy. And I *liked* it. The power to do whatever I wanted to whoever I wanted.'

She sets her jaw and stares into the flames once more, her

shoulders stiff. The cold seeps into my fingers and toes, but I ignore it.

This is my sister; she wouldn't do anything like the others did. She isn't Luciano. She isn't a killer.

'But when they wanted to start killing, you escaped to the Underworld. You don't have to hide from them now. Luciano, Richard Greene, he has to be stopped before it's too late.'

'Luciano isn't Richard Greene.' She blinks, as if the thought is ludicrous.

'But he's the one who tried to kill you, right? He's the one controlling the society.'

Violet rolls her eyes. 'He's just Luciano. Thinks he knows everything. But he's underestimated me, and what I can do, for too long.'

She gives me a brief smile, one that doesn't reach her eyes. The fire crackles as she adds a few dry branches. Scraps of paper, open books and scores of jars litter the ground around us. Even in the Underworld she's still practicing magic. My stomach flips.

'What are we, Violet? Why did we get these tattoos, and why does everyone want us dead?' My mouth is dry as she slowly turns to look at me for the first time.

Her skin is a little paler than it used to be. She's wearing dingy clothes that definitely are not designer, and her eyes burn with something I've never seen in her before.

Desperation.

But Violet Emmerson isn't desperate. She's smart, capable and beautiful. Problems unravel for her and solutions fall at her feet. People bend to her will. This can't be.

'There's a reason we're attuned to magic, to the Underworld. I'm sure you've noticed how easy it is to pick up spells, even stupid, made-up ones from the internet. We can make magic work for us. It comes to us, breathes with us, is part of us. We don't even have to try.'

I shake my head. 'I've never tried. Jae's been helping me.'

Violet looks at me like I'm crazy. 'Who's Jae?'

'A friend from school.' My neck flushes and I trip over my next words. 'He came to Ravenswood to try and solve your murder. He's been teaching me things, but I've never wanted to use magic. I didn't think I could.'

Violet rubs her forehead. 'I thought a psychopomp was helping you. I specifically sent one to Ravenswood to help teach you magic and keep you safe, I guess that must be Jae.'

I squint at her. 'What is a psychopomp?'

'A death guide, of course. Usually they're skilled with magic.'

'I haven't done any magic, and I don't want to.'

'You haven't even *tried*? How'd you get to the Underworld in the first place, or know I was in the marsh?' Violet looks incredulous and crestfallen all at once.

'Jae knows a lot about the Underworld. But that doesn't matter right now, just tell me why everyone in this damned place wants us or our heads!'

'There's your temper,' my sister grumbles. 'I'd almost forgotten how quickly you get mad.'

I scowl. 'I don't –'

She interrupts me. 'Ever since I came to Ravenswood, I could sense something was special. I didn't know it was the convergence of the rivers until much later. But then I stumbled on that yearbook in the library, the one with Greene and the first society. And I got curious. I dug up everything I could. Apparently, they used to practice the occult, but since the sixties it was basically a glorified fraternity until we figured out its true past. Regina, Luciano, Melinda, Eric and I tried a spell I'd found in an old book from the fourteen hundreds. Something stupid, a charm to make a good-luck talisman. But it worked.' She laughs darkly. 'Luciano even convinced his monster of a father to name him heir to the same company he'd tried to force him out of after the last time he bailed Lu out of jail. All because he held that stupid watch I'd charmed.' Violet shakes her head, looking up at the vast cavern like she's still in Ravenswood, watching her first spell come to life. 'After a while, we got bored with parlor tricks. I wanted more. I thought I could find a cure for my cancer. And I did. But that was only after Ossivorus first came to us.'

'What do you mean he came *to you*?'

I've seen shadowy versions of the demon, but he's never been true flesh and bone. Jae said he could only manifest fully during times of liminality or celestial importance, once he's been sacrificed to.

Did Violet summon a demon? No, she wouldn't.

Violet looks down again, knuckles white, her fingers clenched around the stick she keeps poking the flames with. 'It had only been a few weeks since I first found out about the society. About magic. I'd seen Ossivorus' name in a few journals and old texts. I figured out how to summon him.'

'You what?' I jump to my feet, my skin crawling.

'I didn't know any better. Just sacrifice an animal to gain a few moments in the presence of an ancient being with more knowledge than I could fathom. I was curious and had just found out I was sick again. I didn't want to die at eighteen years old!' She throws the stick into the flames, watching as they consume the wood. 'He told me everything. About his deal with Greene, about who I am, and why I was drawn to Ravenswood and to Tooth and Talon. I wasn't scared then; I didn't know how these things worked, or that Greene was still freaking alive and walking around my school!'

I pinch my eyes shut and rub my nose where the bridge of my glasses digs into my skin. 'Just tell me, Vee. I need to know what you've dragged me into.'

My sister stands slowly and looks at me uncertainly. Like I'll burn her at the stake, or hang her, like the puritans in Salem. We don't move to close the gap between us, and for a moment I wonder if we ever can.

'We're not just magicians, Andy. Anyone can do that if they know the right spells, say the right words, or have the right ingredients. We're more than that.' She swallows hard but keeps her eyes on me. 'You and I are descendants of Hecate.'

The ground seems to slip beneath my boots. An earthquake, not the kind you can feel or truly measure, but the kind that shifts your world and destroys the foundations of everything you ever thought you knew.

'Hecate?' I whisper.

Violet is so quiet I wonder if she heard me. But then I meet her eyes and they don't look scared.

She doesn't seem disgusted or frightened or any of the millions of emotions I'm currently experiencing. She seems happy.

*Proud.*

'We're descended from the goddess of magic.'

## 32

'We have to get back to Ravenswood.' I set my jaw and start walking to the waterfall.

Violet chases after me, grabbing my wrist and pulling me to a stop.

'Didn't you hear what I said, Andy? We're demi-gods, or something like it. I haven't really figured out the semantics. But it's incredible! We have more power than we can use in a lifetime. Magic is in our blood; we were born to use it. You wouldn't believe how much I've learned since I figured it out. What I've been taught.'

I pinch my eyes shut and pull my hand away. 'I don't care about magic, about any of it! Who cares if a goddess is my five-million-times great-grandmother? People, young girls, are being murdered back home – and you want to play magician?'

'Andy,' Violet's smile falters, 'I did all this for you. If I didn't learn how to use our powers, demons would be coming after you, smelling the magic in your blood. No one else in our family knows about our powers, or even has them. We're special, Andy. And because of that, demons take note. They want us to help them, or they'll steal our power by killing us. I had to get stronger in order to protect us. To protect you. I knew you'd never be able to do this without me! For over a year I've learned things you can only dream of, all for us!'

'Stop!' I hold my hands out. 'You sound just like Luciano. I don't want any of this. We need to go home, stop Greene, and save those girls before Ossivorus is brought back. Tell me who Greene is, who he's pretending to be, and let's get this over with before anyone else gets hurt.'

Violet's face hardens into a familiar look. 'I can't go home. Luciano and my friends tried to kill me!'

'And we're going to stop them from murdering again! Just tell me who Greene is pretending to be.'

'Richard Greene shouldn't even worry you at this point, I have him taken care of,' she scoffs.

'What are you talking about? The river is still connected to Ravenswood – that means Greene is still alive, and Ossivorus is coming back as soon as your friends finish their sick ritual! If it isn't Luciano like I thought, then who?'

'I'm not telling you.' Her jaw clicks as she clenches her teeth. 'Ossivorus wants me to replace Greene as his anchor. One way or another, that demon is going to be raised. If I take Greene's place, I can help us, help everyone. My magic is a thousand times stronger than his. I could bind Ossivorus, feed him rarely, and banish him again after only a few minutes on Earth. You can't kill Greene until the ritual is complete and I'm grounded to the river, like he is. Otherwise I'm as good as dead, with this sickness spreading through me bit by bit. But this is a good thing, Andy. I'm the only one who can control Ossivorus – Hecate is the goddess of magic, necromancy, crossroads, and everything that keeps demons in their place. Cancer won't kill me because I won't be able to die! Isn't that enough for you?'

I stare hard at my sister. Her face, the one I've spent years admiring, looks fierce and foreign to me now. Her eyes are dark and hard, her lips set in a snarl.

'You're willing to do what Greene did, murder girls to feed a demon, just so you can have what you want?' I don't shout, but she flinches just the same.

'You'd rather I die, waste away while chemo poisons me

265

and takes my hair, my face – everything? I'd never just commit senseless murders. I have a plan, a system.'

I laugh once, dry and derisive. 'What, you'll be a vigilante and only pick serial killers or abusers to murder?'

'Well, yes!' Violet huffs as if I'm the unreasonable one. 'I'd never kill someone who's innocent. And this way, I'll be able to study magic for years without aging, without dying. I don't want to waste my powers on money and controlling selfish governments for my own gain. And I'll be cleaning the streets of another scumbag while I'm at it! I want more than the life I've had, and I'm brave enough to do what it takes.'

'This isn't bravery, Vee.' I hold my stomach, fighting the urge to be sick. 'This is selfishness. We have the opportunity to stop this, once and for all. We can get you treatment – we can find a way to save you with magic, if that's what you want – but we can't do *this*.' I motion to the dank cave in the Underworld where my sister has been hiding. 'It's wrong, and you know it.'

Her face turns scarlet. 'I'm not going back there. Not until I finish my bargain with Ossivorus. This is the only place I can set the enchantment without him sensing what I'm doing. I'm stronger than Greene, than the others. I can bind his power, reduce his need for sacrifices and keep him in the Underworld for far longer. I could summon him to a place far from civilization, where he'd run out of power and be pulled back to his prison in the Underworld before anyone could get hurt. Andy, I promise I can control him. I'm going to take care of everything – I'm going to take care of *you*.'

I press my lips together, the tattoo burning my skin. 'You can't control everything, Violet, when are you going to learn that? Faking your death, hiding for months and abandoning me – don't you see how wrong this is? How much you've hurt everyone who loves you?'

'I didn't *need* you to find me. I wanted to share this with my sister. Not have you try to stop me, to make sure I die a painful, pathetic death!'

'I've already lost you once.' I shake my head, my heart splitting in two. 'I can't lose you again. Not to cancer, not to what you're becoming.'

She doesn't answer, only stares hard at me. Looking through me.

'I have to go back and find Jae and save the girls that are going to die for this.' I start walking towards the waterfall again, wiping at my cheeks. 'You can come and make this right, or you can stay here and hide while I clean up your mess.'

Silence stretches behind me as I walk. It takes every fiber of my being not to turn around and shout at Violet and beg her to see reason. She can't be pushed into doing anything she doesn't want to. But maybe, just maybe, seeing her little sister take control for once will be enough to show her how serious this is.

But she doesn't move. Doesn't apologize or offer to help. I stand, pausing at the waterfall blocking the entrance.

Without looking over my shoulder I say, 'Come with me. We'll stop this and find a cure together. Just tell me who Greene is, and help me save Jae and those girls. You owe it to them.'

Violet's silence is like a knife in my back.

I shut my eyes. 'Please.'

'I can't do that. Without me, you're going to get hurt. You'll understand one day.'

My stomach drops and I fight not to look at her. I square my shoulders and step through the water and back into the Underworld, leaving my sister behind.

\*

Death doesn't find me in the marsh. I walk, mud drying all the way up my calves, until I'm back at the mouth of the tunnel. Amenemopet's silhouette is outlined against the golden cave entrance. His sword is in his hands. The blade is bloodied.

'Where is your sister?' he asks, voice grinding like stone.

'Not coming.' I stride into the tunnel without waiting for him.

The jackal-headed man takes long steps until he overtakes me. He stops, blocking me from storming further into the network of underground passageways.

'Is your sister dead?'

I squint up at him. 'No, she isn't dead. We just couldn't come to an agreement.' I raise a hand and wipe away the tears under my eyes, ignoring the burning sensation behind my eyelids. The way my throat stings as I try to keep my voice steady.

Amenemopet cocks his head to the side in a disconcerting gesture. 'She has made her choice, Andromeda. There is nothing you can do when someone's path diverges from your own. For good or ill, she has made that choice.'

I blink at him through my blurry vision. 'Thanks, Amenemopet.'

The Cynomorpha turns and guides me through the twisting maze below the land of the dead. I study his back, the red-stained blade of his sword, and chew my lip. It's hard not to blame myself for Violet's choice. But how could she think this was the safe option? She wants to kill others, to feed Ossivorus in exchange for health and eternal life. He wants her for her connection to Hecate. How does she think she could control him if Greene never could?

I have to find Jae. He needs my help, and I'm going to make sure I don't lose another person to this terrible hunt for magic.

Sweat seeps through my clothes and into my jacket. We finally emerge from the endless tunnels into the perpetually dusky light of the Underworld. The rivers ripple and weave across the valley and I study their origins, where they split into myriads of deltas. Where the waterfall in the distance feeds them and provides the magic that so many would kill for.

'How do I get back to Earth?' I ask Amenemopet, hands on my knees as I struggle to catch my breath.

His skin isn't even sweaty. His ears swivel, listening for sounds of approaching danger. He studies me without much interest.

'You must use that oil in your pocket,' he nods to the one in question, 'and step through the river until you reach its middle. You must recite words of power when you are there – the words will come to you, if you are using the river to guide you.'

I slip my hand into my pocket and feel the bottle, the cool glass resting against my fingertips. My heart aches as I think of Jae. How long have I been gone?

'Thank you.' I nod. 'I know you didn't have to tell me the way back. Our agreement was just to return me to the valley.'

The Cynomorpha doesn't smile or move or do anything a normal human would do. He simply looks at me, still as a statue. 'You are intriguing, I must admit. You are a rare magic-wielder, one I have not seen in generations. Where your sister has erred and taken a dark path, you have kept magic pure and not used it selfishly.'

'What do you know about magic? About any of this?' My gaze is riveted to the strange man who is not a man anymore. How long has it been since he heard his name? How did he become this thing, set to guard the tombs of the dead for all eternity?

His lips move, almost forming a smile, if jackals were capable of that expression. 'You know I was once mortal. In ancient times, in my homeland, there were many who practiced sorcery. There were many connections to the gods. When a magician and a god worked together, they could create power so vast it could raise nations and empires. But it came at a cost. Often at the cost of the mortal feeding the immortal.'

'Is that what you were?' I swallow hard. 'A magician?'

He shakes his head, eyes trained on the horizon, studying the obsidian buildings gilded in gold on the other bank of the wide black river. 'I was just a soldier who died for his pharaoh. But I had proved myself to the gods and passed my trials in the Underworld. When they asked me what I wished for as a reward, I said I longed to serve my gods for all time. It has been thousands of years since then, and I have seen the endless line of magicians and gods seeking power in this world and the other. I have seen those descended from gods, like yourself, become monsters so foul I was sent to kill them. But I see hope in you. Perhaps you will end the cycle in your little corner of the world. Perhaps you can help us all find some peace.'

'I hope you use the coin well. And maybe our paths will cross again,' I reply.

He nods once before turning back to the tomb he guards. The tunnel disappears behind him. I face the rivers again and jog towards them, trying not to think of my sister beyond, alone in the marsh. Amenemopet is right. She made her choice, and I can't force her to do otherwise.

The wide river sprawls before me. Gray grass and sickly asphodel flowers gently brush the dark sandy bank. Shapes move in the water. Barges float eerily across the surface. Voices drift over the river, the dead enjoying their mansions and endless rest on the western bank.

I step into the water. The cold knocks the breath from my lungs. I thought the palm trees, lily pads and reeds would mean it was warm. But the river is so cold my skin feels like it is cracking and splintering, and I gasp. It takes all my willpower not to scamper back to the dry eastern bank and find another way to get home.

Gritting my teeth, I take another step. The water swirls around my legs, soaking me to the bone. I sink into the water, up to my calves, my knees, my thighs. When I'm almost chest deep in the black river, I finally reach the middle. Soft sand shifts beneath my boots. My teeth chatter as I fumble in my pockets, my fingers numb and heavy with cold, searching for the vial of oil.

Something brushes my leg. I shut my eyes to keep from screaming. The voices on the west bank seem louder than before, their laughter so enticing I want to keep swimming until I'm there, lounging beneath the awnings they gather under. The water tugs at my clothes, making them heavy. I lose my footing a little and slip down the river a short distance, the current strong.

I tighten my grip on the vial and shake my head. Digging my feet into the river bed, I twist the cap off and hold the dropper to my tongue. Three drops. I twist the vial closed with trembling fingers and tuck it into my shirt for safe-keeping. The current seems to pick up its pace, and my legs go totally numb.

Another brush against my leg, firmer this time. I yelp and jerk away, silt swirling around my legs and tickling my skin. What did Amenemopet say I needed to do once I got to the middle? My tongue sits heavy in my mouth as something wraps around my leg.

I wrack my brains, trying to recall the words Jae had recited. What spell had I used to get here? The words slip past my memory like the water around me. The thing wrapped around my ankle tugs me down and my head dips below the water. I flail, my arms heavy as they clumsily slap the surface. I'm barely able to draw breath before I'm dragged below again.

The world tumbles and I scream, air bubbles streaming from my lips. The murky water grows darker as I fight against the thing holding my leg. I can't see much beyond pale skin and dark hair. Wide dark eyes and hissing teeth. Like some sort of siren. I shout again, water funneling down my throat.

I kick off the river bed and suck in more air. I'm still in the middle of the river, but I've floated far down, away from the mansions and towards the rim of dark cliffs that drop off into nothingness. Something waits for me there, I'm sure of it. Something dark and powerful and hungry.

Ossivorus.

My lips are numb as I try to speak. My voice refuses to work and I cough and hack, spitting out the dark water. The pale siren tugs me beneath the water again. The current grows strong and I'm thrown about like a rag doll at its mercy. I kick weakly at the monster holding me down, pushing against the knobby bones of its spine and knees. Its face is hollow and its teeth are sharp. My foot connects with its face and it shrieks, letting me go.

This time, when my head breaches the surface, I yell the words I thought I'd forgotten.

Though I say them in another language, one as old as mankind itself, I feel their meaning deep in my bones.

'*Unto my body may they not draw nigh. Before me may they wreak no evil. Nor follow behind me.*'

An ancient curse against demons, against evil. I can't place the language, or begin to understand how I even know what to say, but the words hold power. Heat ripples through my skin like a thousand hot pokers, familiar and excruciating. Just as that sickly hand yanks on my leg again, golden light ripples across my skin, singeing it, lighting up the dark water.

I close my eyes and depart, leaving my sister alone in the Underworld.

# 33

Groaning, I roll over onto my back, dry leaves and pine needles crunching beneath my weight. They scratch my skin. Cloying soil fills my mouth. I sit up, and a thick layer of dirt and foliage falls off my body.

Like someone tried to bury me in a shallow grave.

Dense forest crowds around the small clearing. But through the branches, and without any thick fog blocking the view, I can see the steep hill where the academy sits. Suddenly, a torrent of memories washes over me. My throat being sliced, hot blood pouring down my front and choking me.

I lurch to my knees, fingers desperately prodding at my neck. It's fine. No gaping wound or gore. I let my head hang between my knees and take a few shuddering breaths. The revelation that I'm totally healed is perhaps more terrifying here than it was in the Underworld

It was too easy to cross through the Underworld by myself. Too easy to use words I don't understand and force the worlds to bend to my will. My body hurts, aching all over from my time in the Underworld. But my skin feels hot to the touch and my head is fuzzy, like I've had a drink or two. Warmth coats my insides. It almost feels . . . good.

My stomach clenches and my skin crawls. I mustn't get used to this feeling.

And then I hear it. Sirens. Their wail echoes through the forest and glens, bouncing off the mountainsides. Even from this distance I can hear them clearly. My heart sinks as I clamber to my feet and limp my way up the hill, all thoughts of what I could do with magic fading as I get closer to the school.

The police are at Ravenswood. That can mean only one thing.

Tooth and Talon has struck again.

By the time I make it into the school, the halls are deserted. Voices drift from the dining hall. I head towards the open doors, slinking in the shadows. The entire school is gathered inside. Most students wear their pajamas and rub at bleary eyes. Teachers and faculty sit at the front, hands twisting in their laps.

'Rest assured that Hemlock Cove PD are doing everything they can to find the missing students. They do believe that this is an isolated incident,' Headmaster Madden says, smoothing his crisp suit. His voice is calm but the skin around his eyes is tight with tension.

Madden nods to a man dressed in a khaki uniform, a badge pinned to his chest and a large cowboy hat perched low over his forehead. The sheriff stands and moves to the front of the dining hall, not bothering to hide his clear distaste for Ravenswood in his stance.

'Your parents have been contacted, your headmaster assured me of that,' the sheriff says, swiping at his gray mustache. 'But we've imposed a curfew on the town and the school. There's a predator out here who is clearly targeting students. Three girls disappeared without a trace two nights ago, and we suspect they were somewhere in town. To keep things contained, until further notice, no Ravenswood student is allowed to leave the school grounds.'

A ripple of murmurs breaks across the dining hall. Older students look annoyed that their off-campus privileges have been revoked. But, for the most part, each face looks worried and ashen.

How many students are missing? I risk a quick glance around the door frame, keeping my body hidden from sight.

'Stay on school grounds, kids. These mountains are remote and the forests are deep. The last thing we need is a group of you trying to find your friends and getting lost, or eaten by mountain lions,' the sheriff says gruffly, blue eyes glowering down at the gathered mass of teenagers dressed in silk pajamas more expensive than his truck.

Madden tugs on his collar and stands shoulder to shoulder with the sheriff. 'We have things under control. This is the safest place for you to be. Rest assured, Ravenswood and the police will do everything to make sure our students and faculty are safe.'

Counselors move around the room, checking in on students as the police file out and head towards the administrator's office. I press myself into a darkened chemistry lab, taking care not to crash into the stands and burettes lining the benches. My throat tightens as I try to figure out what day it is. My phone has been ruined by water – and the battery would be long dead anyway.

I wait until the clunk of heavy boots and the murmur of worried voices fades behind closed doors. Something must be very wrong if Ravenswood is acknowledging it has a problem.

I wait until the coast is clear before I bolt up the stairs and head for my room. Luckily, most students are still gathered in the dining hall, too stricken by fear or grief to do much of anything.

Someone has been in my room. My mattress is flipped over and my clothes are strewn about haphazardly. The contents of my desk are scattered around and every drawer is open. But that's not the only thing that sets my heart racing.

On the other side of the room Munia's bed is in a shambles.

But it doesn't look like someone was trying to search for something. Not like mine.

Slowly, I walk to her bed. The covers have been ripped back, like someone dug their hands in and pulled them half off the mattress. Her desk chair is tipped on its side and the rug at the base of the bed is folded on itself. But that isn't the worst of it.

On the pillow, lying haphazardly on the floor, there is a dark stain. Blood.

I race to her laptop, left charging on her nightstand, and open the lid. It's October 30th. Halloween is tomorrow. I've been gone for weeks. And then I see Munia's tabs. She's been searching for me, contacting friends and family. Her browser is full of research, the very kind that could get her killed.

And now she's gone.

I slap the lid closed and cup my forehead in my hands. The sheriff said three girls were taken two days ago. That means I'm not counted among them.

She thinks I disappeared. Maybe that I died. And she would have known it was Tooth and Talon, even if she knew their club by a different name. My breath comes in shuddering gasps. Munia defended me. Protected me. Worried about me. And they targeted her because of it.

I need a plan. If I survived Luciano's murder attempt, and made it to the Underworld and back again by myself, I can do this.

I dig the heels of my hands into my eyes so hard that stars burst behind my eyelids.

Shakily, I pick through my scattered belongings. Tooth and Talon must have been looking for something in particular when they ransacked my room and took my roommate. I don't know how much time has passed, but based on the dried bloodstain on Munia's pillow, it had to have happened when the other girls were taken. Jae's enchantments must have finally faded. My stomach churns at the implications.

If this isn't brought under control soon, more cops will be crawling over the property. Maybe even the FBI, if word reaches powerful parents.

I grab Munia's backpack and stuff a few essentials inside. There's no way I can just hang around the school right now, not with three girls missing. I'll be questioned, detained. I won't be able to stop any of this. So I change out of my dirty, damp and reeking clothes and into a sweater and jeans. My boots are soaked and crusted with Underworld muck, and I shuck them too, opting for sturdy hiking boots I hardly use.

With one last look over my shoulder, I crack open my window, using all the strength in my weak arms to shove the wooden frame. The air isn't too cold, but I know the unseasonable mildness won't last. Slinging the backpack over my shoulder, I swing one leg over the sill.

This isn't my brightest idea, exiting from a two-story window, but at this rate, it's better than getting caught. I wrap the toe of my boot into some ivy and lower myself down gingerly. My head swims and my stomach cramps as I cling to the side of the building and scrabble for purchase between bricks. Digging my fingers into crumbling mortar, I let myself drop a few feet. Already sweating, I crane my neck and look down. When I can't hold on any longer, I drop the last section, landing on the spongy lawn below, ignoring the jarring sensation in my ankles.

Police cruisers and trucks line the driveway. Officers search the gardens and grounds, dogs sniffing anxiously at their sides. Keeping close to the shadows, I jog into the forest. As I run, I keep close to the treeline, just able to see the school through the openings of the branches.

I have to go back to Violet's greenhouse. I need to find Jae.

When I get to the greenhouse, the sun is rising. Clouds form over the ocean and anxiety rolls in along with them. The tinkling of glass whispers in the quiet as I push aside the decaying plywood door. Shards of broken glass glint at me in the dull filtered light pushing through the grimy panes. I let out a slow breath.

The greenhouse is a mess, but not nearly as wrecked as my room. Tooth and Talon must have rooted through the place, but found nothing of consequence. Most of Violet's ingredients and books are intact, just strewn about as if a tornado ripped through the place.

I drop my backpack and fit the plywood door over the opening again. I hope the police's search doesn't head this way. I need time for what I'm planning, and I can't be interrupted.

I dig through the bookshelf and pull out a weather-beaten, water-swollen copy of a spell book. It's clearly been sitting in a puddle for a while, but the ink is legible enough. Grabbing scattered ingredients, I pray my sister was right.

# 34

The smell of magic lingers in the air. Most of Violet's things are old, making my plan a little more difficult than I imagined. That and the fact that I failed my orienteering course in Girl Scouts.

But I don't have another option.

A wrinkly, yellowed map is spread out before me on the rough table. I set a tripod on either end, with a piece of twine between the jerry-rigged equipment. I weight the bottom of the string with a small piece of amethyst. While it doesn't look pretty, it's the best pendulum I could make.

I take the mortar and pestle at my side and scoop out the fragrant herbal paste I crushed earlier. Smearing the mixture over the glittering purple stone, the scents of rosemary, garlic, caraway and gentian cling to the air. It's hard to see. I only risked lighting one candle, using a soggy box of matches, but I can just make out the colors and shapes on the map. I smooth open the spell book.

My Latin is rusty, but I don't think it matters if I understand every word I say, only that I recite the incantation. I lick my dry and cracked lips and pull back my home-made pendulum. The amethyst swings over the map, the point of the crystal moving wildly across streets and buildings.

'*Ostende mihi illum quem quaero*,' I say slowly, carefully, pronouncing each syllable like my life depends on it. I wrap my fist around the vial Jae gave me, the one with the oil that helps me travel between planes. It was the last thing he touched. The only thing of his I have.

I hold my breath and wait.

The pendulum swings lazily before coming to a rest in its natural gravity-induced position. Just like the last five times.

I throw my head back and drag my hand down my face. Violet said magic came easily to us, that because of whatever strange relationship we have with Hecate, we're able to bend it to our will. But right now, it seems like magic is not bending to the will of Andromeda Emmerson.

Shutting my eyes, I picture Jae. The crinkles at the corners of his eyes when he smiles just right. The softness of his lips. The graceful tilt to his words and the elegance of his hands. I miss him. I want to find him more than anything, to have him wrap his arms around me.

Coldness gatherers at the nape of my neck and inches down my spine. I straighten and stare at the motionless pendulum. The map is wrinkled and aged, with streets labeled that no longer exist. It's from one of the first charters of the town, dating all the way from 1905. But it's the only map I have. Jae has to be somewhere in Hemlock Cove.

A sensation, like a caress, warms my skin. A buzz of electricity starts in my fingers and moves to the base of my skull. I roll my shoulders and neck out, itching at the ghostly feeling. But it's familiar. One I've felt in Violet's room and around Jae.

Magic.

I take a deep breath, screw my eyes shut, and pull the pendulum back. This time, when I speak the incantation from the book splayed on the table, the words are forceful, coming from somewhere deep and primal and desperate.

'*Ostende mihi illum quem quaero!*'

*Show me Jae,* I pray silently.

I open my eyes. The crystal no longer swings. Instead, the pointed end, dripping with my mixture of clarifying and focusing herbs, is frozen unnaturally in the air at an odd angle. Like an invisible hand holds it there. My lungs squeeze and that cold feeling, like a thousand needle pricks, rushes across my skin. Like it did in the Underworld. Like it did when Luciano tried to kill me and I escaped.

I shudder and rub my arms, desperately trying to stamp the feeling down. I bend over the map and trace a line from the point of the crystal. It hits near the bend of the river that weaves through the valley. It's somewhere at the edge of the town limits, where an old orchard once sat. I squint at the yellowed paper and faded ink.

Tracing the roads nearby, I find one I recognize. Elm Drive. The only road that winds up the lonely mountain to Ravenswood. I study the little tracks and offshoots and memorize the name of the curve in the river where the spell says Jae is. Oxbow Bend. I grab a marker from Munia's bag and put a dot on the location. I'm glad I have my hiking boots, because the only way I'm getting to this place is on foot.

As soon as the marker leaves the map, the twine slackens and the crystal dangles limply, like a body from a noose. I wince and yank the pendulum down, scattering the tripods and tucking the crystal into my pocket. The feeling of magic still pebbles my skin. A strange mix of heat and cold and power. I scrub at my hands, willing the feeling away.

It isn't one I ever want to get used to.

I fold the map and stuff it into my backpack and head into the forest. The only compass I have is the one built into a flimsy strap on Munia's backpack. I saw the strap off with one of Violet's rusty blades and hold it in my sweaty palm. For better or worse, I'm going to find Jae. I only hope he's okay.

The light of the afternoon fades as I hike. Stillness and silence prick at my senses and play tricks on my ears. I wanted to stay close to the treeline, monitor goings-on at the school, but that possibility fades with each step. Soon, I'm in the depths of the forest. Vibrant green leaves and ferns decorate the dark soil. Ponderosa pine, oak and madrone trees press in like fingers. Low-lying fog slips between tree trunks, clinging to the branches of a rippling creek.

I stop a few times to check my position on the map, hoping against hope that I know what I'm doing. I do my best to head south-west, in the direction of the old orchard and the bend in the river.

Soon, the meandering creeks grow in frequency until I hear the rush of the river ahead. The ferns grow thicker near the bank and gray stones litter the ground. I pick up the pace, my heart hammering. The sun slips lower, casting warm late-afternoon light across my skin. I break through the trees onto the rocky bank of the river. Setting down the backpack, I take a drink from the water bottle I stashed inside.

I look for signs of an orchard. But the map is so old I don't know when the orchard became abandoned. The trees could be overgrown. Any fences could have rotted. The forest and time tend to eat away traces of civilization if humanity isn't there to push their ravages back.

I check the small compass again and walk for a few more minutes, anxiety twisting my stomach in a vise. After a few minutes, the rushing water jerks sideways, like a snake coiling, preparing to strike. I follow it and soon the deep bend in the river, like the curve of a sickle, appears.

The bend is large, far larger than I anticipated. Tracking the curve of the river with my eyes, I squint into the sun. Light bounces off the water, spotlighting insects that dip and dive along the surface. Shading my eyes with my hand, I lean forward.

A dark shape interrupts the rays of the sun. A dilapidated, beaten old shack rests on a crumbling jetty halfway into the swirling river. It looks like one stiff wind would knock it over, but the weeds choking the slats of the dock are bent. Freshly walked across. My fingers tingle, holding tight to the compass. I break into a run. The backpack bangs against my spine as I go. I barely notice the sting of sharp stone as I trip, grazing my knee. The jarring in my wrist bones as I stagger, putting a hand out to save myself. I haul myself onto the dock, boots pounding on the rotten wood. A door is swollen shut, blocking my view of the interior.

Throwing my shoulder into the wood, I push with all my remaining strength. The door groans and creaks but stays firmly shut. The sunlight feels too hot. The light too bright. I drop the backpack, my breath shallow. He has to be here. Has to be.

I heave my body against the wood one more time. The door swings open and bangs against the inner wall, rattling the entire shack. I stumble inside, coughing at the musty air. It takes a few moments for my eyes to adjust in the darkness.

I blink and rub at my sun-spotted vision. It's an old boathouse. Water sloshes lazily where the river has forced its way inside, shaking the bottom of the shack. Rotten wood clings limply in place. Rusted hooks and decaying ropes dangle from a long beam across the ceiling.

'Jae?' I gasp, fighting a surge of nausea. There, hanging from one of those ropes, is Jae. He's submerged up to his hips in the slow-moving water. His head hangs limply to the side, and his hands look almost purple, suffused with blood.

He doesn't respond.

I curse and fumble across the slimy boards, fighting to keep from pitching into the water. I should have kept the knife, brought some kind of weapon. Clawing my way over to him on the flimsy jetty, I try to keep from crying.

Please be alive. Please, *please*.

'Jae?' I say again, my voice catching. 'Are you okay?'

He groans, barely audible. I bite back a cry and reach for

him, hooking one knee over a splintered railing. His body is limp and cold as I tug on his torso, trying to drag him towards me. But the current is too steady, too strong, and he slips from my fingers as I fight to keep him in place.

I hang over the edge, ignoring the splinters of wood that bite at my flesh and lodge under my skin. I manage to grasp the knot of his rope with my fingertips and pull it towards me, desperate to loosen it. The knot is strong and complex and my shaking fingers slip and ache as I pick at it.

'Damn it!' I scream, hurling my words at nothing in particular.

I swing back over the railing, my breath ragged and too rapid. I'm hyperventilating. I can't stop. I dig in the backpack, searching for something, *anything* to help. My fingers close on Munia's pencil case and I pull out a pair of scissors. They aren't big or terribly sharp, but right now they look more beautiful and deadly than Amenemopet's sword.

Reaching over the railing, keeping one leg hooked over the warped wood, I saw at the rope. Sweat trickles down my brow and runs into my eyes. The rope has hardly begun to fray when I hear something in the distance. Voices? Barking dogs?

I move my arm faster, but it's taking too long. Jae is unnaturally still and his hands look almost black now. His lips are cracked. Tears roll silently down my cheeks as I jump over the railing and into the icy water. Where Jae is only submerged up to his hips, the water engulfs me all the way to my shoulders. I gasp at the cold but work my way over to Jae, hanging onto his belt to keep from being swept aside.

Finally, the rope begins to snap. After one last desperate cut, Jae's arms fall to his waist and he flops into the water. I drop the scissors into the swirling current and wrap my arm around his chest, propping his limp head onto my shoulder.

It takes a few minutes of desperate shoving, but I manage to get his upper body onto the dock. Dripping with water, shivering and terrified, I drag him the rest of the way out of the river. I kneel at his side, pressing my fingers into the hollow of his neck, searching for a flutter. A pulse.

Water. He needs water. I scramble for my backpack and uncap the bottle. I tilt his head up before pouring a trickle over his lips. His Adam's apple bobs and I dare to hope.

'Andromeda,' he croaks, eyes flashing open.

I scream with relief before slapping my palm across my mouth. Without thinking, I throw myself across his body, hugging him as tight as I can.

He lets out a low grunt but I feel his arm lightly rest against my back. 'It's okay. I'm okay.'

'I thought you were dead!' I cry into his chest.

A low rumble, delicious and familiar, vibrates against my ear. His laughter. I can't believe how much I've missed the sound.

'Suspending me over water is the only way to stop my powers. But it takes a little more than that to kill me, I'm afraid.' His hand moves slowly up and down my back as I press my face into his neck. I feel the warmth slowly return to my skin and I breathe deeply, reveling for a moment in his scent.

I sit back, keeping one hand planted on his chest. 'Your hands,' I stammer, the blood draining from my face. 'How bad are they?'

His eyebrows pinch together. 'They're fine. But how'd you know where to find me?'

He tries to sit up but I push him back down, ignoring the way his eyes are focused on my hand planted on his chest, keeping him pinned beneath me. 'I tried to find you, but Luciano – he took you. I had to go to the Underworld to get away from them after they ambushed me in the greenhouse. The whole time I was there, I didn't know if you were okay!'

His nostrils flare. 'You were in the Underworld alone? For weeks?'

I open my mouth to respond, and choke, staring down at where his fingers grasp mine. 'Your hands – they were nearly black. How –?'

'Magic,' he says softly, looking at me with wary eyes. 'You smell like herbs and magic.'

Grabbing both of his hands, I study his pink fingernails, the smooth golden skin of his palms. They look perfect. Even the cracks in his lips fade as I watch. Bruises melting away like they were never there to begin with.

Jae looks at me, an apology etched across his features. I only wish I knew what he had to be sorry for.

'I didn't want you to use magic,' he says softly, his thumb skating along the edge of my fingers. 'I didn't want you to know what it felt like. I didn't want it to change you.'

'There wasn't a choice,' I say, the need to defend myself rising like the tide. 'Luciano tried to kill me, and somehow I got to the Underworld by myself. I used a spell to find you. I did what I had to.'

'Luciano did what?' His voice is low, deadly.

'It doesn't matter right now. There are cops at Ravenswood, and the society took three girls. We have to go.'

He clenches his jaw, tension still tight in his shoulders, ignoring what I said. 'I wanted to keep you safe for a little longer. Keep others from finding out about you.'

My stomach hollows out. 'You mean that I'm a descendant of Hecate?'

Jae jerks back, eyes cautious and wild all at once. 'Who told you?'

'Violet.' When his expression remains as shocked as before, I continue, 'I found her in the Underworld. I used the coin you gave me and she told me everything.'

'You found her by yourself?'

I feel another twinge of hurt at the surprise in his voice. 'You knew what I was and didn't say anything. Why shouldn't I be able to find my own sister in the Underworld?'

'I didn't think it was my place to say.' He holds my gaze. 'Did Violet tell you who Richard Greene is?'

I shake my head and set my jaw, skittering away from his touch. 'No. She wouldn't cooperate – she wants to take Greene's place.'

He lets out a long breath and stretches his cramped limbs. I try to ignore the way his wet clothes cling to his skin. I sigh.

'I worried she might be too far gone,' he mutters, almost to himself. 'Fine. We'll finish this ourselves.' He gets to his feet, moving with such purpose it's like he's going to kick down Greene's hidden front door and choke the life out of him with his bare hands.

'Jae. Tomorrow is Halloween. There are students missing.' I want to scream at him. He isn't hearing me, not truly. 'They've got Munia.'

His face turns ashen, and he drags a hand through his wet hair. 'Tooth and Talon will be back to check on me and use my power to strengthen themselves before tomorrow. We can talk to Pastor Carmichael. Maybe he has an idea who Greene is.'

Jae takes the backpack lying on the dock and strides out the door. I scramble after him, my heart hammering wildly in my chest. The sun has slipped just far enough towards the horizon that the treeline on the mountain blocks the fiercest rays and I can see clearly. More insects buzz along the water-line and cling to the tall grass. But the chill in the air is already returning, chasing the heels of the sun.

'Wait! A few moments ago you were half dead, hanging like a corpse in the water, and now you want to waltz all the way to town?'

I try not to feel hurt that our reunion wasn't more . . . I don't know, special? Besides Violet, I've never fought so hard for someone. I've never wanted to be with someone so much that it makes my heart ache when I'm not next to them. That my lungs feel like they can't get any air. And here he is, acting like what happened to him, to me, doesn't mean anything.

He pauses, just long enough for me to catch up, and then resumes his usual breakneck pace. 'We don't have another option. Greene will be wherever Tooth and Talon is. We find him, kill him, and this is finally all over.'

'Can you stop for one moment?' I make a sound of frustration deep in my throat. 'Tell me how you know about Hecate. Tell me why you wanted to keep me from magic.'

'Magic is dangerous. The more you use it, the easier it is for beings in the Underworld to track you, to use you for their own ends. Hecate is powerful. Her magic runs in your veins. I just want to keep you safe. Keep you hidden.'

'Why? From what?'

'Andromeda, you know why.' He steps forward, one hand cupping my cheek.

It hurts though: that look in his eyes, somewhere between panic and pity. I shove his hand away.

'Stop. Why can you heal like it's nothing? Why does everyone talk about you like you're some sort of freak? How do you know more about me and my sister than I do?'

Jae swallows. 'This isn't the time.'

'It never is,' I say bitterly. 'There's always someone dying, something to chase. But I spent days in the Underworld with nothing but a Cynomorpha for company. I found my sister and lost her all over again. I lost *you*. You can't keep dragging me across this place and asking me to trust you. Not anymore. Not after everything that's happened. Not after I mourned you like you were dead.'

Silence stretches between us. And then finally, finally I see the armor Jae holds tight around himself slip. Just a fraction, but it's enough. He looks resigned and grim. Like a messenger with nothing but terrible, terrible news.

'You already know about my aunt. About my dealings with Egeria and the bits of myself I've lost along the way, searching for my revenge. Turns out when you keep offering yourself to gods, they ask for more and more in return.' His face is dark, his voice even darker. But he moves closer, close enough that I have to tilt my chin up to look him in the eyes.

'What do they ask?' My voice feels thick as he keeps my gaze trapped on his.

'Jae Han spent twelve years wandering the Underworld. He looked everywhere for deals to get revenge on those who killed his aunt in a ritual gone wrong. And he found it, only after he'd lost every scrap a mortal has to lose. He asked Morpheus, Osiris, and yes, even Egeria for favors. Gods long for mortal souls and flesh, a taste of what they once had when they were tangible and real in the world above. So, Jae gave them everything he had if they promised him justice. Revenge.'

My blood turns as icy as the river rushing by.

'Jae,' I whisper, feeling sickness creep into my bones. 'Please.'

'Do you know what it's like, Andromeda, to waste away and become nothing but a shade, a shred of something, when you were once stronger than any human could imagine? Can you imagine the pain of being forgotten, cast aside, buried under sand and rubble for millennia? Jae found his way to the west bank without being dead. There's only one way to do that.'

'How?' I ask, voice barely above a whisper.

Jae nods imperceptibly, like he wants me to ask, wants me to understand the toll that hangs in his words. 'He gave himself up entirely. No soul, no body. But he didn't care, so wracked with hatred and the need for justice and revenge, he would accept oblivion. Most beings of the Underworld would not be able to perform such a task. All but one. Jae searched for years to find the one that rested in an endless slumber. The one that was hungry to taste mortality once again.'

The world spins on its axis, tilting and listing like a sinking ship. *Acta deos numquam mortalia fallunt.* Mortal actions never deceive the gods. A warning written on a scrap of paper so long ago it feels like another lifetime, another Andy who read those words and plunged headfirst into this world of shadows and smoke.

'Gods can see past human squabbles, even if they once took part in them so long ago, when they ruled their patches of desert and ocean. Human piety in exchange for blessings and riches. That's what every mortal has ever offered when dealing with a god. But not Jae. He wanted justice. For things to be made right.'

'Jae.' I take a step back. Another. And another.

His eyes are so dark they could be black.

'No,' he says, that deep sonorous voice I've heard a handful of times before ringing through the small glen. 'I'm not Jae. Not really.'

My fingers close around the compass in my pocket. Air squeezes into my lungs and I blink rapidly, pushing traitorous tears back.

No, no, no.

'What are you?' The words are a whispered curse on the air, torn from my mouth and charged with hatred and fear and betrayal.

His face seems to ripple and change. 'Like I said, Andromeda. Mortals never deceive the gods. It's always the other way around.'

# 35

'You're a god.' My voice sounds hollow. Dead. Every cell in my body screams that I need to run, to flee and hide from this boy, this . . . liar.

He nods slowly. A hunter with its prey held captive between sharp teeth.

'Why?' I gasp, my heart aching in a way it hasn't since I thought my sister died. 'Why possess Jae? Why come here?'

'Isn't it obvious? To feel something again. In the form of a god, I am nothing but power and intangible impulses. Having a body, I can be something. Someone.'

I shake my head, fingers gripping the compass tight. 'Who are you?'

'A psychopomp, a death guide. But it doesn't make me any different, Andromeda. I'm still the same person. I just thought you'd get on better with a boy than a devil.'

'You're a god. A death god,' I snarl, anger overcoming the shock in my frozen limbs.

'Death guide,' he corrects, the ghost of a smile on his lips.

For a moment that glimmer of humor feels so human, so like *us*, that I falter. But that smile, heartbreaking and handsome, doesn't belong on this face. Something swims beneath the surface, wearing Jae's skin like a coat. Nausea whirls in my stomach.

'What is your name?' I press my fingers to my burning tattoo. My thigh aches like a brand, heat curling up my skin. A warning? Violet enchanted this tattoo to protect me.

His smile fades and a certain sadness creeps into his eyes. I ignore it.

'Anubis, Hermes, Azrael – call me what you like. They're all the same to me.'

I squeeze my eyes shut and take a rattling breath. Anubis. Death guide. God. Who is the boy I've been following, the boy I trusted with everything I had? Why did I ignore the signs of his extraordinary abilities? The healing, the strange knowledge, the way others reacted to him. It hurts almost as bad as Violet refusing to help me.

I clench the compass so hard in my fist, the metal edges bite into my palm, cutting, digging in. Hot anger and shame boil inside me and I hurl the compass at his face with all the strength I have left, letting out a ragged cry.

And I run.

Blurred patches of green and gray and blue flash before my eyes. I'm not sure how long I've been running, only that the sun has dipped far enough for dusk to settle on the valley. My throat burns as I try to suck in air and I trip over a slick rock, plummeting to the forest floor. I roll onto my back, tears burning my eyes, coursing down my cheeks.

Jae isn't human. Not really. This is worse than anything I ever imagined. A shiver goes down my spine as I realize a god has been toying with me, using me for weeks. Why? Because somewhere along my family tree an ancestor got a little too friendly with Hecate? Because the boy whose body he stole once lost an aunt like I lost my sister?

Tree branches snap, and I hold my breath. Listen. I wonder if it's the police, their dogs tracking my scent through the forest. I scramble to my feet, sniffing and wiping at my nose. It's hard to see where I'm going in the gray light of dusk, made worse by my stupid, self-serving tears. So, I don't see the strange curl of black smoke emanating from the ground when I take a step forward. Or another. Until I collide with something I thought was a tree trunk but instead is very warm.

I scream.

'Andromeda!' Jae's arm snakes around my waist and his other hand seals my mouth, silencing my scream. 'Stop, just listen to me for a moment.'

I struggle like a fish on a line, kicking and twisting against him. But his arms are like steel bands and I succeed only in tiring myself out and bruising my own skin. Black smoke clings to his body, curling off his arms and face. As I fight, the smoke dissipates and the distinctive scent of the Underworld lingers in the air. He must have traveled through its planes to cut me off. Of course he would – he belongs to the Underworld.

I scream against his palm, kick at his shins, jerk my elbows towards his stomach – but he doesn't flinch. My muscles burn. Fatigue and exhaustion take hold. I don't know how long I struggle, only that I feel drained and broken and hopeless. Finally, when it's clear I'm too tired to fight anymore, his grip loosens and he sets me back on my feet.

'Andromeda, please, let me explain.'

'Don't call me that. You've done nothing but lie to me.' I wipe my cheek and glare into the forest. I can't look at him. I can't see those brown eyes and that smile and risk getting confused again.

'I couldn't tell you what I was. You wouldn't have believed me anyway. But I wasn't lying about my – Jae's – life. His story.'

Despite myself, I look up. 'But you aren't him! You're wearing his face but you're something else. You're everything you warned me about – dangerous and selfish.'

'Andromeda –' He catches himself. '*Andy*, I couldn't tell you. You have to understand that. I've been keeping the promise I made to Jae twelve years ago in the Underworld. I've been hunting down every person connected to the society

293

that killed his aunt. People who tamper with magic for their own gain, who kill and use demons and gods to get power over other humans.'

I grit my teeth, fighting a sense of revulsion at every touch, every thought I've ever shared with him. 'Stop acting like you're being noble. You're everything you've said the gods are. You're getting what you want, the mortal experience, without the pain and death that comes with it, at the cost of somebody else's soul. You're a monster.'

Jae – Anubis – whatever I'm meant to call him, jerks back. 'Jae would have died and faded away entirely in the Underworld if I hadn't intervened. He'd lost every bit of his soul in exchange for deals and was hanging on by a thread.'

'So, you swooped in and took what you could? A human body inhabited by a god, so you could traipse around the mortal world doing whatever you wanted? To whoever you wanted?'

I enjoy the heat of anger. I can handle that. I can't handle the twinge of pain, the ache in my bones when he makes me want him.

He shakes his head, eyes fierce, and steps forward until my back is pressed against the damp bark of a tall pine tree. His brown eyes seem to glow in the dark, and even though night has almost entirely fallen, I can still see the details of his face, the gentle swoop of his hair.

'I thought after all this, you'd know me better.'

I tip my chin up. 'I don't know you at all.'

He speaks slowly, voice bitter and full of longing. 'Jae found me on the west bank, buried so deep in my own magic I'd slumbered for thousands of years. Jae was practically dead. He would have ended up as another lost shade trapped between the banks forever. He begged me to help him, to avenge his aunt and stop mortals from tampering with things that destroy lives and taint the world in evil. I was intrigued by his bravery, his desperation. I'd felt those feelings before, long ago, when I was powerful. When I had a body and could be *more*.'

He looks away, dark eyes reflecting the soft light. For a moment I think I can see his face shift and change in the dark. Move from something lupine to something bright and noble. The face of a god.

'I can't trust anything you say, anything you do. Now let me go.'

I try to slip under his arm, to run again. To escape this feeling growing in my stomach, that rush of heat and fear. But he grabs my arm and pulls me back, placing his palms on either side of my head. I'm pinned in place, caged by his arms. His scent is everywhere, spicy and rich and intoxicating. I want to close my eyes, but I can't seem to tear myself away. His eyes are too deep, too *other* to ignore.

'No,' he says stubbornly. 'You need to hear this. You need to understand why I've been drawn to you, to your sister, to Ravenswood. I didn't understand before, but I think I do now.'

'You're insane if you think I'll ever listen to you again.' I spit as much venom into my words as I can. 'You're a god. A liar. You'll do anything, say anything to get what you want.'

'I'm a god,' he agrees, eyes dark and hard. 'But I don't want to siphon power like Ossivorus or Egeria. I just want to *feel* again. I want to be more than a shadow but not what I was thousands of years ago. I'd give anything to –'

'What?' I snarl, my voice cracking. 'What explanation do you possibly have for all this?'

Jae takes in a sharp breath and releases it slowly, like he's trying to calm himself. Our chests rise and fall rapidly, and I ignore the way our bodies brush together, the electricity that it sends shooting up my spine.

Finally, he speaks, his words almost a caress. 'For the first time in eons I *wanted* to help. As a death guide, I can cross boundaries other gods cannot. My role when I lived above, in the human realm, was to help souls on to the next life. When the last great ancient empires fell, so did I. Jae reminded me of my purpose. So I made a deal with him. He followed the path of Anubis – a way to be reborn. I would save his soul, make sure he could rest on the west bank forever with Min-Jun, and I would get his body. I would hunt down those who were using powers that should not be abused. I would make things right.'

I don't respond. I can only watch as one of his hands moves slowly to trace a line along my neck, his fingers curling at the back of my skull, forcing me to look into his eyes. I try to jerk my chin away, to pull my face from his grasp, but my hair catches on the rough tree behind me. I'm not sure I'm breathing anymore.

'We both got what we wanted. Jae could rest knowing I would finish his mission. And I was torn from my endless purgatory, kept from fading into nothing like so many others. It had been so long,' he murmurs, his thumb stroking the sensitive skin behind my ear. 'Centuries since I could remember my role. I was created to help mortals, to give them peace in their eternity. What could be better than to find a way to do so directly?'

He pauses, as if waiting to see if I'm going to run again. To scream and beat at his chest and curse him for everything he's put me through. For every lie he's told. But I'm pinned by his gaze, by the little shocks running down my skin. And I hate the fact that part of me feels sympathy for him, for a god that has lied to me.

*A trick,* I remind myself. *He's trying to play you, Andy, to use you like everyone else.*

'I wanted to be complete again,' he whispers, his eyes tracing my face. 'To grow and change and learn in a way that's only possible if you experience the mortal world. I wanted to feel everything, Andy. Not just the pleasure, but the pain and loss too, so I could keep my promise to Jae. And when I heard of Tooth and Talon, saw your sister in the Underworld, I knew that's where I needed to go next. But it wasn't just the last step towards finishing Jae's revenge, the last link to the people who killed his aunt twelve years ago. I could sense something was waiting for me at Ravenswood. And I know it was you I was waiting for.'

'Me?' My voice is scratchy and breaks. 'You don't need me. You need Violet to figure out who Greene is.'

Jae shakes his head and leans a little closer. My mouth goes dry and my fingers are numb, hanging limply at my side. I hate him, right? Hate everything he's said and done to me, manipulated me into feeling for him, so he could get information. I should want to punch him in the face, not be admiring the curve of his jaw or the way his eyes spark when he looks at me. But my fists do nothing, betraying me.

'Not for Greene. It's not about Tooth and Talon.' He hesitates for a moment. 'Andromeda, you're a descendant of Hecate, and with that comes power you can't imagine. But you're also a fiercely loyal sister and friend. You're brave and good. I needed you so I could finally understand what drove Jae to do what he did. To sacrifice everything for someone else. To know what it meant to be human.'

'You've figured it out, then? Tell me,' I ask, my voice ragged. 'Tell me what it means to be *human*.'

He leans closer and I place my hands on his chest, stuck somewhere between wanting to push him away and drag him closer.

'I didn't know gods were capable of feeling it.' He licks his lips and my eyes follow the motion. 'But maybe it's because of what Jae did. I don't really care. All I know is that I need you, Andromeda. I need you more than I need to breathe, than I need to sleep. I would burn the world down for you if you only asked. I've never felt that before as a god. Felt *this*.'

His other hand moves to cup my jaw, his thumb tracing my lower lip. I can't feel my feet anymore and I wonder briefly if I'm imagining this. If I maybe drowned in that water trying to cut him down.

'Whenever Tooth and Talon threatened you, when you were scared or hurt or lost, I wanted nothing more than to make it right. To find Violet, to end your suffering and break every law I'm bound by. That isn't what a god is fated to do. To care for someone more than themselves.'

For a moment I think he looks frightened. The aura of power, the strength in his limbs, and the confidence he has seems to waver. He doesn't seem so godlike right now. It's like he's the same boy I've wanted to simultaneously punch and hold for the past few months. Just a boy and nothing more.

Suddenly, he bends down and presses his lips to mine, and every thought flees my mind except for him. How good he smells; how warm he is. How my chest squeezes when his fingers tighten in my hair and pull me closer against him. His lips are soft but urgent against mine. Hungry and desperate, like he's afraid I'm going to turn to smoke and slip through his grasp.

I wrap my arms around his neck, letting myself get swept away by his kiss. I vaguely feel the scratch of bark at my back as he presses against me, like if he can just hold me tight enough everything will be okay. For a moment I don't care that he's a god, that he isn't really Jae. Heat spreads through my body, and when my breath is gone and my lips are bruised, I manage to pull back.

He rests his forehead against mine, his breath equally as ragged. He loops one arm around me, his hand resting on my hip, hugging me close against the heat of his body.

'I care about you, Andromeda. I need you.'

I open my mouth to answer, to do *anything*, but nothing happens. My chest squeezes painfully, aches and burns in a way that isn't entirely pleasant. My silence doesn't deter Jae. He leans in again, and his lips are warm and feel so good I can almost pretend he didn't just say those words. That I don't believe him.

His fingers tug at my hair, holding my head at just the angle he wants. My eyelids flutter and I dig my hands into his chest, run them along his shoulders. His breath hitches and his hands slip under the hem of my shirt, his fingers pressing against my hips and crawling up my ribs.

Just as the tenor of his kiss turns desperate, like he's trying to ply the same words from my lips, a snapping sound startles us both. Embarrassment heats my cheeks as I realize how entwined we are, how his hand is on the bare skin of my hip under my shirt and how I've knotted his glossy black hair between my fingers. How stupid I am for letting that happen. For letting him manipulate me again. I pull myself away from him, as fast as lightning, my heart pounding.

'Did you hear that?' I whisper.

He nods and holds a finger to his lips – his very soft and very kissable lips. My mouth goes dry, loathing and shame battling for supremacy in my heart.

Without my senses being clouded by Jae and his smell and his hands, I can tell where the snapping is coming from. A lumbering sound, like someone running, or an animal fleeing a predator.

'Stay behind me,' he commands.

A flash of red and gray winks between the branches. My

heart thuds. Two people moving fast through the forest, coming from the direction of the boathouse. They know Jae is gone.

Before I have the sense to scream at him to run, our two pursuers emerge from the trees. Regina, her legs spattered with mud and sporting a fresh cut on her cheek, spots me and her mouth drops open. And then Eric lumbers into the clearing behind her.

I forgot how tall he was, how heavily built, like a freaking linebacker. His eyes zero in on Jae and he pulls a gun from his red puffer jacket. A gun? It seems ludicrous for some reason, a logical and powerful weapon, when I've come to expect magic and mirrors. Nausea swells in my stomach as we stare at one another.

Jae is wound tight, coiled like a spring.

'Looks like your little girlfriend found you,' Eric snarls, cocking the gun.

'Eric,' Regina hisses, one of her hands steadying his arm, 'that won't kill him.'

He shrugs her hand away. 'It's worth a try. We just need to slow him down, siphon his powers like Lord Ossivorus asked, and be done with this.'

I flick my gaze between the four of us. Jae doesn't move, but his eyes are dark, a warning scrawled across his stone-like features. Regina's eyes widen as she stares at Eric, and she takes a tiny step back. That's the only warning before the air in front of Eric explodes.

'*No!*' I scream, the sound echoing through the forest with the crack of the gunshot.

The world crashes to a standstill. The forest is silent for a moment. All I can hear is the frantic pulse of blood through my ears. Jae looks down at his chest where a bloom of dark red stains the front of his shirt. He falls to his knees.

'Get her,' Eric commands, pointing the muzzle of the gun at me before I can run to Jae.

Regina flinches, her face so pale I think she might faint. She pulls a matching gun from her coat, her hand shaking.

Jae groans and Eric swings the gun in his direction again. White panic flashes through me and I lunge for Jae, throwing myself between him and the weapon. It doesn't matter if a gun can't kill a god. He's in a mortal body that bleeds as much as it heals. And the sight of all that blood welling between my fingers as I press one hand to his chest feels only too real.

Eric snarls and stalks into the clearing, standing over Jae and me. He raises the gun to my temple, but I kick at him, my boot connecting with his chest and leaving a muddy mark. His eyes blaze red, his blond hair sticking to his sweaty forehead. The shining metal of the gun glints in the low light.

'Wait!' Regina cries.

Eric hardly spares her a glance as he wrestles me to the ground, our hands reaching for the weapon. His fist collides with my temple and the world blurs. My ears ring.

Regina grabs my shoulders and heaves me off of Eric. 'Ossivorus knows she's alive. He wants her for the ceremony.'

Eric hesitates, his eyes bright and wild. After a few heavy breaths he picks up the gun from the underbrush as I roll on my side, gasping for breath.

'You heard Russo. He wants this taken care of. Both of them.' He nods to me.

'Ossivorus won't be happy,' Regina complains, flicking her eyes around the forest. 'What if he gets angry?'

Eric bares his teeth in a grimace and heaves Jae up by the collar. 'Luciano knows what he's doing. Now hurry up, I'll take care of this one.'

She shifts on her feet, chewing her thumbnail. This isn't part of the plan, the agreement. Regina loves rules and approval.

If I can somehow distract her, convince her to listen to me maybe –

Eric hurls Jae's limp body a few feet away. His head thuds against a mossy rock. Blood spills over his cheek and his jaw is slack. I let out an anguished cry at the sight of his body, limp as a rag doll. Blood trickles from my split brow but I ignore it, crawling towards Jae.

Regina finally jumps into action, catching me by the ankle. I kick, but my movements are slow, clumsy. The sky and trees blend together, spinning like a top. She pulls, grunting as she drags me through ferns and underbrush and into the thick trees.

'Jae!' I scream, my head pounding, my pulse hammering against my skull. I vaguely hear another groan and Eric saying something in harsh tones before another shot rings through the air. I scream and scream, venting everything in me, the hatred, the betrayal, the fear, bubbling over.

Regina curses as I twist and buck against her grip.

'Stop it, Andy!' She grunts, dropping my foot. 'Stop or I'll shoot!'

I scrabble on all fours, my nails digging into leaves and moss. I have to get to Jae, have to help him.

Regina moves to my head, grabbing my face between her hands. The cold bite of the metal from the gun stings my cheek as she shakes me. 'Stop screaming! Do you want Eric to find you next? He'll do a lot worse to you than he will to that monster.'

I grit my teeth, blood from my aching temple dripping into my eye. 'Jae's the monster here? What about you? You tried to kill your best friend. You're murdering innocent girls for nothing!'

'That isn't even his real name, you know. He's wearing that body like a suit. He's a god, and he's using you, and you think what *we're* doing is wrong?'

I take in a breath and kick with all my might. My boot connects with her shoulder and Regina sprawls on her back, gasping like I knocked the wind out of her. I clamber to my feet and stumble through the forest, hanging on to trees as I wipe the blood from my eye.

A thudding sound, the snap of skin hitting skin. I gasp and squint in the darkness. Eric lies motionless on the ground, his red puffer jacket standing out like a beacon. Jae hunches over him, his fist colliding with his face again and again. Eric's body flails limply, weakly fighting off the attack.

'Stop!' I race over to Jae and grab his wrist, yanking as hard as I can. 'You can't kill him.'

He looks up at me, eyes wild and angry, seeing right through me. 'Why shouldn't I? He was going to kill you. He was going to make sure it hurt.'

Eric lets out a pitiful groan, and I spot the gun lying a foot away from his bruised knuckles. I move cautiously, like a deer caught in the sights of a mountain lion, and snatch the gun up, switching the safety on before I stuff it into my coat.

Jae watches me, still crouched above Eric's writhing form. His fingers curl into fists at his side as the other boy coughs and spits blood from his mouth. I take Jae's elbow and pull him to his feet.

'You aren't a killer, Jae,' I say softly, trying to ignore the tense muscles beneath my fingers. 'We have to stop the others. Stop Greene.'

'That isn't my name,' he says, eyes flashing unfamiliarly, glaring at his bloodied hands. 'I'm not who you've painted me to be. I'm a god, a god of death. You're right to be afraid of me.'

Something in me breaks a little at his words. I want to agree, to blame him for everything. But I can't. Seeing Eric and Luciano and Greene, the blind violence of everything that's happened, I don't see a monster when I look at him. I see someone not quite human, but close. A person.

I reach out and touch his shirt, still damp from the river and now wet with his own blood. My stomach twists and my fingers freeze. He didn't die. A gunshot straight to his heart and he didn't die. But instead of being disgusted, I'm relieved.

'You're still Jae to me,' I whisper.

I want to mean it, don't I?

The steel and fire in his eyes fade and he blinks at me as if seeing me for the first time. Eric coughs a mumbled curse from his ruined mouth, snapping us from the spell.

'I can't just leave him. He can warn the others.' Jae scowls at the other boy.

'Can't you do something about that, with, you know, your godly powers?'

His lips quirk up in a sly smile. 'It's a little hard to use godly powers when you're in a human body. But I can try a spell, bind him in place.'

'Traitor!' Eric spits blood from his mouth and glares at me through his swollen eyelids. 'You should be working with us, not helping that thing.'

Jae takes a menacing step forward, his shoulders tight and hunched, ready to resume beating Eric into a pulp. But I grab his arm and he stops.

'I hope you enjoy burning in hell. Once Ossivorus is gone, I'll make sure you never set foot on the west bank,' I say.

'You can't stop them,' Eric jeers, words slurring through broken teeth. 'I've given everything to them. We all have. If you think you and a single god can stop us now, you're wrong. Every girl who dies, every drop of blood we spill, is for something bigger.'

'You sound just like Luciano.' I shake my head, disgust

burning the back of my throat. 'But he isn't here. No need to lick his boots anymore.'

Eric curses and tries to get to his feet, his eyes burning. 'You stupid –'

I take a step back as he reaches for me, one massive hand aimed for my throat.

Jae moves fluidly between us, planting his foot on the other boy's chest. 'I think I'll bind that mouth of yours shut too.'

Before Eric can continue, Jae chants in that fluid tongue of his. Faint purple light glows around Eric's wrists and ankles, tightening like an invisible cord.

The injured boy flails uselessly around, his lips unable to move as he tries to scream and grab at us. Jae steps back, a satisfied smile on his face. But my blood turns cold as Regina steps into the clearing, her trembling hands pointing her gun, not at Jae, but at me.

'You can't stop this,' she says, her voice high and grating. 'If you do, Ossivorus will kill us all.'

Jae moves in front of me. 'Regina. Put the gun down. Enough people have been hurt.'

'You don't understand. You'll never understand.' She shakes her head, tears streaming down her cheeks. 'I have to do this. I have to kill her. I failed with Violet; I know that. But I can make it up to him. I said I would.'

'I understand.' Jae holds his hands up and takes a step forward. 'Ossivorus promised you anything you wanted. A way to prove to everyone that you're the best, the most capable. But it's a lie.'

She laughs, a high-pitched, brittle sound. 'If I kill her, he won't kill me.'

Regina pulls the trigger.

I jump, my heart hammering in my throat. But the bullet hits the bark above my head, lodging in the trunk of a sturdy maple. She moves closer, the whites of her eyes so pronounced the faint moonlight makes her look crazed. She reminds me of the Goya painting. Of Saturn devouring his sons.

'Stop!' Jae grits his teeth but remains still. 'Murdering Andy won't help you. Ossivorus is going to kill a lot of people if you and the others raise him tomorrow night. Whatever he's been telling you, whatever promises he's made, they're all a lie. The only one he's bound to is Richard Greene.'

Regina laughs, a sharp staccato burst that sounds as unnatural as it looks on her delicate features. 'You think I don't know that? All of this –' She waves the gun, and I try not to scream as it moves wildly through the air. 'It was supposed to be so simple! But then Violet had to go and ruin it. She couldn't stomach the sacrifices. She thought she had a better way. But Ossivorus made us pay.' She shudders and squeezes her eyes shut, breathing rapidly.

'Regina,' I say slowly, carefully. 'Put the gun down. We can end this. You just need to tell us who Greene is.'

'You think you can stop him? No one can. One way or another, Ossivorus will rise.' She wipes at her eyes and cocks the gun. 'But I can secure my place if I kill you. Ossivorus wanted you alive, but Greene doesn't. You're a risk. You and your sister waste the power you're given. If it were me, everything would be better. *I* would do everything better.'

She straightens, her hand no longer shaking. Jae goes to take another step forward but Regina pulls the trigger again. I try to stifle a scream as shards of wood rain onto my hair.

'If you shoot her,' Jae warns, darkness gathering around him, 'I will rip your head from your body and torture you forever in the Underworld.'

'It's no worse than what Lord Ossivorus will do if I fail. I had one task – kill the sisters. Everything would have been fine if Andy had just died when she cut herself on the thorns of the *Subitae mortem* like I had planned! But you,' she points the barrel at Jae. 'You've been in my way since the beginning.'

The gun explodes. Another scream rips from my throat as the flash of the muzzle illuminates the clearing for a split second. I hear a thud and the sound of a struggle. I lurch forward, blindly reaching as I blink away dark spots that obscure my vision.

Someone screams. Me? I stumble to my knees, the damp bed of leaves and soil seeping into the fabric of my jeans. I feel for the gun in my jacket, my fingers trembling. I try to pull it out, but my hands are cold, frozen.

Another scream, this one of pure frustration.

'I need it to end,' Regina sobs, her wrists pinned to her side as Jae leans over her, wrestling the gun from her grasp. 'Make it end. It wasn't supposed to be like this. Everything is wrong.'

Her sobs break through the clearing as she twists and writhes, mascara running down her cheeks. I kneel a little way behind Jae, feeling the strangest urge to break into sobs with her. Regina's hysterical words, her broken voice, they sting like salt in a wound.

I crawl forward. 'Help us put an end to all the killing. Tell me who Greene is. I want to help you.'

She shakes her head, still fighting against Jae. He looks over his shoulder at me, his face grim. I can tell he feels the same way I do. And as much as I want to hate Regina for everything she's done to me, to Violet, I can't bring myself to hurt her. She isn't to blame, not completely. Greene and Ossivorus are. Their hunger for power and their ruthlessness have ended so many lives, hurt so many more.

'Violet is alive.' I study her face, the subtle downturn of her lips as her fight slowly fades. 'I spoke with her in the Underworld. Whatever Ossivorus tried to make you do to her, it didn't work. You can have a chance to make things right with her. All you have to do is tell me who Greene is.'

'Alive?' Regina's body goes slack even as her chest heaves.

I nod to Jae and he slowly lifts his hands from her wrists and kneels next to me. The heat from his body fights the chill in my wet clothes and I want to lean against him, needing something to anchor me. But I don't. I can't.

Regina doesn't try to run or scream or reach for a weapon. She stares up at the canopy of trees, at the tiny pinpricks of silver starlight shining between the branches as tears stream down her face. 'Nothing was supposed to be like this. Luciano and Violet promised I could have everything if I helped. I could be president, or serve on the UN, anything I wanted. But then Greene said I had to kill Violet. I didn't want to. But he said if I didn't, he'd feed me to Ossivorus next. I need it to end, dear God, *please.*'

Jae's fingers reach out and grasp my knee. 'Then end it.'

Looking into the stars, her face blank and emotionless, Regina is still. For a moment I worry she's passed out or comatose. But then she turns her head and looks at me and she speaks one name.

# 36

I hover next to Jae, crouched in the depths of the hedge that rims the back of the school grounds. Overgrown twigs poke out of the greenery, their shadows stretching along the lawn as the sunrise kisses the mountains.

Jae's warmth radiates towards me, but I deliberately keep our arms from touching. He hasn't tried to kiss me again since we left Regina and Eric in the woods. But I can't risk anything right now. Not while my thoughts are so addled. Not while I look at him and feel nothing but confusion and deep, deep hurt.

'If Regina is telling the truth, the rest of Tooth and Talon will be with the girls now, preparing for tonight.' Jae rubs his jaw, fingering the shadow of stubble clinging to his chin and below his sharp cheekbones.

'Even with the police sniffing around?' I squint at the quiet school, up there on the hill. Bodies, as small as ants, wander around the grounds. They could be cops, they could be students. But they all walk the same, hunched over, tense and searching. Waiting for something.

I wonder if Mom and Dad have been informed that I'm missing; if Munia's parents are aware of her disappearance. If the cops are in league with the school administration and are hiding it for as long as possible. I tug at my collar and shift my aching limbs in my scratchy, dirty clothes.

'How much time will it take?' I ask, keeping my eyes forward.

'Twenty minutes maybe. I just need to sneak inside and

grab a few things. Then we can track Greene and hopefully end this before nightfall.' He checks his watch, but it's broken, the hands frozen from their time in the water.

'And you're sure Pastor Carmichael will be able to help?'

Jae straightens a little, his tall body half hidden behind a pine tree. 'He'll help. He's been hunting Greene far longer than I have.' He leans down and pushes one of my matted curls behind my ear, moving as if to press his soft lips to mine.

Ice grips my chest and I turn my face away.

He pauses, the air as still as death around him. Around us.

When he speaks again, his voice is rough and he clears his throat. 'Stay here, and I'll be back as soon as possible.'

'Okay.'

'Andromeda . . .' He hesitates, and my ribs tighten, but I force myself to look up at him. Hurt flashes across his face before he smooths his features. 'If anything gives you trouble, use this. It's the last one I could find.' He holds out his hand. A gleaming gold coin, roughly hammered, rests in his palm.

I take the coin and slip it into my pocket, flashes of another payment flitting through my mind. Before I can mutter a thank you, Jae presses his lips to my forehead and squeezes my hands.

My breath catches, snagging somewhere near my heart. 'Don't let anyone see you.'

He nods before jogging off into the trees, shadows clinging to him before he disappears within their embrace. I shudder at the sight, at the reminder that he isn't human.

I want to fold myself into him, like I did before. That hazy blaze of heat that connected us before everything fell apart. But every time I consider it, I remember the ways he's lied to me, gone behind my back, and buried things I needed to know. Jae knew my sister was in the Underworld, that he could help me find her. And he knew what we were the whole time.

Ossivorus, Greene, Tooth and Talon – they all want me for some dormant powers resting in my blood. The magic that Violet has been cultivating for years. And I know Jae does too.

I take a deep lungful of air, forcing my shaking breath to steady, willing my eyes to stop burning with the sting of useless tears. And I steel my resolve.

Waning sunlight filters through lopsided gravestones half sunk in the earth and coated in a carpet of moss and lichen. The church sits silently in the near distance, the white steeple weather-beaten and peeling. The scent of the harbor, of brackish water and fishing boats, blows in on the breeze.

I hug an oversized coat, one of Jae's, and breathe deeply. He and Pastor Carmichael crouch together next to a gravestone so battered by the elements I can barely make out the vague outlines of what was once the deceased's name.

Jack-o'-lanterns line the sidewalks. Storefronts are decorated with cobwebs and plastic ghouls. Soon, the street lights will kick on and younger children dressed as superheroes, doctors and monsters will run around the town, knocking on doors and shrieking with delight.

Halloween has taken hold of the harbor, of the valley.

'Take a fistful of soil right by the headstone,' Carmichael instructs Jae, cradling the ornate bronze bowl in his wrinkled hands. 'Sprinkle some inside the bowl and along the rim. Andy, take this bag of salt and make a circle all the way around the headstone.'

We do as we're told.

Jae had emerged from Ravenswood a half-hour after he'd snuck in, with an armful of clothes and a bowl. When we got to the church – after changing into fresh clothes, all of which were far too big for me – Pastor Carmichael had looked at the bowl and gone stark white. The priest had stopped us before we could cross the threshold of the chapel and stared in horror at the thing Jae held in his hands. Now, whenever I look at the dish, my heart rate kicks up a notch.

The men kneel in the dirt as I fiddle with the empty salt bag. Jae couldn't risk crossing into the girls' wing as well, so he'd grabbed some of his clothes for me. I sniff, rubbing at the cold tip of my nose with the sleeve of my borrowed coat.

The khakis I wear are too long, cuffed three times and tucked into my boots. We'd had to carve a new notch in his fancy Italian leather belt in order to secure the pants around my waist. But my skin no longer chafes with sweat and dirt, so rolling up hems is low on my list of complaints at the moment.

I'm tugged from my thoughts as the pastor stands and dusts off his knees. I flick my gaze away from studying Jae's back as the sun dips steadily lower. The bowl rests next to the headstone, and Jae remains on his knees in front of it, his fingers tracing the pattern of ornately carved symbols that spiral around the outside.

'I've blessed it,' Pastor Carmichael says and shoves his hands into his coat pockets. 'It should be able to summon now.'

'Okay, I'll bite.' I lift an eyebrow at Jae, but his lips remain pursed in a thin line. 'What is that thing, and what are we summoning?'

Carmichael looks nervously between Jae and me. 'You didn't tell her?'

Jae's shoulders tighten but he continues tracing the ancient letters with his fingers. My stomach drops as the temperature dips. The graveyard goes unnaturally quiet. The cry of seabirds and the laughter of trick-or-treaters become dim and hollow, like we're behind a closed door.

'What's going on?' I take a step towards Jae, a strange

tingling sensation creeping along my scalp like fingers. The pastor stops me, his arm blocking me from moving closer.

'It's an incantation bowl,' he says. 'An ancient spell in Aramaic, written by a priest of the early Church, is inscribed all around it in order to summon a specific demon.'

My stomach plummets. '*What?*'

'Don't come any closer, Andy,' Jae commands, finally looking over his shoulder at me. 'We've cast a protective circle. As long as you don't cross it, the demon won't be able to harm you.'

I try to push Pastor Carmichael's arm aside, but he's surprisingly strong for a guy in his late sixties. He shakes his head firmly, his fingers wrapping around my wrist.

'Why didn't you tell me we were summoning a demon? We're meant to be killing one, not adding more into the mix!'

Anger burns in my belly and I flex my fingers to keep from launching myself across the barrier of salt and clawing at Jae's face.

'This one owes me a particular favor,' Jae says. 'I've kept the bowl inscribed with his name and location in the Underworld for a moment like this. Believe me, Andy, this isn't what I want to do. But this is the only option we have left.'

My jaw pops as I clench my teeth. 'Why do we need this demon?'

Jae finishes his incantation and the bowl begins to glow red-hot. The grave dirt within melts and swirls into a dark russet color as the smell of spices fills the air. He must sense the venom in my voice, feel the distance I've already put between us after he's tried and failed once again to keep his promises.

Jae stands and looks down at the bowl as it continues to glow and the dirt within swirls and shifts like the grains of a sand dune. 'Ossivorus is far too powerful for even a god to control. But I've been tracking demons and societies for over a decade now, dismantling them one by one. Often, they are fed their power by a lesser demon, one I can easily trap or banish.'

'And this is one of those?' I cross my arms, trying to fight the fear that snakes along my skin as the bowl begins to shake and tremble.

A faint sound, metallic and scratching, begins to emerge from within the vessel.

'This one was running a particularly bloodthirsty sect at a private school near St Andrews. After it had driven three of the society members mad with its attempts to free itself from the Underworld, I and one of Pastor Carmichael's colleagues managed to imprison it back in the depths of the Underworld. Using this bowl inscribed with its name thousands of years ago, we strengthened the spell so it could never whisper to another mortal again.'

Sweat stands out in beads on my forehead as the heat from the bowl becomes almost unbearable. Jae remains still, watching as the rim begins to melt and widen like a giant mouth. But he doesn't move or flinch.

'Harold Clarkson is an old friend, he is a chaplain at St Andrews,' Pastor Carmichael explains. 'He was responsible for introducing me to Mr Han.'

'As a being from the Underworld, I'm unable to use sacred objects blessed by any religion to banish or summon creatures of hell.' Jae looks into the bubbling mess of metal and swirling sand that is growing ever larger and hotter. 'Clarkson had been tracking me for weeks. I'm afraid I was not yet used to the mortal world or human customs, and I made quite an easy target for any discerning holy man.' Jae smiles sardonically at the mess before him. 'When I explained who – what – I was, he agreed to help me. Together we tracked the society that had been committing murders and experimenting with dark magic at the university and found their power source, a particularly mischievous demon named Choshech. Clarkson took this bowl from the anthropology museum and together we bound the devil for eternity. Carmichael is the only one who can activate the trap, with a blessing.'

'But why are you summoning him in the first place?' I ask, my voice high and grating. The bubbling mass of melted metal, spice and sand coagulates and rises from the grave like a . . . well, like a demon from hell.

'Hello psychopomp,' a gravelly voice spits from a misshapen mouth. A tall form, with broken wings that seem to be made of clay, towers over Jae. From its mouth drips molten metal, oozing between sharp teeth. Its eyes glow dark gold, and bony protrusions run along its spine and across its chest.

A strangled sound slips from my mouth and Jae stiffens, but he doesn't turn around.

'Choshech,' he speaks evenly, 'I've come to collect my favor.'

The demon lets out a rasping laugh and flexes its broken wings. Its golden eyes search the graveyard for a way out, but its gaze settles on the circle of salt and the mass of the melted bowl sticking to its feet, and it grimaces.

'You've left me to rot in the bowels of the Underworld with no way to feed myself mortal flesh,' Choshech growls. 'Any favor I may owe you will never be collected.'

My eyes widen as Jae's form begins to shift and change. Mist and shadow gather around him like a cloak. His skin changes from soft gold to deep russet, and an elaborate headpiece resembling a jackal rests on his jet-black hair. For a moment his chest is bare and an ancient linen kilt wraps itself tightly around his narrow hips. My face heats as I catch myself staring, but Jae doesn't turn around.

He steps forward and power ripples off his form like bolts

of electricity. For a moment everything goes cold and quiet, like the throes of death. The demon hisses and twists as if stuck by a hot poker.

'Do not forget who you are speaking to, who tugs on your strings, Choshech. It is only by my grace you weren't destroyed when I banished you from the mortal world. If you do not grant me my favor, then I will finish what I started twelve years ago.'

My skin feels frosted with ice as the god steps closer to the demon. Pastor Carmichael remains rigid at my side, his icy-blue eyes clearly disturbed.

'Tell me what you wish and I will have it done, my lord.' Choshech lowers his horned head in submission.

Suddenly, the god before us disappears and in his stead is Jae once more. He nods, as if satisfied with the demon's response. 'Tell me where Ossivorus is.'

The demon looks surprised, a strange expression on such a terrifying creature. 'Is that all, my lord?' he asks in an overly gracious tone. When Jae does not respond, the creature continues, 'The High Lord Ossivorus waits just beyond the weakened veil at the convergence of the rivers.'

'He is not at the convergence below Ravenswood.' Jae shakes his head. 'I checked.'

'The convergence below that school is merely a way to allow magic to flourish in a place where it does not naturally grow. There is another place, formed by the moon and the tides, that connects to the world beyond. Only five miles from where we stand, on Duskmoor Island.'

My muscles tighten at the name. The island is small, seated in the center of the cove, with only a few rickety cabins lining the craggy shore. They used to be rented during the summer but have long since been abandoned. Violet and her friends went to the island many times during their time at

Ravenswood. If you had access to a boat in the harbor, it was well known as a perfect haunt for the braver teenagers to drink and smoke without any adult interference. The perfect place to murder and talk with demons. The perfect place to try to kill Violet and cover up the truth.

Pastor Carmichael curses at my side. He must be thinking the same thing: we should have suspected that the island was where everything had been happening. At the center of the cove where the bodies of drowned girls had been discovered over the decades. But it explains why no member of Tooth and Talon had been caught in the act. Why so many other girls' bodies had never been found.

'Good,' Jae says. Choshech smiles, exposing needle-like teeth, clearly pleased that his service was so easy to render. For the first time, his dark golden eyes, set in that leathery skin, land on me. His disturbing grin grows bigger. Hungrier.

'Ah,' he licks his lips. 'Child of Hecate. The rumors are true. Come here, girl, and I will unravel all the mysteries of the cult of the mysterious goddess. I can show you your true purpose and guide you on your lonely path. All you need do is break this circle and take the bowl for yourself –'

Jae steps forward, his hand closing on the demon's throat. 'Do not speak to her. Do not even look at her,' he growls, his hair falling in front of his deep brown eyes.

'My lord,' Choshech says gravely. 'My apologies. The girl is merely so tempting, the blood in her veins could feed a horde of demons for eons –'

'Silence,' Jae barks, his form rippling between human and godlike. 'I will take great pleasure in ripping your spine from your body if you so much as breathe one more word about her.'

The threat hangs in the air. Finally, the demon nods and Jae releases his iron-like grip on Choshech's throat. The demon sags and rubs at his neck before glaring at the god that has him trapped.

'You must hurry, my lord Anubis. The hour grows near for the sacrifice. High Lord Ossivorus will rise and complete his plan.'

'Tell me of his plan, demon.'

Choshech's smug expression falters as the tendons on his neck stand out. For a moment, I think he's choking but then his strangled words rip from his throat. Jae's favor must truly be invoked now, because as the demon speaks, his eyes snap with so much fury and hatred I can feel it like daggers in my own skin.

'The King of Demons will use the silly little band of mortals he has been cultivating like wheat to protect his vessel permanently. After tonight, he will be immune to any attack, any attempt to banish or trap him.'

'How?' Jae demands, stepping closer.

Choshech grimaces, as if speaking pains him. 'He will turn the puny human that keeps him from slipping into the lowest levels of the Duat with the rest of us into a god. His vessel will never be able to die, not by any being's hand, and will take the Demon King's place in prison. Ossivorus will merge the Underworld and Earth to rule over every being.'

'No.' Jae shakes his head, stepping back from the grinning demon. 'That is impossible. Demons are bound to the Underworld alone, and gods are born only from ma'at; the worlds of the living and the dead must be held in balance. Richard Greene cannot be turned into a god by Ossivorus.'

The demon laughs, a terrible rattling sound, and then looks at me, the hunger in his gaze pinning me in place. 'Ah yes, but the children of Hecate can transcend their mortal state. Those two sisters, so naive and brave. They have been walking into his trap so nicely.'

Jae lets out a strangled roar and slams his fist into the demon's chest. Choshech winces and curses in a language I don't understand before he melts into the earth, golden eyes disappearing as his clay body crumbles into dust.

The metal bowl perches next to the scorched headstone, inanimate and silent once more.

I remember the symbols scattered on the paintings in Violet's room. The ones where an odd river flowed where it didn't belong. Where a djed and an ankh inked every page. Violet knew. She'd been trying to tell me that in the Underworld, between life and death, she had followed the path of Anubis. Her words behind the waterfall click into place.

My sister wants to take Greene's place; live forever tied to Ossivorus. But she doesn't know that is exactly what the demon wants. He's going to use her power for himself, a sacrifice that will let him roam the Earth freely. For eternity.

The three of us stand in complete silence as the sky bursts into the red and orange billows of sunset over the dark sea. Jae's shoulders are hunched as he picks up the bowl with trembling hands and thrusts it at Pastor Carmichael.

'Mr Han, where are you going?' Carmichael asks as Jae turns and begins to march towards the iron gates of the cemetery.

My heart beats in my throat as I stare at the patch of burned grass and scattered salt.

'I'm going to kill Richard Greene before the veil opens, and send Ossivorus so deep into the Underworld his bones will be crushed into dust.'

## 37

I race after Jae, my legs trembling beneath me. I catch up as he runs through the gate and out onto the street, headed for the rusty beige Buick Pastor Carmichael agreed to loan us.

'Wait!' I cry, wrestling my hand free from the too-long sleeves of my coat.

Jae pauses next to the car, his hands resting on the frame above the driver's-side door.

My heart clenches at the way his face and body shift and ripple and change. Anger distorts his muscles, his skin. Shadows cling and morph around him like running water. I can't make out the details of his features. But I can smell burning hair, and I grab his hands before I can think.

'Stop,' I plead, ignoring the painful heat of his skin. 'You're hurting yourself.'

He takes a shuddering breath and shuts his eyes. 'I'm sorry. If I use too much of my powers, it can burn my human body.'

Slowly, the shadows that follow him like loyal dogs drift back into the ground. His body stops shifting and his skin returns to a normal temperature. He opens his eyes and Jae is back, holding my hands and looking at me in the way that makes my stomach flip.

'You need to stay here, Andy. I can't let you come to the cove; it's too dangerous.'

I drop his hands immediately. 'You can't *let* me? This is my fight too, and it's been dangerous every step of the way.'

He shakes his head and wrenches the car door open, fumbling for the keys in his jacket pocket. 'You heard Choshech:

Ossivorus has been using you and your sister somehow. I can't let you go to the island. What if I can't kill Greene in time?'

I step forward and slam the door closed, narrowly avoiding crushing his fingertips in the metal frame. 'You've had no problem dragging me through danger for weeks. Now you suddenly want to protect me from getting hurt? What about everything you've done to me? Every lie you've told?'

Jae shakes his head, a muscle in his jaw jumping. 'That was before.'

'Before what? Before I learned the truth about you? Or was it before I figured out that Violet and I are related to a goddess? You don't care about protecting me, *Anubis*. You only care about protecting yourself.'

We stare at each other, our chests heaving with labored breaths. So many unspoken words. Realization slams into me like the weight on Atlas's shoulders. I'm right, and the truth is bitter. Jae has been keeping so many secrets from me, he's used me in this strange game, this hunt to find and kill Greene, all to keep a promise to a desperate boy. A human he made a deal with.

Beneath the surface of his skin rests an ancient god. He may pretend to be mortal, but he isn't. I can't allow myself to believe he cares about me in any way that truly matters. I'm a means to an end. A knot in the last thread of a tangle of corrupted societies that is finally unraveling. And once Greene is dead, and Ossivorus has been banished to the depths of hell, Anubis' promise to Jae Han will be fulfilled. He'll be free to experience a mortal body without restraints. Without the weaknesses he's been saddled with for a decade.

'That isn't true, Andromeda,' he says, his voice husky and low. 'I'm not a monster.'

Before I can scream in frustration, he pushes me against the car. The cold sheen of the metal bites into my skin as he jerks my chin up and presses his lips to mine. This kiss is different from the one in the forest. This one isn't sweet and deep. This one is fierce and angry and desperate. I squeeze my eyes shut and bunch his shirt in my fingers, pulling him against me. His lips, soft and warm, are rough all at once as his body molds itself against mine.

The heat from his body contrasts with the cold metal of the car, and a muffled groan slips past my lips as I return his kiss. His fingers dig into my side, tearing at my clothes, as we struggle for control. His mouth is begging me to do as he says while mine is telling him I'll never trust him again. A dance of bodies and lips and fevered emotions.

'Andy.' He murmurs my name, over and over again, brushing his lips against my neck as he trails hot kisses across my jaw and collarbones. I let my head fall back against the car window as his hands and lips draw lines across my body no one ever has before. 'Let me keep you safe. I need you.'

Despite the heat, the desperate desire for him that runs through my bones and invades every cell in my body, I push him away.

Those damned words. *I need you.*

'And I needed you,' I spit at him through gritted teeth. I tear my eyes from his face and swallow back my tears. The cold metal of the car door presses against my shoulder and I lean against it before I can crumple to the ground.

I never realized how much I've relied on Jae. On his smiles and guidance, on any scrap of approval or attention he's tossed my way. Just like I always did with Violet. I've focused on winning attention and affection from those I think are better than me. People with magnetism and charisma and confidence. I've always been a follower, desperate for a place to fit in. A person to fit *with*.

Anubis stands so close I can still feel the hard ridges of his body, smell his intoxicating scent. His breathing is ragged, his lips red and swollen. Before he can say anything, I pick up the keys from the pavement where he dropped them during our blind and desperate kiss. My fingers tremble as I open the driver's side door.

'Get in. I'm coming with you. And once you kill Greene, you can go back to hell.'

# 38

The briny tang in the air triggers memories of drowning as we step onto the shore of Duskmoor Island. The last time I was on the beach in the near distance, I nearly died. Now, as I wobble getting out of the small motorboat, dread washes over me. The convergence of the rivers, one of which runs under the school and through the forest, is located somewhere here. A coming together where people can complete their rituals in safety. It could be a spring, a well, or a stream. I can feel the magic pulsing in the earth below my boots. Like a steady drumbeat it calls to me, lets me know that here, in this land, I am powerful. I push the thoughts away, refusing the temptation. I'm not here for myself, I'm here for those missing girls.

Anubis is silent as he jumps smoothly out of the boat and drags it up onto the beach. We stole it from the harbor while everyone in town was distracted with Halloween parties. The bar by the dock was blaring a steady stream of rock music, covering the sound of Anubis starting the engine.

We've killed the motor and paddled the final hundred yards to shore, unwilling to risk anyone on the small, rocky island hearing our approach.

Waves roll against the pebbly shore, making a strange scraping sound with each lap of water. I square my jaw and squint into the thick trees. Abandoned cabins dot the curve of the island, rotting with mildew and warped by the salty air. But they're empty, devoid of any activity. The ritual must be happening further inland where the pulse of magic beckons me closer.

'It's almost time.' Anubis squints at the sky. 'The moon rises in less than an hour. As soon as it does, they'll make the sacrifices.'

I ignore the way Jae lifts his shirt to tuck a long hunting knife into his waistband, forcing my eyes from the strip of naked golden skin. *Anubis*, I remind myself. He isn't Jae and never was.

I finger the gun in my jacket pocket and chew my lip, tasting the coppery hint of blood on my tongue. There are only two bullets left, and Pastor Carmichael didn't have any other ammo or guns besides antique hunting rifles. The best he could offer were the hunting knives the two of us have strapped to our bodies.

Anubis' eyes glint in the starlight. 'Remember, I'll kill Greene the moment we see him. Without an anchor, Ossivorus will be weak enough for me to banish him back to the Underworld. When everyone is focused on me, you can rescue the girls and put them in the boat.'

I clean my glasses on my shirtsleeve as we press ahead into the forest. The only sounds are our breathing and the soft thud of our feet in the damp earth. Our plan is so simple. But Luciano will be there with Melinda and whoever else is helping them.

'What is it?' Anubis asks, pausing to help me over a large fallen tree.

I let go of his hand the moment I scoot over the log, and shake my head. 'Nothing.'

He sighs and slows his steps. The scent of smoke is faint on the air. It curls around my tongue, presses against my mouth, and turns my stomach sour. We're close. I knew we'd arrive at the place quickly, on an island this small, but I'm still not ready.

'Is it your sister?'

'She hasn't been in contact with me since the Underworld,'

I say, keeping my eyes on the trees. I don't want to confide in Anubis, but at the same time I know I could die soon. 'She will try to take Greene's place. All of this I did for her: coming to Ravenswood, following her clues. I died for her, or at least some part of me did.'

I rub my face, jostling my glasses as the heat of my tears mists the lenses. Anubis is quiet at my side as the smell of smoke grows stronger. He steps a little closer to me and I force myself not to lean into his arms.

'Andy,' he says, voice silky and soft. 'You and your sister are descendants of a world even I don't fully understand. She's focused on the wrong things right now because of her own fears, but you're bonded, you're blood. I have to hope she'll do the right thing.'

I ball my hands into fists in my pockets, my throat tight. Forcing myself to look up and into his eyes for the first time since that kiss by the church, my breath catches. Under the starlight his hair glimmers like obsidian. His eyes are deep and soulful, and for a moment I wonder what Anubis truly looks like. If he's as beautiful as the boy who stands in front of me. But before I can risk another bruise on my heart, smoke pushes through the trees, heavy and suffocating. It smells of herbs and incense. Of magic.

Anubis swears and grabs my hand. 'We need to go. Follow me.'

Ten minutes later, we hover behind a large pine tree and stare at the scene before us. It's like a vision from Dante's *Inferno* – hell itself. A raging bonfire crackles in the center of a small clearing. Bones litter the ground in a pattern I can't understand.

And there on the other side of the flames, lined up like broken dolls, are three girls. More bones surround them, interspersed with bundles of strongly scented herbs. The kind that only grow in the Underworld. A bronze brazier burns on an altar of some kind, spitting out orange flames On top of the altar rests a massive pair of horns from a creature I can't place. Like an offering for a cruel god. Ossivorus.

Three figures, clad in black robes topped with antlers, stand together before the brazier. The flames now sputter an unearthly shade of greenish-purple, like a living bruise.

Luciano and Melinda. The third person must be Greene.

My tongue sticks to the roof of my mouth. I know there are more people, alumni, who are helping the society. Who knows where they are? Perhaps they're hiding across the island, watching us. Ready to pounce.

'Do you see Munia?' I clutch Anubis' arm, desperate to stave off the horror of the scene before us.

'I can't tell, they're all dressed the same.'

He's right. The girls are wrapped in long-sleeved, stained white shifts that fall to their ankles.

I stare at the trio standing before the altar. At the person who is responsible for everything, reborn into a new body.

Though their face is covered, I know the set of their shoulders. And if they were to take off the hood, white-blonde hair would fly free. I grit my teeth, remembering every instance, every glance. Their interest in Violet. In me.

Mrs Bianchi. The new Richard Greene.

'There he is,' I whisper, nodding towards the group of black-robed figures. 'Greene has the largest pair of antlers, and they're gilded.'

The figure in the middle does indeed wear gold-leafed antlers on their hood. They stand taller than the rest, sure of their power. A red sash bisects the black of their robe. And then they begin to chant, words so ancient I wonder if even Anubis knows them. I glance over at him, fear turning my stomach to lead.

'Stay still,' he urges me. I'm going to use the Underworld to cross to them unseen. When I appear, that's your cue to grab the girls. Use this, it should wake them up from their trance.' He hands me a small corked bottle, even smaller than a salt shaker.

'What is it?'

'Ein Al-Afreet, a type of incense that Pastor Carmichael always keeps on hand. It wards off evil spirits. It should break the binding spell they're under, as soon as Greene is wounded.'

He stands and raises his hands, about to sink into another realm.

Before he can disappear, I grab his arm. 'The others are going to try to stop you from killing Greene. How are you going to get away?'

Anubis smiles ruefully and reaches out to tuck a loose curl behind my ear. 'Don't worry about me, Andromeda. I'm a god, after all. Just get the girls to safety, and I'll keep the others from coming after you.'

I nod mutely as he drops his hand, his fingers gently brushing the side of my cheek and neck. He gives me one last look before he disappears into a vortex of shadows. I hold my breath and clutch the bark of the tree, trying to control my breathing.

Time moves slowly as I stare at the ritual, my eyes trained on Greene hidden beneath his robe, like it can shield him from the truth. The manipulations. Greene sprinkles herbs over the bodies of the girls, as if cleansing them. Then the three robed figures circle the flame and link hands. They chant as the flames grow brighter and the smell in the air changes from smoke and plants to rot and death. A smell I remember from the last time they tried to summon Ossivorus.

*Hurry*, I urge Anubis silently. I breathe deeply, holding the air in my lungs. When the pressure gets too great to bear, and my eyes begin to water, I see the telltale vortex of swirling shadows, like black smoke. The next moment, faster than a striking cobra, Anubis emerges from the darkness and buries his long hunting knife deep in the chest of Richard Greene.

I explode from the forest and fly across the clearing, my feet hardly touching the ground. Greene staggers, his own ritualistic blade arcing towards Anubis' abdomen. I keep running, aiming for the three girls, even as Anubis clutches his stomach. I smell the Underworld, the stench of death and ash, and his form shimmers like it did at the cemetery as he calls on his powers.

Greene rips the knife from his chest and throws it aside before lifting his hands, face twisted in a hideous snarl, as he recites the ancient words of a spell. A ragged scream, hoarse and high, rips from Melinda's throat as bones rattle from the ground. I leap over a shivering femur, smothering my own cry. Skeletons cobble themselves together, marching towards Anubis, their master.

A strong wind blows through the clearing, rippling through my hair. And once it clears, a shimmering veil rests between me and the fire, like the one Violet cast for me on the beach. A protection charm. For once, I'm glad Jae is really a god.

I run the last few yards as skeletons collapse at the hands of Tooth and Talon.

'Call the others!' Luciano screams to Melinda. 'We must continue the ritual.'

Dropping to my knees in front of the three limp girls, I pull the cork out of the bottle. A scent, heady and pungent, cuts through the aroma of decay in the clearing. I waft it under the nose of each girl, hesitating when I get to Munia on the far end. Her face is bruised, her lip split like she's been hit. Anger washes over me but I bite it back and focus on what I must do. The other girls are strangers to me, but they have one thing in common. As each one opens her eyes, fear floods her expression, wild with terror, like prey caught in the jaws of a wolf.

'Shh,' I whisper to them, my hands shaking as I pull the knife from its sheath. 'I'm going to get you out of here, but you have to help me.'

Sweat beads on my forehead as the sounds of fighting grow louder. Shouts and the thud of stricken flesh. Flashes of golden light and screams fill the air as I saw at the tight bonds around each girl's ankles and wrists. Once the first two girls are free, they help to work at the knots binding Munia until her arms and legs are loose. I try to pull her to her feet, but she wobbles. She's still groggy, eyes cloudy and pupils dilated. She must have a concussion.

'Where are we going?' asks the youngest girl, her hair wound in tight coils around her face. Her dark skin is streaked with ash and mud but she supports Munia with her slight frame.

For the first time, I risk looking beyond me. Greene lies on the ground, the black hood covering his face. Anubis seems to glow with power as he slashes at Luciano with his knife. Even though Anubis is a god, and is as fearsome and deadly as the army of undead swirling around him, I know he can't hold out for much longer. The aura he has cast in our direction is strong, but it's taxing his powers, draining the energy of his mortal body.

'To the beach with the cabins,' I urge, panting and wiping at the sweat on my forehead. 'There's a boat.'

The girls huddle together, eyes wide with fear. I loop Munia's arm around my shoulder, and we stagger from the clearing. The girls are slow, weak from hunger and dehydration. We barely make it to the treeline before the veil Anubis has cast plummets to the ground and the shimmering gold wall of energy vanishes.

I swear and push them harder, shouting at them to run. We slip and slide onto the rocky beach. The tide is coming in, the dark water kissing the hull of the boat. My hands shake as I help them into the vessel. Rocks slide and clatter together as I help Munia aboard, her head resting on the lap of one of the other girls.

The buzz of engines, the clatter of voices.

The dark smudge of another motorboat appears along the curve of the shore, pushing off from a rickety dock.

Voices shout and one of the girls cries out in fear.

'Get in,' I demand. 'How many others were there?'

'I-I don't know. There were those two year thirteens. Mrs Bianchi was there too. Why was she there?' the girl with the dark skin and coiled hair speaks shakily. 'They said they wanted to kill us. Sacrifice us. They said we'd be doing a great service.'

'How many?' I ask sharply, because I need to know now how impossible it's going to be to save Anubis.

She stammers, clearly going into shock. 'Th-they held us somewhere in one of the cabins for a few days. I saw some people from the alumni lunch guarding us. Maybe . . . maybe four others?'

Her eyes are wide, stricken. Her body trembles. I want to comfort her; I want to rip the throats out of every single society member, every alumnus and parent who started this mess. Suddenly the girls scream, eyes focused somewhere over my shoulder, and I know I'm out of time.

I run to the stern of the boat and yank with all my might. The swirling tide does the rest and soon the boat is lifted by the waves. My pants are soaked to my thighs but I ignore the biting cold and reach for the rip cord with my numb fingers. I tug clumsily. It takes a few tries but the engine roars to life and I push myself away from the whirling propellers, staggering back towards the beach.

331

The other boat scrapes the shore a few hundred feet away as it tries to turn towards the fleeing girls. The motor revs and then stalls as the engine floods. A tiny miracle. Whoever is helping Tooth and Talon will be stuck on this island with me.

'Go!' I shout at the girls as they crest a breaking wave. 'Get to the shore and then to the church. The pastor is waiting for you. Keep Munia safe!'

Luckily, one of the girls staggers to the back of the boat, grabs for the tiller and stops the vessel from being pushed back towards the shore. They look at me and scream. I know what's behind me, I can sense it, smell it. But it doesn't matter, because the girls are going to get away.

'Go!' I scream again.

That's all I can do before strong hands force my head under the water.

# 39

I open my eyes to the burn of salt and endless darkness. This has happened before, being lost under raging water. Once in the same ocean, and once in the rivers of the Underworld. Each time I've come out of the water changed, reborn; a mockery of baptism. But this time is different.

An inhuman hand grips my throat, real and unforgiving. Blood pools in my head, building pressure as I claw at the mottled skin of Ossivorus. His black eyes, sunk in his half-fleshed face, bore into me as he pushes me further and further under the water. He flickers in and out of being, one moment a solid mass looming over me, sharp teeth threatening to tear me apart, the next moment gone.

I can feel the hum of the convergence nearby, a link to the Underworld, a place where magic, dark and sensual, licks at my spine and begs me to use it. For once, I listen. I don't fight against Ossivorus' great weight, pressing me down, down into the depths.

Instead, I let the thrum of power, the prickling sensation that steals over my skin and sends waves of dizziness through me, take over. I listen to the drumbeat of my heart as it falls in line with the convergence. A thread, somewhere deep inside of me, unravels. And all I can think about is stopping the demon from touching me.

A high-pitched sound pierces the dullness of the water. I open my eyes to see Ossivorus contort, his body bending grotesquely. Ribbons of golden light reach through the water, lighting everything with a soft glow, emanating from my tattoo like a beacon. They wrap around my wrists and unleash their power at the demon. His already trembling form, struggling to remain in a realm it does not belong to, is set alight.

Bubbles of heat make the water between us roil, and the demon groans in pain. The warmth from my magic seeps into my bones, pleasant and heady. Power curls at my spine; I feel my body practically purring in contentment. I can do anything, be anything. I want more.

But suddenly my muscles contract, spasming, as if whatever magic just tore from my body was too much. I gasp, inhaling a mouthful of salty water. Kicking hard, I break the surface and strike out towards the shore. The sea behind me boils as the demon shudders, caught in the convergence. Whatever I did isn't stopping Ossivorus, only slowing him down. I reach the pebbly shore and double over, the incoming waves tossing my limp body back and forth. The golden light grows stronger, brighter, hotter. I think I hear screaming.

Cold air slaps my skin. I roll to my side and retch, coughing water from my lungs. Stones scrape my arms and legs, and bite at my palms as I force myself to my knees. I blink hard, eyes stinging from the seawater. My glasses are long gone, floating somewhere in the waves. In the distance, blocking out the cluster of orange lights from the harbor, a white smudge bobs on the surface of the sea. The boat. The girls got away.

The call of magic dulls, fading from a roar to a whisper, but still tapping at my brain, begging me to use it. I shake my head, water flying from my tangled curls. I flex my fingers, staring at them. That feeling . . . that's what drives Greene, Tooth and Talon, to do what they do. If I keep getting a taste of it, let it win a few more times, it will be a drug. A promise of another high, but each hit will take a bigger toll. I can't do that again. I won't.

Water splashes as something huge breaks the surface.

Ossivorus roars in outrage, shaking the pebbles on the beach. The smell of burning flesh pushes its way down my throat, making me gag. I twist, watching as his form flickers again, struggling to remain on Earth without his sacrifices. Those dead eyes turn to me and he reaches out, as if to crush my skull.

I get to my feet, shivering, and push through the dense brush, desperate to get away from the open beach. The angry cries of Ossivorus fade in and out. But until Greene is dead, this isn't over.

I see more people just down the shore as I cross into the small forest. A small group, too old to be students, sees me struggling to my feet and shouts, sounding the alarm, heading for me. Their boat lies useless on the shore. I stagger away, my fingers and lips numb, and stumble blindly into the trees.

The scent of smoke is strong and I follow it to the clearing. The flames still flicker, casting shadows across the grass. Anubis struggles on the cold ground, his face blurry. My eyesight must be warped without my glasses. But that's not it. His form is unsteady, losing its luster. I remember the knife to his stomach, the surge and retreat of his own powers. I gasp and race forward, my legs weak as I reach for the dagger strapped to my thigh.

'Not so fast,' a smooth voice whispers, just before I feel an arm snag around my waist.

The air catches in my lungs as I'm yanked to a stop. I scream and aim my elbow at Luciano's face, but he catches my clumsily thrown jab, seizing my wrist.

'Let me go!' I scream.

He twists my arm hard and my hand opens involuntarily. The knife drops to the ground. Luciano grunts as I throw my head back against his throat, but it's a weak contact. He wrestles my arms behind me and drags me towards the fire, towards Anubis who lies on the ground unnervingly still. No shadows dance at his fingertips. His golden power remains beneath his skin. Only his eyes give away the fact that he's still alive as they flick between me and another body a few feet away. But I can't focus on anything besides getting free.

Melinda crashes through the branches, breathing hard. Behind her three more people enter. Adults, all of them. Alumni from Ravenswood. I recognize two of them from Violet's internships and her circle of friends. The last one, the tallest and most imposing, is Mr Russo, Luciano's father. They must be former society members. Who knows what Tooth and Talon promised each of them if they helped to cover up the society's sins.

'She helped the girls escape and forced Ossivorus back to the Underworld,' Luciano says as he binds my hands with thick twine, jerking them at a painful angle. But he isn't speaking to Melinda or his father. He addresses a shadowy figure standing over the other body I've barely registered in the corner.

'It doesn't matter,' Greene says. 'We will manage with the two girls we do have. Their magic is more than enough to wake Ossivorus permanently.'

Greene's hood is thrown back, the antlers pointed to the ground, sharp and wicked. For the first time, I get to see his face properly. It's Mrs Bianchi's, gently lined and pale, with her blonde hair, and yet it's not. It's as if I can see his original face below the surface, twisting her features into something almost inhuman.

I scowl, ready to argue for the girls' lives, when I notice who is lying on the dais beneath the bronze brazier. A familiar head of black hair, long limbs sprawled at an uncomfortable angle.

*No.*

'Violet?' I croak, my voice breaking as I squint, desperate to be wrong.

This can't be right. She was hiding in the Underworld. A small lump swells beneath her eyebrow. My sister must have traveled here from the Underworld, and been ambushed.

'Look who decided to show up at the last moment to steal our thunder.' Luciano nudges her with his foot.

With a vicious snarl, I lurch forward, slipping my hands free from Luciano's grip. They're still bound behind my back, but I don't care. I stumble towards my sister, her body alarmingly still. I fall forward, landing hard on my shoulder. But I barely register the pain. Inching forward, I dig my feet into the ground. I finally reach her, but with my hands tied all I can do is nudge her with my knee.

'Vee! Wake up, we have to get out of here!' My heart beats furiously in my throat, and my skin, numb only a moment ago, feels feverish and slick with sweat.

My sister remains still. I cry out her name again, wishing I could feel for a pulse, anything.

'Bring them over here,' Greene snaps.

Dark wetness coats the front of his robes, a gash from where Anubis stabbed him. But the wound isn't enough. He hardly seems fazed by the deep cut to his chest, scoring a line between his ribs.

Luciano and Melinda seize Violet and me, dragging us to the feet of Richard Greene. They drop us unceremoniously on the damp earth. Anubis lies a foot away, his skin a disturbing gray. I try to catch his eyes but they've rolled back in his head.

'Let us go,' I demand, trying to flip over.

Luciano presses his knee into the small of my back and I yelp at the pressure it puts on my arms. My cheek grinds into moss and dirt.

'You're not in a position to ask things of me,' Greene says, his face coming into focus as he leans over me. 'You and your sister have been making quite a mess of my Lord's plan.'

'His plan? He wants to banish you to the Underworld in his place! All these lies he told you; don't you know that everything from the Underworld is a facade, mere fakery?'

Richard Greene, the first member of Tooth and Talon, smiles through the face of Mrs Bianchi. Her voice, his voice, blend together for a moment, two people trapped in one body.

'If your sister had been precisely what my lord was hoping for, perhaps she could have had all that he offered and more. But she chose this path the moment she awakened her powers at the site of the convergence at Ravenswood.'

'Chose?' I gape. 'She didn't choose this! No one in their right mind would choose this life. You tried to kill her!'

'She would have hastened my Lord's return with her blood and been handsomely rewarded in the Underworld. But instead, she cast that spell, hid herself away until tonight, for her own selfish pride. Poor Violet, always so cocky. So sure she could have it all and control everything. She wanted to take my place as his anchor, throw me aside, when *I'm* the one who led her to the society, who pulled the strings and guided her. But she's come to me now and brought her sister. Spilling your blood this night is worth far more than a dozen of those other girls.'

A coil of revulsion wraps itself around my stomach. A back-up plan. Violet had slotted right into place, a pawn moved by a hand unseen.

The heat of the flames kisses my skin, the intensity almost painful. Violet stirs, groaning. My heart leaps into my chest. She's waking up, she's alive. And when she opens her eyes and sees what's going on, she'll save us. Her magic is so much stronger than mine; she's nourished it. I just have to give her time to think.

'So, you'll kill us and free Ossivorus? What then – you rot in hell for the next ten thousand years? Is that your plan?' I scowl at the face of my art history teacher. The pale skin and sleek blonde hair shimmer like a mirage. Like Greene is swimming beneath the surface, ready to spring out and squeeze the life out of me, crush my throat.

Greene smiles and turns back to Anubis. 'I'll strip the power from your ridiculous guard dog you dare call a god, to protect myself and my followers. I am not foolish, girl. I have known Lord Ossivorus for over a century. His plan is not pretty, but it is necessary to usher in the next age. To right the wrongs of this world and the one below.'

Violet lifts her head slightly, eyes blurry and confused. I look at her, hoping she's alright, hoping she will fix this.

'Try to kill us, prove me right. You'll have eternity to languish while your so-called lord abandons you, Tooth and Talon, and every other person he's made promises to once he gets what he wants!' I practically scream the words, staring at Luciano.

His mouth twitches and he glances behind him. Melinda and the three alumni. Powerful men with endless supplies of money, funneling their assets into this plan. A plan to free a demon and rule the Earth at his side. A plan they're too foolish to realize is nothing but false promises. That they're necks are just as much at risk as mine.

'You'll have your wish soon enough,' Greene says to me, and kneels next to Anubis. 'You've wasted your power for eons, Anubis. You and the other gods who have languished in the Underworld as the world above changes and forgets. But I won't make your mistakes.'

Anubis opens his eyes, steely and dark, and grits his teeth. 'You'll be dead before you can see your lord rule.' A fit of coughing overtakes him and he struggles to speak.

Greene smiles wickedly and leans over him, hand planted against his chest. 'Is that supposed to frighten me? You gods have all grown so weak, accepting your new place. But I will make sure that everyone knows who I am, that I am not forgotten.'

Greene pushes harder against Anubis' chest until I hear a crack. The gray pallor of his skin grows until he looks drained of life. I can't keep the tears from rolling down my cheeks as I bite my lip to keep from screaming. A god can't die. He can't.

But his mortal body can.

Greene, Luciano and Melinda move around Anubis in a circle, chanting in a rising frenzy as his power is stripped away. Salvatore Russo and the other men join in as well.

Violet twitches beside me as the god housed in the mortal boy's body fades beneath the hands of Greene. She rolls onto her back and contorts, slipping her arms over her legs so they're now bound in front of her.

'Do something,' I plead, my voice a ragged sob.

Anubis begins to scream. Terrible, heart-rending screams that tear at my soul. I want to help him, save him. But that pulse of warmth, of heat and magic, lying dormant in my bones, it frightens me. I never want to call on it again. I never want to lose myself to it. Because I know I'll never win.

'Ossivorus is coming,' Violet whispers as her fingers work at the knots on my wrists. 'You only wounded him. We have to go far enough away to cast my spell without someone stopping us. I'll trap him before he's fully formed and force him to swap me for Greene.'

'Violet, you can't. He's going to destroy everything once he's free!'

'I told you in the Underworld, I'm going to use my magic to control him! I'm stronger than Greene, stronger than anyone before me. Now, focus! The moon is at its apex. He can enter the mortal plane completely for a few moments even without his sacrifices.'

Mr Russo and the other two men tear their eyes away from Tooth and Talon as they crowd around Anubis, their eyes closed as they chant. Violet stiffens as Mr Russo takes a step forward, his eyes on her newly unbound limbs.

'Violet!' I gasp.

As quick as a lightning strike, she lifts her freed hands and mutters a spell. I feel it in my bones, register her power as the magic rattles my teeth. Salvatore Russo and his two companions freeze in place, unblinking, like statues. Greene, Luciano and Melinda don't falter in reciting their spell, totally unaware of the threat.

'We have to save Anubis!' My cheek presses into the cold ground as Violet tugs desperately at my bindings. I taste dirt and the salt of my tears on my tongue.

'There isn't time,' she hisses as the knot on my wrists loosens. She moves fast, touching the tattoo on her thigh, peeking beneath her hiking shorts. The ink flashes gold for a moment, the moon shining brighter than the rest. An answering burn encases my own leg, hot and painful. I choke back my scream as something appears in my sister's palm.

'What are you doing?' I get to my knees.

Anubis begins to thrash, shadows erupting from the earth, tangible and real as they move to protect their master. The scent of burning hair fills my nose as Luciano and Melinda lunge forward to hold him down while Greene's voice rings through the air.

Violet seizes the moment of distraction to grab a bundle of herbs and a jar of oil from the debris scattered on the ground. She uncorks the bottle, dabs a dot on her wrists and ankles, and a final dot on her forehead.

She yanks on my arm and we run through the woods, away from the clearing, racing in the opposite direction to the beach. I don't know how many seconds we have before

Luciano or Melinda notice the others are frozen, and realize that we're gone.

We crest a small hill. The sound of the ocean is loud; we must be near the side of the island that faces the open sea. We pause by a tree and Violet clutches the thing in her palm, some sort of ancient clay pot, and murmurs an incantation over it.

Pain flashes through me, turning my vision white. My leg feels like it's blistering from the inside out. I barely manage to choke back another scream as Violet touches her tattoo. The jar in her hands is no longer made of clay but of deep obsidian. Golden runes dance across the surface, spiraling around the outside. The lid is tightly shut but I sense something within it – dark and ancient.

'I'm sorry it has to be this way,' Violet says, panting and wiping at her brow. 'I'm not strong enough outside of the Underworld to use my own magic. I need to use yours too. This body is weak with cancer and the wound they gave me the night they tried to sacrifice me. I'm sorry.'

'What are you talking about?' I beg, twisting to look behind us. 'Please, we have to help Anubis!'

'He's a god. He doesn't need us.'

'He helped you when you were in the Underworld! He guided you to safety. And this is how you pay him back?' I cry as she leads us from the clearing.

I want to dig my heels in and turn back. But my sister is here. She's alive, and real flesh and blood. I need her. I've always needed her. She's brave. Intelligent. Cunning. These past months without her have been hell.

'We have bigger concerns right now, Andy.' Violet stops next to a fallen, rotten log and crouches, placing the pot on the ground. 'We have to perform this spell before Ossivorus can fully manifest on Earth. He hasn't had any sacrifices. I can control him with this, force him to trade Greene for me.'

I gape at her, at the little obsidian pot on the ground. And my stomach churns. 'It's a devil-trap, isn't it? It's made for Ossivorus.'

She looks up at me, surprise flickering in her expression. 'Looks like you've been studying after all.'

'Where did you find it? Who blessed it?' I demand, my fingers cold and trembling. She sighs and crushes the herbs in her fingers, sprinkling them in a circle around the small vessel. A pot infused with ancient spells strong enough to hold a demon.

'The Underworld. That's why I went there in the first place. I had to follow the path of Anubis, finding a way to partially die and go through the trials of the dead, so I can be reborn as Ossivorus' new anchor, without needing a new body. An ancient priestess of Hecate blessed it before I came here tonight.'

'That's why you were gone, dead for the last eight months? That's why Mom and Dad buried a body that looked like you. So you could find *that*?' I ball my fists.

'Andy,' she says sharply, 'you don't understand any of this. Ossivorus was always going to rise, with or without me. Greene has been sacrificing to him, over and over, growing his strength until he can break free. Tonight is that night. But Ossivorus has to have an anchor, a host. I went along with it for as long as I could. I wanted to bring you into the society sooner, but by the time I realized who Bianchi was, it was too late. Greene knew that I would be more appealing to Ossivorus and tried to kill me. You had to follow the path yourself, partially die, like you did before you found me in the marsh, and then come back, to awaken your magic. You had to uncover the truth so we could control him.'

'Control?' I step back, my chest tight. 'You need my magic; magic I don't even want. You won't be any different. You'll still kill to keep Ossivorus fed so he can grant you power. You're swapping one prison for another, and for what?'

Violet glares at me and wipes her hands on her shorts before standing tall. She has an extra three inches on me, but it feels more like twenty. 'Don't you understand? No one can stop Ossivorus. No one can kill him! If I don't become his anchor, he'll kill you, Andy. He'll kill Mom, Dad, our grandparents, anyone else we've ever met! All because Greene will be his anchor, and we would be a threat.'

'This is wrong. We can stop him – we just have to kill Greene before Ossivorus is fully on Earth, while he's weak and untethered without any sacrifices!'

'Maybe I made a mistake not clueing you in earlier, training you. But you never wanted anything to do with Ravenswood. If I told you I'd started summoning demons and practicing magic, you never would have believed me.' Her breath catches, and there's a wild, frantic look in her eyes. 'My plan is far from perfect, but it's the only one I have that will keep me from dying of cancer. If I'm gone, you're helpless, Andy. Our family is unprotected. Because of what we are, how we're tied to Hecate, we'll always be a target. Is that what you want?'

My stomach twists. I feel like I'm going to be sick as I stare at my sister. All of this – the secrets, the lies, the clues – it wasn't to free Violet. It was to give her what she wanted. Life without death. She never needed me. Not like I thought. She only needed my magic to awaken, so she could use it for this very moment.

Something inside me breaks.

'I won't help you. We can end this, once and for all, by killing Greene. We can save Anubis; you can make things right.'

'You don't understand anything. I've been studying this for years!'

I step back. 'I understand enough.'

'Don't make me do this, Andy! The moon will rise soon, and Ossivorus will be here in his physical form any second!' Violet's voice is ragged and high – alien. 'I need your help to bind him. *Please!*'

'No,' I say through a sob.

Her face falls, panic hunching her shoulders. The moon seems to shine brighter overhead. A ripple of power shudders through the air. The moon has reached its apex on Halloween night. Ossivorus won't be a flickering, half-formed demon. He'll be here completely. Powerful. Deadly.

'Please, please, forgive me, Andy,' Violet begs. 'I need your magic. I can't lose you.'

I don't have time to ask what she means before my chest seizes, white-hot pain flickering from my tattoo and encasing me like a cocoon. I hear myself scream, smell my own flesh bubbling, feel it peeling from my bones. I writhe in the dirt as the scent of burnt skin mixes with the aroma of rotten undergrowth, moldering flesh, and the stench of evil.

A guttural cry erupts from the depths of the earth. My eyes burn as a bolt of bright light flashes from Violet's hands to rise in the air around the circle of herbs. The ancient djed symbol burns on the ground. The symbol of rebirth. What Violet wanted all along: a resurrection. To be reborn as Ossivorus' anchor tonight, and never taste death.

Through my blurred vision I see the tall horns of Ossivorus, his ragged robes, his half-fleshed face and mottled skin, as he rises, knots of magic beginning to tie him to the devil-trap. His hideous mouth opens in a roar I can't hear.

I see Violet looking wildly between me and the demon. Her mouth moves, shouting my name, over and over, panic making her look as crazed as those dark paintings she loves so much. She screams, tears streaming down her face, but she doesn't stop her spell to check on me. Not with the demon barely tethered at her fingertips.

Slowly, the pain fades from excruciating to a dull ache. I lie still, my body empty and broken. I can't hear anything as Violet speaks with the demon. Her face is cruel. The demon is clearly incensed as he rages against his invisible bonds.

The vibrations of footsteps rattle my aching body, and make my temples thrum. I turn my head and see black-robed figures desperately reaching for their lord. The demon raises his hand and they halt. I see Luciano staring at his ex-girlfriend, his eyes fearful and wild. His father stands next to Greene. No one else appears from the forest.

I blink, shutting my eyes for a moment. When I manage to open them again, the people around me have shifted. The ringing in my ears fades until I can hear the commotion. Luciano moves forward, but his father catches his arm and pulls him back.

'Father,' he hisses, 'look at what she's done. She will force Ossivorus into this pact with her instead of Greene! If we do not join her, she will make sure Ossivorus kills us.'

Violet glowers at him. 'You'll die, either way. Perhaps you'll be the first one I sacrifice to your *lord*.'

'You foolish girl. Ossivorus will break free of these bindings and snap your neck and your sister's. And what will you gain then?' Greene curses, and I see Violet flinch at the face of her old teacher. Is there anything left of the sister I knew, beneath that mask of hatred and anger?

'Swear to me,' Violet yells to the demon.

He glowers at her from his massive height. His bare shoulders roll as he considers the girl before him.

'Your power is alluring, little mortal,' he rumbles. 'Perhaps you could be of use to me. If I swear to keep you alive, as I have my other servant, you must give me more in return.'

346

'Like what?' Violet spits.

'Your sister,' he says, face splitting in a grotesque grin.

'My Lord –' Greene gasps, the unanticipated betrayal coloring his face, but the demon raises his hand to silence his servant.

'Hecate is a goddess of endless power. Those foolish Greeks hardly paid her the respect she deserves. She is formidable, dangerous. The blood that runs through your veins is more than rare – it is nearly impossible. But here you are. Sacrifice your sister to me, and her magic will only enhance your powers. You will never die, never need to change bodies like my earlier servant. And to crown the deal, your soft heart will never need to sacrifice another mortal if you give her to me.'

Violet's eyes flick to Greene where he stands, indignant and disbelieving, behind his master.

'I can't kill my sister,' she says raggedly, shaking her head. 'I won't.'

'Then you cannot have your deal. You are outnumbered. My servants will free me and I will feast on your flesh. Your sister's too.' His voice is deep, grating. It skates along my ruined skin. I struggle to move, to scream at Violet, but my vocal cords don't work. I'm helpless, ruined.

'*No.*' Violet grinds her teeth. 'Now swear to me, before the moment passes and you are trapped in the Underworld again. Heal Andy, now!'

Ossivorus moves to the edge of his golden prison; already it seems to sputter like a flame on the end of a wick, close to extinction. Violet's too weak from her cancer. She can't hold her spell for much longer.

'Your sister is already near death. Give her to me. We will both benefit. I will ensure her soul is treated like a queen in the Underworld. She will have whatever she wants, an existence

347

so luxurious she will hardly know she is dead. Your precious little sister will be protected, safe. Her power will not be sought after by others. It is the only way.'

'No. You will fix her when we make our deal. The power I used to summon you with is more than enough,' Violet says, her face twisted with pain. She sways on her feet, her forehead wrinkled as she considers me. 'I never meant to hurt her.'

'Accept my demands or there is no deal.'

Violet shakes her head, mouth opening and closing silently.

Ossivorus waits for a moment before he beckons Greene to come closer. 'Very well. Break the trap and seize the girls.'

Luciano and Greene move together, hands raised. I shut my eyes, forcing my trembling hand to move. I reach inside my sodden, filthy jacket and unzip the inner pocket. The gun rests heavily against my ribs as I struggle to pull it out.

'Wait!' Violet screams. 'If you touch my sister, I'll destroy your vessel!'

My burnt flesh glares back at me as I pull the hammer back on the pistol. How long was it underwater? My jacket may not have protected it. I doubt it will work. But I have no other choice, everything has fallen apart. Anubis is gone. Violet isn't thinking clearly.

I lift my hand. The gun feels heavier than the weight of a thousand stones. My heart clenches and I struggle to aim. A crack rips through the air, surprising even me.

Luciano looks down at his chest where blood drips like a macabre fountain. His eyes widen before he crumples to the earth in front of Greene's feet. Lip curling, Greene steps away from his human shield. Violet smothers a scream behind her hand.

I pull the hammer back again. One bullet left. Luciano's father is stricken, frozen by the sight of his dead son's body. Ossivorus looks at me. At the gun. Greene staggers, his face contorting in pain. He stares at the demon, a look of shock on his face.

Violet gasps and turns towards Ossivorus, her hand outstretched. I can feel it in the air, the moment Ossivorus abandons Greene as his anchor. The snap of power, like a rubber band being drawn back and let go. Nothing, no one, is anchoring him in place.

I level the gun at Richard Greene's head and pull the trigger. The second crack seems louder than the first, an echo of thunder that rolls across the harbor and fills the trees with its cry. The blonde hair of Mrs Bianchi – of the replacement body housing a man almost two hundred years old – turns red with blood.

All that remains of Tooth and Talon is Violet. The first to die. The last one standing. I shut my eyes and let my head fall against the mossy ground, everything suddenly too heavy to bear.

Ossivorus' roar is so loud, I feel my eardrums burst. A wave of scorching power, a swirling inferno of the demon's rage, slams into my already weak body. I feel my heart slow.

The last thing I think of as I slip into the familiar embrace of the Underworld is how I'm not afraid.

Not anymore.

# 40

Black water churns before me. Two rivers cut through an end-less landscape of rolling gray hills and obsidian mountains. I look down at my hands. They're normal, with pale skin and a light dusting of freckles. The pain is gone.

I twist around, searching for a familiar face. Or perhaps it will be unfamiliar? But no one – nothing – is here. A warm breeze, humid and sweet, rustles the gray grass that sways against my legs. Pale flowers bob on the horizon. But Anubis doesn't appear.

'Andromeda Emmerson.'

I whip around to face the boiling river. A man, tall and graceful, with short cropped hair and flawless brown skin, stares back at me. His eye sockets are endless pits of black, so deep I can't tell if he is eyeless or if his eyes simply have no whites. Linen robes billow in the breeze. He stands on a small barge, a long oar in his hand. The prow nestles against the shore.

I swallow, my throat unbearably dry. 'Who are you? Where is Anubis?'

'That god has been gone for many years.'

'He – he might be here. His vessel died.' I wince at the words, at the memories. But the man on the boat doesn't seem interested in answering questions.

'Here.' He extends his hand, palm up. 'Come with me. I will take you to the west bank, where you can finally rest.'

I recoil, stepping out of his reach. 'I can't die. Not yet. I have to help my sister, and find Anubis. You don't understand what's been happening, what the demon Ossivorus has been planning.'

The man frowns but doesn't pull his hand back. 'Each soul only gets one chance to cross the rivers to Elysium, the Field of Reeds, Heaven – whatever name most suits you. If you do not take my hand, you are stuck between banks forever.'

'No, I can't die yet. I have too much to do. My sister, she's making a terrible mistake. I have to know what happened!' I shake my head and take another step back, my legs shaking.

'You must make the choice. Do you wish to rest with other brave souls, or languish with the forgotten and damned?'

'You're Charon,' I recall, clutching my arms around my middle. 'You require payment to ferry dead souls across the River Styx. I have nothing to pay you with, so you may as well go.'

'Aken, Charon, Haros – they are merely names for the same being. My job, my purpose, is to bring you peace, child. Money is not what I take as payment.'

'Then what do you take?'

He smiles, fully this time, his white teeth flashing against his dark skin. 'Memories. I find the dead can only rest when their more *unpleasant* recollections are taken from them. Perhaps that is where the idea of the Lethe, the river of forgetfulness, came from.'

My mouth grows bone-dry. 'My sister, Anubis – I never want to forget them. I'm not ready.'

The pain both have caused me is an open wound. But I would rather live with betrayal, with heartbreak, than forget the way Violet and I were before. To never recall the way Anubis looked at me again.

Charon considers me for a moment, his grip on the oar tightening, muscles bunching as he prepares to push away from the bank. 'If that is what you wish.'

I shut my eyes. I'm really dead. Maybe Anubis is too. I have no way of knowing, no way of contacting anyone. Perhaps I should give up, give in. Mom and Dad will eventually get over losing another daughter. If Violet survives, they'll have that consolation. Munia is safe.

I killed Greene before Ossivorus could use him or Violet as a vessel. Without anything grounding him on Earth, he'll be like he was before Richard Greene ever called to him: trapped somewhere in the Underworld. What else is there for me?

My heart beats in my chest, the flutter of a phantom.

'No.' I open my eyes, shivering. 'I have to stay. I need to find Anubis.'

'After all he's done?' Charon asks softly.

My chest squeezes, a familiar ache now. But I think of what it would be like to never see him again. I don't think I'm willing to part with those pieces of me. I'm not ready to let him fade into nothing.

'Even after everything he's done,' I agree. 'He's a god, after all. I have to assume selfishness is built in.'

'Very well. I wish you luck. And perhaps I can offer you a glimmer of peace in parting.' Charon digs his oar into the bank and pushes away. 'I may not take payment, but others do.'

I cock my head to the side, considering the ferryman as the river's current takes hold of the boat and tugs it along in search of more wandering souls. Before I can call after him, his boat disappears around a bend. I turn from the river, from the west bank where warm light and sparkling mansions speckle the beautiful landscape.

A wasteland of decay and ash stretches before me as I contemplate the ferryman's words. My fingers move to my jacket of their own accord and press down. I gasp, finally realizing what he means.

Others do take payment.

# 41

It takes a long time for me to find a tomb. This one is different from the last, far grander. A mausoleum of marble with two large columns and a relief carved into the face: grapes, satyrs, and a pantheon of gods lounging in various stages of undress. A Roman tomb for a rich person who was somehow forgotten, doomed to be trapped forever between life and death.

A bitter taste floods my tongue. Will my tombstone appear somewhere on these hills? I push the thought aside as I consider the entrance, my fingers tracing the shape of the disk through my coat. Taking a deep breath, I pull the coin free, the metal bright against the shadowy gray of my surroundings.

'Stop,' a deep voice commands.

A guardian already? But they should let me pass, not keep me from going deeper into the Underworld. I turn, expecting to see another jackal-headed man or maybe even a griffin or lamassu. But instead, I stagger, feeling like a hole has been punched straight through my chest.

'Anubis?'

He smiles, those soft pink lips parting into a lopsided grin that twists my heart. He looks like Jae. Black hair swept back, sharp cheekbones and deep, soulful brown eyes.

'Andromeda.'

'I was trying to find you,' I whisper, 'to give you the coin so we could both come back.'

His smile turns a little sad and he moves closer, his hands

stuffed into his pockets. 'I know. I didn't want you to waste that coin on me. I'm not worth it.'

'Are you – did you . . .' I trail off helplessly.

'Did I die? In a way. I don't have a mortal soul like you do. If I were completely destroyed, I would cease to exist.'

'What happened to you?' I knit my eyebrows together and study him.

We stand six feet apart and neither one of us makes a move to come closer. Not after everything that's happened. But a part of me desperately wants him to.

He pushes his fingers through his hair and looks towards the rivers. 'Greene tried to strip my powers but stopped when he noticed you and Violet were gone. He knew what your sister was thinking and went to stop her. But it was too late for me to try and heal myself. My body – Jae's body – died.'

I stare at him in silence.

'I knew it would happen, Andy. Greene and Tooth and Talon outnumbered us; I knew that from the beginning . . .' He pauses, lets his gaze linger on me for a moment. 'There was no way I was going to make it out of there in one piece. And I'm okay with that.'

'But you still look like him,' I say, my voice strangled.

'After a decade with this face, I admit I'm partial to it. Besides, it's the face you're most comfortable with.'

I can't believe he let himself, his human vessel, die. The very thing that other gods have killed for: a moment of control and existence in an imperfect but beautiful world. All so he could help those girls. Help Violet. Help me.

When I speak, my voice is taut with emotion. 'You can't go back, can you?'

Anubis steps forward cautiously, like I'm a skittish deer. When he halts, he's so close I can feel the heat radiating off him. 'I can't go back, not like before. I'll never be able to stay on Earth.'

I nod, not trusting myself to speak. Why does that revelation cut at me so deeply? I look away from him, from the face I've studied and dreamed of for months. The boy, the god, who risked everything and then lost it.

After a moment, I wipe at my eyes and clear my throat. 'What happened to the others?'

He smiles and brushes my hand with his. I'm shocked I can still feel the warmth of his fingers, the pull of his scent. 'You saved the girls, got them away before Ossivorus could rise. You were amazing.'

'I died. Violet, she tried to take Greene's place. She was willing to hurt me to get what she wanted. I am not amazing,' I say bitterly, the gravity of my sister's actions pressing down on my chest like an anvil. 'I failed her.'

And she failed *me*.

'No.' He steps closer. 'You didn't fail her at all. Greene is dead, I can sense his soul awaiting judgment with Osiris even now. He won't pass on to the Field of Reeds or to any eternal rest. He will be punished for everything he's done.'

'But Violet –'

'She survived.' He grimaces. 'And if it is any consolation, she didn't kill you. And the thought of harming you tears at her soul even now. The moment you shot Greene, Ossivorus' already tenuous connection was severed, the shockwave stopping your heart. I've sent some of the lesser death gods to pursue him, bind him so deeply in the depths of the Underworld, he won't be able to call on anyone ever again.'

'Violet's alive.' I process that, stewing for a moment.

'Andy.' Anubis hesitates before he takes my hands, holding them against his chest. 'Andromeda, I – I wanted to thank you.'

'Thank me?' I stare at him dumbly, not sure if I should pull away from him. 'What for?'

'For helping me see what I was always meant to be. I'm a death guide. I'm meant to help people on into the next life, comfort them like I did with Jae. But I lost sight of that, like all gods forget their purposes, I suppose.' He brushes his thumb over the back of my hand and I feel it in my toes. 'I wanted to have a mortal experience without the challenges, like you said. But I was wrong for doing that – selfish. You reminded me what I'm meant to do. I need to focus on my purpose, help others like I did with Jae. Be the god I was created, and help lost and forgotten souls.'

*Oh.* I think I've forgotten how to breathe.

'I'm happy for you,' I choke out. 'But I wish things had gone differently.'

Anubis releases one of my hands and moves to tuck an errant lock of hair behind my ear. His fingers trace a line along my jaw before resting on my cheek. 'The coin I gave you, use it to go back home. This isn't the end for you.'

'What?' I look up and his eyes are pained as they study me. 'I died, Anubis. I'm pretty sure I've run out of chances. I don't even understand how I survived the last time.'

'Andromeda, the way you screamed, I could hear it even as I slipped into the Underworld.' His other hand tightens on mine, crushing it to his chest like he can anchor me there. 'But it isn't the end. The coin can be used to pay your way back; a guardian of the gates will gladly accept it.'

'Why?' I whisper.

He cocks his head. 'Well, the coins allow beings of the Underworld to go where they wish, free of their bonds for a time. It's an alluring prospect to experience life like you did, even briefly –'

'No,' I interrupt. 'I mean, why do you want me to go?'

His thumb brushes a tear from my cheek even as he smiles tightly. 'Because this never should have happened. I should have protected you better, listened to your concerns about your sister. You don't deserve to be here.'

'What if I wanted to stay here,' my voice breaks, 'with you?'

'Andromeda.' He leans forward, pressing his forehead against mine as his arms wrap around my waist.

I fight back the urge to sob as I bury my face into his shoulder. Because this feels too much like goodbye.

I thought this was what I wanted. But I'll never see his smile again, hear his laugh, or feel his lips on mine. And it hurts. Because I know he's right, that I have to go back. Violet needs me. She needs to understand that what she did was wrong. She'll never be able to live with the guilt if I die.

'I can't do this without you.' I dig my fingers into his back, holding him tightly as I fight back another sob.

Anubis lifts my chin gently, forcing me to look at him through my tears. 'This isn't goodbye forever. I'll find a way to communicate with you, to visit you if . . . if you want me to. But I'm not a human man; I'll never be normal, never be able to be there for you like you deserve.'

'I'm sorry,' I say, resting my hands on his chest again, feeling his heart beat hard against his sternum. 'Everything I said to you. You gave up your one chance of having a human life for me.'

'I'd do it a thousand times over. They say gods are incapable of it, but maybe my time in the mortal world has changed me.' Anubis smiles softly, sadly, but he leans close, brushing his lips over my cheek, my nose, my eyelids. 'I love you, Andromeda.'

When he kisses me, I don't hold anything back. I'm tired of fighting what I feel for him, the consuming ache that takes over everything when he touches me. For a moment, I don't care that he's a god, that he will stay in the Underworld and rule alongside other gods over the souls of the dead. And despite everything, I feel a weight lift from my chest.

'I love you too,' I tell him. And I truly do.

His breath hitches and his eyes seem to burn gold for a moment. When our lips touch again, I swear I've never felt more alive.

# 42

*February*
*Four months later*

I turn to the next page in my book as the heart monitor beeps noisily beside the bed. I squint in the low light afforded by the weak incandescent light bulbs behind Violet's head. The hospital is quiet this late at night. The only disturbances come from the various monitors and the sound of the lake slapping against the nearby shore.

'Andy.' Violet's scratchy voice pulls me from the novel I was half-heartedly reading.

I fling it aside and pull the blanket off my lap, moving to kneel beside her bed. Violet's face is pale and drawn. A month ago, we shaved her head when the chemo made her hair fall out in clumps. I touch the soft stubble growing back and help her sit up, holding a straw to her dry, flaky lips so she can drink.

Once I help her settle back against the mountain of pillows Mom insists she have, I hold her hand, careful not to jostle where the IV is taped in place.

'I don't think I'll ever get used to needing you to help me with everything, little star,' she says, sighing and shutting her eyes.

She's right. It's weird for me too. For our whole lives, she's been the protector, the nurturer. But now the roles are reversed and she needs me in ways I'd never expected. I can tell it eats at her, this helplessness. My newfound backbone.

Our dynamic has shifted. I clear my throat and steer away from the inevitable argument that crops up every time we discuss what happened. How we got here.

'How are you feeling?' I ask.

Violet gives a weak laugh, opening one eye to squint at me. 'Like death warmed over.'

'I know how that feels,' I joke.

Immediately I regret it, because she shuts down again. The mask of anger and betrayal veiling her expression.

When I appeared back on the island, Violet was alone as she sobbed over my cold body. Although she hadn't killed me, not truly, my heart had broken. Because even though it was Ossivorus' banishment that stopped my heart, she used me and my magic. Hurt me more than I can bear to remember.

I expected the police to comb the island, carry out arrests and take us away. But it never happened. Mr Russo fled the island as soon as Greene died, leaving behind the bodies of Melinda, the two other alumni, and also Luciano. Pastor Carmichael came to investigate just before sunrise and helped us get back to shore. When I told him about Anubis, he seemed almost proud.

Back at Ravenswood, Tooth and Talon's connections had been hard at work. Luciano and Melinda's deaths, the girls' reappearance, Mrs Bianchi's sudden departure – all of it was explained away by silver-tongued Headmaster Madden. The angry look he gave me when I showed up with my sister only cemented my suspicion that he was one of the many who'd been promised riches and power by the society. But he was useful in the end, smoothing over the disaster that had taken place on his campus.

I'm sure money exchanged hands, or rather massive sums were shifted between offshore bank accounts, and in a matter of a few days everything was explained as a terrible hazing gone wrong. The GSE club was blamed. The alumni who died were painted as irresponsible adults helping to haze new members. Everything went wrong when too much alcohol entered the scene. And then there was my sister's miraculous recovery to explain. Only, she had never been dead.

The past few months of memories had been tampered with and changed. Anubis helped me cast the spell in the Underworld. A way to alter everyone else's memories but mine. To the school, to Mom and Dad, Violet never drowned. There was no funeral. We had simply both gone to Ravenswood together for her last year. And even Jae was forgotten, wiped away.

Sometimes, I wish that was the truth.

'Violet,' I say softly, refusing to let go of her hand. 'You need to stop wishing for something that's impossible.'

'I had so much power at my fingertips that I was barely beginning to understand. And now look at me.' Her jaw clenches and she looks away, out the window to the dark lake. 'A bald, dying girl with no high school diploma whose only plans for next year are picking which coffin she will be buried in.'

I try to hide the hitch in my voice. 'Don't talk like that, Vee. I told you we're going to find a way to save you. There has to be another way, another spell – something we can do. Don't give up yet.'

'I could have been healthy. Immortal. I'd never have to feel like this,' she whispers, her eyes half-glazed with morphine.

My stomach hollows. 'But you would have had to kill others, even if it was to protect me.'

Tears well in her eyes. She pulls her hand from mine and rolls onto her side so all I can see is her back, the knobs of her spine peeking through the gap of her thin hospital gown.

'I would have thought of another way if I could.' Sobs wrack her body, a conflict she can't seem to overcome.

Ever since she came back from the Underworld and I killed Greene, she's been like this. Defeated and totally unwilling to look for a solution to her sickness. I'm sure half of it is punishment for herself, an attempt to atone for what she did to me. How she used me. And the other half is self-pity.

The worst thing is, even as I do my best to look for a spell, there are times when I still believe she wouldn't hesitate to trade me to Ossivorus for another chance. That truth guides me, so even when I study magic, I ensure I never actually use it. The temptation is always there, begging me to tap into a power that runs deep within me. But I've seen what it's done to my sister. It's torn her apart from the inside, and no spell is worth that.

It's so hard doing this alone. Being the only one who knows the truth. Even though Violet is with me, she's never been further away. And I worry she's never going to recover, never see the error of her ways.

'Mom is going to be here soon.' I check my watch to hide the hurt that flashes through me. 'I'll be back tomorrow night.'

'You should go back to Ravenswood, Andy,' Violet murmurs towards the wall. 'One of us ought to make something of herself.'

I hold my tongue. She's been trying to pawn me off on that terrible place since we left. I'd pulled out of the school and transferred back to my old one, switching to online studies to be with Violet and my parents more. I never want to go back there. Not with all the memories, the ghosts that haunt the halls. Not without *him*.

'I'll see you soon.' I lean over to press a kiss to her head. Violet is silent and I try not to let her rejection, her apathy, eat at me. I rub my eyes as I step into the elevator and hit the button for the ground floor.

Mom, Dad and I take turns spending time with Violet.

I usually take the night shift, switching now and then with Mom. I can handle the lack of sleep. But sometimes I wish I never had to walk back into this place that smells like antiseptic and death.

The late February air is cold, nipping at my ears and nose as I dig in my coat pocket for my keys. The orange light from the lamp posts glimmers off of the slick, icy parking lot. I slip and slide my way to the car and work the key into the frozen lock. Just as I crack the door open, the lights wink out. My stomach drops and my fingers tighten on the door. The air feels charged and strange. The crisp winter night smells like rich earth and incense.

My muscles freeze as I consider what to do. Something strange is here, I can feel it. My skin prickles and my breath becomes shallow. Violet warned me that other demons and gods would look for us, searching for my magic that could feed them for centuries, allow them to wander freely.

Snow crunches a few feet away, in the depths of the thick trees shrouding the border of the hospital. I debate throwing myself into my car, but the piece of junk is old and the engine will likely refuse to turn over on the first try.

I dig frantically in my coat for the pocket knife I now keep on me at all times. My fingers fumble to release the latch and I nearly slice into my own palm as the crunching of heavy footsteps grows closer.

'Andromeda,' a husky voice whispers at my side.

I scream, slashing the knife wildly. A strong hand catches my wrist and a familiar low laugh sends a curl of heat through me.

Anubis grins down at me, snowflakes catching on his long lashes. He looks like Jae still; his eyes flash golden for a moment.

'What are you doing here?' I gasp. The warmth from his skin rattles me to the core. He's really here.

'Aren't you happy to see me?'

My heart squeezes painfully. 'How did you get here? I didn't think I'd ever see you again.'

'I asked for assistance from a few gods that owed me a favor. They used their powers to open a pathway for a short time.' His eyes drop to my lips and for a moment I can't think. 'I had to come see you in person, even if it's only for a few moments.'

'Can you stay?' I whisper.

His smile slowly fades. My fingers ache to reach out to him. But I don't know if I can. I can't take my eyes off of him, afraid he's going to disappear and leave me broken and alone all over again.

'No, not without an anchor. I already feel myself being pulled back. But I came here for a reason: I have something to tell you.' He moves closer, his scent wrapping around me. 'I've been looking into some things regarding your sister and Hecate.'

'Hecate?' My heart stutters. 'Why?'

'I wanted to understand your power better. Maybe I could find the source, an explanation, and a way to help Violet. And I think I may have.'

It feels like the ground just gave way beneath me. 'Something to cure her?'

'Maybe. But that's not all.' He licks his lips. 'I found Hecate. She's been sleeping like I was, trapped in her own sub-conscious, fading more and more each day. It won't be easy to get to her, but I think it's the only way to help you and your sister manage your magic. And to save Violet's life.'

'You think she can help? That she'll be able to awaken?'

He nods. 'The very goddess of magic, the one who gave you these powers, would have any answer we need. If we awaken her, she will help.'

'When are you going back?'

'Now.'

'Oh.' My heart twists.

Anubis leans close to me again, his breath, warm and addictive, spreads across my skin. 'Come with me,' he whispers, extending his hand, palm outstretched.

The air smells different again, the tang of the lake and the crispness of the falling snow fading until there's nothing but pine and salt and him. Darkness appears behind him. A path to the Underworld opening to take him away.

I look over my shoulder at the hospital and bite down on my cheek. The image of Violet, her eyes sunken, cheeks swollen and body wracked with pain, haunts me. But I look back at Anubis, his brown-gold eyes warm and sure. And I know what I have to do. Carefully, I take his hand. I smile when his strong fingers wrap around mine.

The smell of ash, of rich dirt and a time forgotten settles on my shoulders like a comforting blanket. We step inside the tunnel, and the passageway behind us closes.

I begin my journey back into the Underworld.

And Death follows with me.

# Acknowledgements

*All The Devils* wouldn't be in your hands without my wonderful agent, Susan Velazquez. I have to thank her from the bottom of my heart for answering that unsolicited email in October 2022. She saw the potential of Andy and Violet, and her instincts led us right to Penguin Michael Joseph. Here is to many, many more books together. And to Stevie Finegan, my UK subagent, for championing ATD so fervently and with such dedication. Christina Zobel, thank you for also joining the ATD train and loving it from the beginning.

To my editor, Rebecca Hilsdon, for falling so deeply in love with Andy and this story. Your excitement from the moment it hit your inbox is the stuff of dreams. Thank you for helping me shape *All The Devils* into the story it is today. And thank you for your cats – I love them and the fact that Raven forever stalks the halls of Ravenswood Academy.

Thank you to Jorgie Bain for your help in editing *All The Devils* and catching the little details you did. To Shan Morley Jones, thank you for your keen eye in copyedits!

And of course, a massive thank you to the team at Penguin Michael Joseph for being so excited for this spooky, creepy book about two sisters. I know we found the right home for Andy and Violet with you.

Speaking of sisters, what kind would I be if I didn't thank mine again? You two have always been the first to hear about my stories, encouraging me and never letting me give up on this dream. Camille has done so much art for this book, and I can't believe how lucky I am that she is forever obligated to continue to do so. This book is a love letter to all sisters, but mine in particular. I miss you guys, and can't wait until we're back where we belong – living in the same house and ignoring our husbands.

And to my own husband, Taylor. From the moment you learned I wrote, you encouraged me. You never let me doubt myself for a moment. Thank you for being by my side, wiping my tears and forcing me to take breaks when my hands cramp. I love you.

To Mom and Dad, thank you for being so supportive and proud of your strange child's stranger books. I promise I don't summon demons. At least not on Sundays.

Finally, thank you to Katie Taylor for being the first person to read the whole manuscript, back when it was very different. You helped me change Andy's character into who she is, and loved Jae as much as I did. Thank you for helping me find the heart of the story.